THE AMBASSADORS

THE
AMBASSADORS

George Lerner

PEGASUS BOOKS
NEW YORK LONDON

THE AMBASSADORS

Pegasus Books LLC
80 Broad Street, 5th Floor
New York, NY 10004

First Pegasus Books cloth edition September 2014

Interior design by Maria Fernandez

Frontispiece: Hans Holbein, "The Ambassadors," 1533

Map on page vii © Scott M.X. Turner

ISBN: 978-1-60598-620-3

10 9 8 7 6 5 4 3 2 1

Printed in the United States of America
Distributed by W. W. Norton & Company, Inc.

For My Parents

Adele Falk Lerner
(1922–1971)
and
Edward Robert Lerner
(1920–2013)

and
for Alyson

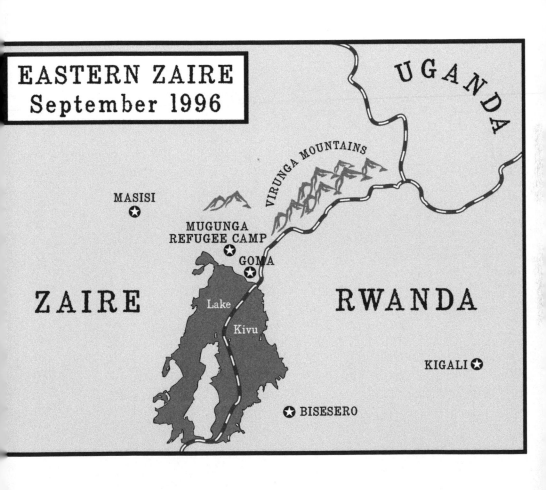

PART 1

1

Brussels Airport
September 10, 1996

THANK GOD I HAD NEVER GROWN SOFT WITH AGE, OR THE PAST four days stuck in this airport would have been hell. Along with our fellow travelers, we had turned luggage into pillows, jackets into blankets, creating a refugee camp in the heart of Europe. At least here we had solid floors and flush toilets, and the displaced persons surrounding us were far from dispossessed. Heading home to Kinshasa, they were hauling suitcases and cartons, nothing like my old friends who staggered out of Auschwitz with only striped pajamas on their backs and numbers tattooed on their forearms.

"Jacob, you know I would follow you anywhere, but how long do you want to wait for this fucking plane?" Dudu asked, squatting beside me in a sumo pose, his legs spread wide, his knees bent, his massive chest ready to absorb a blow.

"Have some faith, Dudu. It'll get here eventually."

Dudu pressed his arm sideways against his torso. "I hope this trip will be worth the trouble."

I could never doubt his strength, nor his loyalty, but his constant questioning of our journey was making me crazy.

"Of course it'll be worth it. There's more to life than lying on a beach in Thailand."

Wincing, he let the arm drop. "It was nice there, Aba. Better than this. What I can't understand is why an old Jew like you, who has spent his life rescuing people, wants to get involved in this dirty business. You should retire already, take it easy."

Dudu had called me "Aba" for years, ever since his father died and I helped him escape Soviet Odessa as a teenager. He meant it as a sign of appreciation, better than I could expect from my own son back in Brooklyn, but Dudu also took it as license to torment me.

"What retire? Can you picture me sitting on the beach like an *alter kocker*?"

"It doesn't sound so bad, Jacob. If I live as long as you, all I will want is a big lady who knows how to use her tongue." His gaze landed on the broad ass of Josephina, digging through her many suitcases for a fresh dress.

"You'd never survive what I've been through, not with your appetites."

On our second night here, Dudu had challenged the heaviest Zairean, wide as a refrigerator, to an eating contest. It didn't turn out to be much of a competition. Dudu overwhelmed his opponent, who lost momentum with each successive frankfurter. Before long, the poor bastard emptied his guts, while Dudu pounded his chest, cursed in Russian, and swore he was still hungry.

By this point, on our fourth morning, there was no use trying to entertain ourselves any longer. We had all settled in for the duration. Josephina and the other ladies were adjusting bright fabrics around their bodies, twirling smaller pieces of the same material into head scarves. Young guys lounged about like fruitcakes in their silky shirts and tight pants. Merchants in dark suits lurked behind huge boxes of contraband. Compared to them, Dudu and

I must have looked like workers in a slaughterhouse. My shirt had lost its starched sheen; the collar felt grimy against my stubble of beard. Dudu's soccer jersey grew more stained with every meal.

"Look, our friend is back." Dudu pointed to the ticketing desk. The Air Zaire representative, who had been bullshitting us for days, had finally shown up to face off against a crowd of disgruntled passengers.

"Do something about the plane," one of our fellow travelers demanded. "Pick up the telephone and call for another one."

"Yes, tell President Mobutu to send his private jet," another said.

"Shut your mouth, or you will be removed from the passenger list," the Air Zaire man said, waving away his countrymen roughly.

We had tried cajoling and flattery, and bribery too. Now Dudu took a different approach. Slipping through the crowd, he wrapped his arm like a yoke around the ticket agent's neck. "All right, my friend, where is that plane that you promised? It should have been here four days ago." Dudu must have been exerting some pressure, because the guy's face began to soften.

"It is coming, Sir. You must be patient. We are awaiting news any minute."

"You told us the same shit yesterday, and when it turned out to be a lie, my boss wanted me to throw you onto the runway. I had to beg him to be merciful."

Glancing at me, the agent promised us free tickets, drinks, all the goodies handed out by First World airlines. It was more bullshit. He didn't have any power to give us freebies, much less a realistic timetable. Satisfied he had made our presence felt, Dudu released the man, and I slipped him a few greenbacks to remember our names—Jacob Furman and David Abramowich—for the seat assignments.

All we could do now was wait. This project that had sounded so promising—to help the Tutsis survive—was having trouble getting off the ground. Our momentum stalled, my thoughts turned back to Susanna. I would have liked to have said goodbye in person. Not that it could make up for a broken marriage, but at least we would have had a sweet memory of parting, in case anything happened.

A group of children edged close to challenge Dudu to arm wrestle. He knelt on the floor, braced his elbow against the hard plastic seat, and let them heave their collective weight against his wrist. The kids soon exhausted themselves, and Dudu slammed his arm down to crush them. As they scurried away, one of the African businessmen, an electronics dealer surrounded by canyons of cardboard, leaned forward to poke into our affairs.

"When we reach Kinshasa," the man said, "I can introduce you to my friend in the mining ministry, if you want to do some business."

He might have been a loudmouth, but Dudu knew not to give anything away. "Talk to Jacob. He makes all the decisions."

Half the lounge turned to hear my response, even though none of them would have grasped the deeper meaning of our journey. The struggle of the Tutsis against the Hutus, the genocide in Rwanda, and the refugee camps filled with murderers were a thousand miles from their lives in Zaire's capital.

"We won't be staying long in Kinshasa. Only a few days, before we fly east to see the mountain gorillas."

Who knew whether they believed me, or whether they just accepted that two foreigners so determined to make it out on this flight must have had a clear purpose.

"Jacob likes to chase the animals, but I prefer the ladies," Dudu said, sidling up to the full-figured Josephina. After all our days in the lounge, she retained a smooth elegance, her dress fresh, her face glistening.

"Mama, you have very good taste," he said, pinching at the fabric of her dress. "I bet you taste good too." Dudu leaned in and whispered something that made her jerk away. Clearing his hand off her leg, she gave Dudu a shove. I couldn't let this pass.

"Please forgive me, Josephina. For years I've tried to teach Dudu some manners, but it's hard to change a man's inner nature. If he offends you in any way, you have my blessing to give him a good smack."

Josephina eyed me with a mixture of suspicion and cheek. "He is your son?"

"No. If he were that, I'd have slapped him down long ago."

Dudu faked outrage. "Mama, how can you ask that? I'm much better looking than he is. Although they say Jacob can still be very charming with the ladies."

"You should be more respectful of your friend." She pushed him again, this time with enough force to send him flopping back onto the seat beside me.

"Are you going to make trouble for me this entire trip?" I said, punching him on his upper arm. Dudu bent over in pain, strangely melodramatic for a guy who must have withstood plenty of hard blows. I figured he was baiting me until he gingerly rolled up his shirtsleeve to expose a fresh tattoo, all red and puffy.

"What the hell did you do to yourself?"

He shrugged. "There was a girl in Phuket who drew it like I asked. She had a great ass too. I could have stayed with her forever if you hadn't called for me."

He dropped his sleeve before I could identify the image in blue, green, and yellow, or the black lettering that wound into his armpit.

"I meant: what kind of Jew gets a tattoo? I didn't help you escape the Soviets so you could mark up your body like a barbarian."

"Oy, Jacob. Don't tell me you're turning Hassidische in your old age."

"It's not Hassidische to believe that the only tattoos our people should bear are the numbers they received in the camps."

"Ach, Jacob, this is the problem with you. You saw so much shit fighting Hitler that you have death on the brain. Before it was

Auschwitz and Buchenwald, now it's the Tutsis and Rwanda. It's like when you hear about genocide, your eyes light up and you become the happiest person in the world."

"Happiness has nothing to do with it. These are debts we owe to the dead."

"I can't afford any more debts, Aba, not even to you. After this trip is over, my bill is repaid."

Dudu had turned ungrateful, as bad as my own son. Just like Shalom, he lacked any perspective on history. Ah, well, all I could do was live by example. Leaving for the bathroom, I faced the mirror and felt the prickly patches of white wire covering my face. It would have been simpler to let the beard grow, but that would have failed to honor the survivors whose stories still haunted me. Compared to what they had suffered, I couldn't exactly complain about a few days trapped in an airport. I pumped the faucet to let the hot water flow, pulled out a razor, and cleaned myself up.

Returning to the lounge, I found Dudu in pitched battle with the Africans. The fight was always the same, over who was the best soccer player in the world. Dudu appeared to have finally conceded that his guy, a young Brazilian tearing up the Spanish league, couldn't match the popular favorite: a tough Liberian playing in Italy.

"Why are you wasting time arguing over a stupid game?"

"Come on, Jacob. It's better for men to fight about football than to start killing each other over a piece of earth."

"You have a ridiculous way of viewing the world. Can't you take anything seriously?"

"What could be more serious than a beautiful goal?"

Reappearing across the lounge, the ticket agent weaved his way through the encampment to our seats. "Good news. The plane is here." He pointed across the tarmac to a battered junker that looked like it was patched together with buckles. Even the insignia of a golden flying leopard was missing paint. A couple of Belgian officials were peering into the engines and poking at the flaps. Too bad their propensity for safety hadn't applied when the Nazis rounded up the Jews of Antwerp.

"How long before that one crashes into the ocean?" Dudu asked.

"Not today, Dudu. Today it will take us to Kinshasa."

"You are a man of great faith."

"About some things."

"Not me." His fist pumped his chest. "I have learned never to trust in anything. Not even in you, Aba."

Despite Dudu's cynicism, the sight of the plane, no matter the condition, roused the lounge to action. Our fellow travelers all rushed to the gate. We could afford to take our time. As the others jostled for seat assignments, I slid the ticket agent a few more bills to wave us down the gangway. We were crossing the tarmac when Dudu nudged me.

"Jacob, you've been like a father to me, but isn't it better to die at home, with your wife by your bedside, than to be lost fighting someone else's war?"

I couldn't fault his attention to risk. It was, after all, his job to protect me. What I didn't need was him digging into my personal affairs. Dudu's attitude toward women was too rough for him to understand the nature of my regret, especially in terms of Susanna.

"Don't worry, Dudu. It'll be worth it in the end."

Boarding the plane, I settled into my seat, fastened the frayed belt, and ignored the cracks in the side panels. As we shot down the runway, I breathed in deep, glad to commit myself one more time to the fight. Even if this business ended badly, at least my sacrifice would be for a higher purpose.

2

Brooklyn
September 12, 1996

PEEKING IN AT SHALOM, I SUCCUMBED TO MY DEEPEST MATERNAL impulse and swooned over my grown son. The need to protect him felt overwhelming, even at a time that impelled me to attend to my own well-being. Faltering at the parlor door, I watched him engage his comrades in the band. Shalom deserved to hear my news, but not yet, not when he presented himself before his friends as their guide to a new world. The last thing he needed, as they assembled for another of their interminable meetings in my living room, was to confront the eschatological anvil hanging around my neck. A little delay wouldn't change anything.

"Hey, Mom, I didn't realize you were home," Shalom said, catching me spying on him. "Come on in. The guys want to say hello."

"Please don't let me interrupt. You must have much to discuss."

"That's all right. You remember Delacroix. And Ismael, our musical director."

His companions, dapper musicians from West Africa, rose with a deference that recalled the formality of my childhood in Europe. Ismael, the sullen saxophonist, nodded while gripping his horn, while the drummer Delacroix extended his hand and thanked me for allowing them to gather in my home.

I wanted to leave before Shally noticed the telltale signs of my unease: the frayed breathing, the trembling hands, the drowning in an afternoon cup of tea. If my son recognized this discomfort, he said nothing about it as he pressed on through the final introduction. "And you know Sang Froid from his music."

The pianist bowed at the keyboard, as if facing a recital audience. All afternoon, the sounds of his practicing had resonated through the brownstone. It had provided a lovely distraction.

"Yes, of course. I have enjoyed your playing. The piano gets so little use."

The Steinway, in its long peripatetic existence, had probably never been asked to deliver anything quite like Sang Froid's jazzy compositions. For years it had brooded in silence, its only action coming every few months when Jacob dispatched an aged Holocaust survivor to keep it tuned, in case I should change my mind and take up lessons. My former husband, long ago consigned to his basement netherworld, was a man who stuck fast to his dreams. He had never stopped hoping my resolve might weaken.

How odd that life with Jacob should come back to me now. It had certainly been an afternoon for reflection, after the pathology report confirmed my darkest fears, that the black moles across my shoulder, long ignored, had burrowed too deep to be excised fully. My oncologist had outlined a rigorous course of chemotherapy, offered without enthusiasm, as the best available treatment. What felt strange was my own response: not the panic that had pursued me through my days, but an eerie sort of relief. After a lifetime of neuroses—aerophobia, claustrophobia, and hypochondria over every imaginable ache—I didn't have to worry any more. The diagnosis was absolute and assured. And yet, much as it provided me with a measure of resolution, I dreaded the burden it would impose on Shally. It had comforted me no end to watch him set sail on his own odyssey with these African troubadours, whose music inspired him more profoundly than my anthropological tractates. Now that he had finally found his way, I couldn't allow him to be sucked into the whirlpool with me.

Excusing myself to the kitchen, I set the kettle atop a burner and plunked a fresh tea bag into my mug. Behind me, a cigarette lighter scraped the air. The whispers and successive draw-back of breath informed me that my son was assuring his friends that his mother was too immersed in thoughts of language and evolution to notice the rich scent of cannabis spreading through the house. I didn't object. Better to let him enjoy himself while he still had time.

The water had nearly boiled when the telephone bolted to life. In normal times, I never rushed to answer. My years with Jacob had steeled me to expect nothing good to come across the telephone lines. Now, after an afternoon of grim revelation, I was struck by a unsettling notion: what if it had been a mistake, a lab mix-up, a misinterpretation of scans, a cruel joke. The thought, once broached, cracked my insouciance like the discovery of scientific fraud. Lifting the receiver, I became acutely aware of my hand shaking.

"Good evening, Madame Professeur." A man addressed me with the same Francophone lilt as the dignified musicians occupying my living room. "It is Pascal. Might I to speak with Shalom?"

Denied a reprieve, I called for my son. As Shally strode across the parlor, I marveled at how little of Jacob there seemed to be in him. He lacked not only his father's evasiveness and capacity for deception, but also his imposing physical bearing. Instead, Shally resembled my own father, Dr. Sigismund Sussman, fixed in my memory through a handful of photographs. So handsome they both were: my father looking somber in his medical clinic, with reclusive smile and stern, dark brow; and Shalom among his friends, casual and dashing and, despite all my efforts to guide him, perpetually lost. They must have been about the same age: my father fossilized in the few black-and-white images that survived my escape from Poland, and Shalom—the living, chattering impresario, whose setbacks never seemed to deflate his ambitions. One who I could barely remember, the other who had drifted beyond my reach.

Shalom's thumb brushed against my wrist as he relieved me of the phone. It had been ages since he held my hand, not since his childhood, when he would accompany me to record baboon vocalizations at the zoo. Of course, he still kissed me in greeting or parting, but the unimpeachable attachment of a boy to his mother had vanished into the murky pond of memory and regret.

Addressing his friend, Shally sounded testy in spelling out directions from the train to our brownstone. As he spoke, I allowed the words to blend, until all I could perceive was the ineffable chattering that had propelled me through a life in science: the buzzing of the larynx, so low in the trachea that it gave birth to a morphological cacophony; the marvelous flexibility of the tongue, so thick and lithe and muscular that it could carve vowels from the air and pound consonants off the teeth; and the creative genius of the *Homo sapiens* brain, spinning out an infinite array of sentences, each of them unique in the universe. All together they produced language, so essential, but perhaps not exclusive, to being human.

"Everything all right, Mom?" Having completed his call, Shalom faced me with an alarming degree of expectation.

"Of course. What shouldn't I be all right?"

"You seem a little frazzled, that's all."

It was comforting that he could read my mood, even if he knew nothing about the dark cells coursing through my lymphatic system.

"Oh, no, I'm fine, just fine. I'm just contemplating the epic descent of the human larynx. You know, the usual stuff."

"All right, cool. You don't mind if me and the guys hang out for a while?"

What I minded was his tortured grammar and poor diction, but the time had long since passed when it would have been appropriate to correct him. In any regard, he wasn't really asking for permission, as much as informing me of his plans.

"Of course, don't worry about me. Go entertain your friends."

He turned to leave, but paused at the doorway. "Say, Mom, we've got a show this weekend. You should come out, if you have time."

I weighed whether to reveal my condition right then, if only to deflect any further invitations. The words stayed inside me. My son had such a vibrant spirit and so much enthusiasm for his newest project that I stopped myself, hating to box him in with me. Jacob had always accused me of coddling him, of trying to shield him from every little bruise, as if wishing to spare him all the anguish of my own refugee childhood.

"Oh, Shally, you don't want your mother embarrassing you in front of your friends." This answer was preferable to another truth, that crowded spaces incited my claustrophobia and dark nightclubs triggered my flight instinct.

"Don't be crazy, Mom. You'd never embarrass me. Plus, the guys love you. Sang Froid is even working on a piece called 'The Susanna Variations.'"

"That's very kind, Shally, but I have a mountain of departmental paperwork awaiting my attention. You remember how busy it can be right before the semester."

I cringed at my excuse. It was insensitive of me to remind Shally of the Anthropology department that had expelled him without mercy before I could help formulate his defense. My son had been so gifted as a listener, and so attuned to music and stories, that his ambivalence as a scholar broke my heart. Standing before me, he didn't seem offended by my reference to the department, only impatient for his final bandmate to arrive. Ever since childhood, my son had been in constant motion. I could never keep up with his intensity, his need for activity, and he in turn seemed to feel immured by my research. Even as a boy, he had tugged against the constraints of my discipline and teased me for my dreaminess, forever admiring images of skulls—ape or hominid. "Skull gazing," Shally called it, pretending that I had some special gift to reanimate bare bone with flesh and muscle.

The water finally boiled after Shally returned to the parlor, and I refilled my mug when once again the phone ruptured the evening calm. By this time, Dr. Bradley would have finished his clinical rounds, making this the last chance for him to lift the severity of the decree. I picked up the receiver, which seemed to have grown heavier in my hand, and tried to contain the disquiet in my voice. What emerged was an untempered quailing; the two syllables of "hello" hovering between despondency, desperation, and anguish.

"Good evening. Did I call at a bad time? You sound troubled."

It took only a moment to recognize Jacob's voice: the commanding, resonant bass that had coaxed countless compromises from me.

"It's not an especially bad time," I said, recognizing myself to be a poor, unpracticed liar. "I'm simply surprised to hear you break radio silence. It's not like you to reach out from your travels."

Given our history, I wondered whether Jacob had an inside line on my medical condition. It didn't seem likely. For all his skill at deception, he had always respected my demand for privacy.

"Well, Susanna, at the risk of violating our established boundaries, I wanted to call one more time. This may be a hard trip, and before I dropped off the map, it felt right to say goodbye." He paused for a moment, sizing up his words. "In case anything unexpected happens, you should know that I was thinking of you."

His banter transported me back to an unwavering courtship, when he presented his credentials as a fellow orphan and wore me down with a surfeit of ever more opulent gifts. The material items didn't charm me as much as his vow of devotion. If he could only have honored that commitment, I might never have thrown him out.

"Jacob, I hope for your sake this undertaking isn't unduly dangerous."

"It's tough to know what will happen, even for a guy like me, who can predict the future." His old joke about prescience, manifested in a purported ability to recognize when an airplane would plummet to earth, brought me back to our times together. It had comforted me once, to believe in him, but that was only because I had been deceiving myself.

Jacob reminded me of the emergency cache of funds stored in his cabinet downstairs. It was a habit of his, to prepare for every contingency. "Would you mind taking care of my bills over next few months? The power company always threatens to turn off the lights if I miss a few payments. I hate to come home to chaos."

The last thing I needed was another chore, but refusing him would have required its own explanation, and so I consented. The old temptation stirred within me, to pry some hint of his antics from his disciplined jaws. What a futile endeavor that would have been. Jacob remained as sturdy as ever. His hair had given over to white but had lost none of its thickness. His exuberant stride had barely slowed, his barrel chest served as a bulwark against the slovenly spread of most men his age. His eyes retained the same alertness, a falcon patrolling from on high, watching all activity below.

"One more thing you should know," he said. "My will is next to the cash."

How ironic that he should speak of wills on this particular day. If it continued in this vein, he would soon be reminding me of his preference for being interred in the orthodox fashion—in a plain pine box, as if it made any difference to the dead, especially compared with the involuntary cremation of both sets of our parents.

"Wouldn't it be better for Shalom to handle that for you? He would be most directly affected."

"No, he'd only screw it up. Anyway, you're still the principal beneficiary."

It didn't surprise me that Jacob remained faithful in this final regard. I even felt tempted, for a moment, to share my news, if only to test him, whether he would abandon his clandestine enterprises and dash home to attend to my care. It wasn't worth the risk. As the sun set on this harrowing day, the last thing I needed was any more disappointments. Once a man—be it husband or father—betrayed you, promised one thing and did the opposite, there was no turning back to the *status quo ante*. In my entire life, the only one who had been true to me was Shally. For all his flaws, he was the only one I could trust.

"Would you like to speak to our son?"

"That's all right. He won't want to be bothered," Jacob said. "What's he up to?"

"Shally is meeting with his musician friends, the Africa Rumba Express."

"If they were smart, they'd ride that express far away from him. What does he know about the music business, anyway?"

Throughout our years apart, Jacob had never failed to be charming and solicitous of me. Yet, for all his courtesy, and his acceptance of my boundaries, he refused to show any respect to our son. What motivated his disdain for Shally no longer concerned me, except insofar as it added to our son's burdens. Shally might have failed to live up to his father's standards, but he deserved better than condescension and competitiveness. Now, more than ever, a son would need his father.

"Jacob, try to be kind. Shally has always had a good ear, and a gift for listening. Perhaps this will be how he finally finds himself."

"If he's got such a good ear, why didn't he ever listen to me? I tried for years to get through to him."

Jacob let it drop, and we reverted to the formality that had guided us since our marriage came apart in October 1973, in the wake of war and betrayal. I promised to attend to his affairs, and he wished me well and hung up, leaving me as alone as ever.

The rumble of a jet engine drew my attention out the window to the carousel of airplanes beginning their final descent to Kennedy Airport. Each one flickered in the twilight as it emerged from the horizon and grew gradually larger until it passed overhead. Years ago I used to track the flights in horror, worried that one might tumble to earth and incinerate a row of brownstones. Now, given my current diagnosis, the threat seemed irrelevant. The engine noise blended into the ambient sounds of the street and even provided some consolation that, after lifetime of aerophobia, I need never again gaze through the portal of a departing plane.

Shally leaned into the kitchen. "Hey, Mom, was that Pascal calling again? He should have been here by now."

"No. This time it was your father."

"You're kidding. What kind of skulduggery is he up to now?"

"He wasn't terribly forthcoming."

"No, I wouldn't imagine. Did he say how long he'd be gone?"

"He didn't specify, but it sounded as if it would be several months."

"Cool, then we'll use his place downstairs to rehearse."

Returning to his friends, Shally proclaimed that they now had a space to practice. I couldn't bring myself to object; father and son would have to sort out their differences at a later date.

When he left, I turned to the poster that had kept me company since my early days with Jacob. This framed image of a Holbein painting had been a gift from my husband before he started taking himself so seriously. *The Ambassadors* comprised two men standing over a table laden with the articles of their trade—tools of navigation, maps and a globe turned to *Affrica*, spelled so strangely. Each of the figures somehow bore a striking resemblance to Jacob, except for the beard of course, but it was the burly Ambassador on the left, with his resolute posture and aura of command, that had always reminded me most of my former husband. At their feet, floating above a marble floor, was a surprising modernist twist: a skull distended through some trick of light and lenses, as if the Ambassadors brought death with them, carrying the fate of nations within their mantle of power.

That Jacob should have called, on this of all nights, challenged my disbelief in supernatural spirits. While I remained steadfastly skeptical of an omniscient being, Jacob's timing made me wonder about a god of irony. Such a fickle presence could account for my ambivalence toward him a quarter century after he betrayed me in Ethiopia. No, impish deities, like mercurial husbands, were merely romantic distractions. My faith was embedded in language alone. With time running out, I needed to get back to work.

3

Brooklyn
September 12, 1996

DAD'S DISAPPEARANCE CAME AT THE PERFECT TIME. THROUGHOUT my life, he had always been dashing off somewhere, but this was the first occasion when his travels actually provided me with a tangible benefit. His vacant basement apartment meant no more schlepping around instruments and no more burning pricey studio time waiting for Pascal. All we needed to do now was to shift Dad's dumpy furniture to one side and set up for rehearsal.

"Guys, this is great news. My father could be gone for months."

The four leading members of the Africa Rumba Express didn't share my excitement. Gathered around Mom's coffee table, they tinkered with their instruments or gazed at their hands, until Delacroix tapped out a beat and said: "Shalom, this will be a great intrusion on your father. What will he say when he returns?"

Back in their countries, the guys must have lived by a more rarefied sense of filial piety than I did. As far as I was concerned, lending us his place downstairs was the least my father could do to make up for a lifetime of condescension and neglect.

"Don't worry, my mom gave her blessing, and no one can challenge her authority in this brownstone."

"But our playing will be very loud," Sang Froid called over from the piano. "It will disturb the professeur."

"Believe me, she's too immersed in screaming baboons to notice," I said. "Her research puts her into a trance."

Reaching into my guayabera, I pulled out a joint, the third so far this evening. Or maybe it was the fourth.

"Shalom, you should not smoke so much. It is bad for the piano," Sang Froid said, brushing his finger along the keyboard.

"That piano must have survived worse that a little ganja." I took a deep puff, eyed the Steinway and stubbed out the joint.

The one whose voice counted most, Ismael Camara, our musical director, hadn't yet said anything. He was busy tending to his saxophone as if dressing a small child for winter. After testing the action on the keys and valves, Ismael applied the oil that made the brass smell like an engine, one that plied the ocean currents between Africa and the New World. Around the table, the guys waited for him to render his opinion. To his left sat Delacroix Soumarahu, the Clark Kent of our band—UN investigator by day, conga player from Côte d'Ivoire by night, a judicious presence in either incarnation. At the piano was Sang Froid, whose real name was Mouhamadou Bah, but who had adopted a bracing *nom de guerre* to avoid any administrative conflicts with the City University, where he taught higher math. And in the chair facing me was Pascal Sidibe, a fast-talking hustler who spent his days peddling knock-off handbags along Broadway. He sang a spirited vocals, but never stopped questioning whether my managerial instincts matched their musical talents.

"Our problem is not the practice space," Pascal said, removing his sunglasses and clipping them onto his open shirt. "Our problem is a manager who does not have the correct strategy to promote our music. My friends in Europe are performing at the biggest festivals, but you bring us only to very small clubs."

Pascal fed me this horseshit all the time. What he really wanted was to seize the mantle of headliner, to call the band his own, "Pascal Sidibe and the Africa Rumba Express," when in reality it was Ismael who gave form and pace to our music.

"We've got to be patient," I said. "It takes time to build an audience, and I have an idea that could change things for us."

"You always talk about the big ideas," Pascal said. "We do not want to play before any more festivals of the renaissance."

That particular gig, at the Robin Hood Country Faire, sure hadn't worked out as planned. My idea had been to reach out to the crunchy types who actually listened to World Music. Unfortunately, this Faire turned out to be a gathering of dorks and hippies pining for "Greensleeves." Only a handful of them even bothered to break away from the maypole to listen to the Rumba Express.

Ismael wiped the excess oil from his horn and kissed the bell, as he did before every performance. "Shalom, you work like a donkey to support us, but it was not worth driving five hours to play for people who dress up in crazy costumes."

It was always hard to get a read on Ismael. He seemed dreamy, contemplating a galaxy of notes beneath the dark kufi that covered his close-cropped hair, but he had a clear sense of direction forged by years of struggle. The saxophone that he cradled on his lap had been his most intimate companion, closer even than his wife and children in Senegal, more reliable than his bandmates, and far more essential than his manager.

"That's true, *compañero*, the Faire was a big disappointment, but this next idea could really change everything."

I called him *compañero* as a nod to our shared passion for Cuba. Ismael had grown up in Dakar listening to the old records of the great Havana bands, and developed his sound to reflect the melding of African and Cuban strains. My ties to old Havana were far more corporeal: a doomed summer of anthropological fieldwork spent cycling through the beds of various *muchachas*, the bill for which came due on my return home when the department spurned my ethnographic take on seduction.

"Shalom, why do you always need to change everything?" Pascal piped in. "It is not your place to tell us how to play the music."

"I don't want to do anything to the music, only present it a little differently."

"What do you suggest?" Delacroix asked.

"That we make our image more political."

"You are crazy, man." Pascal rolled his head back in laughter, as if the village idiot had suggested rising up to overthrow the government. "No one cares about politics when they come to listen to me sing. They want to drink the beer, meet the girls, have a good time."

He had a point: women and wine were certainly what drew me out at night.

"*Compañeros*, believe me, Americans only give a shit about the world if they can shed their grace on it. What I'm proposing is that we adapt our name, to let our audiences feel like the saviors of lost children."

"What name do you propose?" Ismael asked, inserting a fresh reed into his mouthpiece.

"The African Refugee Mega-Stars."

The parlor went silent.

"But we are not refugees," Delacroix said. As one who translated victims' testimonies for war crimes prosecutions, Delacroix demanded precision in language, the same exactitude that went into his impeccable suits, the flawless starched shirts, the glistening sheen of his perfectly shaved head.

"You're forgetting about Robbie," I said. "That's his official status, so we wouldn't be deceiving anyone, or at least not completely deceiving them."

A flicker of nods recognized that Robbie Benson, the session musician who played the timbales for us, was indeed a refugee.

He'd escaped Liberia's civil war right before the rebels rolled into Monrovia chopping off the hands of anyone in their way. Fortunately for him, Robbie found passage on a freighter out of the burning city. Functioning hands were pretty much a *sine qua non* for a drummer.

"In fact, you guys could all be considered refugees," I said. "You came here seeking a better life. You shouldn't be required to have run from an invading army to use that term."

My argument sounded crass, even exploitive. These were professional musicians seeking a broader forum for their art, not a six-year-old Susanna Sussman fleeing Hitler. All around me, brows were tightening, chins were being scratched.

"I do not like this name: African Refugees," Pascal said, wriggling a fake Rolex on his wrist. "In Senegal, we have known peace since independence. Our people live in cities with great culture and learning. The warlords and child soldiers on your television are not part of our reality. You should not think that all Africans are the same."

Delacroix rubbed his hands together slowly, as if milling the evidence into a just conclusion. "Pascal is correct. The designation of 'refugee' has specific legal requirements. You must have left your country due to what we call a 'well-founded fear of persecution.' None of us here can claim that, not that we could prove before a judge."

Nothing was ever easy. Even a simple name change set off a grand ontological debate.

"Guys, it doesn't have to mean anything cosmic. The name is only a way of playing into the American vanity that the whole world revolves around them. We want to give our audiences a reason to cheer for us, to see the underdog make good."

Looking around the table, I longed for some of my father's clear sense of conviction, or at least his forcefulness. If I had learned one thing from a lifetime of dealing with Dad, it was never to show your critics any doubt, or they would use it to crush you.

Survival rested on the certainty that when you stepped out onto a frozen river, the ice would act as a bridge to carry you across.

"Hey, *compañeros*, this is something you obviously have to decide among yourselves. But this issue may be symbolic of something bigger, about the direction of the band, and whether you want to proceed with me as manager. If so, then we should press ahead together, but if not, I'll step aside and let you go your own way."

My threat of resignation was meant to blast away their resistance. No such luck. Power plays were never my strength. Delacroix thanked me for my candor and informed me they would consider my recommendations. He smoothed out his tie, turned to his bandmates, and addressed them not in French, which I could have followed, but in Wolof, which he had picked up during a long stint with the UN in Dakar. Much as I didn't appreciate Delacroix's shift in language, I could recognize that any hope of retaining my position rested with his capacity to plead my case. If he still believed in me, and I had every indication that he did, then at least I had a fighting chance. He was fair, prudent, and circumspect. Music was more passion than vocation for him, something to take his mind off the testimonies of butchery he dealt with during his days sorting through evidence for the UN war-crimes tribunals.

For all of Delacroix's temperance, Pascal seemed to be angling for a fight. His voice rose quickly, and he pointed to me while laughing derisively. It wasn't hard to peg Pascal as echoing my father, who swore that incompetence tainted everything I touched: Shalom the fuck-up, Shalom the dilettante, Shalom the reverse-alchemist, turning every golden opportunity into lead. Not that I hadn't given Dad plenty of ammunition—what with getting thrown out of grad school and embarking on a slew of far-fetched schemes. This time was different, though. Now I had a real plan, and a resolute commitment to see it through. Provided the guys didn't fire me right here in my own mother's living room.

I rose from the couch and drifted toward the bookshelves running floor to ceiling along the parlor. Serving as the pillars of my mother's world, the stacks bore the lode of all four branches of anthropology: from linguistic to biological to archeological to cultural. The volumes that had once informed my studies now stood as totem to my failure. I never should have tried to keep up with her, something that became clear from my first breath in graduate school.

"Shalom, come back to us. You must be present for this discussion," Delacroix called out. He was standing as the rest of the guys looked away, leading me to conclude that the decision had gone against me. Girding myself for the inevitable dismissal, I wondered how I would recast my life yet again.

"Tell him," Delacroix instructed Ismael. "Do not make him wait any longer."

Fingering his sax, as if rehearsing a tune, Ismael slowly revealed his judgment: "When Shalom joined us, we were playing in the metro, waiting for the police to push us away. Then he found us a place at the Shamrock, with five people in the audience, but the next week, ten others came to hear us, and each time since then has been bigger clubs and more people. So I say 'yes,' let us stay with him as manager. We will become, as he says, the 'African Refugee Mega-Stars.'"

It didn't sound like much of an endorsement, but at this stage I couldn't afford to take offense. The guys all rose to celebrate the renewal of our vows, and I made my way around the circle shaking hands with each of them.

As soon as we sealed the deal, my beeper came alive, tingling around the hip. Squaring the little box before me, I recognized the number as belonging to Mia, a spoiled ex-dancer now studying for a doctorate in my mother's department. She had a penchant for ganja, an open expense account and a lithe body.

"Guys, I gotta go."

"But Shalom, what about the practice?" Delacroix asked. He had stood up for me, and now I was standing them up.

"You go on downstairs. I'll be back as soon as I can."

I dropped the keys to Dad's apartment, grabbed a few dime bags from my stash upstairs, and bolted. It would take me an hour to reach Mia uptown, and she would want me to stay while she sampled both product and messenger. Sure, it was more time wasted in a lifetime of wasted opportunities, but I couldn't help myself.

4

Goma, Zaire
September 16, 1996

As the plane turned toward Goma, I peered out the window at a dark lake ringed by green mountains. To the north, barely visible through the storm clouds, a string of soaring volcanoes shot up to the heavens. These must have been the Virunga Mountains, looming over Lake Kivu and the sprawling city below.

"What the fuck is that?" Dudu asked. He was pointing west, to a crazy mosaic of reds, greens, and blues spread across a vast field.

"It must be one of the refugee camps."

"Aba, you promised this wasn't going to be like Ethiopia."

"Don't worry, we won't be doing any rescuing. Not this time."

The camp below was filled with Hutus, the perpetrators of genocide, who had hacked to death a million Tutsis faster than Hitler had exterminated the Jews of my father's Galicia. One thing I knew for certain: those murderous bastards wouldn't get any help from us.

We bounced down on a bumpy airfield. As the brakes slowed our momentum, the plane shot past a succession of broken aircraft that had been left to rust just off the runway. Arriving in what passed for a terminal, we walked through a crowd of hustlers making like we were old friends.

"*Muzungu*, come this way. I have a taxi. Let me take your bags."

"*Muzungu*, I have a good hotel."

Dudu didn't hesitate. Pushing straight into their midst, he opened a channel through their groping hands. Denied a day's pay, the men turned nasty, fingers pinched together, moving up and down as if milking a cow, the same motion we had seen in Kinshasa, where every loafer wanted a handout. They hounded us until we came to a short fellow holding a sign with my name— Jacob Furman—written in block letters.

"You must be Patrice," I said.

The others fell away, the hunt was over.

"Yes, that is me. I have come for you."

He was so small that he looked stunted, with a big smile and a head too large for his body. Loading our bags into his car, I directed him to the Hotel Bruegel and we headed out into traffic behind a truck marked with the initials WFP that was bouncing all over the pockmarked road. As we entered a rotary, the truck slowed before a pothole as big as a bathtub, rocked back and forth, and then turned west as a volcano appeared through the mist.

"That is the way to Mugunga," our driver said. "They are delivering food for the Rwandans."

"Rwandans, you mean the Hutus?"

"Yes, the ones who came two years ago. Our government let them stay in the refugee camps after they lost their war. You are coming with the UN?"

Dudu leaned over the front seat with a big smile. "Do we look like do-gooders?"

Patrice shrugged. "The man who contacted me only said you would arrive on the morning flight."

The last thing I needed was for Dudu to stir up any confusion. "We have some business here," I told the driver, "some people to see."

We slogged through the center of town, past open-air markets where peasant women sat on blankets with produce stretched out before them. Young guys straddling motorbikes waited for passengers to taxi across town. Outside the storefronts hung battered signs illustrating diamonds and gold; inside, the brokers weighed the fruit of the mines. On the corner, big women in colorful robes held calculators in one hand and wads of cash in the other, the same posture we had seen in Kinshasa, a profitable enterprise built on the collapsing value of President Mobutu's banknotes.

Passing through the commercial district, Patrice turned right at another traffic circle and headed into a neighborhood of fine villas guarded by high stone walls, making the place look like a Swiss lake town. A checkpoint appeared. A half dozen Zairean soldiers leaned over the car ahead of us, leering into the windows, waving their Kalashnikovs like toys, pretending to spray the occupants with automatic fire.

"Here we go, Aba. More fun," Dudu said, turning to see our retreat blocked by cars behind and stone walls on both sides. He leaned forward to wrap an arm around Patrice's shoulder: "Stay calm, my friend. You can't outrun a bullet."

Spotting our car, the gang of soldiers rushed toward us. Their shirts hanging out, they banged on the roof, rubbed their bellies, and made the same up-and-down pinching gesture as the airport porters.

"Give us something, *Muzungu*. Give us some money."

"A sweet, give us a sweet. You have plenty."

Dudu patted my arm to indicate he would handle this. Bribes, like beer, were his specialty. Opening his window halfway, he passed them enough to buy a round.

"Enjoy, my friends. Think of us when you are drinking tonight."

The soldiers who scrambled over the money weren't satisfied with his generosity. "That's not enough, *Muzungu*. The price of beer has gone up since last week."

Dudu slipped a few more bills more out the window. "All right, go spend this fast before the cost rises again."

The thugs moved on to their next victims, and Patrice wasted no time putting the car in gear. The road led along Lake Kivu, whose shore was lined with palm trees and fancy homes. Reaching the Hotel Bruegel, we found a restored colonial villa transformed into a luxury lakeside resort, albeit one filled with shaggy relief workers. The do-gooders paraded through the lobby, kibitzing in a dozen languages, wearing tan vests emblazoned with the initials of their particular aid group. Damn fools, aiding the Hutus as if they were any other refugees. Avoiding them, we proceeded to the marble reception desk, registered with the uniformed concierge, and were led upstairs to adjoining rooms facing the lake. Alone at last, I flopped on the bed and allowed myself to be seduced by an afternoon nap, nestled by the trees rustling in the breeze. The scene was nice and peaceful, but if I had learned one thing from history, it was that tranquility never lasts.

A thunderstorm rolling through Goma woke me in the late afternoon. After the rain passed, I returned to the hotel lobby and found myself surrounded by more do-gooders. Craving some privacy, I strolled out onto the hotel's back lawn. Beyond the grass lay Lake Kivu, cold and dark as oil, the waves slapping the rocky shore. Somewhere up north, another wave of thunder boomed, still far off. To the east, already shrouded in darkness, was Rwanda, where the trouble all began two years ago. Out on the lake, the oranges and reds of dusk reflected in the water. It was a glorious vision. A real Eden that brought me back to an earlier time in Africa, when Susanna went digging for the bones of our ancestors.

Susanna always considered my nostalgia to be a curse, but it saddened me to think of Ethiopia, how we could have built something enduring, what the rabbis called "palaces in time." If only she had trusted me, if only she could have had faith in my intentions. Back then our lives had seemed intertwined, like the

31

Havdalah candles lit by observant Jews at the end of Shabbat, three discrete strands of wax braided together, so that the wicks burned separately but at the same time. It was a sweet, romantic notion of togetherness. Even though she was lost to me now, I was glad to have called her a few days ago from Kinshasa, to remind her that my feelings had never changed, not from the moment she first stumbled into my arms.

"Aba, what are you doing out here all by yourself?" Beer in hand, Dudu slipped in behind my chair. "It's no good for an old man to be left alone with his regrets." This was what made Dudu so dangerous. Somehow he could see right through you.

"Have you ever known me to look back in regret?" I replied quickly, not wanting to give him even the slightest opening

Easing himself quietly into a lawn chair, he still moved as if on night maneuvers through hostile territory. "Not you, Jacob. You don't allow anyone to peek into your heart, beneath all the scar tissue."

"Don't worry about me, Dudu. My heart is plenty strong. Otherwise I could never have survived so many disappointments."

He looked me up and down, like a fighter scanning for weakness. "This is what makes me so crazy about this assignment, Aba. Why did you let yourself get mixed up with Salik again? You may be a *nudnik*, but you've always been an idealist."

Dudu deserved an answer, for our many travels together, beginning with my placing him and his mother on a night train out of Odessa, after the Soviets hounded to death his *refusenik* father, and culminating with the last great Ethiopian airlift, when he helped me transport thousands of Beta Israel out of Addis Ababa, the planes taking off so full that whole villages vanished into thin air.

"I'm still an idealist, Dudu, that's why I agreed to Salik's request. The Tutsis need our help."

He downed a big drink of beer. "Oy, Jacob. You're going to make a mess here."

A loudmouth like Dudu couldn't comprehend the scope of the tragedy, how the Hutus had slaughtered the Tutsis without mercy and had then stolen the mantle of victimhood for themselves.

"This mess existed long before us. Now it's time for justice."

"It will take a hard man to watch that, Aba. You don't have the stomach to be so ruthless."

"Just watch, it may surprise you how ruthless I can be."

"Not the Jacob who I have known. Not the man who lives to save people."

He lifted his shirtsleeve and placed the beer bottle directly against his left arm, high up, by the shoulder. He rotated the arm stiffly, as if opening and closing a lock.

"Still bothering you, eh?" I asked.

"The damp annoys it."

The weather made my fingertips ache, but at least my pains weren't self-inflicted. "Serves you right for getting that stupid tattoo."

"Aba, you always talk about remembering the past. Well, this is my memorial to bad times in Lebanon. It's guaranteed until ten days after death."

The story, as it had been passed on to me, was that, during the early days of the Lebanon War, a rocket-propelled grenade had wiped out half of Dudu's unit. For years he hadn't wanted to discuss it, and I never pressed him. Now he had the whole saga painted onto his arm.

The last vestiges of daylight illuminated the lake like a painting of Moses and the revelation at Sinai. The scene before us, of course, looked nothing like the desert. It was far too wet for that, with the lake disappearing in the mist and dark clouds to the east promising a fresh tempest.

"What a beautiful place," I said.

He lifted the bottle from his tattoo and took a drink. "Beauty is no good, Aba. It tricks you to believe in illusions. This is how we got stuck in Lebanon. We couldn't see the truth, only what we wanted to believe."

This kind of sentiment I might have expected from Susanna or Shalom, but not from Dudu, who had loved guns so much as a teenaged immigrant to Haifa that his poor widowed mother worried for his sanity.

"When did you turn into a peacenik?"

"What peacenik? I only refuse to live in a fantasy world, thinking that what you win in battle will ever last."

Our conversation was cut off by the shouts of fishermen rowing out onto the lake. Darkness was creeping in, but we could still make out the men in their crazy-looking boat—three canoes lashed together with long poles—arguing over how to clear an obstruction in their nets. One of the fishermen tried to dislodge the object with his oar, but soon he needed to lean over the water and tug hard at the net. A few shakes set loose the unmistakable shape of an arm and a torso, rolling across the surface. Easing their catch onto open water, the fisherman went back to rowing.

Dudu rubbed his head as if it were hurting him. "So, say you eat the fish from there, would that make you a cannibal?"

"What are you, a philosopher? You think that after the shit you saw in Lebanon, you can write a new Guide to the Perplexed?"

"Not me, Jacob. I leave the philosophy to you. The best lesson I learned in Lebanon was to be careful of the food. This is why it will be steak tonight for dinner. At least you can trust a piece of meat."

Out on the dark water, the fishermen had paddled out of sight, and the body had disappeared beneath the surface. Whoever it was, its presence had vanished as completely as Dudu's tattoos would do, ten days after death.

5

Brooklyn
September 13, 1996

I LOOKED UP IN WONDER AT THE BOY WHOM I AFFECTIONATELY called Yorick, and he stared right back, inasmuch as a skull can stare, through wide sockets that millions of years ago had contained his eyes. His sightless visage made me reflect on the deep past, and on all the twists of the hominid evolutionary tree leading to our existence. Yorick's photo posted on my wall, even in his silence, brought me back to all my basic questions about the birth of language, and to what I might have accomplished if I only could have kept digging through the dust of East Africa.

"Skull-gazing again, Mom?" Shally asked, breaking into my musings. He stood in my bedroom doorway, ready to depart for the evening. "Haven't you sucked old Yorick dry by now?"

Shally's brashness had always masked a terrible vulnerability. When he was a boy, upset about his father's criticism, I used to strum my hands through his hair and console him with the assurance that I would always be there with him. He kept his hair too short for that these days. And no longer could I deceive him with promises in perpetuity.

"You might be surprised at the power of continued observation."

Shally glanced at the photo. "Say, Mom, have you ever wondered what early humans talked about when they first figured out this language business?"

"Food, I would imagine: the hunt, the search for seeds and berries. And war too, the struggle against common enemies."

"Not sex?" Shally had always been forthright about physical intimacy. Even now, he carried himself with a sly smile that I found unsettling. Much to my dismay, he had acquired a terrible reputation as a rake that had often led him astray, most notably in his louche, misguided essay on Cuba.

"Oh, Shally, be serious."

"I am serious, Mom. Mating is a primal influence."

He never introduced me to his girlfriends, which was probably just as well. Shalom set his standards far too low, and it would have crushed me to see him tied to a woman who failed to match his gifts.

"I suppose that may be true," I said. "Courtship could well have been a driver of language formation."

"It's sure something we talk about in terms of the band, how to generate the magic that will charge up an audience."

Turning back to Yorick's picture on my wall, I noticed the bleached outline around its edges, marking where Jacob's antique marriage contract had once hung.

"I can't offer you much advice there. I'm somewhat immune to the effect of music and dance."

"Maybe that's because Dad wasn't much of a romantic."

"Well, he certainly didn't take me dancing."

We both laughed at the image of Jacob as dancer, and I wondered whether this might be the moment to inform Shally that his mother might soon be as silent as poor Yorick. It would have been simple. He had nothing more pressing than another night out with his friends. Yet for the tenth time, I deferred the inevitable and let him slip out the door. Speech, despite my decades of study, had failed me. The only option left was to reach for pen and paper and to inscribe what came out less as confession than elegy.

> *Dearest Shally,*
>
> *Forgive the shocking nature of this note. It is so terribly difficult for me to communicate troubling news. This past week I sought medical attention to address the dark moles on my shoulder.*

I stopped to steady my hand. Feeling flushed, I reached for the bedroom window to let in a little air. So much had happened since I conceded to the haunting fear and went trembling to my physician, hoping for him to dismiss me once again as a hypochondriac. Logic should have driven me to the doctor months earlier, when I first spotted the strange shadow as I twisted out of the shower. At that point, the sight of moles had made me collapse onto the bathroom floor, wet and shivering, covering my mouth so that Shally—sleeping off another late night in his bedroom upstairs—wouldn't hear my weeping. Then, abhorring the sight of my own body, I ignored the threat, echoing the response of my father, who had failed to flee Poland until it was too late, until all he could do was to assure me that everything would be all right, that we would meet up again in America, as soon as my parents could secure passage out of Łodź.

> *Pathological results confirmed my deepest fears. It is cancer. Melanoma. Further tests will determine its spread, but my physician has counseled me to prepare for an arduous battle.*

Since the diagnosis, bathing had become an apology. My hands avoided the moles, as if each stroke of the washcloth, each tracing of soap could speed the cancer cells through my body. My intensive study of human physiology allowed me to envision the ineffable wasting: the dissolving of breasts and cheeks, the bony protrusions of shoulders, ribs, hips. Foresight was a curse, as damning now as with Cassandra before the fall of Troy. Facing the mirror, I imagined stepping into the looking glass, fleeing this vale of tears and sparing myself the chemicals and radiation, the needles and nausea. But fiction, like myth, was nothing but an escape, an exercise to concentrate the mind in metaphor. Truth brimmed with far more anguish.

Whatever happens, Shally, I want you to know of my love for you. From the morning you were born, I have always tried to protect you. You can't imagine how sad it makes me to inform you of this news.
All my love,
Mom

Completing the note brought me little relief and no catharsis. After subduing another bout of hesitation, I leaned the paper against Shalom's door and returned to bed, but a toxic cocktail of insomnia and guilt roused me to every creak in the house. Seeking something soporific, I picked out a copy of Chomsky from the bookshelf. My old friend Chuck Rosenfeld would have raged at me for indulging in something as whispery as linguistics, but if anything could lull me unconscious, it was *Language and Mind*. As my eyes glided over the thickets of sentence mapping, I felt myself drift off.

Hours must have passed before the front door thumped open downstairs. Roused from a quarter-sleep, I listened to Shally stumble in and begin his death march up the stairs. As he staggered past my bedroom, I regretted binding such a grim, unflinching prognosis onto paper. Perhaps I should have persisted in the fiction of normalcy through whatever lay ahead. No, much as it might hurt him, he deserved to know. As Jacob used to remind me, I couldn't coddle him forever.

Shally took his time poring over my words, before he returned to knock at my door. When he entered, letter in hand, he looked pallid, shrunken, as if he had aged ten years in these past few hours.

"Mom, what does this mean?"

A monumental question, to which I could offer only a Delphic response. "The doctors aren't sure yet. All they can say definitively is that it will be difficult." Then, in my desperate wish to avoid hurting him, I offered him a sanctuary in which I had little faith. "They want to start me on chemotherapy next week."

Shally shook his head slowly, as if refuting the reality presented to him. "Have you told Dad?"

As if by reflex, I looked at the wall, not at Yorick, but behind him, to the ghostly shadow of the vanished *ketubah*. Shally probably didn't remember the marriage contract that had once hung there, but its loss still clung to me. Jacob remained present even in his absence.

"He didn't exactly leave a contact number, even if I wanted to tell him."

"Uncle Effie could track him down."

For as long as I had known Jacob, he had always instructed his corpulent, wheezing friend Effie to be a point of contact during his travels.

"The last thing I need is Effie mixed up in my personal affairs."

"It's up to you, but Dad could really take charge in this kind of situation."

"That's just it. I don't need anyone taking charge."

My tone was harsher than I had intended. The rigors of the past week must have taxed me. I reached out my hand, and Shalom clasped it and bowed his head, as if showing obeisance to a queen.

"Oh, Ma." His words sounded like a gasp, his fingers tightening around mine, a drowning man searching for solid ground and grasping only driftwood. "I was hoping this might be one of your crazy neuroses."

Poor Shally had suffered through a thousand of my imagined ailments: strained breathing equating to lung cancer; headaches seeming like signs of glioblastoma; or chest pains feigning cardiac infarction. It was his tolerance of my various fears, and his sensitivities as a listener, that convinced me he would have made a good anthropologist.

"Sadly, even hypochondriacs suffer from real illnesses."

He shook his head and sighed. "What happens now?"

The quivering tenor of his voice drew me closer than ever before to the terrible choice faced by my father, who had lacked the courage to admit there was no hope for our family as he bundled me onto a children's flight out of Łódź. Facing my son at this awful moment, I reverted to cliché, another form of cowardice, and abandoned a lifetime of refusing to look on the bright side.

"We'll do the best we can."

"Okay, but what does that mean for us on a tangible basis?"

"No, not us. Me. Let me fight this my own way. I don't want cancer to be definitional. We have to look past this diagnosis and press on with our lives. If that means attending a musical performance with your friends, then you must do that. We cannot allow anything to change. That would be giving in to the disease."

My request must have sounded like a bromide out of self-help literature, but it was the best excuse I could manage. Shally retreated upstairs to sleep off what remained of the darkness, and I felt imbued with an acute sense of wakefulness. For once, however, it wasn't purposeless insomnia as much as crisp vigilance. Denied any real hope of arresting the disease, I took consolation in binding my work into a coherent valediction, before decades of research and colloquy with colleagues dissipated into the fog of cancer's endgame.

6

Lower Manhattan
September 14, 1996

THE SAPPHIC SANCTUARY WAS PACKED THE NIGHT AFTER MY mother dropped the worst imaginable news on my door. It felt strange to be out clubbing, but my guilt over complying with Mom's demand for normalcy was assuaged by the sight of Mercedes Mendoza making her way along the bar. Mercedes hadn't come for the hip, tattooed women who mobbed the place. She was here for me. And of course for my band, exiled to a table in back. Holding my arms tight against my chest to guard against any misconstrued poke, I snuck through the sweating sapphos to catch up to her.

"Buenos noches, *compañera*. You have no idea how good it is to see you."

Mercedes stretched up to kiss me on both cheeks, our first physical contact since a brief dalliance last year. "You wore me down, mi amor. All your messages about the Africa Rumba Express piqued my curiosity."

"I hate to disappoint you, but we're the African Refugee Mega-Stars now."

"Mega-Stars, that sounds ambitious. Was that voted on by the UN High Commission for Refugees?"

"You might say it's an unofficial title. After all these guys have been through, they've earned the right to a few linguistic liberties."

Mercedes looked much as I remembered her: a tiny Mexicana with hair dangling to her waist, with a working woman's ass that kept firm time with the music. Dispensing with the high fashion of the Latina elite, she dressed like a hippy campesina: her sandals crafted from tire rubber and her funky vest woven from rough alpaca. Moving closer, I considered whether it was bad form to hit on a woman in a dyke bar. The last thing I needed was any personal drama, considering what a saga it had been to book a band of African *salseros* here. The Sanctuary's manager had been skeptical, but I won her over with a generous supply of weed and a pledge that the Mega-Stars could inspire any crowd to dance.

"You really must be loving it here," Mercedes said, her attention drifting across the room. "Surrounded by all these beautiful women."

"Don't worry, I'm all business tonight."

During our time together, I had burdened Mercedes with the details of my various misadventures until, like an asshole, I abruptly stopped returning her calls. And now, however venal it must have seemed, I had tracked down an old lover for professional courtesies. She was, after all, a music critic versed in everything from Congolese soukous to Cuban son. The Mega-Stars could use her on our side.

"Shally, I was surprised to hear about you representing a band of *salseros*. You always made it sound like your time in Cuba was a bitter memory."

"Music wasn't the reason for me getting tossed me out of school, *compañera*. It was just the wrong fit. One thing Havana did teach me was how to recognize when a band has something special."

My pitch must have sounded like a bad pickup line, but it was better than confessing the insufferably earnest truth, that the sound of Ismael's winding sax runs and Sang Froid's sharp chords provided me a kind of transcendence, a way to look past all the world's hate and hostility and see a real brotherhood of humanity. This I didn't dare explaining to tough little Mercedes, who couldn't stand what she called my bourgeois fantasies of saving the world.

"What's with the kufi?" She reached up to tug at my skullcap. "Have you turned African since we last met?"

I could have cited my mother's anthropological evidence that we were all Africans, the entire human species descended from common origins. I held my wit in check; it served no purpose to come across as patronizing.

"It's not a kufi. It's a Bukharan kipah, traditional to the Jews of Central Asia."

"Ah, getting in touch with your roots. That's new for you."

"A man without roots is a man without mooring, or so my father says. Mostly, I thought it looked pretty bad-assed."

It was all for the better that she couldn't distinguish my Galicianer forebears as being as far from Uzbekistan as they were from Senegal. Mercedes wouldn't have taken to my philosophy of culture: how in a globalized world, you picked what fit best.

"Would you like to meet the guys?" I asked.

"That's why I'm here. I'm excited to hear them sing of the refugees' plight."

When I presented Mercedes to the Mega-Stars, Pascal lowered his sunglasses and bent deep to kiss her knuckles. Wise to such hustles, she snatched back her hand and pressed on through the circle until she reached Ismael cradling his saxophone, his head bobbing to some internal music. They made for a striking couple: the dreamy African artist cloaked in a long blue boubou and the gritty Latina writer in her *huaraches* and earthen vest, determined to draw out the hidden alchemy between the notes. A mellifluous match would have benefited all of us.

"Shally's description of your musical philosophy intrigued me," she said. "It's well known how Cuban music has its roots in Africa, but I wanted to hear how, for you, the sounds traveled the other direction."

Growing up in Dakar, Ismael had been inspired by the great Havana bandleaders to form his first group, the Ambassadeurs d'Amour, to create a salsa that plied the musical trade winds between Senegal and Cuba. None of this was privileged information, but Ismael preferred to let the music speak for itself.

"Yes, we liked the Cuban records very much," he said.

Mercedes seemed to take his reticence as a challenge. "What did you hear in the son and guaracha and rumba that inspired you to form your own sound?"

"The old style was how we learned the music, so we sang it with our languages."

I would have loved for Ismael to expand on his philosophy, but the club's DJ signaled that our time had begun. Not wanting to waste a moment, I prodded the guys on stage. Draped in ankle-length robes, they looked mighty distinct from the Sapphos wearing tank tops and shorts on this hot night. As the Mega-Stars tuned their instruments, Pascal removed the microphone from its stand and strutted across the stage with unmitigated gall, a sexy beast, untroubled by the reality that this audience didn't give a damn. He held a flower like a lovelorn crooner, making me worry that our cocksure singer might have some fanciful ideas about raiding the henhouse. After a few plaintive sniffs, he handed it to a fetching girl in front.

"Bon soir, ladies, this is African music, brought here for your enjoyment," Pascal said. "We come from countries where people know what it is to suffer, but we turn life's pain into music: salsa African style."

Pascal introduced the Mega-Stars, who each spent a moment in the spotlight: Sang Froid's fingers pranced across the keyboard, playing a few measures of a piece he called "Number Theory";

Delacroix pounded on the congas with a heavy hand used judiciously in his investigations into genocidal crimes; and Ismael kissed the bell of his saxophone before belting out a clarion call to mark our arrival. Then Pascal proceeded to the session musicians who hadn't yet won admittance into Ismael's inner circle: Ousmane Diabate on electric guitar and his cousin Abdoulaye on bass—Guinean members of an ancient clan of griots, who were barely conversant in French, much less English. Ousmane, his deeply lined face seeming antique, picked out a tune on guitar that borrowed equally from his storytelling ancestors and the Cuban big bands. Abdoulaye, who worked so many menial jobs that he could barely stay awake, tried to keep up a bass riff. Finally there was Robbie Benson, the quiet timbalero from Liberia who had unwittingly lent us his refugee status. Taught by war to watch his mouth, Robbie expressed himself through his drumsticks, which churned out a beat so fast they became a blur.

Pascal kicked off a raucous number, singing in Wolof seasoned with Spanish and French and Fula. As many times as I had heard this song, the words all fused into one common blur. It was hard to imagine what my mother had drilled into me when I was young, that all language had evolved from a scraggly band of hominids eking out a life in the African Rift Valley. She told me stories of language evolution on regular pilgrimages to the zoo, where she plopped herself in front of the baboons and captured every sound on her tape recorder. The monkeys were disgusting. The males pranced about with big erections, and the females shook the bright red corpuscles coming out of their asses. When I whined about being bored, she hugged me and pointed out the little nuances of baboon behavior, the grooming and petting, the cuddling and preening, the combing of that crazy natural weave in their hair, like some silly glam-rock band. With their long, distinguished faces, they looked so peaceful, until one of them violated some obscure rule of etiquette and they all started screaming and snarling. For all her fixation on the baboons, Mom took no interest in the nearby playground, where a group of boys my age were playing King of the Mountain, climbing to the top of the jungle gym and pushing the others down, shrieking and posturing like our monkey cousins. I would have loved to join the melee, but Mom put her hand through my hair and told me that I didn't need to fight, that we could find a better way to live.

I had tried to follow her direction, but had inherited none of her patience and circumspection. Even now, as Mom lay at home, I had failed her. A good son, a decent human being would have scrapped his evening plans and stayed by her side, if only to reassure her that she would never be alone. That son wasn't in me. I could picture Dad cursing at me for having left her. Sure, he cursed at me in any regard, but this time I would have deserved his contempt. My only justification rested with the desperate need to make this band work. Mom couldn't see me fail again.

On stage, Pascal ceded the floor to Ismael, who blasted out the opening bars of his signature song, "Coumba," a winding uphill passage. It didn't seem possible for so much power to emerge from his narrow frame, but our ears rang with the proof. It wasn't as if Ismael had Coltrane's barrel chest or lung capacity. He made up for the deficit with boundless energy: smiling between every burst of music, bouncing around the stage with such passion that the big horn seemed weightless, a broomstick for this *brujo* to fly away.

The Sapphic sisterhood ate it up, stomping so hard that the floor began to wobble. Ousmane joined in, so that sax and guitar argued like an old married couple, still squabbling after decades together: the trans-Atlantic salsero and the traditional griot swapping licks, taking alternate routes up the mountain. As Pascal picked up the vocals, I could see that my gamble had paid off; the African Refugee Mega-Stars were kicking it.

"They're great," Mercedes said. "Ismael especially."

"Yeah, I told you these guys had something special."

"Amazing what a group of refugees can come up with."

I started to defend our generous redefinition of the term "refugee," but she pinched my side. She was just fucking with me. Putting her notebook away, Mercedes began to dance with the rest of us, her little ass moving for the Mega-Stars as it had once moved for me. Sturdy legs and a strong will. I might have failed in so many ways—my studies, my half-baked business ventures, even the basic duty of accompanying my mother through her time of need—but at least I had managed to win a music critic to our cause. A small victory, but at this point I'd take what I could get.

7

Iceland
August 25, 1996

THE PLANE TOUCHED DOWN IN A SUMMER SQUALL SO INTENSE
that the signalman was nearly blown sideways as he waved us to
the gate. The rough ride from New York hadn't bothered me. Turbulence was an occupational hazard, something I had spent years
trying to convince Susanna was worth enduring. Even after our trip
to Ethiopia, she remained so afraid of falling out of the sky that she
refused to leave Brooklyn. Nothing could change her mind at this
point. She had stopped believing in me a long time ago.

Effie waited at the gate holding a sign, like one of his drivers.
On it he had written "Dr. Hausmann," the name of the Nazi
scientist we had once chased into the Alps.

"Very funny," I said. "Let's get started. No point in dragging
this out."

"There's a problem: Salik was delayed leaving Rome."

"Shit. How long?"

Effie pointed at the arrivals board. Salik's connecting flight
was already three hours late. So much for his promise of a quick

meeting halfway across the Atlantic. Nothing to do at this stage. Whatever Salik wanted to discuss, some special project in Africa, a place I hadn't visited in years, would have to wait. Our more immediate concern was the thankless burden Effie had borne: baby-sitting a big donor.

"Nu, how was it?" I asked.

Effie shrugged. He didn't like to complain. "What can I tell you? The guy's a pain in the ass."

"Might as well introduce me. We've got time to kill."

Effie led me into the duty-free shop, where our guest, Stanislaus Auerbach, was sizing up packages of salmon. No one actually called him Stanislaus, but he kept the full name to remind himself of his Lithuanian roots, even after he left the ghetto for the gold coast of south Florida.

"Would you believe this? Five dollars for a whole chunk," Stan said. "Fresh too."

"We didn't come for the fish," I said.

Stan greeted me with a manicured hand, his fingers decorated with knuckles of gold and cut stones. A thick silver bracelet dangled on his wrist. His white hair looked as seeded as the forests around Jerusalem, planted in rows across his scalp. He had made millions producing action flicks dubbed into a dozen languages, where the hero got the girl and the bad guy met his just end. Salik had thought my presence might coax the movie mogul to open his wallet.

"Let's go, there's no sense waiting here," I said. "Salik will know how to find us."

"You want to go out in this weather?" Stan flagged his silky shirt, as pink as the salmon, offering little protection against the gale outside.

I draped my leather jacket over Stan's back. "Here, wear this. The cold doesn't bother me."

He made an unconvincing effort to hand back the coat, but I was already moving quickly out of the terminal to hail a cab.

"I would have dressed better if I had known where we were going," Stan said in the taxi. "All Effie told me was to be ready at five A.M. with my passport."

"We try to be discreet," I said.

Stan nodded enthusiastically. He didn't want us to think of him as a whiner. "Oh yes, of course, yes."

An outline of smokestacks appeared in the mist, followed by a moonscape of steaming pools. The sight of the blue lagoon, looking like a witch's brew, seemed to frighten our guest.

"I hope this bathhouse isn't going to be anything wild," Stan said. "My fortieth wedding anniversary is next week."

This idiot must have thought we were taking him to some sleazy massage parlor. Sanctimonious piece of shit. He couldn't claim to be any more attached to his wife than I was to mine, even if my time with Susanna had expired long ago.

"It's not that type of place. No one's going to touch you."

Inside the spa, we rented towels and swim trunks and made a quick dash through the chill to ease our aging bodies into the lagoon's milky warmth. Bobbing off the bottom like a hippo in the mud, I led them to the far end, where we could speak in private.

Stan seemed drunk over the scene. "It's wonderful, it's really wonderful. They won't believe it in Palm Beach, that you can sit outside in the freezing rain."

"It would be better if you didn't mention this trip to anyone."

"Oh yes, of course." Stan cupped a handful of the milky broth and held it up to his nose, like some kind of ritual offering. "I love the smell of salt water," he said, breathing in deep. "I can never get enough of the sea."

"Tell Jacob about your boat," Effie said, egging him on.

"Oh, don't get me started," Stan laughed, pleased with himself. "We need a full crew to take it out. You can imagine what it costs."

His lines sounded well-rehearsed, the terrible financial burden to roll out his floating palace and act like lord captain of the high seas.

"So it's a big boat?" I asked, remembering Salik's request to humor the bastard.

"Big?" he said, loud enough to make the Icelanders look in our direction. "They had to clear room in our marina to fit it. When you get out onto the open water, it's like the whole ocean is yours. Have you ever sailed on a boat that size?"

"Not in many years."

"Oh yes, what kind of craft was it?"

"Nothing so glamorous. Only a banana boat bringing survivors from the death camps to Palestine. That was the first time Salik and I worked together."

Stan couldn't have imagined the old hulk, barely seaworthy, bought off the scrapheap in Baltimore and retrofitted in Italy for human cargo. A half century later, my arm still ached from all the sawing and hammering we did to build bunks for the thousands of souls crammed below deck. The survivors didn't worry about drowning at sea or squaring off against British frigates. It was worth the risk, they told me, even after the Brits captured us and shipped them back to Germany, of all places, to be confined again behind barbed wire.

"What a terrible story," Stan said, sinking back into the warm water. "So what happened when the British caught you?"

"Let's just say they left a lasting impression."

"What do you mean?"

"They ripped out his fingernails," Effie said. "Those polite English officers wanted to know about our operation. But Jacob wouldn't tell them a fucking thing. They couldn't even figure out his native language. You should have seen him after his release. For three weeks, he couldn't grip a knife and fork. I had to cut his meat for him."

Stan shouldn't have been so shocked. He must have made a hundred movies where the hero gets beaten half to death.

"You know, Jacob . . ." His voice slowed. "I really admire how you've led your life. It's men like you that make me want to contribute."

God damn it, Salik should have been here to deal with this shit. This was his business, securing whatever donations he needed.

"We all contribute, Stan, in our own way," I said.

"Yes, well, there's no point leaving anything to my son."

I had heard something about his boy living a wild lifestyle and didn't need the details, but Stan couldn't help himself. "My son, well, you see, he likes boys, in those filthy nightclubs. Men dressing like women and doing disgusting things to each other. What's the use in talking? He is lost to me. This shouldn't be my legacy. No, I want to leave a mark, so that when I'm gone the world will know I existed."

It seemed crazy to pretend any kind of relatedness, but the guy seemed to be in real pain.

"It's like that with kids," I said. "You give them everything they could ask for, and they still tell you to fuck off. That's how it is with my son as well."

"Your son's a homo too?" Stan asked.

"Shalom? No, he has plenty of girls, too many, in fact. My son has a different problem: incompetence. He fucks up anything he puts his hands on. And there's no fight in him. He gives up at the first sign of frustration: graduate school, a crazy scheme to send hippies into the jungle. Now he wants to be a big macher in the music business."

"It's hard to imagine your son would be this way, with you being so decisive."

"Shalom never listened, at least not to me. Every time I tried to instruct him, he did the opposite."

Effie had been bobbing off the bottom, letting me do the heavy lifting with Stan, until he couldn't hear any more about Shalom. He wasn't strictly observant, nothing like his Hassidische son, but he upheld *lashon hora*, refusing to speak ill of others. "Be merciful to him, Jacob. You have been criticizing the boy since he was six years old."

"Come on, Effie. You know what he put me through."

Effie shrugged. He had always looked out for me, through all my trials. "Not every son can be exactly what we want. Maybe he sensed you were never so convinced about fatherhood to begin with."

"I just wanted him to show some guts."

"Let him be who he will be. You can't measure him against yourself."

"You sound like Susanna. That's what she used to say."

"She was always smarter than you, Jacob."

Smarter to be sure, but also unforgiving, even if I had never given her much cause to be forgiven. That would have forced me into false apologies and empty promises of change, and I had already deceived her enough. Effie couldn't understand. He had never been asked to make any sacrifices. Only to assist me along the way.

"Enough of this crap. Where the hell is Salik already?"

"Relax, Jacob, we've spent fifty years waiting on him. He'll show up eventually."

He always did, reaching out to ensnare me again. This was what Susanna hated about Salik. She blamed him for calling me away without notice, for insisting on complete discretion, for demanding loyalty above all else. What I could never admit to her was that the fault also lay within me, with my compliance, with my inability to refuse him, with my recognition that his assignments gave me a sense of purpose.

I had nearly lost faith in Salik by the time he burst through the door from the locker room. His shape had changed in the half century since he first challenged me to fight. By now, the tough old bulldog had let himself go; his belly protruded so far sideways that it looked like it might topple him. He hadn't, however, lost an ounce of his willpower, or his cunning.

"My friends, I am sorry to be late. At least you had a nice place to wait for me," Salik said, his heavy body turning weightless as he floated across the water. "Isn't it beautiful, Stan? It reminds me of that trip we took to the Dead Sea."

Salik got right to work. Within minutes, he'd secured a large donation from the movie mogul and dispatched him to procure some lox at the spa's gift shop, so he could have a quick chat with me before we all returned to the airport.

"What did you want, Salik?" I asked as soon as Stan drifted away. "It sounded important when you called."

Stretching his body after the flight, Salik swam circles around us. "It's a delicate matter. Something you can help with." He described a crisis in Central Africa, among a community that had suffered its own holocaust. "We need to know if we can work with these Tutsis."

Effie interrupted, as protective as ever. "Salik, what do you want to send Jacob for? Find a younger man to go instead."

"We need a man with Jacob's sensitivities. It's a messy situation, and we fucked it up already by dealing with the old Hutu regime. Now the Tutsis are upset with us." He splashed some water on his face. "Look, Jacob, the world is changing, and it's important to build new alliances. The Tutsis are coming to visit us soon in Jerusalem, and they want materiel to protect themselves from another genocide. Think how we would have felt in their position, and what a mitzvah it would be to stop the *shoah* before it started."

Even after all these years, the old devil still knew how to wrench me out of shape. I could never be like Stan, lounging about on his yacht, playing poker at his country club, not when there were battles left to fight.

"And why should I take on a mitzvah to strangers?"

"Because that's what keeps you strong. I have always had faith in you, Jacob. You may have failed at marriage, but you're a genius at outsmarting death."

Anyone else making light of my marriage's dissolution would have earned himself a punch in the jaw. Salik, however, couldn't be dissuaded by physical blows. This much I'd learned long ago in Bavaria, along with the lesson that one man alone could do little when the world was against him.

"There is no outsmarting death, Salik. All I can do is outmaneuver it for a while. Let's say I make this trip; will you give me someone good to take care of security?"

Salik glided through the blue soup. "What about Dudu? Would that make you happy?"

"Dudu? All he wants these days is to roll around a beach in Thailand."

"He would come back out of respect for you."

"I didn't think he respected anything."

"Maybe not so much. That can be good, though. At least he can make sure an old romantic like you doesn't fall in love again."

I had to laugh. Romance was one thing Salik didn't need to worry about. The world was filled with killing and cruelty; there was no sense in getting sentimental about any of it. At least that was how it seemed as I soaked in a milky bath on a frozen island, waiting for the storm to subside so I could fly back to Brooklyn and prepare for the journey ahead.

PART 2

8

Bavaria
August 14, 1945

HITLER, O HITLER, HOW I PRAYED FOR ADOLF HITLER TO LAND in my hands the final night before Major Jimmy Williamson shipped out for home. Goebbels could have served just as well, giving me another king to challenge Williamson's hold on the poker table. Either of those bastards would have shown my fellow officers, and by extension the whole U.S. Army of Occupation in Germany, that I hadn't given up the fight. All I needed was a little luck. Resting my cards on the table, I raised a single finger: "One."

Williamson leaned close to inspect my face. "All right, Lt. Furman, I can tell you've got something under there."

The major considered himself the sharpest guy around, but the great operator had never uncovered how I had conned my way into the U.S. Army at sixteen with forged papers, and had even convinced them to send me off to Officer Candidate School.

"That's the question, Major. Am I devious enough to beat you with nothing?"

Williamson checked his cards again. "Very good, Jacob. Never give anything away. Let your enemies cook up their own theories about what you're thinking."

Colonel Burckhardt dealt the draw. Our commanding officer had an aversion to risk, ever ready to appease the Germans under our occupation, meaning the hand would come down to me and Williamson, and the single card resting before me. The deck itself was Russian, showing Hitler, Goering, Himmler, and Goebbels as kings, followed by a succession of Nazi party hacks in descending order of importance. These cards must have been groped by innumerable hands, most of them dead by now, all the way from Moscow to Berlin, but now they were in the firm grip of Major Williamson, who had bought them off a Soviet commissar on the gamble that they might have some novelty value back in Virginia.

Tilting up the draw card, I saw the black swash of hair, the ridiculous toothbrush moustache, the arm extended in a Heil. For years I had spit at every image of that son-of-a-bitch. Now, a third king in hand, I forced myself into a calm indifference, as if we were back in the Ardennes waiting to ambush a German unit advancing across open ground.

I slapped a ten on the table.

Williamson took another hard look at me, probing my face for weakness, before checking his cards again, as if doubting his own resolve. "All right, you little bastard, since you won't show me anything, I'll trust my instincts."

Reaching into his stack of cash, he called my bet. I dropped my cards: three kings of the Third Reich: Hitler, Himmler, and Goering, sitting between a pair of sixes.

"So that's where Hitler was hiding all this time," Williamson said. "That's all right, you can keep your full house." He flipped over his cards, four of a kind led by Mussolini masquerading as the Queen of Spades. All evening, no one had drawn anything better than triple jacks. Now the cards seemed to change faces at his command.

"You're getting better, Jacob," Williamson said as he collected his winnings. "At first, you gobbled up all the Army's horseshit about freeing the world from fascism. Now you're every bit as cynical as the rest of us."

Williamson didn't give a shit about anything, so he couldn't comprehend what had changed in me during the final gasp of war, back in April, when a special nighttime mission sent us high into the Bavarian Alps to track down a notorious scientist. As our caravan of jeeps climbed a treacherous mountain road, I leaned on my driver—the dimwitted Private Ephraim Grossberg—to hurry, to beat the others to the villa.

"Drive faster, you stupid idiot, drive."

"I'm pushing it as hard as I can, Lieutenant," he said. "The road is very dangerous."

As the company's only other Jew, Grossberg might have understood my reasoning, but I couldn't take the chance of sharing my plan with him. He had earned a reputation as the dumbest blockhead in the U.S. Army. He took forever to clean his rifle or dig a foxhole, and responded to every order by bobbing his head like a grinning ape. Maybe it was a question of language. Grossberg had been born in Breslau and would have been tossed in the ovens himself if his parents hadn't shipped him off him to America. I had tried to protect him on the long slog across France and Belgium, but after he got his hand stuck in a can of peaches and wandered into a minefield searching for a place to crap, I wondered how any Jew could have been so stupid.

As Grossberg raced around the snowy curves, the two enlisted men in back complained about the wild ride. I told them to shut up. We had our orders, I said, and they didn't need to worry why the other jeeps had disappeared so far behind. Reaching the cottage at dawn, ahead of the others, I rushed inside to find the scientist at his desk, working on computations to save his crumbling fatherland.

"Doctor Hausmann?" I asked, confirming him to be the evil genius responsible for blasting rockets across the English Channel.

He looked up from his papers. "Yes, congratulations. You have found me. Now I ask you, in the tradition of Archimedes, do not disturb my circles."

The Germans and their goddamn philosophers, spouting bullshit to the very end. For me, the answer to his riddle was clear. I dragged him outside and flung him into the snow. Almost without consciousness, I threw myself upon him and punched freely, landing hard crosses, right, left, right, right, left, as if I were back in Bernie's gym hurling all my strength into the heavy bag. The German lifted his arms to cover his face and cried out for me to spare him, for God's sake, confessing that terrible things happened in war.

Ripping my pistol from its holster, I aimed at the blubbering rocketman, and in that electric moment felt pure vindication, as if blowing out his brains would make up for all the bombings and blitzkriegs, all the graves and gassings. It would have only taken an instant, as quick as a sneeze, to achieve retribution in the name of the dead. And yet I couldn't pull the trigger. It wasn't conscience or fear of the consequences, but a terrible distraction: the memory of my sister, Nesia, and her parting words before I boarded the bus south from Boston for basic training. Weeping and pounding my chest, she begged me to stop fighting the world. We both somehow knew this would be our last meeting, though neither of us could have guessed it would be me, not her, who would survive the war. What had happened to my sister and my parents was a holocaust in its own right, something I had been as powerless to prevent as the deportations in Galicia. A nighttime fire had swept through our home in Roxbury. My family didn't suffer, the neighbors wrote, as if anyone could know what it felt like to be gassed, whether inside a burning house in Boston or the showers at Birkenau.

The memory of my beloved Nesia seized me long enough for the three enlisted men from my jeep to realize their lieutenant was about to execute a valued prisoner. Before I could take aim, they tackled me into the snow. The big oaf Grossberg hugged me from behind, wedging my arms straight up, as if trapping me in a chimney, while the other two privates hurried the Nazi inside.

"Let me go, you idiot," I ordered Grossberg.

"I can't, Lieutenant. I can't let you do this."

"Don't you know who that bastard is? He built the rockets that blew up London. He used Jews as slave labor, and then had them murdered."

"I know, sir. I know."

Locked in Grossberg's grip, all I could do was curse his stupidity until Colonel Burckhardt's jeep pulled up to the cottage. At that point, Grossberg released me into the snow, and I dropped the pistol, no longer any use to me. I prepared a story that Dr. Hausmann's injuries came from an escape attempt, but the colonel didn't care. Ignoring me, he ordered that *dummkopf* Grossberg, who spoke the best German in the company, to transmit an invitation from the U.S. Army to discuss his research with our brightest minds. Forced to watch, I clenched my jaw and fumed that Grossberg failed to take any liberties with the translation. The least we could have done was to make Dr. Hausmann think the hangman would be waiting for him at the bottom of the mountain.

For an hour, while our men collected the scientific papers that the U.S. Army wanted to keep from the Soviets, I staggered off into the woods, through snow rising to my knees. The chill barely penetrated my open coat. I was too steamed, punching the air and the occasional tree until the pain forced me to cool my swollen fists in the snow. By the time the colonel dispatched Grossberg to collect me, I was spent, resolved not to fall for any more delusions that we could change the course of history.

After the card game wound down, Major Jimmy Williamson was determined to cap off his final night in Bavaria with one more tilt at the biggest black marketeer in town. Summoning Private Grossberg to serve as chauffeur, we drove over to the home of Baroness von Hassan and roused her from bed. Williamson wasted no time tearing into her storeroom of fine china in search of the perfect set of Herend.

"Come on, boys, don't give up now. Momma's counting on me to bring home a dinner set for Christmas. You can't get plates like this in Leesburg."

This was the first time he had ever mentioned a mother.

"I don't know why we're bothering," I said, surveying the piles of rejected settings, cast aside for the slightest crack or imperfection. "These dishes are sure to be all busted up by the time they reach Virginia."

Opening a fresh carton, Williamson combed through the stack to discover a full complement at last, without any obvious defects. "Don't worry, Private Grossberg here will pack them up real careful for safe passage across the Atlantic."

It seemed crazy to entrust such a delicate job to Grossberg, who hulked over the fine china like a gorilla sipping afternoon tea. Not that I cared about any damage the big galoot might do. If it had been up to me, I would have smashed the baroness's entire china collection in the town square to warn the Bavarians against profiting from the misery of others. It was no use. Much as I had tried, I had never been able to touch the baroness; she had powerful friends, among them Colonel Burckhardt and Major Williamson, who had already acquired enough goods to fill a quartermaster's depot.

"Be careful with those dishes, Private," the major told Grossberg. "At this stage, they're worth more than you are."

Hoisting up a soup tureen, Grossberg squeaked his thumb against the surface. "Major, these look just like my mother's Passover plates. The bowl even has the same little bump on the inside."

Williamson shook his head, refusing to give up his prize. "Not very likely, Private. I'm sure the baroness has all her documentation in order."

The major offered a deep, theatrical bow to our hostess, watching from a nearby sofa. He didn't speak much German, but Williamson seemed to have a special ease with this widow of a Wehrmacht officer who had frozen to death at Stalingrad. She smiled like an aging actress caught in her boudoir. Time had bleached her blond hair into a silky white; a tall man's trenchcoat covered her to the ankles.

"That set belonged to one of our finest families," she said, lying to me when I pressed her about its history. "It is a tragedy how our people must dispose of heirlooms passed down through the generations."

I could have ordered her to cough up some proof, but Williamson had dibs on this Herend. As always, he held all the cards. All I could do was hope for Grossberg to chip a few dishes while the major stalked the house in search of anything that might have resale value back home.

"What do you think, Furman?" Williamson asked, holding a stormtrooper's shirt up to his chest. "How does this look?"

Trailing behind, the baroness picked some lint off the shirt and assured him it would fit fine. She didn't grasp that Williamson didn't want to dress up like a Nazi, only to peddle this crap to souvenir hunters stateside. When the major offered her a cigarette, she bent close to suck in the flame, and there they remained, connected by a tiny bridge of fire. She blew smoke into his face, and he held fast, entranced.

"Furman, see if she has any overcoats my size."

I passed along his request to the baroness, who seemed to ponder something more weighty than clothing.

"Perhaps," she said, leading us to a special closet in back, which opened to an orderly rack of coats and suits, fine material, camel and cashmere, dusty and smelling of mothballs. "These belonged to my husband."

Williamson didn't balk at diving into a dead man's wardrobe in full view of his widow. He yanked out a heavy cashmere overcoat, too hot for a summer night, and asked my opinion. If there was one thing I knew, after a childhood helping my father, it was outerwear. Brushing Williamson's shoulders, tugging at the fit, I felt carried back to Boston on Saturdays when my father opened his coat factory to the public. Those days measuring customers had persuaded me to break away from the rag trade. Ironically, with my parents gone and the business shut down, my wish had come to pass. I was free.

As Williamson moved on to a pile of *lederhosen*, we heard a clanging from the old carriage house outside. Private Grossberg, having finished with the dishes, had discovered a collection of grand pianos lined up like cars at an auto factory.

"Listen to this one," he said, testing the action on a Steinway. He hunched over the keyboard, his fat fingers barely able to navigate the notes. As he started to hack out a piece of what sounded like Chopin, my mind drifted back to Roxbury, where my mother listened to concerts on the radio. She had wanted me to take up music, but my hands were less suited to ivory keys than boxing gloves, mixing up hooks and jabs down at Bernie's. The idea that our radio must have been incinerated along with everything else in my parents' home left me with an unalterable conclusion. This Steinway belonged to us.

"Baroness, you must have heard about the special commission to repatriate assets stolen from Jewish families. We will need to see the full provenance of this piano."

She protested that all such documentation had been destroyed in the Allied bombing, so I jacked up the piano's lid and started noting down the identification number. My little act must have scared her. She told me to send men to collect it after daybreak and went off to bed, muttering that we should show ourselves out.

Williamson seemed surprised by the arrangement. "She's going to let you have the Steinway? That's nice of her."

"Yeah sure, very nice. The real owner probably ended up at Buchenwald."

He lit himself up another cigarette. "Not much use he'll have for the piano then."

We loaded the major's haul into the jeep, and Grossberg drove us to the house where a few local girls rented out their nights in exchange for cigarettes and canned meat. Hearing us arrive, one of them leaned out the window and called for Williamson.

"Coming, dear," he said in German, one of the few expressions he had picked up. Then he turned to me. "Listen, Furman, if you want to get your revenge on these Krauts, what you should do is go back and fuck that baroness. She may be old enough to be your mother, but the two of you had a little spark there."

How he could confuse hate for lust was beyond me.

"No, thanks, Major, I'll leave that piece to you."

"Too late for me, buddy boy. My time's up. But not before a grand send-off. The girls have been planning this one for weeks."

He rushed into the house, leaving me outside with Grossberg, who had pinched a bottle of Slivovitz from the baroness's liquor cabinet. The private offered me a taste, but the Army had strict rules against fraternizing with enlisted men. Anyway, I hadn't quite forgiven him for betraying me in the Alps.

"You okay out here, Grossberg? The major may be a while."

"That's all right, Lieutenant. You go have a good time."

The squeal of fraüleins sounded from inside. Williamson was probably promising them U.S. visas in exchange for special privileges.

"I'll be glad to be rid of him," I said. "Williamson would have tried to ship Hitler's carcass back to Virginia if the Russians hadn't burned it first."

Grossberg gave his usual dullard nod. Even between us, he refused to speak badly of our superiors. "I'm going to Buchenwald next week, sir," he said, "to look for some record of my parents. You could come too, if you'd like to visit the camp.'"

The prospect of two Jews bearing witness to a death camp sounded like a far better use of time than plundering the baroness's storeroom. "Yeah, I'd like that, Effie. We should see what happened there. It'll be something to tell our children."

One of the fraüleins called for me, claiming that Williamson needed help with his German, and I went inside to fall into her arms. No risk of fraternizing there. No peace, either, even if the war was over and work crews were clearing the rubble from the town square. Pity we hadn't saved a few atomic bombs for these bastards when we had the chance. Now it was too late. My only taste of retribution lay in reclaiming a magnificent piano that I didn't even know how to play. It wasn't much, but at least it was something.

9

Bisesero, Rwanda
September 23, 1996

THE TUTSIS WANTED TO SHOW ME WHAT IT MEANT TO SURVIVE at Bisesero. All around were steep hills, untilled, no sign of the farmed terraces that stretched across nearly every slope in Rwanda. This place was wild, and hard to climb. Struggling up a trail better suited for mountain goats, I brushed off the arm of our escort, Captain Ezekiel Hakizimana, who had remained behind to guide us up the path.

Stopping before a large boulder, the captain suggested that we rest for a moment. "We are approaching the mountaintop, Mr. Jacob. Soon the way will become easier."

I could have used a break, even a drink of water, but not now, not today. "That's all right. Mountains have never been a problem for me."

Before I could press on, Dudu flopped himself down on the rock. "Come on, Jacob, the captain is right. A man your age shouldn't push so hard. Sit here with me and enjoy the view." Dudu patted the stone as if to soften it for me, and when I ignored him, he turned to our escort. "You have too many hills in this country. Why don't you Tutsis find a nice flat place where no one will bother you. Maybe try Madagascar."

Dudu could never take anything seriously, not even on a day as somber as this. He had been complaining all week, ever since we crossed the Rwandan border at Goma. First it was the rain, then it was the lack of cold beer and ample women. Most of all, it was the company, the somber Tutsi military officers who refused to humor him. This morning he had campaigned for a day of rest and reflection, but I didn't want to pass up the invitation to Bisesero.

"Don't pay any attention to Dudu," I told our escort as I settled myself down on the boulder. "He doesn't mean to be disrespectful. It's just how he is."

Captain Ezekiel nodded intently, as if absorbing a bit of unwelcome intelligence. He was a serious young man, confident and courteous, and clearly unaccustomed to Dudu's incessant gibes. The captain seemed every bit as determined as we were, but he acted cooler, more restrained, not so combative. If you asked me, he looked too lanky to be a fighter. Ezekiel had shoulders wide enough to serve as a sail upon the passing breeze, and his limbs were so long they might have been stretched on a rack. He took easy, loping strides, what Susanna would have called languid, as if never in any rush. His army pants were tucked into rubber galoshes, the kind that children wore in nursery rhymes.

"How can you walk in those?" Dudu asked, bending down to pinch the rubber toes. "Where we come from, they are only for little girls and farmers. A soldier like you needs some good heavy boots."

"These fit our climate," the captain said. "When it rains, we pass through the mud with no problem. We could find a pair for you, but I think your feet are too big."

Dudu stretched out his legs to show off the lumbering construction boots he wore through every situation. "Not me. I would never go to war without strong support for the ankles. If

70

you tried those rubber things in Lebanon, the Hezbollah would catch you and chop off your head." Laughing, Dudu drew a finger across his throat.

The last thing I needed, around guys as serious as these Tutsis, was for Dudu to crack jokes about the dead.

"All right, Dudu, stop screwing around. The captain doesn't care about Lebanon. He has his own enemies to worry about. That's why his commander invited us here. Isn't that right, Captain?"

Reminded of his mission, Captain Ezekiel straightened himself up to his full height and filled us in on what had transpired here during the genocide. "We call this the 'Hill of Resistance,'" he said, explaining how two years earlier some fifty thousand Tutsis had sought shelter in these mountains from the Hutu genocidaires with their Interahamwe militia. "By the time our army liberated this place, only one thousand Tutsis were remaining alive. The dead fell all around where we are now standing. After a heavy rain, we still recover bones from the ground. You must be careful where you step."

Looking over these hills, two years after the genocide, I thought it fitting that evidence of the slaughter still peeked up out of the earth. It had happened so easily, to the Tutsis as to the Jews, for our neighbors to turn against us and condemn us as cockroaches or rats, as tall trees to be chopped down, or vermin to be exterminated, all because of our noses or our height or the cut of our pricks.

"Captain, you are making Jacob very happy with all your stories about death," Dudu said, spoiling the mood. "Be careful, the old man may try to adopt you as the son he always wanted."

Damn it. Dudu always found new ways to embarrass me.

"You'll have to excuse me, Captain," I said, "I have never man-aged to convince Dudu in the importance of honoring the dead."

The Tutsi officer peered down at the dirt between his boots, as if to inspect the earth for hidden bones that he could hold up as examples. "Perhaps your friend will appreciate our situation after he has seen the victims," the captain said, starting back up the path.

As we rose for the final push to the summit, I kept my eyes fixed on the ground before me, taking care with each step to avoid crushing any human remains. Behind me, Dudu tromped along in his heavy boots. He didn't give a damn what he stepped on.

The path leveled off at a hilltop panorama, where we caught up at last with the Tutsi military command. Standing apart from his aides, General Roger Gitarama was surveying the wild hills that stretched west to Lake Kivu. When we had met the general down below, he greeted us with what seemed like indifference, his hand as stiff as a wire birdcage, his gaze looking past me, making me feel like an unwanted guest at a wedding rather than one who had flown thousands of miles to attend his big event. Even now, after I passed his test by hiking up the Hill of Resistance, the general barely glanced at me as he pointed across the landscape.

"Look around, Mr. Jacob, and try to imagine the struggle of the local Tutsis," he said. "They were simple cattle herders, without any weapons or military training, but they held off the Interahamwe for two months."

The surrounding hills formed something like a natural fortress, making me think of Masada, where a thousand Jewish Zealots fought back a Roman legion until at last, their walls breached, they chose suicide over slavery. What would my choice have been, Salik had pestered me during our early days working together. My answer then was the same as it would be today: to find another way off the mountain.

"General, our history has shown us that mountains can shield the persecuted, but only for a short time," I said. "You have to act fast to rescue your people."

For the first time, the general seemed to unwind. The faint etchings of a smile welcomed our relatedness. With his gold-rimmed glasses and soft face, he looked almost academic, albeit less aggressive than some of Susanna's old colleagues. If not for his uniform, the same dark green fatigues and rubber boots as his men, I might have mistaken him for a philosophy professor, rather than the commander of the most effective fighting force in Africa. Who knew what horrors the general had witnessed, what terrible decisions had been forced upon him, when his men were outnumbered, outgunned, chased through malarial jungles, where his rebellion was nearly crushed before it could regroup in the frozen mountains, saved by discipline and pure devotion to the cause. All this I had learned from Salik—how the general's enemies couldn't defeat him in battle, so they decided to exterminate the Tutsi civilian population instead. And the world did nothing. Just as during the *shoah*.

The general beckoned us to follow him inside a dimly lit shack that stank of rotten blood. As our eyes adjusted, we could see hundreds of skulls laid out in rows. Some of the skulls were in rough shape, smashed like porcelain. Others looked untouched, like the specimens Susanna used to gaze at in wonder, as if they were speaking to her. On a separate rack lay piles of bones: legs and arms and backs all jumbled together.

"We have established how many were murdered here," the general said, "but to match the names to these bones remains beyond our technical capabilities."

It made me think again of Susanna, and whether she could help them separate man from woman, adult from child, to give these bones back some dignity. She would have loved it here. The terrain wouldn't have bothered her at all, not with her strong calves from always taking the stairs. If I ever made it back to Brooklyn, and if she were willing to listen, I would hold out Bisesero as a prime spot to dig for human history. That would have to wait, of course, until the war ended, until these Tutsis achieved some peace and security. But then, maybe, if she could find her way to forgiving me, we might give it another chance.

Returning outside, the general invited me to sit with him beneath a shaded tree. As a group of Tutsi officers gathered behind their commander, Dudu stood at my shoulder and kept quiet for a change. Maybe the sight of skulls had finally persuaded him to tone down his act. That was my hope, at least. A soldier carrying a tray of soft drinks offered me a choice of cola. After the hike, it would have been nice to partake, but this was a boundary I refused to cross.

"Today is Yom Kippur, our day of atonement," I told the general. "We don't drink or eat on this day."

The general looked perplexed. "We did not realize you were a religious man."

"Even in Auschwitz, my people kept this promise."

The general rocked his head slowly. For a moment, the only sound was the fizzing of the soda, until the general sent away the tray. "Today we will all be as Jews."

This simple act affirmed Salik's purpose in sending me here. For all the difficulties, I was glad to have accepted the role of emissary.

The general leaned close, as if divulging a confidence. "Consider, Mr. Jacob, how your people would have responded if Hitler's army had been allowed to escape Germany, and the world treated them like innocent victims. This is what we have been forced to endure—an entire field of genocidaires camped out just beyond our borders."

I tried to imagine, just for a moment, what it would have been like if Himmler and Goering and Eichmann and a million engineers of the Nazi regime had decamped for Austria, living in plain sight, and we were denied the right even to disarm them, much less to bring them to justice. Worse yet, if we had to watch them tended to by the do-gooders of the world.

"General, if I've learned one lesson from history, it's that justice is a fruit you must pick for yourself."

The general stared at me, as if he hadn't heard my response. Then he adjusted his glasses up the bridge of his nose; the golden frame might have been the only thing at Bisesero that didn't jump to his command. Reaching forward, he gripped my knee. "You seem to be a moral man, with a sense of history and justice. If that is true, then you owe it to us to help stop the next genocide."

He nodded to Captain Ezekiel, who ducked into a nearby building and returned escorting two trembling figures enshrouded in flowing blue fabrics. At the captain's urging, one of them, an old lady, wobbled forward and unwrapped her scarf to expose a wad of bandages across her scalp, stained brown where the blood had seeped through. Her eyes cast downward, she revealed a story in bursts, flinching with every breath.

"This lady was living with her son, the pastor of their village, when the Interahamwe came to their home," the captain translated. "Her son went out to face them, and they struck him with their machetes. She could do nothing to save him, so she fled, but as you can see, she could not run quickly enough."

It confused me why her wounds looked so fresh. The genocide, after all, should have ended long ago. Ezekiel explained that these women, the old lady and her daughter-in-law, came not from Rwanda, but from the mountains of Masisi, across the border in Zaire. Born into the Tutsi diaspora, they had been spared the Rwandan genocide, just as my family in Boston had avoided the *shoah*. Now these ladies had fallen prey to the Hutu genocidaires, who had regrouped in the refugee camps around Goma.

The old woman started again, her voice growing hysterical, her arms flailing around wildly.

"There was a baby too," Captain Ezekiel said. "The child of this young lady here. The Interahamwe tore him away from her and cut him too. They swore there would be no more Tutsis in Masisi."

Trembling, the old lady retreated to her daughter-in-law, who folded her back within the protective blue scarf. There was something Biblical about these women, echoing the story of Naomi and Ruth, two widows clinging to each other to bear the loss.

"You see, Mr. Jacob, these ladies were my neighbors," Captain Ezekiel said. "They come to us from my home village in Masisi.

I ran away from there as a boy, after my father was murdered by our enemies."

"We became his new family," the general interjected, poking my knee again to demand my attention. "Ezekiel grew up among us. Now it is time for him to return to Masisi to liberate his community. So that no more babies are slaughtered."

The general spoke with a calm clarity, outlining the campaign before them. All around us, his senior aides were nodding, admiring the man who seemed to be more than just a military commander. With his tactical genius, his absolute commitment to the fight, and his vision of the future, General Roger Gitarama had the presence of a patriarch. This was the role I had hoped to provide for Dudu in rescuing him from the Soviets. Unfortunately for me, Dudu had a different way of showing his appreciation.

"You Tutsis are as bad as us Jews. We could never stay in one place either," Dudu said to the general. "Like I told your captain: It's no good to fight forever. You should find a nice island somewhere and try to live in peace."

Shit. Maybe I should have left him in Odessa after all. That way, he wouldn't still be tormenting me all these years later.

"Please forgive my associate," I asked the general as his aides rumbled in protest behind him. "Dudu has seen a lot of war, but he took the wrong lessons from our struggles. He thinks they give him the right to say whatever he pleases."

The general glared at Dudu with an intensity that made me wonder whether that stupid idiot might soon find himself locked in a dank cell—or, worse, marched off to face wartime justice. No one could blame the general. It took a hard man to lead a people back from annihilation. This much I knew from Salik.

Breaking away from us, the general rose and addressed the women directly. Everyone, even Dudu, grew silent. When he finished, the Tutsis all nodded in what seemed like agreement.

"What did you tell them?" I asked the general.

"I promised that soon there will be no more massacres."

Speaking for the first time, the daughter-in-law directed a question my way that made the chorus of Tutsi officers rustle behind us.

"She asks why the world is supporting the genocidaires in their refugee camps when they commit such terrible crimes," the general explained.

Observing her, I recognized something familiar: a resilience through tragedy, a rugged determination to persist, and a terrible grace and beauty, all of which reminded me of Judith, the Auschwitz survivor whose presence lingered with me a half century later. As a young soldier, I had learned from Judith what it meant to fight, a lesson I failed to appreciate until it was too late, and she was gone. Cowardice was a mistake that I vowed never to make again.

Claiming the privilege of age, I approached the daughter-in-law and framed her face between my hands. She smelled of blood and dirt and fear, a perfume familiar to me from a dozen evacuations. As she bent her neck modestly, I kissed her forehead.

"Tell her this *muzungu* will not stand by and watch another genocide."

Releasing her, I stepped back and pounded my chest with a closed fist, like in the Yom Kippur vidui, confessing not my own sins but those of the world, which had abandoned her people as surely as it had once abandoned mine. Who knew how much the ladies understood, but the murmurs from the military men sounded approving. The women covered themselves in their veils and were ushered away. When they were gone, the general took my arm and led me back down the mountain, where we waited for dusk and the chance to break our fast.

10

Brooklyn
September 19, 1996

THE TREK UP SEVEN FLIGHTS OF STAIRS TO MY DEPARTMENTAL office left me panting. Gripping the metal banister, I struggled against the panic that the cancer might have already spread to my lungs. It behooved me to inform my oncologist, in case it might obviate the need for chemotherapy. No point in suffering through the nausea, exhaustion, and hair loss if it wasn't going to matter anyway. I had become terribly forgetful lately, perhaps another sign of metastasis. Either that, or I was simply distracted by all that had happened. My only certainty was that, on this final day before plunging into a seething ocean of cytotoxins, when all I wanted was some quiet time to plan a conference on language evolution, I had left my address book at the office.

Rising to the seventh floor, I found the anthropology department buzzing with the frictive tension of a new semester. To my undying relief, I was able to slip through the halls undetected. The last thing I needed was to be confronted with the mundane details of university life. I had nearly succeeded in avoiding all such entanglements when I discovered Mia Greystone, my most irksome graduate student, sitting outside my office door.

"Hello Mia, did we have an appointment today? I must have forgotten."

"That's okay, Susanna. I wasn't waiting long. You had promised to speak with me about the situation with Kaveh."

If there were a saving grace to the winding down of my earthly days, it was being relieved of my duties as graduate student adviser. The kids were sweet enough, but I never felt quite comfortable in the role of mentor, with acolytes seeking my guidance. Most demanding of the lot was the narcissistic waif scrambling to her feet before me. Mia expected me to adjudicate every petty dispute, the most recent involving a formal charge of sexism against Assistant Professor Kaveh Ali for spurning her post-feminist take on matrilineal power structures.

"All right, let's try to get through this quickly," I told her.

Striding in behind me, Mia mounted the opposing chair, slipped off her sandals, and bent her bare feet beneath her thighs, lotus position. She had been a dancer once, and her flash of cleavage and bare midriff were far too spicy for my inherent modesty. My aunts had instilled in me a distrust of strangers, women in particular, and Mia's reputation had done nothing to defray my instincts. Recalling the widespread complaints over her cloying need for attention and her gratuitous manipulation of male intent, I felt relieved that Shalom had been ushered out of the department, lest he fall inexorably into the thrall of our resident Circe.

"After reading your essay, Mia, I have to concur with Kaveh. It's a mess."

"Really? Was it that bad?"

She teased her hair with all the fragile vanity of a shampoo advertisement. The act was as infectious as a cough in a concert hall. Before I could stop myself, my hand was combing through my own hair, my only physical attribute that gave me joy. Soon this too would be lost, if I proceeded on a course of dubious medical utility.

"Bad? My dear Mia, it's terrible. Sentences drop off without conclusion. Spelling mistakes abound, and one of the pages appears to be missing. Worst of all, there is no underlying thesis. Did you even read it over before submitting it to Kaveh?"

"I did, I swear, but my computer screen was cracked."

"That shouldn't matter. At the graduate level, you must stand behind your work."

Cumulonimbus clouds developed across her face. Mia's tactical predilection for weeping had carried her through two years of graduate coursework and had bedeviled most of my colleagues. Even while recognizing her tears as a ploy for sympathy, I couldn't cope with such a lachrymose performance on a day like today. Reaching across the gulf between us, I took hold of her wrist and shook it.

"Mia, please, you will need to develop a thicker skin if you hope to produce a master's thesis on as speculative a subject as the anthropological origins of dance."

Nodding intently, Mia was now apologizing, her voice lifting. "You're right, Susanna, you're so right. If it's not too late, I can withdraw my complaint over Kaveh. I never should have made such a fuss. It's just been a difficult time for me personally."

Her swift acquiescence made me cringe. Mia could never have withstood life with Chuck Rosenfeld, who raged at the first blush of self-doubt.

"Mia, let me give you some advice. Don't show your emotions in a professional context. We are your colleagues, not your friends, not your allies. If you need to cry, find yourself a boyfriend, or if you prefer, a girlfriend."

Back when I was Mia's age, studying under Chuck, I used to hide my frailties as if my career depended on it. Wary of exposing my neuroses, I attributed my avoidance of the elevator to a need to "maintain my figure" and my resistance to air travel to "family commitments." The only one who knew the truth was Jacob, who allowed himself to be cast unfairly as the domineering husband so as to obfuscate the truth of my phobias.

Mia, much as her neediness chafed at me, might not yet have found someone to grant her that license, and so I gave her a chance to rewrite the essay based on emotional stress, especially since she had offered to withdraw the complaint against poor Kaveh Ali. It was a generous gesture, too generous perhaps, but generations of students had tagged me as a softie, always amenable to adjusting the rules. I would have made similar provisions for Shally, if only he had allowed me to help.

Wiping her face dry, Mia composed an ode of gratitude that sounded as studied as her weeping. Her surfeit of thanks confirmed my urgent need for a sabbatical. There was no other way to organize my conference in peace. As soon as she gathered her papers and breezed out the door, I pulled out my address book and started down my list of invitees. The first challenge, as always, would be to convince my oldest, most disputatious friend to make peace with his enemies. Dialing his number, I reached Chuck in Seattle, where he was taking a break between efforts to record the vocalizations of orcas as they hunted harbor seals beneath Alaska's tidewater glaciers.

"The sound of your voice, my dear Susanna, eases the pain in my joints," Chuck said, detailing a mild case of the bends. He loved these aquatic predators, their directness, their unity of purpose, their familial bonds. Poor Chuck. If he could have devised a means of breathing underwater, he would have stayed with them forever, seeking in cetaceans and pinnipeds all the relationships he couldn't manage with *Homo sapiens*.

"I hope you're being careful," I said. "Skinny as you are, you would make a tasty snack."

"No chance of that, my dear, not when I have my sound equipment to shield me. Any orca that wants to taste my flesh will have to chew through a mouthful of metal."

The idea of Chuck swimming through ice floes, inured to cold and risk, reminded me of his New Year's Day excursion with Jacob into the waters off Coney Island. The Polar Bear Club had served as a macho competition between them, another manifestation of their incessant jousting. They used to spar in my parlor with open hands, testing and probing each other's weaknesses—Jacob's heavyweight bulk against Chuck's lean body of a trapeze artist. It had stirred up far too much male aggression for my taste. I had hoped they might get along: for Jacob to appreciate Chuck's disdain for academic pretense, and for Chuck to view Jacob as a proxy for an early hominid, obsessed with the survival of his clan. Instead they had acted like Achilles and Hector outside the walls of Troy. The memory of their battles made me reflect on my poster of *The Ambassadors*, as if Jacob and Chuck—soldier versus scholar—represented Hans Holbein's two characters come to life. The image didn't quite fit. Given his pathological resistance to compromise, Chuck could never be anyone's idea of an ambassador, unless it were to a pod of killer whales.

"If the intrepid Chuck Rosenfeld would indulge me in a special request: please stay clear of the ice. It would break my heart to hear you've been crushed by a calving glacier."

"Susanna, if I have the ill fortune to be entombed under ice, then at least my death will have been in the service of science. There is more to fieldwork than watching baboons masturbate."

Chuck reveled in trying to shock me. Entering his class on the biology of language in 1960, I found him berating his students with such intensity that none had courage to sit in the front row. When he finished the lecture, I pleaded to be admitted within his corona. Ever skeptical, Chuck challenged me to a merciless apprenticeship, filled with courses on acoustics and gross anatomy, even an assignment to attend primate autopsies at the zoo, all to grasp the basic mechanics of the vocal tract. Up to that point, I had dithered in English, taking apart Emily Dickinson line by line, despairing that the play of poetics could ever untangle the mystery of the words themselves. What Chuck offered me was a tangible theory of language origins, of what united us as humans and linked us to the natural world.

"My dear, I have a proposal for you," I said, spelling out my plan for a conference on the evolution of language. He had argued for decades that language came about through natural selection, in accordance with the biological processes that had produced the ear, the eye, and the tongue, and didn't just appear 150,000 years ago thanks to some magical genetic mutation, like a gift from the gods, Athena springing from Zeus's head.

Absorbing my proposal, my old mentor didn't interrupt, he didn't argue, he didn't rage. In fact, he didn't say anything until I was finished.

"Will those idiots from linguistics be there?"

There was no getting around decades of loathing. Chuck had long ago dismissed linguistics as little more than mysticism. During each of his legendary duals with Chomsky and his protégés, I had faithfully served as Chuck's second, trying to soften his sneering and his provocations, and to negotiate wider acceptance of his theories.

"I'm inviting them of course."

"Then don't expect me anywhere near your latitude, unless you need my help grinding them up for fish food. We've had this same fight for thirty years. It's time to stop worrying about the blindness of fools."

I considered the moral argument, that a consensus on the roots of language could help countermand the history of human brutality, dating back at least fourteen thousand years to Jebel Sahaba, the first known massacre site, discovered in the upper Nile. No, idealism wouldn't work with Chuck. I needed a more powerful form of coercion, even if it contradicted my long-held aversion to sharing my personal weaknesses.

"You might want to reconsider, Chuck, if you would like to see me again."

"Is that a threat, my dear? Hardly the love poetry of the virgin princess who threw herself upon my tender mercies in 1960."

His reference to my poetic sensibilities made us both laugh. Back then, everyone thought we were a couple and so we were, in every way but the romantic. Chuck was too combative, and too committed to men's bodies for anything beyond intellectual intimacy.

Indulging in my first tactical maneuver of our long friendship, I spelled out the medical prognosis that defined my narrowing corridor of time, and capped off my dirge with a clear, unwavering warning. "You see, my dear, if you choose not to participate, I don't know how much more communication we will actually have."

Chuck seemed overcome. His impish arrogance withering, he confessed that he couldn't imagine life without me. As he promised to preserve the third weekend in April, I thought it ironic that my frailty, which I had sheltered from Chuck for so long, should have finally provided me the means to ensnare him. If nothing else, it showed me to be more devious than I had ever considered possible. Maybe Jacob's influence had rubbed off on me after all.

11

Bavaria
September 17, 1945

THE SCREAMS FROM THE BACK YARD ALERTED ME THAT OUR housekeeper Angela had caught a thief. Angela was a brute, 180 pounds of Rhinemaiden wielding her rolling pin like a spear against anyone who dared pilfer our supplies. Looking out the kitchen window, I saw her fat ass and flabby arms shaking with pleasure as she poked at her latest victim. I rushed outside to watch the action, but instead of coming upon a greedy Bavarian, I found a starving woman with short hair lying in the dust. The way she lifted her bony elbows to ward off Angela's blows made clear this was far from her first beating. Along her forearm I spotted a shadow. Numbers.

"Angela, what the hell are you doing?"

"Lt. Furman, this little rat was stealing from us." The house-keeper held up a can of meat, smashed open.

The bedraggled thief looked so emaciated that it was hard to imagine her having strength to bust open a can. Kneeling beside her, I reached out in a language she could understand:

"Don't be afraid. Zei Gezint. You'll be safe here."

The sound of Yiddish convinced her to lower her arms. She smiled for an instant, her teeth shrouded in brown rot, and then checked on the proximity of our housekeeper. After all this girl had been through, I wasn't going to allow her to be intimidated.

"Get out of here, Angela."

The housekeeper must have recognized the purity of my anger, generally directed at the town elders who denied any complicity with the Nazi regime. This afternoon, as Colonel Burckhardt dined with the same local bigwigs, Angela knew not to screw with me. She beat it before I needed to raise my voice again. With Angela gone, I helped my guest rise from the dust. There was so little left of her, she practically flew into my arms.

"You could have knocked on the front door," I said. "We would have prepared you a decent meal. Nothing kosher, but better than you could find in a can."

Unsmiling, she bowed her head and trailed me into the kitchen. Recalling my father's labors on evenings that my mother attended Hadassah meetings, I lit the stove and laid a steak onto the hot pan. When the meat was cooked, I placed it before her and watched her lash into it roughly, shoveling big chunks into her mouth.

I begged her to slow down, and assured her she could eat as much as she wanted, but she wasted no time devouring the food. Months had passed since liberation; her hair had begun to grow back, and she had swapped striped pajamas for filthy rags that hung off her. There was nothing to do about the numbers. Those would be with her forever.

"What's your name?"

"Judith," she mumbled between bites. Suddenly, she looked alarmed, as if troubled by something inside her. Rushing past me, she made it halfway to the back door before retching on the floor. Holding her steady, I tried to comfort her that it was all right, that she had just eaten too quickly, but as soon as she caught her breath, she dropped to the floor to scoop up the chunky mess with her bare hands.

"No, no, stop. Let me do it," I said, grabbing Angela's apron to wipe up the gobs of bile.

I invited Judith into the parlor, and we sat on opposite ends of the couch like awkward teenagers on a first date. Back home, my sister had coached me how to chat with her friends, chirpy girls who fluttered in my presence as if astounded that a Jewish boy should know how to box. It was long ago, but I thought back on Nesia's counsel: act confident and never waver, just like in the ring. Women want a man to be sure of himself.

"You are safe here," I said, holding up my revolver. "Under my protection."

Judith eyed the gun like a snake in the trees, not an immediate threat, but something over which to maintain steady vigilance. To disarm her, I placed the pistol on the table. A guarded silence crept over the room. Failing to ease her distrust with words, I opted for something tangible. Beckoning her to the bathroom, I handed her a fresh bar of soap and a clean towel. Take a bath, make yourself at home, I suggested. She tested the lock before accepting the offer.

No one could fault her caution. She must have been through a hell that I could only imagine from my afternoon visiting Buchenwald with Effie Grossberg a few weeks earlier. The sign at the gate, which might as well have read "Abandon all hope who enter here," had a different kind of poetry: "Jedem das seine," to each his own, to all deserving his own place. By this time, the crematoria no longer spewed smoke, the electric fence had lost its juice, and the wooden bunks where prisoners clung to each other for warmth were empty, the few survivors shipped out to displaced-persons camps. A thousand years could have passed since the atrocity, as if the earth itself had conspired with the Germans to cover up their crimes. We walked onto a freshly tilled field that contained the ashes of innumerable Jews, including perhaps Effie's parents and my father's cousins from Galicia. A bird pecked at the soil. I wondered whether the worms tasted different here.

Stopping on the field, Effie swapped his army cap for a brown yarmulke. In his hands was a small prayer book, worn and stained.

"Where did you get those?" I asked.

"I carried them with me, sir. This siddur belonged to my father. My mother packed it in my bags when they sent me out of Breslau."

That he had hidden the siddur and skullcap in his army gear all the way across Europe astounded me. Throughout the march east to Germany, Effie had earned his reputation as a dumb jackass, the butt of every battalion joke. Tired of hearing him mocked, I had tried teaching him to fight, to put his weight into a punch, but despite having the strength of a mule and an immunity to cold, he never responded to the abuse. It was hopeless. There was no way to fill his heart with fire.

"Would you like to share the book with me, sir?" he asked.

"Stop calling me 'sir.' There's no rank between two Jews standing in a cemetery."

Opening the siddur, Effie commenced a kaddish, which I joined with intermittent amens. When he finished, we stood over the field, on the kind of gray day where the clouds shrouded the horizon and obscured the thin line between heaven and earth.

The memory of Buchenwald stayed with me as I listened to the rush of bath water and imagined Judith lowering her wasted body into the tub. Soon she would emerge and we would return to our prickly discomfort on the couch, unless I could somehow reach her. There was only one man who I could trust to help. Reaching for the phone, I rang up Effie and ordered him to return to the baroness for some women's clothes.

"What kind of clothes?" he asked.

What little I knew of women's wear came from my sister's admiration for outfits she saw in magazines. "Dresses, sweaters, that kind of stuff. Just make sure they're cut small."

My guest was still splashing around when Effie dropped off a box with enough options to clothe three women. Depositing the clothes outside the bathroom, I called for Judith to pick out what she liked. When she finally returned to the parlor, she looked like a child playing in her mother's wardrobe. The sleeves stretched to her knuckles, the skirt and stockings drooped so low that they threatened to trip her. Cursing Effie's incompetence, I requisitioned some safety pins and recalled my father's lessons in alteration, taught to me Saturday afternoons at his shop. Fingering her waist, I tightened her skirt, and then pinned back her sleeves. She flinched as my hands brushed against the soft underside of her wrists, but I stayed cool and took my time, wondering what it felt like farther up her arm, whether the numbers were hot to the touch or bitter to the taste.

When it was finished, she lounged back on the couch and brushed a hand through her hair, still wet, as untamed as in a tragic play where the mad heroine puts out her eyes or butchers her children, and the chorus wails for the ruined city. A queen of such dark sentiments might have cried out for vengeance, but Judith told only of exhaustion after liberation, when she floated back through the shadows of her former life in Łodź.

"My feet carried me to familiar places, but everything had changed. Strangers were living in my father's house. His office had been seized by the Gestapo and then taken over by the communists. No one was left from my past. I felt like a ghost."

When she finished her story, Judith gazed at our piano, untouched since its arrival from the baroness. Seeing her tempted, I invited Judith to try her hand. She went to the piano and felt for the keys lightly, as if testing whether they might burn her. Then she rolled up her sleeves, which allowed me to make out a letter "B" and the number "1," the digits stretching like an arrow along her left forearm. It felt rude to stare, so, joining her at the keyboard, I closed my eyes and listened to her launch into what sounded like Chopin. When she finished, Judith bent her ear toward the keys, as if expecting to hear an echo.

"That was beautiful," I said, breaking the silence.

Before I could press her for more, a voice rang out from beyond the parlor door: "Lt. Furman, what's this all about?" It was Colonel Burckhardt, returning from dinner with the burgomeister. As I stood to salute my commanding officer, Judith shifted back on the sofa and lifted her knees up by her chest, as if to prepare for another beating.

"Official business, Colonel. This woman has critical intelligence about the SS networks still operating across Bavaria."

Burckhardt removed his hat and wiped a hand across his big head. We used to take bets whether any complex ideas penetrated that thick skull. If he had been born a thousand years earlier, we might have used that head as the tip of a battering ram.

"Well, she can't stay. It's a clear violation of protocol, and the burgomeister will ask questions."

"But Colonel, she walked all the way from Auschwitz. We can't just put her out."

The name of the camp should have shamed Burckhardt to relent; but regulations, not basic human decency, were the only things the colonel held sacred. "I know, it's terrible what happened to these people, but the DP camps are there to help those like her. Make sure she's placed first thing tomorrow morning."

I nearly damned the consequences and belted him. One punch to make up for months of backstabbing compromises. Only the memory of Judith warding off the housekeeper's blows reminded me that my court-martial wouldn't help her cause. The rage passed, the colonel retreated to his room, and I was left to admit the limits of my power.

"My colonel is a real son-of-a-bitch," I said, rejoining Judith on the couch. Explaining his orders, I offered to escort her to the closest displaced-persons camp, where she would be guaranteed twice the calories as those rationed to the Germans.

Her response was to reach into the sofa cushion and to pull out my pistol, which she must have pinched from the table. "I would sooner shoot him while he sleeps."

The gun pointed toward the door, she displayed all the courage that I lacked.

"Please, Judith, he can't force you to do anything. The decision is yours."

Placing the weapon on the table, she brushed back her hair, still not fully dry. That hair had its own magic, tempting me to run my hands through it. This was no time for monkey business, though, not after all she had been through.

"What will you do now?"

"I will keep walking."

I nearly questioned her plan, but I had no right to pry, not when all I could offer was one night's sanctuary. Pulling a blanket from the closet, I unfurled it over her as she stretched out along the couch. Retrieving my sidearm, I turned my chair to face the door. Unable to guide her to safety, the least I could do was to guard her while she slept.

"Don't worry, you'll be safe tonight. Rest now."

"Wait." She grasped my hand and tugged me beside her on the couch. Rolling up her sleeve, I exposed the tattoo and kissed the numbers. My lips traveled lightly along the digits, B-164732, but it must have been sensitive, because she snatched back her arm. I was forming an apology when she lay back and opened her arms wide. "Come."

I bent down to her, and as our lips came together, I tasted something pure, free from any expectation or hope, or even faith, free from the burden of worrying about the future. My fingers swam through her hair, short strokes in dark waters, and I sniffed in the fresh scent of her bath. There was no bucking the sense that it was wrong, terribly wrong, for me to proceed, but we had both lost everything, and there was no one left to judge us. Even the rabbis had been fed into the ovens.

I hesitated, reluctant to cross that river, until she coaxed me forward, shifting her bony hips into the center of the couch and tugging my shirt loose from my belt. Floating above her tiny frame, all skin and bones, I tore open the clasps that pinned her skirt in place and slid down her stockings. Awaiting me, she closed her eyes, not in bliss, but with a determination to persist.

When we were finished, she shifted to one side for me to squeeze next to her, As she buried her face into my shoulder and drifted off, I listened to her breathe and damned my cowardice. A real man would have refused to abandon her, no matter the consequences. I was still cursing myself when the light in the sky affirmed the inevitable. Morning had come. It was time for her to go.

I wanted to send her off with enough cash to carry her across Europe, but too many reckless nights with Williamson had tapped me dry. Whatever inheritance awaited me back in Boston was useless to me now. Once again, I could count on only one man for support. I rang him at daybreak.

"Effie, do you have any greenbacks?"

"How much?"

"As much as you've got. It's for the girl."

When Effie showed up, he handed me a wad of bills collected over months of saving. He was a mensch, proving to me that in a land that had devoured our people, I had found an unlikely brother.

Judith accepted the bills without word and slipped them into her waistband, the skirt pinned tightly to fit her frame. I had one more gift for her, my revolver and a small cache of bullets, which she tucked into her bag. It wasn't much, but it might protect her from another beating. Then she pulled a black scarf from the bag and tied it behind her neck. Fingertips to her lips, she blew me a kiss, a final gift before she disappeared through the ruins of the town square.

12

Brooklyn
September 25, 1996

IN THE WEEK SINCE MOM BEGAN CHEMOTHERAPY, SHE HAD turned her bedroom into a Library of Babel, assembling a jumble of books and papers all around her as if gathering her tribesmen to repel an invading army. She ravaged the bookshelves downstairs, leaving big gaps, like missing teeth, in the stacks. Half her filing cabinet shared the bed with her. Her focus on the descent of the human larynx had grown so intense that it was getting harder to coax her to come down for dinner. All she wanted to do these days was to lie around in her bathrobe and pore over her notes.

"How's it going, Mom?" I asked from the doorway. "The place looks more chaotic than usual."

She pushed aside some papers to clear a little space on the bed. "Come, Shally, sit with me if you have time. There's something I want to discuss."

It hadn't tended to be good news lately when my mother had something to discuss. My whole life, she had avoided any subject that might upset me, but every word these days ushered in a more ominous reality. Wary of her revelations, I faltered at the threshold, and yet there was no way to avoid stepping inside. It wasn't as if she asked much of me. The least I could do was to keep her company before meeting the Mega-Stars for a late-night show.

"Sure, Mom. What's going on?"

"I'm sponsoring a conference on the evolutionary roots of language. All the leading figures, even Chuck Rosenfeld, have promised to attend."

"Don't they mostly use language to curse at each other?"

She laughed, a rare moment of lightness. "This time it will be different."

"Not if your old pal Chuck has anything to do with it." My childhood was marked by Chuck's periodic visits en route to intimate encounters with aquatic mammals. The cranky old queer always put on a good show, with pictures of whales breaching or dolphins screwing, and killer impressions of their mating calls.

"Chuck promised to behave himself this time," she said.

"I hope you didn't have to sell your soul to wring that promise out of him?"

"Not quite, but it did use up most of my remaining credits."

Mom must have really worked some magic to muster a peace between Chuck and his intellectual enemies. Those feuding gasbags lived for their ridiculous lines in the sand.

"You could help me organize the panels," she said, "if you're not too busy."

I tried to contain my laugh, but it burst from my mouth as a cough, or more like something in between: a lough. In the three years since my expulsion from the department, I had never looked back, not once, at what had been the academic equivalent of an evolutionary dead end.

"As I'm sure you remember, Mom, my last adventure in anthropology didn't end so gracefully."

She smiled vaguely, distracted again. "Of course, I wouldn't want to force you into anything uncomfortable."

No, she never did force me into anything. All she did was plant suggestions, hints as to her preferred path, invariably difficult to follow, like the books she brought home to inspire me as a boy: highbrow girlish fantasies about space and time and mirrors. The pressure to plod through those books was excruciating. As Mom listened to her recordings of baboon chatter, I stretched across the carpet in her study staring at the same page until I finally begged to be allowed to watch Magilla Gorilla on Dad's television downstairs. I was no better off in college, when she guided me toward a physiology class where a professor in medical scrubs unveiled a breadloaf-sized bundle wrapped in wet cheesecloth that turned out to be a human brain, the spinal cord dangling like the tendrils on a jellyfish. As the instructor sliced up the brain with a kitchen knife, I couldn't stop thinking it had the consistency and color of tofu. It led me to months of doubt: is that all we were in the end, this majesty of human existence, nothing but bean curd?

Later, when weighing graduate school, I succumbed to Mom's guidance yet again when she suggested ethnography, given what she saw as my natural propensity for stories. More than ever, her brilliance shadowed me. Borrowing copies of Malinowski and Lévi-Strauss and Geertz and Mintz from her bookshelves, I discovered her scribblings in the margins, haunting the arguments, forcing me to conclude that I would never be as wise, as intellectually agile, as gifted as she was. Adding to my grief were the grumblings from my fellow anthro students about nepotism, which reached their pinnacle when the department offered me a generous grant to conduct summer fieldwork on Cuban political consciousness. Reaching Havana, I found myself stuck listening to dull clichés that the regime wanted to foist upon us gringos. After a fruitless month hearing nothing but state dogma, I changed my focus to what came naturally—women and music—and suddenly I found informants everywhere. The hustlers hanging around Old Havana were dying to tell of their exploits romancing European girls on vacation. It didn't matter whether they spoke the truth, only that their stories reflected how they felt about their poverty, their underdevelopment, their sense of manhood. All right, it was banal, but hell, in this case banality equated with freedom. There was no point resisting when Fidel's spies were everywhere. Might as well enjoy life, a perspective that made sense to me, as I joined their revolution and spent the summer seducing French and Swedish girls who believed my accent to be Argentine. The Cuban hustlers roared at my gall and cheered my expressed ambition to hear the ecstatic "Oh My God" in a half dozen languages.

The summer turned out to be far more engaging than most academic fieldwork, and it yielded a startling, if heterodox, paper: "Sex on the Beach: The Dialectic of Subjugation among Marginalized Cubanos and their Wealthy Gringa Mistresses," a title that both solidified my reputation as a Don Juan and incited the fury of my compatriots in the department, who didn't buy my reinterpretation of the participant-observer relationship. When I presented the essay in seminar, a host of fellow grad students accused me of subverting departmental funds for my bohemian pleasures, of reaching a preposterous, sexist conclusion, and of misrepresenting myself to the poor European women who fell for my lies. The worst subjugation, they charged, had been conducted by the anthropologist himself.

My expulsion must have been a terrible blow to Mom, but it came as an incalculable relief to me. Every time I'd tried to broach the prospect of leaving anthropology, she'd persuaded me to persist, offering to tutor me in the canonical texts or to intervene with my professors. She couldn't help herself from trying to save me, and would no doubt have tried again had I not sabotaged myself instead. It had to be done, and in the most public way possible, so as to leave no bridge unburned. There could be no chance of turning back.

"Shally, there is something I need to ask you."

My mother and I had never discussed the incident. It hung between us like a death, unmourned, unacknowledged, barely referenced obliquely. If there were ever to be a time to hash it out, it would have to be now. Breathing deep, I readied a long-overdue apology.

"Sure, Mom, anything."

"I would like you to shave my head."

"Excuse me?"

She brushed her hands back through hair so thick that her fingers became entangled. "My doctors say it will all fall out as result of the chemotherapy. They recommend shaving it beforehand, so the loss won't be so unsettling."

Her request floored me. If there had been one bit of continuity in my life, it was my mother's fulsome hair. As a kid, I imagined it to be the source of magical powers that allowed her to speak to animals not like some silly Dr. Doolittle, but as a real mad scientist: reaching out to monkeys in their language, struggling with pitch and intonation, and all the nuance that made communication between living beings so confounding.

"I don't know, Mom. The Mega-Stars are expecting me soon."

"You could do it now, if you have time."

My electric clippers had served me well since my break with anthropology, when I snapped on the number two attachment and shed the long hair that had carried me like a crown prince through an academic career. Since then, a biweekly shearing had given me an odd sense of clarity, confirming my decision to put away childish vanities. My affinity for the razor, however, didn't make it any easier to turn the blade on my mother, no matter how her doctors described the effects of chemo.

"Mom, don't you think the ladies at the salon should take care of this?"

Her sole concession to vanity consisted in monthly visits to the "colorist" who prevented gray from seeping into the roots.

"I would prefer it to be you."

Presented this way, I couldn't exactly refuse. Resigning myself to the job, I yanked the razor out of my cabinet and returned to her bedroom, when my beeper started buzzing. Mia had been pestering me all day, missing me, so she said.

"Do you need to answer that?"

"No, Mom, it's just a friend of mine being choresome."

"Choresome?"

"You know, a pain in the ass. Isn't that the right word?"

"I don't believe so."

I could have sworn that the very word sprang from Hamlet, spurning the priest over Ophelia's grave, but Mom recalled it as churlish; and when we checked the reference, she was, as always, correct.

"Don't feel bad, Shally, language is formed through necessity. Perhaps your inventiveness will start something that lasts for centuries to come."

She had always been absurdly generous to me. Even a basic grammatical mistake could be testament to my inherent creative impulse. I didn't feel like arguing.

Clippers in hand, I could see there was no avoiding, only enduring, this miserable task. I placed a stiff chair in her bathroom and instructed her to face the mirror. Once seated, she closed her eyes, her lips moving slightly, as if in prayer. Standing behind her, the blade like a scythe in my hand, I reached out to touch her hair, the way I used to do as a little boy. As my hand floated across the space between us, I stopped dead. Stroking her hair seemed far too intimate, the violation of a terrible taboo. I wasn't a child any more.

"Let me know when you're ready, Mom."

"Yes, I'm ready. Please go ahead."

The razor buzzed to life like a chainsaw gearing up to hack through an ancient forest. Her eyes still shut, she nodded a few times, either in concentration or as a final push for me to proceed, so I pressed the clippers to the base of her skull and carved out a clump of hair. I tried to catch it, but my hand clutched at empty air as the hair fell lifeless to the bathroom tiles. That hair, like the rings on a tree, spoke to her journey, her passions, her life itself. With one swipe, I felled decades of accumulated experience. It was a tragedy, and yet I had to press on. Raising the blade again, I took another pass, and another after that. Mom barely flinched, not even when the razor jammed in the thick undergrowth. Bit by bit, I transformed her into a Raggedy Ann doll, and then buzzed her within a half inch of the skin. When it was done, I bent down to her ear and peered at the two of us side by side in the mirror, mother and son with an inch of dark hair between them. It made us seem more connected than ever.

"That's it, Mom."

She opened her eyes and blinked at the sight, her hands instinctively rising to touch the soft undercoat we all carry beneath our vanity. A little yelp came out: shorter than a wail, but still tough to bear. Mourning fluttered on her face and then disappeared, as she recomposed her dignity with a quick nod.

"Thank you, Shally. You did a fine job."

She brushed off her shoulders and reached for a broom to sweep up the mess. Careful not to let her see me, I palmed a lock of fallen hair. She didn't notice my theft. She had already returned to the books awaiting her attention.

13

Bavaria
November 28, 1945

Staring out my office window, I kept hoping to catch Judith in her scarf strolling across the square, having abandoned her journey and returned to my care. No such luck. The only ones trudging through town were German: the aged haberdasher with the greased-back hair, the teenage bricklayer rebuilding city hall, and the young mother carrying her toddler. Life had returned to normal, and the local bosses all wanted to pretend that the war had never happened. Assigned to the process of "Denazification," I spent my days investigating those who had contributed to the Nazi regime, but none of them were willing to bear responsibility for their crimes. My efforts turned out to be a monumental waste of time. The U.S. Army of Occupation paid no attention to my findings. Colonel Burckhardt even ordered me to stop haranguing the town fathers with my "inquisitions." Let the Germans report any bad apples, he said, we needed the civilian leadership to clean the streets, distribute the ration cards, and deliver the mail.

At the colonel's instructions, I left my office door open to any Germans willing to denounce their neighbors. There were no takers, at least not until a stranger knocked on the door requesting an audience.

"Lt. Jacob Furman, I need to speak with you."

That he addressed me in English, with the twinge of a British accent, made me reconsider the colonel's warnings to watch out for Russian spies. Until now, it had sounded like typical army horseshit, meant to justify our refusal to tighten the noose around a nation of Nazis. Facing this stranger, I could no longer be so sure.

"All right, who are you and what do you want?"

This visitor sure fit my image of a Red: faded wool jacket, workingman's cap, the smug assurance that pegged him as a true believer. From his square build, rutted face, and big dirty hands, he looked well traveled, accustomed to a good fight. Breezing in, he pulled a chair close to my desk.

"You have a reputation for being a capable man, but your skills are being wasted here." He scanned my office, filled with boxes of evidence destined for an army storage depot in Maryland. "Jacob, Jacob, Jacob, a man like you needs something to fight for."

No civilian in Bavaria had ever dared to address me so informally. Pushing back my chair, I rose fast and stepped toward him. He bounced up as well, so the two of us stood chest to chest. My visitor was a few inches shorter than me, but solid, with a nose that looked like it had been broken before.

"Who the hell are you to pass judgment?" I asked.

"Did you show this much fight when they ordered you to send a helpless young woman into the wilderness?"

I didn't ask how he knew about Judith. I just smacked him. A solid right cross to his chin that knocked him to the deck. Most guys would have folded, stayed down and avoided antagonizing a bigger man, but this little bulldog popped right up and hit me with a rapid combination of tight blows to my ribs, so quick and hard that they staggered me. But he didn't press the attack, and as

I heaved him back and regained my footing, ready to pound him into the rubble, the stranger held up his hands and started to laugh.

"Enough, please. You've done me a great service and answered a classic question from the Torah."

The Biblical reference made me wonder what game he was playing.

"Why are you worrying about the Torah? The rabbis were all lost in the camps."

"The rabbis may be dead, but I remember as a boy in *cheder* listening to the arguments over your namesake, Jacob, when he wrestled the angel in the road. They could never agree whether the angel was literal or a manifestation of Jacob's spiritual conflict, his doubt. Now, thanks to you, I have an answer: he was just a stubborn fool."

Neglecting the prohibition from Bernie's gym against showing any hurt, I rubbed the ribs that ached from our tussle.

"And you're an angel of God sent to deliver me?"

"No, I am Salik Landsman. And as for delivering you, I couldn't care less about your spiritual awakening. What we need is your help, to move thousands of survivors to Palestine. You, better than anyone, know they can't stay here. You've seen these 'Displaced Persons' camps."

After Judith left, I had searched for her in all the nearby DP camps, just in case she had found sanctuary there. Behind the gates I had met the survivors, mostly men, who made a deep impression on me. None of them had seen her, but they explained how they had made it through Auschwitz and Buchenwald and Gross-Rosen by remaining clean-shaven, using any sharp edge, even broken glass, on their beards, just so the SS wouldn't think their strength was slipping and dispatch them to the gas chambers.

"You're crazy. The DPs are in no condition to go anywhere."

"They are already moving on their own, thousands of them, on the roads, on trains, even on foot, going south to the sea. When they make it to the Mediterranean, we will put them on board ships. A man like you, who has commanded troops, could be a great asset."

His plan took shape before me. A risky, lunatic scheme.

"The British will never let the boats through. You're wasting your time."

"Strange thing to tell the man offering your life purpose. What else do you plan to do when the U.S. Army releases you in a few months? You have nothing more waiting for you in Boston than the survivors have in Łodź or Jasło."

I didn't bother asking how he knew about my family. This Salik, whether angel or devil, understood that my impending discharge would leave me rootless. Such freedom was what I had hoped for as a teenager looking to escape my father's rag business. Never would I have expected that war, and fire, would relieve me of any obligation to go home again.

"Watch your mouth. My parents' house may have burned to the ground, but their lives counted for something."

"Fair enough. You will have to forgive me. I am used to speaking bluntly. The survivors don't have time for pretty talk."

He outlined plans for a new state, a haven for the Jews, a Zion that would come too late for the millions who had perished. It had always seemed to me an impossible enterprise, to gather up the wanderers scattered over two thousand years in exile. There was no telling that to Salik Landsman. He had his vision and he did not waver. Soon, I found myself with only one remaining question.

"How did you come to me?"

"Think about it, Jacob. Who is the one person left on earth to care about your welfare?"

There was only one suspect. After Salik left, I rushed down the hall to the office of Private Effie Grossberg and grabbed him by the collar.

"You lousy rat, you had no right telling anyone my personal business."

"Jacob, I was thinking of your future, our future. We should focus on the living, not the dead."

It was only then that I recognized Effie's famed stupidity to have been an act, more convincing than any of Williamson's bluffs at poker. Unlike Williamson, Effie stayed in character long after the last card was dealt. If anyone had been the *dummkopf*, it was me, and my mistake was made worse by my failure to recognize the meaning of Salik's offer. I released my hold on Effie's jacket.

"All right then, let's toast this new future of ours."

"Won't that be a problem for you? Fraternizing with an enlisted man?"

"Fuck it. If the colonel bothers us, we'll tell him it's a Jewish holiday."

"*Hine Ma Tov,*" Effie said, mumbling to himself what sounded like a prayer.

"What was that?"

"It's a Hebrew song: 'How good and sweet to sit together as brothers.' I can teach it to you. You will need a few songs for the sea voyage to come."

Yes, do that, I said, throwing my arm around his shoulders and leading him out of the office. As brothers, orphaned brothers, we returned to my place, broke open a bottle of Slivovitz, and drank to a new beginning. If the U.S. Army could turn to the next war so easily, then so too could we.

14

**Kigali, Rwanda
September 28, 1996**

BINOCULARS TRAINED ON THE EASTERN SKY, CAPTAIN EZEKIEL Hakizimana called orders into his walkie-talkie with a forcefulness that brought me back to the final minutes before an operation, when thousands of lives depended on the smooth execution of our plan. If anyone could understand the nature of my life's work, it was this young Tutsi officer. Watching his serious intent, I recalled scanning the sea for British warships that were determined to block our banana boat full of survivors from reaching Palestine. That mission, my first with Salik, ended with me holding firm under British interrogation, convinced in my course even as they tore every fingernail from my hands.

"No sign of the plane?" I asked the captain.

"Not yet, Mr. Jacob, but it won't be long now."

A unit of Tutsi soldiers waited beside us along the tarmac. Singing along softly to a lady's voice on the radio, they seemed as disciplined as Captain Ezekiel, a far cry from the Zairean thugs who had pestered us for beer money at all the checkpoints in Goma.

Leaning back, Dudu tapped the captain's rubber boot. "What's that word—'Jeshi'—in the song? It sounds familiar."

"Jeshi is the army. The song is about the sacrifice our soldiers made in the war."

The answer sent Dudu's mind racing, always a dangerous business. "Hey Captain, you know what: the Arabs have the same word—Jaish. I heard it all the time in Lebanon."

What Dudu meant with this comparison wasn't at all clear. I didn't want to take any chances.

"When did you become such a student of linguistics, Dudu?"

"It's good to know when people are cursing at you."

The "Jeshi" song sounded more like a lamentation than a march to war. No one could blame the Tutsis if they liked sad melodies. Some of our best—*Kol Haolam Kulo, Hine MaTov*—were composed in a similar mood. Not that I could claim to be a music critic. That job was best left to my son. For a moment, I wished we could have brought Shalom with us to Rwanda, if only to show him what it meant to fight for a cause. The Tutsis never would have suffered his piddling about, trying this and that, and failing at all of it. He might have turned out different if I had rowed him out to sea, tossed him overboard, and forced him to swim back to shore on his own. Instead, Susanna had coddled him, and who was I to challenge a mother's love? However much she resisted any link to Judaism or the Jews, she had proved herself to be a Yiddische Mama at heart.

The music on the radio switched to something bouncy and light, and a sergeant seated nearby made a suggestion in Kinyarwandan that seemed to amuse the captain.

"The sergeant would like me to teach you some of our dancing, Mr. Jacob," Ezekiel explained. The Tutsi soldiers all turned my way, awaiting my response.

"You've got the wrong customer," I said. "Dancing has never been my thing."

Dudu heaved himself up. "Let me try. When I was young, they wanted me for the Bolshoi. Until they worried I might eat the ballerinas."

The soldiers didn't seem to get his Bolshoi joke, and yet the platoon rose with him, relishing the sight of the big *muzungu* lining up beside their lanky captain. They made for an odd couple facing us, but it was an odd kind of dance, which the captain demonstrated by bending his knees and weaving his arms, like a stork bobbing and dipping across shallow water. Dudu got the footwork all right, but his arms flapped too heavily.

"Easy now, Dudu," I said. "You look like a fat vulture swooping down to pick at the dead."

"Not me, Aba. I leave the dead for you. And Captain Ezekiel too."

Mimicking the captain, Dudu soon got used to the moves, pressing down his hands as if to keep a woman's skirt from blowing up in the breeze. He did well. Maybe there was some truth to his having formal training in dance.

The walkie-talkie suddenly started to squawk, and the soldiers pointed to a distant speck on the eastern horizon. The dot grew larger until a beat-up old Antonov, marked only by the symbols EW-46524, shot down on the runway and taxied over to us. This was the end of a long, clandestine journey. It had taken off in Minsk, picked up cargo in Bucharest and Lod, and then made refueling stops in Djibouti and Mombasa for the final hop across Africa.

"You are lucky that piece of junk didn't drop into the Red Sea," Dudu said. "What will happen, Aba, when your good fortune runs out one day?"

"On that day, when I walk through the valley of the shadow of death, I will fear no evil. Until then, I have you to protect me."

Dudu shook his head, refusing to humor me. "This dirty business is no good for you, Aba. It's better that you go home to your wife before you regret what you've done here. You aren't hard enough to live with blood on your hands."

What a pain-in-the-ass Dudu had turned out to be. I needed his tactical assessments, not his pseudo-rabbinic judgments on the nature of good and evil.

"Enough of this bullshit. Haven't you noticed what's at stake? These people are facing genocide."

In the old days, Effie never gave me such *tsuris*. He simply looked out for my interests and helped me navigate any obstacle. Back then, it was Susanna who picked apart my morality, on the rare occasion I allowed her to peek behind the curtain. Ah, well, the only upside to the dissolution of my marriage was that it spared me the burden of justifying life's compromises.

As the plane slowed to a stop, the Belarusian flight crew opened the cargo bay door and started to unload heavy pallets onto the tarmac. Captain Ezekiel got to work counting crates, comparing the numbers against his requisition list. After confirming everything to be in order, the captain cracked open a box the size of a child's coffin and pulled out a machine gun.

"Mr. Jacob, these weapons are a blessing," the captain said. "It is a shame that no one gave your people such aid during the *shoah*."

Over the past week, Captain Ezekiel Hakizimana had paid close attention to my accounts of Buchenwald and Bavaria, and of our rebuilding after the Holocaust. Traveling across Rwanda, visiting massacre sites and battle bunkers, we had shared a sense of solidarity that stretched beyond words. What a mitzvah this trip had turned out to be, something rarely bestowed on a man my age, to watch a persecuted people scuttle across that narrow bridge back from extermination.

Hoisting the mag above his head, the wiry captain made like the Biblical Joshua raising a shofar against the walls of Jericho, calling his troops to action. The big gun was unwieldy for him, but what Ezekiel lacked in muscle mass he made up for with determination. Gathering around, the soldiers began to clap rhythmically, breaking into another military anthem, this one more joyous than the songs that had come before.

Dudu, now practiced in Tutsi dancing, tried to join the chorus, but he couldn't keep up with the words, except to repeat what sounded like "Intsinzi." When the song wound down, he called for the captain's gun.

"Let me see that mag."

Dudu gazed over the weapon with the same admiration that he displayed over a busty mama. Sighing, he stroked the wooden stock, steel barrel, and trigger mechanism. Then he hugged it to his chest and closed his eyes in mock adulation, a show of intimacy from many nights sharing the same bed.

"An old girlfriend?" I asked.

With a rapid swing, he popped back to attention, a rare show of discipline, as if on parade before his commanding officer.

"Nothing like that. This fucking thing almost dragged me down."

With the whole platoon watching, Dudu hoisted the butt to his shoulder in one fluid motion and made a "rat-tat-tat-tat-tat" in his throat. Undeterred by the mag's weight, he seemed to draw strength from the earth, his stocky legs planted as heavily as an ancient Assyrian warrior king, like the one who conquered Jerusalem and enslaved our ancestors, who was remembered by history for the massive stone carvings that Susanna had dragged me to see in the museum.

"Come on, Dudu, stop messing around. These guys have work to do."

"I'm not messing around, Aba. I just wanted to see if it still feels as heavy as it used to. We had many difficult times together."

Lowering the mag, he rolled up his sleeve to show off the tattoo that he had previously shielded from my sight. The Tutsi soldiers gathered around to watch him narrate the illustration: a kneeling Hezbollah guerrilla firing an RPG; an armored vehicle in flames; bodies lying all around; and one figure returning fire with a big gun.

"This shows what happened on the road to Beirut. We were riding along, and then boom: the rocket hit us. Three guys from my unit died right away, but I was only lightly wounded on the shoulder. As soon as I got outside, I opened up with the mag until our enemies were all finished. By the time the army sent help, I was the only one left alive. Me and the mag."

Looking over his arm, I noticed another image, the scratched outlines of a table, the illustration much cruder, as if drawn with a pen, with some squiggly writing beneath it, what looked like Arabic script.

"What's that all about?"

Dudu rolled down his sleeve. "That's a different story, Aba, without such a happy ending. We'll save that for another time."

He held the mag out to me like a young mother offering up her newborn to a wayward father. "Here, Jacob, if you want to be in this business, you should learn to carry this fucking thing. Maybe the captain can give us some bullets to show you how it fires."

Back in my soldiering days, I had operated plenty of guns, but that was long ago. The last thing I needed was to expose myself as an old sap who'd lost his handle on modern weaponry.

"Cut the crap, Dudu. Captain Ezekiel has better uses for his ammunition than to have us piss it away."

Complying for once, Dudu slid the weapon back inside its crate and slapped the lid for the soldiers to carry it off to the trucks.

"What about the special package we requested for the captain?" I asked.

"Shit, I forgot," Dudu said, jogging after the plane as it prepared to take off again. He shouted up to the cockpit and someone tossed a flight bag out the side door. When Dudu returned to us, I inspected the bag and presented it to our escort.

"Captain, this is something we want you to have, in thanks for your guidance."

Ezekiel looked perplexed, even a little unsettled. "I cannot accept any gifts, Mr. Jacob. We have strict rules in our army."

"First see what it is, then you can decide."

Reaching into the flight bag, he pulled out a holster containing a late model Glock. He tested the pistol's feel and aimed it down the runway. Promising to seek permission from his superiors, the captain thanked me and fastened it to his belt.

"We will see you soon, Mr. Jacob. As soon as we are able."

The crates loaded on board the trucks, Captain Ezekiel waved the convoy to proceed, and we climbed into a jeep for the ride back to Goma, to wait for the fighting to begin.

15

Brooklyn
October 6, 1996

DELACROIX SHOWED UP BEFORE I COULD FINISH WATERING THE plants. Arriving early for rehearsal, our conga player knocked loudly enough for me to freak out that the Feds might be busting in on Dad's basement. What I found upon opening the front door shocked me: the dapper Delacroix in a complete state of disarray. His collar was dirty, his tie hung unraveled from his neck, and his suit was rumpled, as if he had slept in his clothes. Even his head, generally perfectly shaved, was showing some roots.

"What happened? You look terrible."

"It is this new job, Shalom. The stories of the victims keep me awake at night. It has become so bad that I am afraid to face my dreams."

He had always made it seem that working for the war crimes tribunal constituted a pretty good gig. It paid well and was guaranteed to last a long, long time. There was no end to the list of atrocities.

"You've got to take it easy, man. It's just a job."

Delacroix yanked off his tie. "I have learned of crimes that I could never imagine—a mother who watched her four children killed by her neighbor. The priests who sent the murderers to their congregation, and the doctors who turned on their patients."

His response to genocide—grief and confusion—was so different from my parents. When it came to the *shoah*, Dad had lectured me endlessly, but his lessons were overbearing, as if I had neglected the victims just by being alive. God only knew what Mom had witnessed. She never talked about it. The subject was a dark cloud lifted only by the biannual visits of old Mr. Stolbach, who came to tune the piano, and afterwards read to me from his *yizkor* of Jasło, the Furman ancestral home in Galicia. Mr. Stolbach told me *what* had happened, but I didn't understand *why* the Germans had murdered all those people, so I asked my father. "Because they were Jews" was his wholly unsatisfying answer. When I posed the same question to Mom, she gave me a scientific discourse on the evils of tribalism, traced back to the first recorded massacre, somewhere in Nubia long before the pharaohs. Given the differences between my parents, it seemed strange that the *shoah* should have brought them together, but it did, precisely in what manner they never shared. Maybe it was just too bitter a memory.

Facing Delacroix before me, I felt pretty confident he didn't need a bunch of banalities about the nature of evil. He just wanted to unload his burdens before the others arrived. The best I could do for him was to shut up and listen to his descriptions of human beings slaughtered like animals.

"It is shocking what a machete can do to the body," he said. "Since this job began, I have not been able to eat meat of any kind. I cannot even look at it."

We had all noticed how Delacroix ordered potato pierogis rather than chops or stuffed cabbage at our post-show meals at The Kiev. He never justified his changing tastes, not even when Pascal tormented him for being an African vegetarian.

"Delacroix, are you sure you want to bother with practice?" I asked. "Maybe you should go home and get some rest."

He shook his head definitively. "No, please. The music is my only relief."

A knock at the door turned out to be Ismael, sax case dangling from one shoulder, and the two Guinean cousins, the guitarist Ousmane and bassist Abdoulaye, who were playing with us regularly these days. Their arrival transformed Delacroix. He straightened his posture, fixed his tie, and rubbed his hands together slowly to warm them up for the congas. One by one the Mega-Stars showed up and settled in to their places, until we were left waiting, as usual, for Pascal. The guys practiced riffs and went through the instrumentation, but we needed our vocalist to mount a real rehearsal.

"Where the hell is this guy?" I asked. "Did anyone hear from him?"

No one ventured a guess. Ismael, who should have cared, was busy testing a new sequence on his sax. When Pascal finally did arrive, an hour late, he wheeled along a massive suitcase, as if he had packed for a big trip. Much as I was hoping he might announce his imminent departure for Paris, he opened the bag to offer a profusion of sunglasses, each wrapped in plastic, a fresh shipment of knock-offs. The guys all rushed to select a pair for the bargain price of five dollars apiece. I hated to credit Pascal for anything, but the shades did look mighty boss.

"Hey, Shalom, what about you?" Pascal said. "I will give you a special deal: only ten dollars." He picked out a pair of aviator-style glasses and fit them onto my face.

"Twice as much for me, why's that?"

"Because you make me twice the trouble. If you find us a real studio, then you can pay $5 like the others. This place is no good. The African Refugee Mega-Stars should not be hiding in a basement apartment filled with marijuana plants."

There was no use arguing with Pascal. He didn't care how hard I worked, or how these nights shepherding the band through downtown clubs represented time stolen from my ailing mother. All he wanted was results.

"Be nice to me, Pascal. I just booked us a big show."

"Not another lesbian club."

"No, a Saturday night slot at CBGB." I paused for effect, letting the name fill the air with possibility. "Rock it hard, and we will rip this fucking town apart."

The guys didn't need a translator, or a history of the downtown music scene, to grasp that this show represented a major breakthrough. The Mega-Stars surged forward to congratulate me, and each other, in turn. Finally, we had the chance to prove ourselves on a big stage. The mood turned electric with possibility. As the guys began to play, all the discord faded.

PART 3

16

New York City
May 16, 1963

THE AUDITORIUM WAS SEETHING BY THE TIME I SHOWED UP to hear the debate on the nature of Nazi conformity. With only three weeks left before my oral exams, I should have devoted the time to refining my grasp of hominid vocal anatomy, but the announcement that a renowned philosopher would be addressing her thesis on Adolf Eichmann coaxed me from the library. Eichmann, architect of my parents' extermination, had been hanged by now, his ashes cast to sea, but I retained an inconsolable dread that the Nazis might yet appear on my stoop. Against this terror, the notion that the former SS officer had acted out of petty bureaucratic need held an unexpected solace, that such hate might have a clear explanation, like the biology of the pharyngeal tract.

The assembled audience didn't seem to share my intellectual curiosity. Here a whole battery of damaged souls waited to argue over Eichmann's crimes. With the tension manifesting itself in an epic scramble for the few remaining seats, I spotted an open place deep within a central row and waded through waves of uncrossing legs. As I reached the seat, a burly man stood to allow me past, and in my clumsiness I stumbled and barreled right into him.

"Oh. I'm so sorry," I said. Regaining my footing, I looked at the gentleman who had prevented me from smashing my teeth against the floor. His face seemed weathered, his skin seasoned by crossing too many meridians to count, his nose and cheekbones slightly flattened, as if pressed by a strong headwind. Flecks of gray spindled through his dark hair. He had a wry smile, the kind sported by the damaged hero in a war movie who flies off on a doomed mission and leaves his dame to weep over what might have been.

"That's all right," he said. "I've taken worse blows."

As a student of the human voice, I soaked up the deep timbre generated within his broad, jutting chest. This was how I imagined an Old Testament prophet to have sounded, calling on his people follow him to the promised land. It was a voice that had a strange, unsettling effect on me, inspiring me to speak more than my wont.

"I'm surprised to see it so packed."

He gazed slowly over the maelstrom. "They must think that shouting will bring back the dead."

"If so, then they're bound to be disappointed."

"Only because they don't appreciate that the dead have their own eloquence."

It sounded like mystical claptrap, but he uttered it with absolute confidence. At an event where most men donned a sports coat, he wore instead a leather jacket, less the studied nonchalance of a jazz critic than the off-hours fatigues of a roustabout. His informality made me feel overdressed in my standard academic garb, a tight-fitting tweedy dress suit. Taking my seat, I noticed him peeking at my knees and shifted my raincoat to cover them.

The crowd hushed as the guest speaker strode into the hall. Smiling awkwardly, she presented a summary of her thesis before opening the floor to the legion of critics who had come to swing at her. A heavy woman trundled forward to relate how she had watched her mother and sister marched into the gas chambers. A bearded man demanded she retract her critique of how the Jewish leaders had organized the ghettoes for deportation. Another accused her of being infatuated with German culture. Her expository responses did little to tamp down the audience's fury. After an hour of abuse, the philosopher fled though a final torrent of shouts.

"So, did you hear what you wanted?" asked the man who had saved me from falling. He stood beside me, waiting for the row to clear, and offered to help me into my coat.

"Not exactly. I would have liked for her to expand on Eichmann's supposed normalcy, how such a banal man, in the right circumstances, could turn into a butcher."

He grunted, the sound emanating from deep within. "I'm not so sure about this banality business. It may have only looked that way because the guy was in exile so long. This philosophy lady should have judged him when he had power over life and death, not after he had been living like a lamb, a few steps ahead of the hangman."

"It wouldn't have been very practical for her to interview Eichmann while he attended the Wannsee conference," I said.

"No, not practical, but that's what it would have taken to discover his true nature."

His eyes shot behind me to glare at a nosy man snooping on our conversation. He scowled at the interloper, who promptly scurried away. The curtain drawn tightly around us, he turned back to me.

"Something tells me that you're a survivor," he said, dropping his voice on the word "survivor," as if shielding a candle from being extinguished.

"No, I'm not that. My parents sent me out of Europe as a child, before the war, before they were deported."

I must have sounded defensive in shaking off the ill-fitting cloak of martyrdom.

"Don't be offended," he said. "I meant it as an honor. Your eyes have the distinctive sorrow."

"Am I really that transparent?"

"Only to a close observer—one who has seen the camps."

It wasn't like me to tarry with a strange, presumptuous man, keeping up a macabre flirtation as we edged out of the hall. And yet the banter had an odd feeling of liberation.

"What else do you see in me?"

"A mysterious smile, and a powerful mixture of intelligence and resilience. I am biased, though. I've always admired women who are smarter than me."

"You certainly presume an enormous amount based on a brief encounter."

"Perhaps, but I figured that there must be a deeper, more personal cause for a woman who dresses so elegantly to schlep out on a rainy night."

"And what do you think that cause may be?"

"You're seeking answers for those you lost in this lady's theories."

"Is that what brought you out tonight?"

"Not especially. Philosophy wouldn't be the place for me to search for answers."

"You're not much for introspection, I take it?"

"Only if it has a substantive purpose. What interested me was whether she had any tangible clues into Eichmann's comrades still hiding out in Argentina. They say Mengele may have been living in the same neighborhood."

"It sounds like your interest is somewhat professional in nature."

He laughed. "Don't get carried away. I only like to stay informed."

Remembering the rain outside, I reached into my pocket and pulled out a scarf to cover my hair. As I extended the ends beneath my chin, the silk would not hold a knot, so I tied it off behind my neck. My companion seemed entranced.

"Your scarf reminds me of someone I once knew."

"An old girlfriend?"

"No. A survivor of Auschwitz. She didn't have your beautiful hair, though."

He certainly had an odd way of paying a compliment. His skills as a charmer could have used some practice.

"Funny, I had hoped the scarf would make me look more like Maria Callas," I said. My unruly curls had always drawn attention. My aged aunts had compared them to an operatic madwoman's when beseeching me to submit to a good styling. I rejected all such appeals. Even as I tried to obscure any semblance of a refugee past, I maintained the vow made at age six to preserve my hair exactly as my parents had last seen it, so they might recognize me if they returned one day.

"Maybe the scarf is a little like Callas," he said, "but your accent is different."

"Accent? I don't have an accent—a foreign accent, I mean."

"It's very faint. I can't imagine many would notice."

No one ever did. Still, it troubled me that my words could betray me, even after years of twisting my mouth to mimic native American English. "Since you have such a gifted ear, where do you think this accent comes from?"

He tilted his head, as if listening for a single instrument in a full orchestra. "As the son of a Galicianer, I'd say somewhere in Poland."

His insight triggered a primal fear in me. Feeling flushed, I struggled to contain the swelling sense of panic. It wasn't rational. The war had ended long ago, and this man, whoever he was, surely wasn't looking to betray me.

"Your instincts are correct. My family came from Łodź, but I don't speak Polish. Not anymore."

"Wodj," he said softly, amending my pronunciation. He spoke with a kind of wonder, as if the phoneme itself had revelatory power. "I thought it might be there."

He held the door to usher us outside, where we discovered that the rain had stopped. As I drifted down Fifth Avenue, he matched my steps and offered me his elbow to escort me back to the library. Judging by his formidable build, he was a real man, nothing like the soft-skinned academics who Chuck had always predicted I'd marry. My infrequent dates with those intellectual types had generally petered out meekly. At first I figured it was my talk of hominid speech formation that set their jaws as slack as Neanderthals, their eyes as glazed as bathroom tiles. Then it dawned on me that these erstwhile suitors were wary of prying too deep into the life of a former war orphan, for fear of exposing an open wound. This stranger, who introduced himself as Jacob, didn't have any such hesitation. What else made him different, he had so far managed to obscure.

"I'm curious: what do you do that gives you such insight into the life of a man like Eichmann?"

"Nothing very interesting; I help some old friends with their import-export business."

"I see. What kind of goods do you ship?"

"Oh, lots of things—fruit, olive oil, appliances. Mostly, I have to travel overseas to wait for some petty bureaucrat like Eichmann to sign off on a transport."

"It doesn't sound as if you enjoy your travels."

"They're more of a professional necessity. I'm not much of a tourist."

It didn't seem quite credible that a man with his forceful presence would be engaged in such tedious enterprises. He didn't have any obvious need to lie, and yet an air of mystery hung upon him. My academic study involved sifting through obscure clues of the past, so I was accustomed to piecing together the fragments of a life. What puzzled me was why Jacob made it necessary: the veil of secrecy; the hushed tone that forced me to lean closer just to catch his words; the presumed import of what few morsels he actually shared.

We reached the library, a moment when most gentlemen would have checked their watches, remarked on the late hour, and apologized for rushing off. Given my history, as well as the somber tenor of our impromptu meeting, I expected this same treatment. To my surprise, Jacob faced me squarely.

"If you'd allow me to call you sometime, we could talk more about Łódź and Galicia and other places neither of us will ever see again. I could even help you hide that accent so deeply, no one would ever uncover it."

It was a bold request; but for all his boldness, he understood something intrinsic about me: not the arcane details of linguistic theory, but the biographical trauma that made others squirm. Jacob had seen the camps, the gas chambers and the crematoria, and refused to look away—or, even worse, to look on the bright side. This took a special kind of courage, to stare undaunted through the doorway to the abyss. It was the sign of a real man. The kind of man who could stand resolute on my stoop and protect me from harm.

I jotted down the telephone number of the anthropology department and handed him the paper. Gambling on the goodwill of a stranger wasn't much like me. My spinster aunts had raised me to be suspicious of male intentions. And yet, now that they were both gone and I approached the end of my studies, I felt ready to fly into the unknown.

17

I RECOGNIZED MY BLUNDER AS SOON AS THE WAITER LED ME AND Susanna past a bunch of orthodox guys praying so hard that it nearly shook their table from its mooring. Effie had sworn that this joint on Delancey Street had the best blintzes in town, and hell, I had to figure women liked blintzes. What he'd left out was that it wasn't exactly a spot for intimate conversation. Not with all the religious types benching at race-car speed after finishing their meals. Served me right for taking romantic advice from a guy like Effie, who thought only with his stomach and turned to his rebbe to find him a wife.

"This place comes highly recommended," I told Susanna. "No meat here, though, only dairy. I hear good things about the blintzes."

She held the menu by its edges, as if it might soil her hands. She had cause for concern. The waiter had barely swabbed the table before seating us. As he clanged the previous diners' plates into a big tub, he left us a metal bowl of pickles and a breadbasket of challah.

"I can't remember the last time I had blintzes, but that sounds fine," she said, laying down her menu, looking relieved for the guidance. This wasn't her kind of food, any more than Yiddish-keit was her kind of culture. She came from a refined world of philosophy and science, a long way from the rough edges of my Galicianer ancestors. For an uneducated guy like me even to court her was a sign of the disruptiveness of our times.

As we placed our orders, soup and kugel for me, blintzes for her, I watched her every move: how she shifted her hips in the booth, how she peeked around cautiously with a faint, obscure smile, and how she twirled a loop of hair around her finger and nibbled at it nervously.

There was no point in allowing her to devour herself, so I offered her a slice of fresh challah.

"Good," I said as she took a tentative bite. "I don't believe in this society's nonsense about women starving themselves. It's important to keep up your strength. You never know when the next *shoah* will begin."

"Don't tell me you're waiting for that."

"Sure, I keep a bag packed at all times."

She swallowed her bread and shook her head. "Not me. Being forced into exile once was enough for one lifetime."

"Well, rest assured, I'll have a plan to get us out when the time comes."

"Walter Benjamin thought he had found a way out," she said, shrinking back into the booth. "After the Nazi invasion of France, he escaped across the Pyrenees, but the Spanish threatened to send him back, so he took an overdose of pills. I believe it was mor-phine. They say he was carrying enough to kill a horse."

"It sounds like your friend Walter ran into some bad luck. There's generally more than one route over the mountains, and I make it my business to scout out all possibilities. If we've learned one thing from the *shoah*, it's to be prepared for anything."

I offered her a pickle from the bowl of half-sours, but she shook her head. She put down her bread and grew quiet, her eyes cast down at the table, her mouth open, her breathing strained.

"I'd sooner go quickly next time," she said, "rather than suffer through a long, drawn-out exit. At least in his Spanish hotel room, Benjamin had some control over life and death."

This grim line of conversation didn't suit my purpose at all. What an idiot I was for trying to turn the *shoah* into pillow talk. "Forgive me, I shouldn't speak this way. Sometimes I lose myself, thinking about what I witnessed on the field at Buchenwald."

She sat up suddenly, once again composed, as if reminded of her scholarly authority. "That field represents how most people die: anonymous and forgotten."

"That may be true, but that's the thing about us Jews: we remember our dead."

"A lot of good that does. You're still dead."

"The dead command us."

It was an expression I'd picked up from Stolbach, my father's landsman who had written a yizkor of those who perished in their hometown of Jasło. The kosher butcher, the tavern keeper, the beet farmer, and the lumbermen, not to mention the rabbi, had all been marched into the forest and shot, with no one left to say kaddish in their names.

"Yes, I suppose that's true," she said. "The dead do command us." Her voice dimmed, as if she were contemplating her own debt to the past. It was a subject that I felt I had special insight into.

"If you'd like, I could make some inquiries about your parents. Maybe we could find their names in the Nazi records, discover what happened after they were deported."

"Do files like this exist? I would have thought they had all been destroyed."

"There may be traces left behind, and my people are very good at searching."

Reaching out, she pinned my hand on the table right beside the bowl of pickles. The first significant crack in her survivor's shell. "That would be invaluable to me. If you could discover anything at all."

Her grip was strong; her hands free of nail polish or jewelry. Unable to resist, I peeked up her sleeve to check for numbers. The arm was clean. No sign of B-164732, and no returning to that night with Judith. For years, Salik had scoured the official records for her, until he finally pounded on the table and shouted at me to find another girl. Now that girl had fallen into my arms. I couldn't just let her slip away, not this time.

"Congratulations on completing your oral exams," I said. "Have you decided what you will do for this dissertation of yours?"

"It's complicated. I'm trying to work out a new theory about the formation of human language. In general terms, you might say I'm looking for the first word."

"Really? But you don't even remember your Polish."

She laughed, a good sign that we had moved beyond the *shoah*. "Actually, my research is deeper than any particular language. It looks at the biological roots of language itself and how it evolved from the basic structures within the brain." She paused to check on my attentiveness. "I'm sorry, I don't mean to bore you."

"That's all right, I'm pretty good at language. Please go ahead."

"Only if you insist. My work is based on the theory that language evolved as a biological process, like bipedalism or the opposable thumb. We want to show how it is that language is uniquely human but also emerged from the natural world."

Putting my opposable thumb into action, I tore off a piece of challah and dabbed it into my bowl of mushroom barley soup that had just arrived. "So tell me, why did a woman with your intelligence and abilities choose something so, how should I say, esoteric?"

She looked as surprised by my use of the word "esoteric" as by the fact that I was still paying attention.

"Because language proves our common humanity, and links us to an epic chain of living beings, making our wars and brutality all the more senseless. Given our powers of reasoning, this delicate little worm of life shouldn't be chopped up with no regard."

Her voice picked up speed, and as the waiter finally brought out our blintzes and kugel, she rattled off terms that had no particular significance to me: morphology, pharynx, generative grammar. These crazy ideas seemed to set her on fire, so I shut up and let her ramble.

"Now I really must be boring you," she said, noticing my eyes wandering toward the kugel before me. "I'm not terribly adept at translating academic discourse outside our narrow frame."

"Not at all. I was enjoying listening to you speak."

She tried to show me what she meant by morphology, and in between bites, led me through the basic exercise of sounds, "Ta": tongue banging off teeth; "Pa": lips popping together. Her mouth trilling, pronouncing each in an exaggerated, fiery manner, she was growing more attractive by the moment. Watching her, I began to think what might lie ahead.

The waiter offered dessert, but babka and rugelach were too heavy for her, so I escorted her home to Brooklyn. Leaving the IRT, we walked down wide slate sidewalks, shrouded by heavy trees that swayed in the light breeze. When we reached her brownstone, I breathed deep to appreciate how, after decades rescuing thousands of exiles from peril, here was my chance to save one lost soul. She didn't invite me inside. Undeterred, I took her hand right out on the dark street.

"I have to tell you something. Work is calling me away again. But when I come back, I want to spend more time together."

"Can't you tell me where you're going this time, or how long you'll be away?" Her voice had a injured lilt to it, strained and sad, rising in pitch, as if she already knew the answer.

"I promise to be back as soon as possible."

"At least reassure me that you're not off seducing some beautiful girl in Paris."

"I've already found the girl for me." I took her other hand and swung them both together. "Trust me. I never forget my commitments."

She pulled her hands away and stepped back to the iron railing that marked the brownstone's tiny front yard. Shaking her head, she breathed heavily a couple of times, as if readying herself for a deep dive. "You are so secretive with any detail of your professional life. If we are going to progress any further, I have to ask something: Are you Mossad?"

She was too smart for me not to take this moment seriously. Given the range of possible responses—embellishment, dissembling, outrage, or even disregard, I chose to laugh. "Is that what you think? That I'm some sort of spy? That may be the funniest thing I've ever heard. I would never have figured olive oil to be such a nefarious enterprise."

"Uchh," she said, her exasperation expelled in a breath. "You have no idea how maddening your evasiveness can be. It's like being at a theater where the curtain drops every time you reach a crucial bit of dialogue."

There wasn't much I could do to make my stories more convincing.

"Susanna, what's been entrusted to me is not mine to share, not even with those I feel closest to. All I can ask is for you to have faith in me."

Without even a kiss goodbye, she started up the stoop. "Blind faith is a lot to ask, especially with life already so uncertain," she said, unlocking her front door.

Watching her disappear into the brownstone, I wondered whether she would vanish into her own set of ruins, just as Judith had done so long ago. My only chance at a happier resolution rested with the hope that she enjoyed my companionship as much as I reveled in hers. What lay between us was a clear sense of possibility, that together we could build something new, something enduring, to honor the past and create a new future, if only she could learn to live with my limitations.

18

Brooklyn
April 12, 1964

FROM THE TOP OF MY STOOP, I STRAINED MY EYES FOR A SIGN of Jacob's arrival. On this Sunday morning, the block looked as solid and secure as it had in the quarter century since my Aunts Fannie and Clara, ancient even then, had welcomed me to their quiet street, where rows of ruddy brownstones were lined up like silent witnesses against any violation of genteel behavior. As a young girl, I had been afraid to shout too loud or to make too much fuss, lest some intrusive neighbor inform the authorities about the strange orphan living among them. We had mostly kept to ourselves: my aunts too old and ornery to socialize, me too guarded against any vestige of an accent slipping through the fog of innocent conversation. Wary of strangers, I practiced speaking into the mirror, crafting my words to make them sound less like my imperious, European aunts and more like the American voices reaching out over the radio. All these years later, long after my aunts had left for the warmth of Florida and then the cold of Mount Lebanon

Cemetery, I had never quite stopped worrying that soldiers might show up at my door.

A dark car pulled up and released Jacob onto my street. He bounded up the stoop with his usual vitality, as if each step represented something new to prove.

"Where are your friends?" I asked as he reached the top.

"Running late. The religious only show up on time for their prayers."

"Then it makes sense to wait inside."

Jacob had escorted me home after all our dates, but this was the first time I had invited him across the threshold. Over the past few months, I had wanted to keep something in reserve, some way of countering his elusiveness. Now, given the grand scale of his gift, I couldn't hold him back any longer. He trailed me into the parlor, the floorboards creaking under his weight. The brownstone must have seemed a lugubrious place for a single girl, this grand dark home, its once-posh molding now sagging, its paint chipping and its narrow staircase grooved by thousands of footsteps, as if the wood stored the record of every past inhabitant.

"The place could use a little sprucing up. My aunts let it go in their later years."

He rattled the wobbly banister and rapped his knuckles against the bulging walls. "It reminds me of my parents' home in Roxbury. As a kid, I used to threaten my sister that I would push the whole house down."

"I bet she didn't like that idea."

"No, she begged me not to do it. She must have thought I was trying to be another Samson. What she didn't understand was that I knew I was smart enough to get out before the building collapsed on my head."

He stopped suddenly, his bullfrog chest expanding mightily to suck in more air. The booming voice, its volume always slightly above comfort level, seemed to quaver, as he recalled the house fire that had consumed his family. I touched his cheek, as freshly shaven as ever.

"I'm sorry to remind you of them."

Jacob shook his head as if rejecting an offer, and held out his arms to measure the doorway width. "It should fit right through here. We'd better clear enough room before Effie arrives."

My aunts would have shrieked at any tampering with their established decor, which hadn't changed since my arrival on their stoop as a six-year-old refugee. Even after they had bequeathed me the brownstone, I resisted moving even a lamp, less out of fear than inertia. Now, offered a competing domestic vision, I helped Jacob to reposition the couch by the bay window where it would afford a view of the street. As we sat together to test the new location, Jacob reached over, as he did so often at the movies, and fondled a lock of my hair between his fingers, describing it to be as wondrous as history. It was a strange metaphor, but I never tired of him extolling my beauty, praise that would have made my aunts, had they survived, ever more suspicious. I could picture them bombarding him with questions about his vocation and decrying his deferrals as unacceptable. After much reflection, I decided that it didn't make any difference to me what he did for a living. I accepted the terms of our social contract, that his profession would remain beyond my ken. Much as I felt devoted to my aunts' memory, I had no pressing need to follow their example, to grow into an old maid, and to spend my decline struggling down the stairs to fill a pot of tea. No, I wanted everything they had denied themselves: a husband and a child, a family to replace all that I had lost.

With my aunts gone, I introduced Jacob to my mentor, Chuck Rosenfeld, who sneered at Jacob's rough manner and figured him to be up to no good, immersed in what he termed the transience of the present. "You will read about this man's exploits in the papers one day. Either that or he'll disappear without a trace, and you'll learn his fate when the telephone rings with bad news."

Whatever Jacob's work entailed, it carried him overseas on a recurrent basis. His affinity for flying was incomprehensible to me, in light of the terrible morning four years earlier when a dying aircraft had smashed into nearby Sterling Place, igniting ten brownstones similar to mine, the bricks turning out to be no more sturdy than skin.

"Don't you worry that each flight increases your odds of disaster?" I asked him.

"Not at all. I can predict these things. It's not my fate to die in flight."

His claims of premonition were preposterous, but they felt reassuring, like lucky numbers to a scientist playing the lottery. True to his prediction, Jacob always did return, and he carried with him extravagant gifts: conical earthenware for roasting complex Moroccan stews; decorative tiles of deep blue resonance, glazed in the old Iznik style; an ornate necklace of unburnished silver, the prize of a Yemeni bride; and a Persian carpet with geometric petals and swirls woven in deep reds and browns. I wasn't prone to material possessions, but the gifts—so much the focus of early anthropological theory—tied me to him more deeply than ever.

My favorite present came from a museum gift shop when, after indulging me with a visit to the painting galleries, Jacob caught me admiring a poster of Hans Holbein's *The Ambassadors*. The poster now hung in my kitchen, and I invited Jacob back for a look.

"You see how these gentlemen keep me entertained in your absence. They make for fine companions when I cook."

"They look good there, like they're presenting their credentials."

"The heavy one reminds me of you," I said, pointing out his odd physical resemblance to the courtier, laden with stately furs and medals. "In my imagination, that's the secret behind your travels, that you're cycling back in time to pose for Holbein. Surely you can see the resemblance?"

"Not really. I've never grown a beard in my life. I couldn't, not when so many were forced to shave to survive. Plus, that guy is too fat to be me."

It wasn't the Ambassador's barrel chest that struck me as being like Jacob. It was the man's authoritative mien, with its twinge of arrogance. Even the metal case in his hand resembled one of the *tchotchkes* Jacob had brought back from abroad.

"When I look at those two men, I imagine them to be drawing a new map of the world."

"You've got some funny ideas of what ambassadors actually do."

"Maybe that's what the skull is all about," I said, pointing to the anamorphic image in distended bone stretched grotesquely at their feet. "The cost of rewriting the maps."

My house tour was interrupted by the sound of a truck lumbering down the street. "That must be them," Jacob said, hurrying to the front door as Effie drove up to the curb. Sitting beside his friend were two Hassidic men, not the kind of scrawny boys who scurried down Eastern Parkway, but an older, rougher lot, who had left their black coats at home. Jacob shouted directions to the men, and together they hauled the massive trunk up the stoop into the space we had cleared in the parlor. Effie attached the legs to assemble a grand piano. As soon as Jacob opened the hood to let the instrument breathe, the Steinway transfigured my aunts' dusty parlor and charged it with new life.

"Well, give it a try," Jacob said.

Not wishing to seem ungrateful, I approached the keyboard and played a basic chord, as best as my unpracticed hands could manage. The piano issued a discontented clang that made the movers clutch at their ears.

"She sounds terrible," Effie said.

Jacob cuffed him across the neck. Their years together seemed to allow this kind of roughhousing. "You were supposed to find her an instructor."

"I did. Stolbach said he would come. He kept it conditioned all these years."

"Good, Stolbach will teach her many things."

When Effie and his lifters left us, I wondered how to thank Jacob. All I had done to precipitate this present was to mention that music represented a potential forerunner of speech. Little did I suspect he would respond with such magnanimity.

"Jacob, this is too generous a gift for a novice like me."

"Don't consider it a gift, think of it as a rescue."

"Well, I don't know how to thank you."

"You can start by sharing some pictures of your family."

I couldn't exactly refuse him, not any longer. He had offered to trace my family's fate for me, but I had never shown him what they looked like. Like the house itself, it was something I had insisted on keeping private. Upstairs, I burrowed into my bottom drawer for the carton containing my few mementoes of childhood. My aunts had viewed the treasure chest that had traveled with me from Łódź as a modern equivalent to Pandora's mythic box, within which swirled only sorrow, loss and longing. They thought it wiser not to tempt the gods by prying off the lid. The child within me retained their innate caution. Now, bowing to Jacob's pressure, I opened the box to reveal a crude cardboard medallion lying atop a stack of papers. An unknown hand had scrawled the number "44" on the cardboard and fashioned it into a crude necklace with a piece of yarn.

"What's that?"

"Nothing," I said, sliding the medallion beneath some of the letters.

"It didn't look like nothing."

"Doesn't a person have the right to keep some things private? You are certainly secretive enough."

"I wouldn't call myself secretive, just discreet."

"Tell the truth but tell it slant."

"What was that?" He missed the Dickinson reference, and it was just as well.

"Nothing, just a line from a poem."

I reached into the box to remove the small cache of photos, wrapped together like pressed flowers, the images still crisp. The pictures, packed by my mother into my suitcase on that terrible last day together, represented the only physical reminders of my family's corporeal existence.

"Do you remember much of your childhood?" he asked.

"I left too young to be considered a reliable informant. My memories are infected by the photographic evidence."

"I wasn't asking for a scholarly deposition. Just a few impressions."

My few remembrances were redolent: the heavy wool of their carpets, the tang of antiseptic on my father's hands. They couldn't compete with the steely realism of these four photos. The first showed my father and mother as newlyweds posing at a country villa. Then there was our family at home, with me as an infant cradled by my parents. An antique studio shot showed my mother as a teenager posing among her sisters. The fourth image came from my father's clinic, where Dr. Sigismund Sussman stared skeptically at the lens before a background of books and lab instruments. In the picture, my father appeared as a man of dark radiance, his brow focused on some profound problem. I had spent years wondering whether he was contemplating the resolution to a difficult case or was worrying about the impending storm about to blow in from the west.

"Did you hear anything from them after you left Łodź?" Jacob asked.

"A few letters at first, and then silence, nothing after the middle of 1942. I waited every day for the postman, but he never carried anything of interest with him."

I didn't mention the final letter, which I discovered hidden among my aunts' papers after their death. In it, my father related how he had surrendered all their savings to pay for my flight to London and lacked any more resources to bribe their way out of

Łódź. My parents' sacrifice was something I would never have supported if they had offered me, then six years old, the chance to be heard. Better for me to have remained with them than to be pried from my home and stamped with an indelible memory of departure: the chaos of an airport filled with screaming children and broken parents. As I prepared to board the flight that would deliver me to safety, my doomed father whispered into my ear one last time, assuring me that it would be fine, that I, his wild-flower, needed to take this first step in our eventual reunification. I believed his words, even though the rationalist in me knew it was impossible. My final enduring image came when the plane's door sealed me inside, and I peered out the window to watch my parents waving wildly. Right then, I vowed never to fly again, at least not until my father fulfilled his promise.

Jacob took my hand as a violinist might hold his instrument, purposeful and firm, careful not too exert too much pressure. "We have discovered some information about your parents that the postman could never have delivered."

"What is that?"

"Their names appeared on a list of those deported from the Łódź ghetto to Chełmno. The Nazis liked to make everything official. I can provide you with the date, in case you want to light a yahrzeit candle."

It had never seemed possible that they could have survived. Here at last was the tangible proof. "Thank you, no. I have everything I need."

Jacob released my hand and collected the photos. "These pictures are a great treasure. You're fortunate to have them."

"Fortunate" was not a descriptive I would have readily applied to my biography.

"They are torture to me."

"It may feel that way, but one day they will make a precious gift for our children."

"Children? Is that a suggestion?"

"Why not? Someone has to carry on this legacy. It shouldn't end with us."

After months of courtship, this was the first time he had addressed the looming question of our future. As orphans, neither of us tended to look too far ahead.

"If I can't bear these pictures, how could I impose that burden on a child?"

"It wouldn't be an imposition. It would be a blessing."

"So you consider me a personal mission—to honor this past."

"Well, it is personal. . . ." Leaning over, he gathered me in and kissed me. He had kissed me before: sharp pecks on the lips to remind me of his intentions. This one was more forceful, determined.

". . . but it's far from a mission," he said, diving deeper still.

19

Goma
October 3, 1996

BIDING OUR TIME IN GOMA, ON THE EVE OF A JUST WAR, DUDU dragged me back to Sunny's Thai Cafe. It wasn't my kind of place, but I couldn't fight him on everything. All week, Dudu had sworn that Sunny's cooking reminded him of his favorite spot in Phuket. He was full of shit. Any idiot could tell it was the hostess herself, and not the lemongrass soup, that provided the real draw. Parking us at the usual table, with a clear view of the entrance, Dudu lunged after her silken ass before Sunny could finish taking our order.

"Sit with us, Mama Sunny, I'm hungry for some hot chili."

"Stop it, you dirty man," she said, unwinding his arm from her hips as if escaping a massive python. "My other customers want to eat too."

As Sunny slipped away to a table of three women, the only other patrons in the place, Dudu feasted on her tiny body, framed by a slinky red dress.

"I thought you liked the big girls," I said.

"The spicy little ones taste good too."

Sunny looked more Filipina than Thai, but the Bangkok mystique must have sold better on the aid circuit. She had a pretty savvy business model, following the refugee gravy train around the globe. Her walls were decorated with photos from a succession of hot spots—Somalia, Iraq, Pakistan, and now Goma.

"Say, Aba, maybe there's a ticket for me in this restaurant business. When our job for Salik is finished, I'm going to see if she wants some help."

"What do you know about running a restaurant?"

"What's to know? You boil some noodles and pour on a spicy sauce. Maybe she and I can cook up a special recipe for Yiddische-Thai chicken."

The restaurant was quiet on this final night before the fireworks started. At the next table, three ladies—two African and one European—peeked over at us. They reminded me of the aid workers prancing around the Hotel Bruegel as if their benevolence would save the world. We generally tried to avoid these do-gooder types, who liked to pretend the million Hutus sheltered in their refugee camps were the innocent victims of an Act of God rather than the perpetrators of a genocide.

One of the three at the next table, an African woman wearing a white medical coat, glanced my way again. Her hair drawn back tightly, she had a sharply defined face and a calm demeanor, what must have made for a lovely bedside manner. She sipped her soup with a quiet precision as her two friends chattered away.

"Look at that doctor, Jacob. I bet she could take good care of your body," Dudu said. "Maybe we should make an introduction. You could use a nice girl to make you stop thinking about this war business."

"What would I possibly have to say to these do-gooders?"

"You shouldn't hate them so much, Aba. They're just like you, always wanting to solve other people's problems."

"Don't worry, Dudu. The problems here will soon find their own resolution."

A week had passed since we left Captain Ezekiel Hakizimana on a Rwandan airfield, and war was creeping close. Even at this moment, a small contingent of Tutsi Banyamulenge was poised for the opening salvo, a surprise assault at dawn, far to the south of Lake Kivu. This was what Salik had sent us to observe, how David could fight two Goliaths at the same time, as the Tutsis took on both Mobutu's Zairean army and the Hutu genocidaires operating out of the refugee camps.

This evening gave us one more chance to dine in peace, at least until three Zairean soldiers stomped into the restaurant. Staggering from drink, swinging their rifles around, they shouted that they had a license from President Mobutu to impose a special tax at all restaurants. It didn't take long to pick us out as the most likely source of revenue.

Holding his arms wide, Dudu welcomed them loudly. "Good evening, my friends. Did you come for the noodles? They are much more delicious than fufu."

The leader of the goons waved his gun in Dudu's face. "We don't eat this food, *muzungu*. Give us a sweet instead."

Without blinking, Dudu slid a bill across the table, as if making a discreet offer on a piece of property. "Go buy yourself some beer, with our compliments."

The soldier snatched the money and counted it in outrage. "Are you crazy? We need more than that."

Dudu's smiled deepened, as if he were reassured by their growing agitation.

"All right, you can take this," Dudu said, sliding over another bill. "But no more. With the inflation, we must have something left for Mama Sunny."

Before the soldiers could object, a woman's voice carried across the restaurant. It wasn't Sunny, who was hiding out in the kitchen. No, the voice belonged to one of the African ladies from the next table—not the doctor, but her buxom friend. "Please, gentlemen, this is not how we should treat guests in our country. What will Colonel Njeli say when he arrives for his dinner?"

The soldiers turned to each other, doubts rupturing their nerve. "Colonel Njeli comes here?"

"Of course. The colonel cannot live without Thai food. Mama Sunny is his favorite cook in Goma. In fact, he's later than usual tonight."

Discipline in the Zairean army had broken down quickly, but if one thing still bound these boys to their duty, it was a crushing fear of their commanding officer. Wasting no time, they bolted from the restaurant, making do with whatever Dudu had provided.

When they were gone, the lady turned to us. "We apologize on behalf our countrymen. These soldiers do not understand the consequences of their actions."

All my instincts screamed for me to watch out. The last thing I needed was to be swept away by another chance encounter. And yet we owed this lady some basic courtesies after she had intervened on our behalf.

"That was well done," I said. "We've run into soldiers across Goma and never escaped so cheaply. I'm curious: Does the colonel really eat here?"

Laying her hands on her chest, she laughed as if I were a simpleton. "Oh, no, I would be shocked if Colonel Njeli has ever tasted Thai food in his entire life. But circumstances have taught us to be adaptable. Since we cannot challenge their guns, our only means to help our cause is to appeal to the men in power."

She introduced herself as Germaine Buzera, born here in Goma, and described how she had joined the relief effort two years ago after the refugees started pouring in from Rwanda. Full-figured and solid as an anchor, Germaine was wrapped in a stately blue dress. She wore her hair in dignified curls, product of some elaborate chemical process, but there was nothing artificial about her invitation to join her table. It didn't serve to be rude, so we sat down with the three women of Blessed Relief, a Scandinavian aid group working with the orphaned children of Mugunga refugee camp.

The woman in the white coat was Dr. Chantal Kayiranga, who attended patients at their tiny clinic. Trained in obstetrics, she had switched to emergency medicine, treating everything from gunshot wounds to malarial fevers.

"It's good to know that if we had taken a bullet from those soldiers," I said, "we would have had someone to take of us."

"Fortunately that was not necessary," the doctor said. "Germaine is very skilled with the military men. She keeps them at a safe distance from our tents."

"I take it from your coat that you are always on duty."

The doctor smiled demurely and laid down her spoon. She had navigated an entire bowl of noodle soup without spilling a drop on her white jacket.

"It is a habit of mine. I would feel naked without it."

Her talk of nakedness led me to imagine her disrobed. It was crude of me to picture this elegant, composed lady without her clothes. All this time with Dudu must have rubbed off on me.

"What has brought you gentlemen to Goma?" asked Karina Bronkhorst, the third of their party, who had come from Holland to direct the Blessed Relief operations. Slouching over the table like an elongated shoehorn, she dressed as sloppy as the typical *muzungu*, wearing an Indian schmatte that hung loose across her chest. Not much to talk about in terms of a chest, either. Her smile looked as if it demanded strenuous effort, something out of the fairy tales Susanna used to tell our son about the big bad wolf.

"We came for the famous gorillas, up in the Virunga Mountains."

"What a terrible sense of timing you have," the Dutch lady said, her smile ever more strained. "Don't you realize it is very dangerous to travel to the Virungas?"

"Yes, well, unfortunately, we made our arrangements from afar. With life being so uncertain, we wanted to see them before it's too late."

"It seems very strange to choose this time for such a trip. Why would you want to look at monkeys when human beings are suffering?"

"They're not monkeys, they're apes," I said, recalling Susanna's lessons on the primate family tree. "And if we waited for an end to human suffering, we'd have to postpone our visit until the oceans dried up."

Karina sniffed sharply, as if someone had passed gas. "Is that sulfur in the air? I wonder whether Nyiragongo is growing restless again."

The name "Nyiragongo" referred to the nearby volcano, but why it should have made this Dutch lady so hostile was beyond me. I nearly pushed off and wished them a good evening when Germaine laughed. "We are happy to discover that at least you will not use science to uproot us." She explained that the mountain drew foreign volcanologists worried, the next eruption would pour fire and brimstone down on the refugee camps below.

I couldn't resist the obvious question. "If the volcano is unstable, why not just send the refugees back to Rwanda?"

"Our guests are afraid of the past," Germaine said, "and we cannot judge them. Peace between peoples is the only way to restore the refugees to their homeland. All we can do is attend to their basic humanitarian needs."

It was a real cop-out, her refusal to address the Hutu crimes against humanity, but I restrained myself from snapping at her. The memory of my parting with Nesia, who had begged me not to rush off to fight the Germans, stayed with me all these years later. Losing my cool, I had thundered at my sister that if men like me didn't act, Hitler would burn us all. It was true, of course, but it was also too forceful. The thought of Nesia's weeping still shamed me all these years later. It provided an enduring lesson: I should always treat women gently.

"You have a very idealistic way of looking at the world, Germaine, but it risks excusing some terrible cruelties."

Germaine leaned across the table to clasp my wrist, as if to guide a frightened child through the darkness. "You cannot consider all the Rwandans to be perpetrators of cruelty. Look at our friend: Dr. Chantal. She is one of the refugees, and she is the most ethical person I have ever known."

"It's true," Karina said. "Dr. Chantal has worked miracles at the clinic. Thanks to her, we were able to stop a cholera outbreak, and she has managed to immunize thousands of the children against a whole spectrum of diseases."

The doctor seemed embarrassed by the attention.

"Is that true, Dr. Chantal, that you fled Rwanda with the others?" I asked.

She nodded briskly as if compelled to confirm a dreaded diagnosis. "In our hospital in Butare, we treated all people the same. We never considered who was Tutsi or Hutu before the war. Then everything fell apart."

I watched her paddle her spoon through the milky broth left over from dinner. She had beautiful hands, so delicate and composed. They must have taken the measure of innumerable pulses and countless fevers, but I couldn't help but wonder whether those hands had blood on them. It was a question only our Tutsi friends could answer.

The meal complete, Germaine announced their need to drive Dr. Chantal back to Mugunga. "You must come visit us," she told me. "Once you see our work and meet our orphans, you may remember us fondly with your support."

It was a ridiculous suggestion. The last place on earth we needed to visit was a camp full of butchers, regardless of how captivating I found the doctor. Still, there was no point making enemies, so I promised to keep it in mind, provided it didn't interfere with our visit to the mountain gorillas.

20

Brooklyn
June 1967

OUR CHILD'S IMPENDING ENTRY INTO THE WORLD CAME AT AN inopportune time for Jacob. Throughout my late pregnancy, my husband was consumed by rumors of war, tensions in the Middle East that had overshadowed the growing shape of my belly. The early summer had been hot and terribly humid, making me feel as if I were carrying two babies, one embedded within and the other wrapped around my body like an infant monkey clinging to its arboreal mother. Then, as I lay splayed out across the parlor couch, ever more sympathetic to our primate cousins seeking shelter in the cool forest canopy, the telephone rang and Jacob answered with his typical hush. Ten minutes later he stood before me to announce that he was being called away.

"That was Salik. He needs me."

I could have asked why or where, but those questions never elicited any useful information.

"How can you go now? You know how far along I am."

He glanced out the window, as if even at this moment, with my time nearly upon us, he couldn't wait for the car to pick him up. "It's an urgent situation."

Excited over my pregnancy, Jacob had painted the upstairs bedroom, repaired the exposed wiring in the kitchen and tightened the loose banister on the stairwell. He had even attended Lamaze classes with me. Now, on the cusp of fatherhood, he prepared to abandon all of it, to take part in another man's war. Spotting his suitcase poised by the stairs, I understood his departure to be already in motion.

"When do you leave?"

"The car will be here any minute."

In the three years since we walked along Eastern Parkway to be bound together by a somber Hassidic rabbi, I had never challenged my husband's flights into the unknown. His absences were the price I paid for marriage, a bill submitted by this distant Salik, whom I had come to loathe. Jacob never proclaimed any fondness for him. Nor did he wax nostalgic over their shared sacrifices. For all I knew, this Salik might have been fictional, a composite of all the hard men Jacob had encountered in the field. Whoever Salik was, he generated a strange obeisance in my husband that made me wonder whether Jacob had sold his soul to him long ago. What exactly did Jacob owe this man, that his calls took priority over all else?

"Can't you wait until the baby is born? I need your help just to make it up and down the stairs."

Much to my surprise, he flinched, caught his breath and studied the suitcase waiting for him. Then, quick as the sound "pa" expelled from human lips, the stain of doubt vanished.

"We'll make the bed for you down here on the couch," he said. "Effie can send over a nurse, and he'll have a car ready when the time comes."

He bent over to kiss my forehead, and whispered something I couldn't quite make out. Maybe it was an apology, or maybe some sophistry about husbands leaving their wives to march off to war. Whatever it was didn't matter, not after a car horn sounded outside and Jacob vanished down the stoop.

True to his promise, Effie dispatched a nurse, a Hassidic lady named Drora, who had vast personal experience with childbirth. It was hard for me to show her much gratitude. I didn't want a stranger in my house: I wanted my husband, who had promised me devotion and loyalty on ten thousand occasions and had stamped that commitment onto a *ketubah* writ in ancient Aramaic. Jacob couldn't follow the words, but Drora knew them well, so after he vanished, I asked her for a translation, not just of the marriage contract, but of his faith overall. I wasn't seeking to find God, only to piece together the fractured mythologies that my husband used to justify his behavior. Unfortunately, this remedial Jewish education failed to answer any of my most profound questions.

The war broke out a week or so after his departure. For six days, I held my breath as the television broadcast images of fighter jets shooting across the sky, tanks rolling through the desert, and prisoners lifting their arms in surrender, sweat and fear clouding their humiliation. When it was done, I exhaled but still heard nothing from my husband, his silence as absolute as the God in whom he believed without inquiry or expectation. I had to wonder, as it grew more difficult to rise to refill my cup with tea, whether he would ever return, or whether he had failed, in his haste, to mark our doorway for the angel of death to pass over.

They didn't lack for ambition, Jacob and his compatriots: to take six days to reenact the fables of creation and reconstruct the framework of their world, to unscramble the eggs of human history and carve out a sanctuary for their tribe, to fashion a new Eden defended by advanced weaponry and a modern tongue reconstructed from liturgical tradition. It was hard, very hard to breathe in the aura of euphoria and to recognize that the dusty Sinai revealed nothing but vanity, a striving after wind. Every morsel of scientific truth, and everything I sensed in my heart, informed me it had taken far more than six days to create the world, and would require more time still to recast it. Life was far too complex, far too intricate an instrument to do anything but evolve in fits and turns, filled with dead ends and extinctions over uncounted generations, absent any intervention from a supernatural being or a modern Abraham.

Such were my sentiments late one night, deep into the aftermath of a short war, when my water broke. I had sent Drora home earlier that evening to tend to her seven children. She had objected to leaving me alone and even called Effie to intervene, but I held firm. This was a passage I would handle on my own. Hardly the first solitary journey of my life. The Russian driver dispatched by Effie begged me not to risk going all the way to Manhattan, but I insisted that arrangements had been made at Mount Sinai, the only institution I trusted, not as a source of divine law, but as a haven for neonatal care.

"Please, just drive," I urged him, gripping the back of his seat in pain. "There's still time."

We reached the hospital with hours to spare; and for the rest of the night, I struggled through the contractions, sweated and squeezed, and focused on my breathing, until finally, near dawn, when my child was ready, he emerged from hiding into a still-darkened world.

A nurse bundled him up and offered him back to me as a clean package of flab and wrinkle. He looked pained, as if wincing at the pressure, all the prodding and the jostling that must have felt so alien as he completed his evolutionary transformation into a fully formed human. Gazing upon his face, full of confusion and disquiet, I couldn't stop myself from laughing.

The delivery nurse, a smooth-skinned woman with a Spanish accent, seemed perplexed. "What's so funny? Is everything all right?"

"It's fine. I'm just surprised that he looks so familiar."

What I saw in the face of the baby who lay upon my chest was the image of my father. The visceral nature of this memory could have brought me to tears, but instead it made me laugh, again and again, to think that I, of all people, had survived to give my parents a grandson they would never know, to recognize that the vast cycle of life, death, and regeneration had been affected by one whose very existence had nearly been extinguished in childhood. I laughed at the irony, the absolute shocking irony, that one who might have disappeared unnoticed from this earth should now stake a claim to something beyond words, beyond the sound of air passing across my larynx. I had a child. Our line, very nearly ruptured, would persist.

It was at this critical moment, after they took a print of my son's hands and feet and measured and weighed him, that the nurse returned him to me with a question to frame his days: what would we name him?

"Shalom. We will call him Shalom."

"Unusual. What kind of name is that?" the nurse asked as she noted it down.

"It means peace, for the times in which we are living."

The nurse showed me her chart to approve the spelling, Shalom Furman, and the arbitrary nature of symbolical language that served as a spine to our consciousness made me laugh again. I snuggled close to my son's pinched body, still accustomed to swimming inside me, and laughed some more.

Jacob called shortly after dawn, already aware of Shalom's birth. His sources must have briefed him.

"I hear wonderful news. We've had a lot of that lately. So, it's a boy," Jacob said.

"Were you hoping for a daughter?"

"It doesn't matter now. We don't get to make that choice. I hope the delivery wasn't too difficult."

His cheeriness infuriated me. How simple it all was for him.

"It was difficult, but I managed. When will you be coming home?"

"As soon as I can. Effie will arrange for the Hassidische lady to stay with you until I get back."

When Jacob returned three weeks later, he bounded up the stoop with his typical exuberance, rushing through these final few steps as if it would make up for lost time. Breezing into the bedroom, he bent close to my ear and breathed deep, absorbing the scent of my exhaustion.

"You can't imagine how much I missed you," he said, running his hand through my hair, as he had done during our courtship, failing to grasp how his old intimacies had lost their potency.

"Would you like to hold your son?" I asked.

He peeked at little Shally curled up beside me as if he were an unappetizing cut of meat piled onto his dinner plate. "Sure. Let me try." Picking up the tiny infant, Jacob looked as uncomfortable as a circus bear forced to ride a tricycle.

"You should be happy," I said. "Now you have a child to contribute to the restoration of the tribe."

"Of course I'm happy. I'm only surprised that you settled on Shalom."

During my pregnancy, we had failed to come up with any consensus on a name. For a girl, Jacob had pressed for Nesia, after his sister, which stuck me as terribly old-fashioned, an awkward reminder of the ancestral Galicia he would never stop idealizing. For a boy, Jacob had suggested something monotonous and monochromatic, Dani or Uri or Miki, lacking circumspection or subtlety, precisely the kind of man I didn't want our son to become. Our indecision had left a void that I filled on my own in Jacob's absence.

"What's wrong with Shalom? I thought you'd appreciate something traditional."

"It's better than Avshalom, I suppose."

What an odd reference for a new father: to compare himself to King David, guarding his throne against his rebellious son.

Jacob separated the blankets that swaddled the boy, snapped open his onesie and peeked at the wound left by the circumcision.

"If only you had waited, we could have had a nice *bris*. It didn't have to be done at the hospital. I'm sure Effie could have found us a *mohel*."

The pettiness of his gripe was lost on him. I wasn't inclined to be charitable, not after Drora briefed me on the circumcision ritual.

"You must have forgotten that Jewish law dictates that the *brit milah* take place on the eighth day of a boy's life. That was two weeks ago."

Shifting the baby, Jacob checked his watch, the telltale sign that the clock was running out on his time with us. "Here, take him for me," Jacob said, placing our son back on the bed. "Salik will be calling any minute."

I received the baby with relief, glad for Jacob to take his business downstairs. Something subtle had changed between us, as if the moment Shally arrived, my tolerance for Jacob's fixations seeped away. If he refused to value our lives above the grand sweep of armies, then I couldn't indulge his dreams of a domestic idyll. Having disappeared into a faraway war, my husband returned not as Odysseus reclaiming the throne of Ithaca, but as an incessant wanderer, impatiently waiting to be summoned again across the sea.

21

Brooklyn
October 12, 1996

A TROUBLING NOTION HIT ME AS I LOOSENED MY GRIP ON MIA'S ass and tried not to come too soon: that I might have been conceived in this very same bed. It didn't seem possible. I had to figure that Dad, for all his nostalgia over married life, couldn't have taken the bed with him when he moved down here to the basement.

Mia noticed my shift in rhythm. "What's wrong?" she asked, looking back at me.

"Nothing, sorry. I was just distracted a second."

We were somewhat pressed for time, given that the Mega–Stars would soon be arriving for a late morning rehearsal, so I recovered enough for us to wrap up in unison, and when it was done, and we were lying back enshrouded by the lush, nearly mature plants, I reached into the nightstand for a joint.

"I'd hate for your Mom to see us now," Mia said, "her darling son and her most despised student."

Mia was insecure in a pathetic kind of way. The chivalrous thing to do would have been to stroke her vanity, to assure her of her likeability. The trouble was that she was right. Mom really couldn't stand her. It wasn't as if I brought it up. For all Mom knew, Mia and I had never exchanged untoward glances. No, it was my mother who broke from her usual discretion to rail against this student of hers who abused feminism: flirting outrageously with anyone who might help her, weeping deceptively to cover any attempt at criticism, and foisting upon Mom what she called an absurdly speculative thesis on the origins of dance.

"If it makes you feel any better," I told Mia, "my mother doesn't hold personal grudges. She's pretty rational in her opinions."

Mia seemed to take a particular thrill from screwing the wayward son of her academic adviser. She spent half her time pressing me for details about my mom, and the other half extolling her visions of an anthropology of dance. Fortunately for her, I was a good listener, willing to lie back, puff on a joint, and absorb her endless babble about the roots of joyous movement—the early cave paintings, the various free-form tangos found among birds and wolves and even some great apes.

"It's a shame you didn't stay in the department," she said. "It would have been fun for us to take classes together."

Fun wasn't generally something I associated with my graduate studies.

"I could never have held out that long. Our classmates had their knives drawn for me."

"The story I heard was that you tried to pass off as research your time as a gigolo in Cuba."

"Oh, the trouble started long before Havana. That paper was only a final excuse to frog-march me out."

"Your mom couldn't protect you?"

"Thank God, no. I worked hard to leave them no alternative to expelling me."

Mia brushed a hand through her hair. It was thick and healthy, but much as she waved it in my face, I avoided it like fire. The memory of shearing my mother made me resistant to anything quite so ephemeral.

The joint winding down, I pulled out my special roach clip, pinched from Mom's anthropological toolkit. The tweezers seemed to be standard fare, but they gave me pinpoint control. When the roach was spent, I crushed what remained into the floor.

"Shally, how about an ashtray?" Mia said, slapping my arm.

"Hey, better the floor than the night table."

"This place is such a mess. Don't you ever clean up?"

The answer was no, not really. My presence in Dad's apartment, the living room furniture cast to one side, the cannabis plants and grow lights, the blackout curtains were all jabs at the man who I could never box face to face.

"I keep meaning to tidy up, but every time I think of my father, I decide to let it lie. It's my petty way of getting back at him for years of neglect."

Dad would have fumed to hear me discussing our family ties so freely. "Don't say shit to anyone" was the mantra throughout my childhood. He avoided parent-teacher conferences as if they spread infectious disease, and ignored the few friends I brought over to hang out. The very act of blabbing about our lives seemed a fitting payback to his obsession with secrecy.

"What did the poor man do to deserve that?" Mia asked, rolling onto my chest.

I didn't even know where to start. At the outset, he was a blowhard, yelling "listen to me, listen to me," as if I could possibly avoid hearing him. "It's like he viewed my very existence as an anchor, not to moor his boat in the water, but to tie him by the ankle and drag him beneath the surface. Mom always thought he resented the commitments of fatherhood, and so he blamed me for everything that went wrong between them."

"Wow, you must really hate the guy."

"Hate's not the word for it. It's more disbelief. I don't believe in him, his sense of purpose, his sanctimoniousness, all his precious secrecy."

"What is he, a spy or something?"

"I always figured he was like Rimbaud, giving up poetry to deal arms in Africa."

"You're kidding, right?"

"Yeah, it's a joke. My mom is the poetic one. Seriously, I have no idea how he spends his time. If you press him, he'll give you some song and dance about import-export work, honey or olive oil or some such, or he'll talk about dealing in oil pipeline equipment. He's an expert bullshitter."

My father's contradictions had never been more evident than leading up to my bar mitzvah, when Dad dragged me to a jerky Hassidische rabbi who had dandruff all over his black suit and contempt for how I spoke Hebrew. Dad wanted me to learn old-school Judaism, without any of the liberal compromises enjoyed by the other kids my age, who got to have a big party and to hear how great they were.

"When I was thirteen, I spent every day learning how to box," Dad told me when I complained. "You wouldn't even know how to defend yourself against a rainstorm."

"But Dad, this rabbi stinks."

"What are you, an expert in rabbis now?"

"No, I mean he really stinks. He smells so bad that it's hard to concentrate. It's so bad, they probably have a special name for it in the Talmud."

For a second Dad looked like he was going to crack up. Then he reverted to his usual overbearing seriousness. "Hold your nose and be grateful for the opportunity. If this were Odessa, you wouldn't even be allowed to study your Torah portion."

On the day I became a man, I stumbled through my parshah over constant corrections from the stinky rebbe; and after it was done, we drove out to Brighton Beach with Uncle Effie, to a

Russian place on the boardwalk, where the waiters brought plates of blini and caviar, and everyone told me how grateful they were to my father, who had rescued them from the communists. Some of them cried as they spoke, and hell, even at that age I knew that Russians didn't cry in public. For all the crap he put me through, Dad was loved and admired, more than I could ever say for myself.

"I'm sorry you had to go through that," Mia said, cozying up to my side, all eager for intimacy. "What made your parents split up?"

If Mom shared one thing with Dad, it was a predilection for privacy. Out of respect for her, I held back the details of their fateful trip to Ethiopia, which hadn't ever been fully explained to me, at least not in any coherent way.

"My mother would never say: she was really discreet. As for my dad, he's stayed so loyal to her over all these years that I bet he never had another girlfriend."

"Really? I didn't think men felt that kind of loyalty."

"Some do. Not me, though."

Pulling away from me, she shoved me with both hands. "You really are a shit."

"Maybe so, but at least I'm honest about my limitations." Leaning over to the window, I peeked out the black curtains to check on the morning light. "Come on, we better get dressed. Delacroix likes to arrive early, to regale me with stories of genocide."

The prospect of being discovered naked in bed roused Mia to action. Scrambling for her clothes, she tripped over the plants that took over more of Dad's bedroom every day.

"Why won't you let me meet your friends?" she asked, tugging on her pants. "You're always talking about Ismael and Delacroix as if they were the saviors of human civilization. I'd love to come to one of their shows."

"It's too risky. If my mom showed up, it would be bad for all of us."

She mumbled a vague consent. This thing with her couldn't last. And yet, here we were, hanging on, tempting fate, just like my cannabis enterprise. So far, Mom remained blithely unaware of either perilous venture. If I had retained one lesson from my father, it was how to separate the different sides of my life. So much for his complaints that I never listened to him.

22

Addis Ababa
August 11, 1973

JACOB'S SNORING PROVIDED A COMFORTING RUMBLE AS WE floated above the earth, its colors diffused by the atmospheric haze. It was a marvelous sensation, to drift across the sky, to revel in a serene, unflustered bliss as a pressurized chariot carried us to the birthplace of humanity. This must have been what Jacob had enjoyed all these years, crossing vast distances like a modern god, shrinking the world to his will. For me, the flight to Ethiopia represented liberation, a reprieve from a lifetime of aerophobia.

To reach these heights, I owed an immeasurable debt to my husband, sleeping beside me as peacefully as ever. Jacob's generosity of spirit had made this entire trip possible. He had coaxed me down the gangway, calmed me through takeoff, and consoled me during rough weather over Greenland. On a deeper level, he had championed my ambition to rewrite human history. The journey ahead would open up a continent and give me license to address some of the most profound mysteries of human existence, all hidden beneath a layer of sand. To discover those truths would take courage and resolve, and since I lacked both in sufficient quantities, I had to borrow them from my beloved, whose strong hands had not faltered in ushering me through the turbulence.

With little time left before landing, Jacob had dozed off. It was typical of him. Through all our years together, as I suffered through endless bouts of insomnia, I couldn't recall Jacob missing even a single night's sleep. He never seemed haunted by guilt or anguish, or, for that matter, doubt. Nestled into a cramped plane seat, he breathed in regular, solemn measures, his hands folded over his belly as if lying in state. Those hands bore scars that must have had their own stories, but I despaired of ever revealing their truths. At this point, given the stunning scope of his generosity, it no longer seemed to matter.

This journey to Ethiopia had sprung from the latest anthropological conference, where Chuck Rosenfeld insisted on playing matchmaker, presenting me, whose marriage he had never quite accepted, to an obscure French scientist.

"This guy is really on to something, Susanna. If he's right, it could change our whole vision of human evolution."

Chuck led me into a room where Marcel Elmaleh was laying out a proposal to survey an undisturbed quarter of the African Rift Valley. He described the Afar desert as the ideal fossil laboratory, even more promising than Olduvai Gorge, where the Leakeys had discovered a golden cache of hominid remains.

"Now you see why I brought you here?" Chuck asked.

"Not exactly. My bones are too old to take to the field."

"Don't say that. It's never too late to uncover the truth. Find something of consequence and your name will ring out in history."

When the lecture ended, Chuck lunged forward to introduce me to Marcel as an eager volunteer, willing to break her back to help narrow the gaps in the fossil record. What an unlikely candidate I must have seemed, lacking formal training in excavation, already approaching middle age, with a young child, advanced enough toward tenure that sweating through an East African dig didn't constitute an obvious career path. None of this seemed to discourage Marcel, who was in no position to refuse help, particularly from an associate of the renowned Chuck Rosenfeld, however ill-suited she might have seemed.

"We would be very happy, Susanna, for you to join us. The expedition would benefit greatly from your insights."

His invitation restored the thrill of my early days in anthropology, when all the potential of our discipline lay before me. I nearly assented right away, until I felt my enthusiasm clipped by a cascade of trepidations. Foremost among those: my old resistance to flight, which thwarted any possibility of traveling to East Africa. Begging off, I blamed my husband's steadfast objections to my participating in field expeditions and the extraordinary demands of raising our son.

Even when rejected, Marcel kept up a spirited graciousness, inviting me to reconsider over the coming days. Chuck showed no such restraint and railed at me as soon as we reached the corridor.

"That scoundrel husband of yours has no right to interfere. This could be the chance of a lifetime. If he screws it up, I'll strangle him with my bare hands."

"Don't be silly, Chuck. He's bigger than you are, and tougher too."

"Fine, then I'll tear up that stupid marriage contract you persuaded me to witness. You have to go to Ethiopia. I insist on it."

A drill sergeant in the army of rationalism, Chuck viewed emotional frailty as the enemy of science. I could never share with him the true nature of my phobias. Cowardly as it might have seemed, I took shelter behind the image of Jacob as overbearing zealot. He, at least, was sturdy enough to withstand Chuck's curses.

Returning home, I found Jacob stretched across the couch, bare feet on the coffee table, arguing with the newspaper over tribal tensions in his holy land. Our son was watching a cartoon of an intrepid mouse committing heinous acts of brutality against a gangly cat. Over Shally's protests, I turned off the mindless dross as the cat died miserably, and sent him upstairs so I could relate Marcel's invitation.

Jacob folded up the paper. "Nu, no one's stopping you. The department must owe you a sabbatical by this point."

"It's not so simple. I don't even have the basic equipment for a dig."

"Let me know what you need, and I'll take care of it."

I considered the gear required for my toolkit: a gardening trowel; a set of tweezers; some brushes. Nothing too difficult to procure. The real problem lay deeper.

"Jacob, we can't all be so enthusiastic about climbing on board an airborne coffin."

"Oy, Susanna, not this *michegos* again. If it'll make you feel better, I can accompany you across the Atlantic. Remember, I have a sixth sense for plane trouble."

His claim of prescience made me laugh. "It's an awfully long way to go just to hold my hand."

"True, but long flights never bothered me. They give me a chance to rest, without having to worry about the phone ringing."

He seemed so sincere, so supportive that it felt churlish to point out the obvious complications.

"Jacob, what would you possibly do on an anthropological dig? You'd be bored senseless."

"Don't worry about me. I can make a little tour, take in the sights. You're always raving about Africa as the cradle of humanity. That sounds worth seeing."

The whole scheme sounded ludicrous. Jacob had never voiced the slightest interest in Africa. His investment in human origins stretched only as far back as the Biblical Abraham and his mythic departure from Babylonian Ur.

"What about Shally?" I asked. "We can't exactly drag him along. It's no place for a child."

"We'll send him to Salik in Tel Aviv. He'll have a good time on the beach."

It was hard to imagine handing over my son to that loathsome Salik, who didn't hesitate to call my husband off to war, but never acknowledged my sacrifice or the reality that his assignments, whatever they entailed, might mean the end of my family.

"Shally can't even speak their language."

"So he'll learn. Salik's sons can show him around, give him a chance to become bilingual."

His reasoning had a compelling logic, that Shalom would benefit from early exposure to another tongue, even one of such limited utility as modern Hebrew. Such was the power of temptation, that it could evaporate an ocean of fear.

An hour before landing, a fresh wave of terror swelled back over me. It materialized out of thin air, with ferocity and venom, just when everything seemed safe. I felt a sudden bump, a jolt, and a flurry of tremors, leading to a harsh, punishing drop. Outside my window loomed a jagged mountain range, no place for a plane to put down. Gripping the armrests, I became conscious of the fact that nothing, neither the grumbling engines nor the pilot's instruments, could bind me to a secure point in space.

The turbulence failed to rouse my husband. Only when I called for help did Jacob awaken in his usual manner, with a quick stern snort, alert from the moment his eyes opened. Undisturbed by the jolting airframe, he wrapped an arm around my shoulders and pulled me close.

"It's always like this crossing over the mountains," he said. "The updrafts catch the plane and make it bounce a little. We'll be through it soon."

Just as Jacob had predicted, the aircraft soon settled into a steady groove, smooth enough for me to peer out at the valley below. From this height, the landscape was free of artificial demarcations: no geopolitical borders or warring tribes, only the brackets of agriculture that segmented the earth into a tattered quilt.

"Anything going on down there?" Jacob asked, leaning over me for a look out the window.

"It's hard to make out any details."

"That's because all you care about is bones. You're only interested in people after they've lost their meat." He pinched my ilium for emphasis.

"Stop," I said, swatting his hand away. "I care more than you know. My loyalties simply don't bind me to any particular flag."

Stretching my arms around his substantial trunk, I rested my head against Jacob's chest and listened to the determined coursing of his heart. Steady as ever. There was no hesitation or inconstancy in him, only a solidity that comforted me all the way through our descent into Addis Ababa. When the cabin doors opened, he guided me through passport control and on to a frenzied terminal, where a horde of angry men pecked at us from all sides. Out of this din someone called my husband by name. Greeting the stranger, Jacob presented him as Mulu, our driver.

"Jacob, do you actually know this man?" I asked.

"He came to me through some friends. I never like to arrive in a foreign place without assistance."

Glad for him to handle the arrangements, I didn't question how Jacob had exercised his authority from abroad. I simply followed him to the waiting car. On our drive into the city, soldiers stalked the streets, guarding the intersections, glaring at anyone who passed. Here were more armed men than I had seen since my childhood watching the doomed Polish army prepare for the Nazi invasion.

"What is happening?" I asked my husband. "Why do they need so many soldiers?"

"They are going through some turmoil. It may not be long before the military seizes power from the old emperor."

The menacing signs of a mobilized army left me feeling entrapped. If I had known this country would be so troubled, I would never have left Brooklyn. Jacob, sensing my panic, took hold of my hand.

"Don't worry, Susanna. The army couldn't care less about an anthropological dig. All they want to do is to crush their own people."

Our plan had been to linger in Addis just long enough to secure the official permits, but this task turned out to be complicated. At the antiquities ministry, we were passed from one bureaucrat to the next, each one poring over my passport, visa, and the formal letter from Marcel inviting me on the dig. When at last we appeared before a military officer, his uniform and demeanor filled me with an unmitigated sense of dread.

"What is the purpose of this expedition?" the officer asked, repeating a question posed a dozen times already. Our mission was outlined clearly in Marcel's letter, but this officious man uttered every word as a kind of accusation.

"We are hoping that by unearthing the remains of our ancient ancestors, we will fill in our understanding of human evolution," I said, worrying that my quaking voice might be interpreted as betraying some ignoble intent.

"You will be digging up the ancestors of the Ethiopian people?"

A man like this could never comprehend my search for the roots of language. His resolution to an epistemological quandary would have been to rend it asunder, like a Gordian knot. Desperate to refute the premise of his question, I descended into a plaintive wail of "no, no, it's not like that," and might have unraveled the entire situation, if Jacob had not taken charge.

"You have to understand something about my wife," Jacob said calmly, without any of my breathless desperation. "The struggles we face today don't mean anything to her. When Dr. Sussman looks at the world around us, her mind wanders back millions of years. But you should know: she makes no claim on the bones that lie under the ground. Whatever she discovers will be handed over to the national museum, so the Ethiopian people can benefit from her work."

Jacob's words seemed to cast the right balance, reassuring the officer-in-charge that I had no capacity to meddle in his country's internal squabbles. When the military man stamped my papers, I felt overcome by relief and exhaustion, as if our escape represented a hard-won freedom. To celebrate, Jacob took me out for a luxurious dinner at our hotel's fancy restaurant, offering a panoramic view of Addis. The sight of the city at sunset, the waiter pouring honey wine, and the recognition of Jacob's kindness led me to a teary confession.

"Jacob, I'm so grateful. None of this would have happened without you." My words sounded maudlin, as if mouthed by a Victorian heroine swooning on the moors. Not exactly the role I had hoped to cast for myself in switching from English to Anthropology.

"I wanted you to have this opportunity." He toasted me with honey wine. "Now here's something to protect you from the sun."

He presented me with a thin package, loosely wrapped in tissue paper. Opening it, I found a rich green scarf of finely woven cotton.

"Jacob, this is too lovely. It will be ruined in the field."

"Don't worry, a scarf like this is meant to be worn, not to sit in a closet. It comes alive around a woman's head."

Bowing to his insistence, I gathered my hair and tied the scarf behind my neck.

"Beautiful," he said, humming in appreciation. "You look like a kibbutznik."

"And that's a good thing?"

"It is to me. It means you're a real pioneer, not afraid of working the land."

"That may be true, but I'm extracting from the earth rather than planting in it."

"All right, you win. I'll leave the metaphors to you."

He held my hands the way he had early in our romance, sitting on my aunts' couch. For years I had longed to recapture that closeness, even as the telephone kept tearing him away. Ironic that it took our traveling so far from home to restore the life that had seemed lost to us. Facing him now in the restaurant, I no longer needed to dwell on the sudden separations or the equally unpredictable reunions. As we drank honey wine and watched the dusk dissolve into darkness, I felt myself unwind and sensed the beginning of a new understanding, a new way of being together. The evening ended in bliss, in our hotel suite, high above a strange city rippled with soldiers.

I slept so soundly that Jacob had to shake me awake at daybreak for the long drive across the desert. He carried our bags outside, where our driver Mulu stood waiting alongside an older gentleman, who was presented to me as Tezera. Jacob handed the bag filled with my gear, trowels, brushes, tweezers, and a new scarf as well, to the old man, who loaded it into his waiting vehicle.

"Jacob, what is going on? Why do we need a second car?"

"Tezera is Mulu's uncle, a very responsible driver," my husband said. "He's going to take you the rest of the way."

Back in Brooklyn, when consenting to Jacob's proposal, I never could have envisaged the political realities of this place: the fearsome patrols of roaming soldiers, the guardposts at every public building, the constant demands for our documents. Now that we were here, the world seemed to be spinning too fast, a geophysical impossibility, to be sure, but an emotional certainty. To be deprived of my Virgil, my guide through this foreign land, seemed terribly reckless.

"Jacob, can't you come with us to Hadar? The situation here really frightens me."

"Don't worry, no one will bother you. Tezera will drive you straight across the desert to Marcel's camp. You shouldn't run into any roadblocks."

"Still, it makes me nervous. Won't you even consider joining me? I'm sure Marcel could use an extra set of hands. You're always talking about making the desert bloom."

"It's not my kind of desert, and it's not my kind of work either."

"What if you didn't have to do any digging? You could organize the field camp, catalogue the specimens."

He kissed my forehead. There would be no changing his mind.

"You'll see me in a few weeks, after I finish my little tour. Mulu has been telling me all about some beautiful spots up in the Simien Mountains. We must have passed over them on the flight in."

It only took a slight wobble in his tone, a few cagey words, to alert me that something deeper was at play. In an instant, Jacob had transformed, reverting to his impenetrable norm. It occurred to me now that he had obscured his itinerary, left me no way to contact him, and hadn't even told me how long he would be missing. I should have sensed it from the beginning. He had been so kind in responding to Marcel's offer, so generous, teasing me with an altruism that seemed pure, lacking any ulterior agenda. Now I could see it had all been an act. Perhaps he could give himself fully to others, to the thankless men who called out to him from afar, but to me, to his wife, his generosity was always tempered by discretion, or more precisely, by deception.

"Please, Jacob, I hope you're not getting yourself into any trouble."

"Believe me, that's the last thing I plan on doing."

His assurances were so bland that they ended up confirming all of my doubts. Alas, just as during my childhood in Łodź, there was nothing, absolutely nothing I could do to stop the unfolding of events. As he opened the car door to usher me inside, I grew compliant, dumbstruck. My hands groped instinctively for a medallion hung around my neck, as if I were an abandoned child delivered once again into the arms of strangers.

23

Goma
October 15, 1996

THE LATEST DISPATCHES WERE GIVING ME HEARTACHE. IN THE ten days since the Tutsis launched their uprising, we had lounged around the Hotel Bruegel's back lawn and waited for the fighting to catch up to us. Somewhere south of Lake Kivu, Tutsi rebels were rolling back the Zairean army and sending hordes of Hutu refugees home to Rwanda. It sounded like justice to me. Not so to the foreign newspapers that decried what they called an extermination campaign, casting the Tutsis as aggressors and the Hutus as victims. Shameless fools. They hadn't learned a damn thing from history.

"Tell the truth, damn it. Don't slant it," I shouted at the newspapers.

"Aba, why are you getting so upset?" Dudu asked, resting back in his lawn-chair. "You've never worried about what other people think."

"It's the hypocrisy that kills me. These idiots are calling for an international army to come save the Hutus. Where the fuck was this heroic intervention when the Tutsis were being hacked to pieces at Bisesero?"

Dudu sighed dramatically, to show me how bored he was with this argument. "You have too much faith in war, Aba. All it does is give you more bodies to bury."

I felt a twinge deep within my chest. It was bad enough to suffer through the news, but Dudu's commentaries were going to give me a heart attack. In the face of trials, some men turned into parrots, chirping like idiots and repeating whatever they heard. Others turned to stone, holding firm to their mistakes. Dudu had borrowed from the worst of both.

"How can you, the son of a Soviet refusenik, object to helping others?" I asked. "What would have happened if we had left you to rot in Odessa?"

He tossed up his hands, appealing for divine assistance to straighten out a poor old fool. "Good for one is bad for another, Aba, when your business is moving around whole populations. Sure, you let me escape the Soviets, just like you flew all those Falashas out of Ethiopia, but you never worried what it meant for the Arabs who used to own my mother's house in Haifa." He paused for a drink of beer. "That's how it is. The world is a terrible place. Some of us don't want to spend our whole lives fighting."

He didn't make any fucking sense, mixing up unrelated issues, but as I fumed, the pinching in my chest gave way to a terrible belching, soon accompanied by a ferocious pounding in the ears.

"I don't feel so good." Unfastening the buttons on my shirt, I loosened the collar and spread it wide.

The sight of man my age rubbing his chest, trying to push out a belch, shook Dudu into action. Grabbing my wrist, he timed my pulse. His face clenched tighter with each successive beat.

"Your heart is going too fast, Aba."

For one who could crack jokes at a mass grave, Dudu had turned awfully serious.

"Let me rest here for a little bit. Maybe it'll go away."

"Bullshit, Jacob, this is serious. Salik made us stay in this fucking town, and now you have pains in the chest. We are getting you to a doctor."

"A doctor? Where?"

The local hospital probably hadn't seen a clean needle since the Belgians left. There was no hope of crossing the border at this hour. So close to sunset, the last flight had left hours before. Dudu knew this.

"What about the doctor we met at Sunny's. The pretty one in the white coat, who works at that refugee camp."

This might have been Dudu's worst idea yet. Mugunga was the epicenter of evil around here, the base from which the Hutu genocidaires launched their pogrom against the Tutsis of Masisi. Its existence was the very problem that Captain Ezekiel and his comrades needed to solve.

"Are you out of your mind? We can't go there."

"There's no choice, Aba. I have a responsibility to Salik. To your wife too."

My chest tightening by the moment, I lost the will to fight. Funny that he had mentioned Susanna. All I really wanted was to reach her one more time. My last phone call, made from Kinshasa, had gone the way of all our conversations: formal, proper, lacking in passion. It was sad. She had never forgiven me, not even after all these years. The only resolution would have been to apologize, but at my best, I could offer nothing more than regret for the way things had turned out in Ethiopia. It wouldn't have mattered anyway. Words couldn't make up for the years we had pissed away.

"Come on, Aba, let's go," Dudu boosted me to my feet and ushered me across the hotel lobby.

"Wait, I have to make a phone call."

"Not now. First we get you to the doctor."

Dudu stuffed me into Patrice's car, and our driver raced across Goma's empty streets. The money changers and diamond brokers had cleared out for the day, fleeing before darkness gave way to drunken soldiers applying nighttime taxes. Avoiding the check-points, Patrice veered onto bumpy back roads until a wall of lights appeared ahead.

"There it is," Patrice said. "Mugunga."

The gate in sight, I felt my conscience snap back. "Wait," I blurted out. A righteous man would have refused to enter the pit, to plead for help from those who served the genocidaires. My heart beating faster than ever, my ears pounding even louder, I started to feel my hands tingling. My vision grew clouded.

"Don't make trouble, Aba," Dudu said, "and don't let them know you're sick."

Zairean soldiers surrounded the car as we approached the gate. "Why are you bringing the *muzungus* so late?" the officer asked Patrice. "The camp is closed for today."

Dudu stuck his head outside. "Come on, brothers. I want to go fuck my girlfriend. Have pity on a man, and let me buy a round of beer."

His bribe cracked open the gate and released us onto a maze of crowded lanes. Closing my eyes, I felt the car jolt through the camp until we came to rest before a blue sign of the cross. Inside, a long tent was filled with cots, and dozens of patients stared at me in disbelief, as if no *muzungu* should ever grow ill. When Dr. Chantal appeared, dressed like an angel in her white coat, she showed no sign of alarm, or even surprise. She led us quickly to a closed-off section of tent that served as examining room. Swiftly unbuttoning my shirt, she leaned in close and pressed her stethoscope to my chest. It gave me a little charge to have this lovely doctor so intimate. If I had to face my end in a foreign land, with a war closing in, Dr. Chantal would be a lovely shepherd through the final moments.

"The rhythm sounds normal," she said, pulling the stethoscope out of her ears. "A little tachycardia, but that could be anxiety." She wound a blood-pressure cuff around my arm and pulled me close to her body, as Susanna used to do when accompanying me into the evening. "Pressure is fine."

"I'm confused. What could be wrong then?"

"It could be indigestion, or anxiety. Both can present symptoms of a cardiac episode. We will test your blood to be sure, but I do not detect any structural damage."

Relief flushed over me. The heart rate eased, the pounding in my eardrums faded. It was a soothing sensation, but it left me with a damning conclusion. Despite all my tough-talk, I had become a *nudnik*, as helpless as Susanna before her fears.

For her part, Dr. Chantal showed herself to be sympathetic and kind. Her hands moved across my body with a lovely, delicate touch, giving me cause for hope. Not just that I would survive this ordeal, but that I could rekindle some joy in my life. Breaking open a fresh needle, she drew blood and instructed me to return the next day for further monitoring.

"You don't want me to stay?" I said, suddenly aware of my shirt hanging open, my chest sagging. I tried to straighten my posture.

"That wouldn't be possible. You are not a refugee." Smiling for the first time, she rested her hand on my chest. "Don't worry, we will see you through this."

As the doctor left, blood in hand, Dudu admired the hips draped by her exam coat.

"These do-gooders are not so bad after all, Aba. You look better already."

"I told you it was nothing. You should have let me sleep it off."

"Then you would have missed the touch of a pretty girl on your body. Who knows what else those hands could do."

"She's a medical professional. Can't you show her a little respect?"

"Aba, be merciful, there's nothing wrong with having feelings for a woman, even at your age. Remember King David, they brought him a pretty virgin when he got old."

"You ignoramus. The story was that King David slept with her to stay warm, but he did not 'know' her."

"Too bad for him. That would be the time when I say: enough of this life."

Before I could contend with his nonsense, we were joined by Karina Bronkhorst, the Dutch boss of Blessed Relief who had been so hostile to us at Sunny's Thai Cafe. Karina looked unwashed, compared with the dignified doctor, but her tan vest, marked with a blue cross, lent her an air of professionalism.

"Dr. Chantal informed me of your situation," she said. "I am sorry you were feeling unwell."

"It turned out to be a false alarm. My friend Dudu was just overly cautious."

"He was wise to be so, especially at a time like this," she said. "Germaine will be sorry she missed you. She was excited to show you her work with the orphans."

"Maybe tomorrow, when we come back to the see the doctor."

A deep boom sounded from somewhere up north. It could have been thunder or something more ominous. Karina breathed in the night air, as if she could smell the impending assault. "Did you ever succeed in reaching the mountain guerrillas?"

I ignored her funny shift in pronunciation, guerrilla instead of gorilla. "Not yet, maybe when I'm feeling better."

"I wouldn't recommend traveling to Virunga until the fighting settles down, whenever that will be. The government swears it will crush this rebellion, but every day more refugees arrive from the camps farther north. Their stories give us concern for the future." She looked mournful, as if this city of tents was worth mourning, as if these Hutus could stay here forever. "Can you tell us what is really happening?"

"I'm afraid we can't be much help. We're just observers here."

"Well, I hope you will entrust us with whatever you do learn. Consider it fair compensation for your treatment."

It was a strange twist on the Hippocratic oath, to swap medical care for intelligence. Held hostage by her demands, I vowed to pass along anything useful. It was a lie, of course. I could hardly sacrifice one set of lives for another, especially if it meant choosing the killers over their victims.

Escorting us out to Patrice's car, she pulled a small decal from her pocket and slapped it on the back window. It was a silhouette of a Kalashnikov encircled by a red stripe, the universal prohibition on carrying arms.

"This will protect you on your next visit. You shouldn't get too close to the military men."

Glancing at each other, Dudu and I broke down over the irony at being cast as accidental pacifists. Laughter was good. It eased the strain on my chest.

24

Hadar, Ethiopia
September 14, 1973

I HAD PASSED THROUGH PLENTY OF SHITHOLES ON MY TRAVELS, but few were quite as desolate as Susanna's field site. Driving into camp, I couldn't imagine what would have drawn any living creature, least of all our early ancestors, to this dusty wasteland. Even crazier was the idea that Susanna and her fellow anthropologists might stumble upon a few shards of bone in all this desert. Not that it mattered to me. If this was what it took to spring her from her fears, then so be it. It might as well have been the Garden of Eden.

Mulu parked the car near the big tent, pitched on a bluff overlooking a muddy river. The flaps of the tent were rolled up, opening it to the desert like a wedding huppah, letting in the afternoon breeze. Spread across the bluff were a smattering of pup tents, where the scholars spent their nights. Hell of a way to live.

A crowd of Ethiopian camp hands emerged from the shade to greet us. From the general excitement, they didn't appear to get many visitors. One of the workers jogged into the desert to alert the team to my arrival, and a half-hour later Susanna appeared in the distance, picking her way along a dry ridge. As she approached, I observed my wife, as if for the first time. She looked stunning, her hair bound up in the scarf I had brought back from Fez, its deep green fading into the brown dust that covered the landscape. The sight of her, fit and sweaty after laboring in the field, like a kibbutznik harvesting the bones of our ancestors, reminded me of the passion we had rekindled on our last night in Addis.

I hugged her, but she let out a sharp cry and pushed me away. "Stop. It hurts." She pulled down her shirt collar to expose a blistering sunburn, its outline defined by the tank-top she must have previously worn into the field.

"You've got to be careful," I said. "The sun can kill you."

"That's been the least of my concerns."

She untied her scarf and shook out the dust. Her hair, tinted tawny by the sand, looked as thick and lush as ever. "You've got some gall to show up here at last," she said.

"Susanna, please, don't be sore. My tour of the mountains took longer than expected. It's a beautiful country, but the roads here really stink. Anyway, I figured the last thing you needed was a clumsy oaf like me stumbling all over your discoveries."

"Well, you might as well have stayed away. After you abandoned me in Addis, I learned to cope on my own."

Through all our years together, this was the first time she had ever tried to banish me from sight. I had figured she might be annoyed, even enraged, by our most recent parting. The reality turned out to be far worse. Her response was steely, without compromise, like nothing I had seen before.

"All right. If that's what you really want, I can take off again tomorrow morning. I hate to do it, especially on these terms, but it's your choice."

By this time, the other members of her expedition had begun to emerge from the surrounding *wadis*. As she watched her pals hike back to camp, her tone softened. "All right, fine, you can stay for now. But only if you promise to behave yourself. I don't need any more complications."

"On this I give you my word. My best behavior from now on."

We were joined by a half-dozen anthropologists, filthy from digging all day under the sun. They gathered around, grateful for the company, and welcomed me to their midst. One of them, a bearded guy with a French accent, introduced himself as Marcel, who had invited Susanna to Ethiopia.

"We apologize for failing to greet your arrival," he said. "Your wife could not be not certain when you might come."

"It seemed fair to let Susanna settle in," I said, "but now that I'm here, feel free to put me to work. My shoulders are plenty strong for hauling dirt."

Susanna jolted at my offer, and might have objected, but her boss had his own ideas. Reaching down, Marcel picked up a handful of sandy earth and let it slide through his fingers. "We would be very happy to have your assistance, but be careful what you invite. This is a job that might not ever end."

Susanna stuck close beside me, almost within breathing distance, wary of my every word. She had always hated to have me mingle with her people, even with that old fool Chuck, as if I might let drop some insight that she didn't want shared. In the end, she valued discretion as much as I did. Maybe that was the secret to our marriage.

At dinner, the cook brought out pots of roasted goat and beans, served with their spongy bread, the same stuff I had been eating for weeks. Dropping the flaps on the big tent, the team gathered around the central table, and Marcel pressed me on my travels. Encircled by the scholars, I described a pilgrimage to the glories of medieval Abyssinia: a church hewn from the solid rock; obelisks soaring higher than those of the pharaohs; and a chapel that supposedly housed the ark of the covenant, given by King Solomon to the Queen of Sheba. The anthropologists gobbled up my stories. None of them suspected that these tidbits were culled from a guidebook on the long drive down from Gondar. The only one who seemed skeptical was Susanna, who listened to each of my tall tales as if it might reveal a secret to my inner being.

After eating, Marcel invited me to witness what they had harvested from the earth. At the specimen tent, the Frenchman showed off an array of fossils, including a set of elephant tusks as long as our car and a hippo skull that needed two men to lift. Pointing to an ancient pig jaw, he informed me it had been discovered by Susanna.

"Your wife has a gift for identifying bones. A tiny fragment can barely be protruding from the earth and she will pick it out. It is uncanny, how she can recognize the slightest disruption in the landscape."

Susanna shook her head, as if compliments might jinx her with a *kenahora.* "Please, Marcel, you're giving me too much credit. All I've uncovered are a few ancient pigs. It's not as if I've found a hominid."

"Not yet, but they are out there," he said. "And you could realize something magnificent tomorrow. We need your eyes, Susanna. They are the finest in the expedition. With your help, future generations could look back at this time as a defining moment in discovering how we came to be human."

This guy was a dreamer, pulling dry bones from the valley and making them come alive again, if only in his imagination. No wonder Susanna liked him. He shared her passion for unsettling the dead.

The tour complete, the camp bedding down for the night, I trailed Susanna to her tent and crawled into the cramped space beside her. Shielded by the darkness, this might have been the moment to consider what she had long resisted: another child, a daughter this time, who we could name Nesia, for my sister. Here in the desert lay our chance to create something new, to light a fresh Havdalah candle that would braid our lives together. Reaching around her, my hands meeting by her belly, I pulled her toward me.

"Jacob, stop." She jerked like a horse shaking off its rider, so forceful that I simply released her.

"Why don't we try? No one will hear."

"Forget it," she said.

From the mess tent, where the camp hands were still cleaning up from dinner, a radio blared the song "Lucy in the Sky with Diamonds."

"We could call her Lucy," I said, "if you still think Nesia is too old-fashioned."

She spun around, facing me. "It's not the name, Jacob. It's you. You show up here after weeks of silence, and refuse to admit what you were really doing all this time. How could I possibly trust you?"

I had hoped that my good behavior would have tempered her bitterness, but no, she wasn't buying it. "Susanna, we've been through this before. There are some things I simply can't discuss."

"Fine, but don't expect me to buy any of your nonsense about touring medieval churches. You wouldn't notice a piece of art or architecture unless it came crashing down on your head."

She jerked herself back toward the tent wall and feigned a sudden sleep. It was a poor bit of acting. I could tell she was still awake from the stiffness in her shoulders, from the taut pace of her breathing. We lay that way for a few minutes, a testy quiet, until she turned around viciously and went after me again.

"Salik must be mixed up in this somehow. How else would you know so much about life here: the language, the customs, the politics? Why else would we have had a driver waiting for us, ready to take us exactly where we needed?"

She had put it all together. I had warned Salik this might happen, that we couldn't count on her remaining oblivious to the signs right in front of her. An acceptable risk, he said. This trip was simply too good an opportunity to pass up. Now all I could do was try to limit the damage. So, setting aside a lifetime of discretion, I leaned close enough for my lips to brush against her ear.

"It's true. Salik sent me to look in on the Jews." My voice shielded beneath my hand, I made my confession—a journey into the mountains of Gondar, where, in a desperate poor village, Mulu presented me to his father, the *kes* of a besieged Jewish community. The old rabbi, looking like a prophet in his flowing white robes and turban, listened to my offer, that they no longer needed to live as "Falashas," strangers in a strange land, that we could open the skies and help them make their exodus.

Taking in my story, Susanna lay back and stared at the tent's roof, flickering with the light of the kitchen campfire. "So, this was your plan all along, from the moment you offered to accompany me here."

She wasn't entirely wrong. Her dig had provided a simple cover. It wasn't fair, however, to accuse me of deception.

"My offer was genuine, and I kept my word," I told her.

Tossing away all discretion, she raised her voice loud enough to rouse suspicions. "If I had known it was just a pretext for your own purposes, I never would have consented to this trip. Not when you could sabotage everything we've done here."

"What sabotage? I've been very discreet."

"Are you mad, or just completely reckless? You saw how much trouble we had convincing the ministries to sign off on my papers. Now, if the authorities find out about you, they could accuse Marcel of inviting in foreign spies. The entire dig would be put in jeopardy."

I could have tried to reassure her that, with a revolution in Addis coming any day, the authorities had more pressing concerns than the antics of one foreign tourist. There wasn't much point tilting with her. She was too angry, sitting up now and raging at me.

"How could you do it, Jacob? You knew what this expedition meant to me. But you cast me overboard anyway. And not just me. You sent your own son off to that terrible Salik, and pretended it was all for a little boy's edification. How could you tell us so many lies?"

She seemed to be waiting on an apology, a grand outpouring of remorse and repentance. It wasn't fair to ask this of me. I couldn't prostrate myself, wrap myself in sackcloth and ashes, when so many lives were at stake.

"Susanna, please, try to understand. We have only a limited window. It won't be long before the military seizes power in Addis, and once that happens, those guys will never let our people go."

"You're always rescuing other people, Jacob. What about your own wife and child? When do we get to be rescued? Don't we matter at all?"

"Of course you matter, but you, better than anyone, should know the significance of a humanitarian airlift."

She flopped back and cried out in exasperation, loud enough to wake the dead, even the fossilized dead. After that, there was silence, and I wondered whether the entire camp might be listening for what would come next.

"I'll never forgive you for this," she said softly, in a state of absolute calm, "for what you did here. I will remember it as long as I live."

Words doing me little good, I reached out to touch her shoulder. She flinched and cried out again, louder than ever this time. Shit. I had forgotten the sunburn. It must have been agonizing. Lacking any salve, I decided to let her be. All night she fussed and fumed, until close to dawn she prodded me awake.

"As soon as it's light, I'm going to resign from the expedition."

"Don't do that, Susanna. Let me disappear again, like you said. I can drive back to Addis and fly straight home to Brooklyn."

She shook her head. "No, we can't take the chance. The whole expedition would be placed at risk. The only ethical choice is for me to leave."

"But it's not necessary. You'd only be hurting yourself."

"That may be so, but I can't live with your deceptions. You find it so easy to pretend that everything is normal, but for me, the lies impose an overwhelming burden. If the army questions me again, they'll recognize in a heartbeat that I'm hiding something."

There was no use trying to bargain with her. An inability to compromise was truly the curse of brilliant women. As daylight spread over the desert, Susanna withdrew from the dig. Whatever glories lay beneath the surface here would fail to be associated with Dr. Susanna Sussman. Her name purged from the official records, it would be as if she had never existed.

25

Mugunga Refugee Camp, Zaire
October 16, 1996

PATRICE'S CAR ROLLED PAST MOBS OF REFUGEES, THE WHOLE place afoot, clogging what passed for thoroughfares. No wonder Rwanda had seemed so empty. The Hutus were all here, strolling through Mugunga. Patrice had to stop short to avoid striking an old lady who hobbled past with a live chicken.

"Come on, lady, hurry up out of the way," I called out the window. "We have to be somewhere."

The old biddy shook the bird at me and slowly shuffled along. Watching the exchange was a crowd of young men drinking beer at an open-air café. So much for the trials of exile. One of the dirty bums called out an insult, presumably at my expense, and I responded with a hard glare. Their mood turning serious, they pushed the chairs away and rushed over to our car.

"Where are you going, *muzungu*? What do you want here?"

It didn't take an interpreter to figure out these were Interahamwe. Dudu jumped out of the car to address them.

"Don't be angry, my friends," he said. "The old *muzungu* has a heart problem that makes him crazy. He's excited to see the doctor so she can give him an electric shock."

He jolted as if suffering a seizure. Big fucking joke.

"What the hell are you playing games for?" I asked as Dudu returned to the car. "You don't need to tell them a damn thing about our business."

"They must know already. Listen Jacob, we have to be careful. We don't have friends here. If you make trouble, these guys could cause you some real chest pain, not just the kind in your head."

Son of a bitch, shaming me with my own weakness. This must have been how Susanna felt through the years, stricken by her neuroses, so embarrassed that she took refuge in blaming me for her fears.

I tapped Patrice to press on, but a skinny boy blocked our passage. He rubbed his belly, his face twisted in agony, the standard plea for cash.

"Buy me a sweet, *muzungu*. I need to eat."

Another goddamn delay. Little shit.

"Get out of the way, kid. I have an appointment."

A strong hand suddenly yanked him to the side. It turned out to be Germaine, the formidable lady who had stared down the drunken soldiers at Sunny's. Shaking the boy hard enough to rattle his jawbone, she introduced him as one of her orphans.

"Fulgence will do anything to avoid his studies," she said. "I have had to chase him all across the camp."

"I don't envy your job. It was hard enough for me to raise one son."

"Oh, I have three sons of my own in Goma, but Blessed Relief has given me responsibility for twenty-seven orphans. They are mostly girls, but it is the boys who make the most trouble, and nothing is more dangerous than a rebellious boy turning into an angry man."

It was too crowded to drive, so Germaine offered to escort us to the medical tent. Traveling on foot would take longer, but at least now I had a guide through this city of the plain. Leading us past row after row of tents, she pointed out the various aid groups administering to what had become the biggest population center in eastern Zaire, a metropolis three times the size of Goma. All around, refugee women were stirring cauldrons of bubbling gruel, hanging their wash on clotheslines that stretched in every direction. We passed a slaughterhouse where a man was carving up a carcass. It looked like strenuous work, but the guy really knew how to handle a machete. Covered in blood, he disassembled the animal without conscience, hacking through bone and muscle, peeling back the hide, and turning a formerly living creature into parcels of meat. Butchery seemed to come naturally to him.

"It looks like the people eat well here."

"Yes, there is fresh meat every day," Germaine said. "It has become very reasonably priced."

A stockade of bony cows waited for their appointed hour. Poor bastards couldn't tell what was in store for them.

As we approached the Blessed Relief sector, a gap between the tents gave space for a crowd of boys to attack a soccer ball. There was a wild flurry of kicking, followed by another wave of pushing and yelling. The ball burst free for a moment before the swarm overtook it again.

"Your boys could use a little discipline," Dudu told Germaine. "They don't play as a team."

"Oh yes, we would like to find a coach, but it has been difficult to locate the right person. We do not approve of the men who our boys admire."

"I could be your coach," Dudu said, before turning to me. "As long as it's okay with you, Aba."

Shit. What the fuck was he doing, acting like a big macher. It was one thing to seek medical attention, another to tie ourselves to the wheel of relief. Then it dawned on me that Dudu's coaching would spare me his endless commentaries and allow me to consult with the doctor in private.

"Go ahead, if you think you can teach these kids something."

Germaine needed some convincing. "You, Mr. Dudu? Do you really know about football?"

Dudu had the side-to-side waddle of a samurai, constrained not by a long sword but by the unwieldy shape of his own body, arms too broad to rest comfortably by his side, thighs built for great heaves rather than long runs, and a chest cast in hardened rubber, able to absorb a direct blow.

"I used to play goalie." He clapped his hands and bent his knees as if to prepare for a shot. "You would not believe it, but I was very graceful, with good reflexes."

"Mama, will you let him coach us?" Fulgence asked, pulling on Germaine's arm.

Dudu smacked the kid in the belly. "What position do you play?"

The boy stared straight at Dudu. "Attack."

Dudu grunted. "Can you do this?" He shuffled his feet fast, a phantom ball between them, then made a feint right. It looked ridiculous, but Fulgence mimicked the movement. Then Dudu pulled the invisible ball backward and spun his body completely around, the ground shaking as he landed. The kid parroted that one too.

"You know Baggio?" Dudu asked.

Fulgence looked puzzled until Dudu motioned behind his head to illustrate a ponytail, then he nodded. Of course, he had seen pictures.

"How about Weah?"

This one Fulgence had heard of. Everyone knew George Weah.

"He needed help from me to stay in shape." Dudu pounded his chest so confidently that even I, accustomed to wading through pools of his bullshit, nearly believed him. His act seemed to impress Germaine, who called out for the boys to come meet their new coach. Surveying their ranks, Dudu started dictating his rules—no fighting, stay in position, pass the ball to the open man, work as a team.

Leaving Dudu to his new assignment, Germaine led me into the tent that served as their school. Upon our entry, a dozen girls rushed up to hug her, so many at once that it reminded me of the nursery rhyme about the old woman who lived in a shoe. Afterwards, the girls went back to shouting lines from a shared sheet of paper. Germaine explained this was a rehearsal for *The Tempest*, translated into Kinyarwandan, a language that she, being neither Hutu nor Tutsi, couldn't actually speak.

"Isn't Shakespeare a little challenging for these orphans?" I asked.

"We want the children to learn about the world outside this camp. The next generation should hope for a better future, for something more constructive than war."

The Tempest had been Susanna's favorite, and I remembered how she had dragged me to a performance in Central Park, where right at the final speech, as Prospero's charms were all overthrown, the skies opened up with a ferocious downpour, sending us running for cover, laughing at the irony.

"So it's an all-girl cast?" I asked.

"The only roles the boys want to play are soldiers. We will allow them on stage with spears during the performance, if they promise to stand peacefully."

Germaine asked her Prospero to recite a passage for me, and the tent trilled with laughter. Prodded forward by her friends, the girl hesitated at the opening, then found her stride, delivering the lines with great passion. I couldn't follow the words, but the cadence transported me back to that *Tempest* with Susanna, before parenting, before the wars, back when the trajectories of our lives seemed so intertwined. The sweet memory of my wife curling close for warmth on a shivering subway ride back to Brooklyn reminded me that my exile had dragged on longer than Prospero's. That was all so far away now. It wasn't as if I could conjure up any magic to restore my place.

"We will be ready to perform the play in a few weeks, if you would like to attend," Germaine said.

Surveying the troupe, I wondered whether a Tutsi Ariel, unable to forget the crimes committed against his people, would drop the final curtain on this place by then.

"It will depend on whether we are still in Goma. As yet, we are waiting for our guide to take us into the mountains."

At last, Germaine led me to the medical tent, where I found Dr. Chantal Kayiranga looking as glorious as ever. Her hair tied back, her coat impeccably clean, she seemed buoyant as she glided from one patient to the next.

"I have to complete my rounds," she said, "if you would like to join me."

Matching her pace, I watched her tend to patients overwhelmed by their injuries. Most were new arrivals who had fled from camps farther north. One man was recovering from a gunshot wound to the shoulder; a teenaged boy had broken his ankle jumping from a truck; a lady suffered from a horribly swollen leg, infected by days running through the forest. Its stench wafted through the bandages.

"It must be difficult for you to face patients in these conditions," I said.

"Unfortunately, this is not the first time I have had that obligation."

Dr. Chantal paused at a catatonic man with a bandaged head and drew a small flashlight from her coat. Beaming it into his eyes, she checked for brain activity. If only guilt or innocence could be read so easily.

Her rounds complete, Dr. Chantal brought me back to the private room for my examination. She had me open my shirt, and put her scope on my chest, listening intently to the sounds deep within. At each breath she nodded in approval, as if my heart had achieved something noteworthy.

"You seem much improved. The heart rate is more regular, and your pressure is much reduced."

191

Years had passed since a woman of substance had paid such close attention to my inner life. Too bad our exchange was defined by the cold end of her stethoscope.

"Visiting your clinic must have put me in a better state of being, although it's still a little strange for me. I never would have considered coming to Mugunga if not for your presence."

"I never considered it would be my fate to be here either."

Her placid smile vanished, her eyes drifted behind a veil. Her mood seemed to hover between numbness and sorrow, reminding me of the persecuted Falashas, of the passengers on my banana boat to Palestine, and most of all of Judith. Before losing all perspective, I needed to know whether the doctor deserved this place of honor in my heart.

"Dr. Chantal, I have to ask: what made you flee here? I can't imagine you did anything during the war to be ashamed of."

My question, posed at a whisper, seemed to frighten her. Turning quickly from me, she peeked through the open tent flap to make sure no one was listening. "This is something very dangerous for us to discuss. And it is painful, terribly painful, to revisit."

In a low, hesitant voice, she described how the Interahamwe had shown up at her obstetrics ward in Butare. "They came to kill my Tutsi patients. I begged them to stop, showing them that these ladies were about to give birth, but it was hopeless. All I could do was to persuade them not to cut the women in their beds. I thought that if I could save the bed, then I could treat the next victim, when the madness finally ended."

"But it didn't end."

She shook her head. "It wasn't just at the hospital. The Interahamwe appeared at our house to demand that my brother Michel join them. He refused, so they killed him with their machetes. These were men from his football club, friends who he had known all his life. They murdered him anyway. I was spared only because of my white coat."

"Then why did you flee Butare with those same men? The killers must have posed a great danger to you."

"There was no choice. The Interahamwe pushed us all out with them." Her voice slowed, struggling to find its pitch. "And also, I was afraid, afraid that what they said over the radio was true, that the Tutsis were coming to kill us all, to strike back for what we had done to them."

She paused. "I was afraid the Tutsis would judge us all to be the same."

She breathed in heavily, straightened her coat, and announced her need to attend to some bloodwork. Watching her retreat once again behind a physician's mask, I found myself contemplating the strange truth that she too was a victim, trapped among the killers, in a doomed ghetto. The generous response would have been to reassure her she was not to blame. Much as I wanted to be sympathetic, it wasn't my place to offer forgiveness. That right was held by those who spoke for the dead. All I could do was to hope she would not be judged harshly.

26

Brooklyn
October 6, 1973

JACOB HAD ALWAYS TRIED TO MAKE AMENDS ON KOL NIDRE, and so on this evening, shortly after our ignominious retreat from Ethiopia, I waited for my husband to offer me some form of apology. According to Jewish tradition, Yom Kippur absolved the sinner before God, but it was up to the individual to repair his relations with other people. On this particular night, which followed weeks of avoiding me, Jacob failed yet again to address the harm he had caused. What he did instead was to hoist our six-year-old son onto his lap and paint my family history in golden strokes.

"You are the heir to a glorious tradition," Jacob told him. "Your grandfather, Dr. Sigismund Sussman, was a brilliant surgeon, the only Jew in his medical school. He could spot a tumor with three taps on the belly. When he cut open a patient, he already knew what was waiting inside."

Shally gazed rapt and reverent at his father, the master of manipulation, as if he could do no wrong. I couldn't blame the poor boy. These fables represented all he knew of his grandfather,

194

whose few extant photos were sealed, too painful to be exhumed, in a cardboard tomb inside my bottom drawer.

"Enough already, Jacob. My father wouldn't recognize himself from your stories."

Jacob stopped, as if reluctant to steal any more from me.

"Susanna, the boy should understand where he comes from, especially on a night like this." He rested his hand on our son's little shoulder. "It's up to you, Shalom, to preserve the memory of your grandparents. They gave up what they loved most in the world, your mother, because they recognized it was the only way to save her."

Jacob had placed me in an impossible position. I couldn't contest his paean to my family without further confusing our son.

"Okay, Shally. Time for bed." I yanked him up from Jacob's lap. He must have wanted to stay, because the boy let his body go limp, forcing me to drag him up the stairs. After tucking him in, I returned to the parlor to let Jacob have it.

"You had no right to appropriate my family history. Those are *my* stories."

"Susanna, I want him to feel connected to his roots, to the beautiful legacy you have given him."

I hated when he tried to pacify me with claims to a higher purpose. "Shally is too young for the big existential questions. Lecturing him about the camps could give him nightmares."

"I didn't say anything about the camps. Not yet anyway. You should have a little faith in me."

Have faith in him, this was his constant appeal. What he couldn't recognize was that I despaired at ever breaking through his denials, his evasions and his self-righteousness. We had barely spoken since Ethiopia, and I was determined to charge him full price for forgiveness. No cheap entreaties, no unctuous bromides would wash with me. His renewed efforts to help around the house—preparing dinner, patching up the chipped paint, taking out the garbage—only fueled my outrage.

The night of Kol Nidre ended, as they all had in recent weeks, with a cold war playing out in our bed. If he had been more attuned to my feelings, he would have taken up sleeping on the couch, but Jacob couldn't grasp a basic human sentiment like empathy. He was too busy grappling with how to move whole populations.

I knew from experience how Yom Kippur would unfold. Jacob wasn't overtly observant, but he would lecture us that this Day of Atonement was essentially a rehearsal for death, and thereby he would put on his kittel, a silly white robe, which he wished to be dressed in when laid out in a pine box. It was all very melodramatic, and I made it my mission to shield Shally from his father's grim histrionics.

When the telephone rang early the next morning, Jacob answered as he always did, with both feet flat on the floor. It was just past seven, but I heard shouting on the other end, a surprising state of agitation. Jacob mumbled a response, put down the receiver, and retrieved a packed bag from the closet.

"What's wrong?"

"It's war. A surprise attack. The Egyptians have crossed the Suez." He muttered something about tanks and sammy missiles as he yanked a cache of bills from the top drawer and stuffed it into his bag. The telephone sounded again. This time the voice on the other end was calmer, more measured. Jacob concurred with whatever the man was saying and hung up.

"I have to go."

"Now? I thought you were celebrating Yom Kippur."

"It's a disaster. Effie will be here any minute."

Grabbing his bag, he filed straight downstairs, not pausing until he reached the stoop. I trailed behind, waiting even at this final moment for him to say something, anything, to recognize how he had hurt me, before he vanished again, perhaps for good. And still he couldn't face me, as if a single glance might anchor him in place.

"Don't you want to say goodbye to your son?"

His eyes didn't veer from the street. "Do it for me. You're better at that kind of thing."

When the car pulled up, Jacob tossed his bag in the trunk and looked back at me. In that instant, I thought he might waver, stop his inexorable rush and choose not to abandon us. Instead, he ducked his head inside and rode off to another war.

Before he could turn the corner, I decided to bear no more of this. No longer would I play the role of Penelope, weaving and untying her tapestry as she awaited Odysseus' return. My collected bitterness took shape as a dark wish, that Jacob wouldn't come back at all. It was a terrible thing to consider. No wife should wish her husband to disappear; but his wars, and the pointless squabbling over a patch of land, were a plague on us, on humanity in general.

Closing the front door, I turned to find little Shally huddled on the staircase in his Spiderman pajamas. He didn't speak, not even to ask where his father had gone. Cradled in my lap, he lay quietly until I offered to prepare his favorite breakfast: waffles and syrup. The Yom Kippur fast didn't count for a six-year-old; and in any regard, he had suffered enough. As I stirred the batter, Shalom flicked on the television and immersed himself in the casual violence and impermanent death of his cartoons, interrupted when a dour newscaster broke in to announce what I already knew: a new war in the Middle East, a surprise attack, on a day that my husband claimed to be holy. Worried that the report might frighten Shally, I switched off the set and spent the day reading him stories of secret gardens and white rabbits. His father had taught him enough about suffering and war.

By the time sunset ushered out the Day of Atonement, I flicked back on the television to find it filled with images of smoke rising from the desert, young men in tanks and warplanes rushing off to murder their enemies, another generation reduced to splotches on the sand. What a futile exercise, these sacrifices to a nonexistent god of war, the parties obeying a tribal imperative to slaughter the other side.

Over the following days, the war went badly, then it went well, whatever that meant. Still I heard nothing from my husband. Then the telephone woke me at dawn, cleaving night from day, past from future. My hand shook as I lifted the receiver. Only the sound of Jacob wishing me a good morning allowed my anxiety to bleed back into anger.

"Well, it's good to hear you're still alive," I said.

"I am. Many of my friends were not so fortunate. Salik lost his oldest son. They blew up his tank in the Sinai."

Jacob meant to elicit my sympathy, but I couldn't feel for Salik's loss, not when that terrible man showed no concern for how his calls affected my life.

"When will you come home?"

"As soon as things settle down. It's still very bad here."

Hanging up, he abandoned me yet again. That week brought news of a cease-fire, later broached, and still we waited for some sign of Jacob. It wasn't until the end of October that a dark car rolled down the block at dawn and deposited him on our stoop. By the time I put on my robe and went downstairs, my husband was stretched across the couch, his stinking bare feet resting atop the coffee table. He had lost weight, and dark rings sagged beneath his eyes. His hair, which had been drifting from pepper to salt for years, now looked uniformly white. For the first time in our life together, he appeared spent, unable to hide his exhaustion.

"You look awful," I said.

"I haven't been getting much sleep lately."

"Neither have I. The telephone has been like a noose around my neck."

Rousing his strength, Jacob leaned forward and issued another misplaced call for sympathy. "Susanna, you have no idea how close we came to collapse. It was terrible. The commanders rushed reinforcements to the Sinai knowing those boys didn't stand a chance." His chin wavering with emotion, he shook his head, as if to dispel his own doubts. "There was no alternative. We couldn't survive another *shoah*."

For all his gifts as a polyglot, Jacob didn't understand me at all. I didn't seek his insights into the moral dimensions of conflict, only a recognition that we too were worth fighting for.

"I've always wondered what makes you run every time Salik calls. Now I realize that it's cowardice. You're so afraid of failing him that it doesn't matter whether you betray us."

Despite his exhaustion, my words ignited a rage in him that seemed almost chemical in ferocity.

"What the hell are you saying? I've never betrayed anyone in my entire life."

It was the first time he had ever raised his voice with me. In his anger, he jumped up and knocked over the coffee table, spilling books and papers onto the carpet. Watching my research go tumbling, I reacted less in fright than outrage, that he dared, after all he had done, to act like the injured party.

"No? Then what would you call your behavior in Ethiopia?"

"A sacrifice. For the sake of the living." He flopped back onto the couch and sighed, as if irritated to recall the facts of a settled dispute, one that wasn't even worth contesting. "Susanna, those bones of yours have been buried for four million years. Would it have harmed them to stay underground a little while longer? You could have always gone back to dig them out. The Falashas didn't have the luxury of time. Nor, for that matter, did Salik's son in the Sinai."

His rationalizations astounded me. To him, my role was merely to be a sacrifice, no longer Penelope but Iphigenia, offered up to the gods to secure favorable winds to Troy. I hadn't signed up for this. These were not my wars, and he had no right to conscript me.

"What happened to you, Jacob? You used to be charming."

Restoring the table upright, he started picking up the scattered books. "The responsibilities have worn me down." For a moment, he seemed to falter, as if his outburst had exposed some hidden vein of conscience buried deep within. The fury in his face dissipated, and I thought he might deliver a long-delayed apology. Instead, he reminded me of the bargain that had framed our lives together. "I didn't mean to shout, Susanna, but you've always known my priorities. I've never misled you."

If only he could have expressed some remorse, some doubt, I might have relented. Alas, his conformity, and his acquiescence to strange men reaching out over the telephone wire, had always been his tragic flaw. More than anything else, it was what made me decide to leave him.

"It's not a bargain I can live with anymore. I want you out."

He could have argued, he could have pleaded, he could have even begged me to change my mind. He did nothing of the sort.

"Are you sure?"

"Yes, absolutely sure."

He nodded, as if answering a call summoning him off to another war. "Then I'll have to accept your decision."

With a deep breath, he slapped his thighs, as he did when rising from bed each morning and preparing to begin anew. Then he posed an outrageous question. "Do you think I could stay in the basement for a little while, until I find another place to live?"

I would have lashed out again, but my anger was interrupted by the sound of a toilet flushing upstairs. Shally must have heard everything. Despite my fervent efforts, I had failed to protect him. Another reason to hate Jacob for what he had done to us. But to my great surprise, as I prepared to rush up the stairs, I found my husband right behind me, no longer so exhausted.

"What are we going to tell him?" Jacob asked.

"I don't know, but we have to come up with something."

It would have been simpler for me to do it alone, but the terms of our marriage had already granted Jacob far too much freedom to duck his responsibilities. He trailed me up to our son's room, where we found the little boy wrapped in the Snoopy blanket he liked so much. Not even a doting mother could soften this blow. Adults deluded themselves over the impact of their decisions, but a child could carry a lie forever. Shalom deserved better than to hear false hopes.

Sitting on the bed, I stroked his head. "Shally." What I meant in affection came out as a lament. "Do you understand what is happening?"

A little shake of his head. No. For the first time, I wished for him to have a whiff of Jacob's hard edge, or maybe a touch of my willfulness, to steel him against the hurt.

"Shally, your father and I have decided . . ." I paused as my control wavered. "We're going to live apart from now on."

Shally didn't show any anger, sorrow, or even surprise. He simply stared at the wall. "He doesn't like me. That's why he's going away."

"No, no, that's not it at all." I tried to tell him it wasn't his fault, that this was between adults, but Shally looked inured to all comfort, the way I must have seemed when my parents placed me aboard a flight to London. The familiarity of that anguish made me reconsider Jacob's outrageous request, not for our shared, intractable past, but for our separate, still shared future, embodied in the little boy before us. No matter my resentment, I couldn't deny Shally a father. I couldn't repeat my parents' mistake.

"Your father's only moving down to the basement. It won't be so far."

Shally didn't look up. I had seen him sulk before, a baleful gloom settling over him during his father's absences, as if he were absorbing all the disconsolate loneliness into his own chest. Unable to break the spell, I stood paralyzed until the bass timbre of a professional liar shook us from our torpor.

"You can come down any time," Jacob said, reaching down to pat Shally's foot. "We'll give you your own set of keys so you can watch all the cartoons you want. Is Bugs Bunny still your favorite?"

Shally shook his head. "I like 'Underdog.'"

"Okay, Underdog it'll be. Let me move some things, and I'll set up the television downstairs."

Jacob's invitation flouted my restrictions on television time, but an excess of brainless cartoons seemed a petty misdemeanor in this world of murderous passions. The prospect of "Underdog" even drew a little smile from Shalom, who checked the clock and bounded out of bed to seek his father's permission.

"Can I go now? It's coming on soon."

Jacob deferred to me, and I lacked the heart to object. As our son scrambled downstairs, we were left to contemplate the future over his empty bed.

"So I can stay?" Jacob asked at last.

"We can try it, as long as we establish clear boundaries about your presence."

The idea of "boundaries" seemed to trouble him. He repeated the word, ruminated over it, as if wistful. To make myself clear, I defined a Berlin Wall-style separation, barring him from ever crossing my threshold. There would be no showing up uninvited in the parlor, no poking about the kitchen, no ordering around Shalom in my presence.

"All right, I will honor your boundaries. You have my word."

It took Jacob little more than an hour to load ten years of marriage into a few suitcases, as if he were merely going on a longer trip than usual. After carting his bags down to the basement, Jacob returned to our bedroom one last time before the new boundaries were locked in place.

"Would you mind if I take this with me?" He reached up to remove the *ketubah* from the wall. I couldn't imagine why he would want it. He could barely even enunciate the words, much less respect its deeper meaning.

"What for? Its terms are null and void now."

"You know I'm a nostalgic guy."

Take it and be gone, I thought. He carried our marriage contract downstairs with him, leaving behind a faded mark on the wall that looked like a spot of pale flesh rarely exposed to sunlight. At some point I would replace it, but for now the empty space signified the end of our days together. I had no doubt about my ability to reconstruct a life without him. What I refused to do was to give in to nostalgia. No, nostalgia would only have convinced me to trust in the lies of a man as elusive as the roots of language.

27

Lower Manhattan
October 19, 1996

As the Scrotum Tighteners cranked out their set, I ushered the African Refugee Mega-Stars through a roiling mob of slam-dancing teenagers. The onslaught of a hardcore punk band must have shocked the Mega-Stars, but I couldn't worry about offending their aesthetic sensibilities. This was our big chance, a Saturday night slot at CBGB's. We couldn't afford anything to go wrong.

Reaching the safety of the green room, the Mega-Stars looked as if they had survived a traumatic ordeal. Clutching his sax, Ismael put off his elaborate ritual of preparing his instrument for the show. Delacroix stroked his conga drum and tried to comprehend why, in a world of unremitting violence, American youth would hurl their bodies at each other with such rage.

"Shalom, tell us the purpose of this terrible music," Delacroix asked. "Those young men play their instruments as if they are angry with them, and the singer is shouting at the audience."

Pascal, shielded behind his shades, was equally perplexed, "The way they dance does not allow the men to get close to the women."

I didn't have time to define the punk zeitgeist. We had to focus on the challenge at hand. "Don't worry about those kids. They're not our audience. We have our own people showing up in force, dying to hear us play."

"Our people will be deaf by the time I begin to sing."

"Come on, Pascal, don't be so negative. This is our night. Let's have a show to remember."

Pascal didn't appreciate how difficult it had been to secure this booking. He didn't care how it had taken every ounce of my persistence and a few more ounces of my weed, and even then we'd been bumped three times by bigger acts. With the moment finally upon us, I thought about the old adage passed on by Mercedes, that most bands drew their biggest crowd at their CB's debut. Leaving the guys backstage, I went out to check on the response to my promotional campaign. The seeds of a strong crowd stood clustered by the bar, where our supporters were spared the mayhem of the mosh pit. After greeting a few fans, I spotted a guy dressed in biker boots and leather jacket, with long strands of stringy hair, leaning over a loaded blonde stuffed into a tight mini-skirt. It was Tommy Oppenheim, scout for one of the record labels and a former college classmate of mine. For all his biker regalia and bad manners, Tommy was a son of privilege, rich enough to have started his own record company. When I called his name, he left off scoping his girl's thighs and turned to me with a discernible lack of surprise.

"Hey Sha-loam-me, what's going on? The last I heard, you were hooked up with a medicine man in the jungle."

It wasn't exactly a happy memory, my ill-conceived venture to send narco-tourists to the Amazon to sample ayahuasca with an enterprising shaman. "Ancient history, Tommy. Actually I have a band coming up next: the African Refugee Mega-Stars."

"Those are your guys? The Refugees?"

"Yeah. They're hot. You should stick around."

"World Music's not my thing. The label gave me responsibility over the punk acts, and some hip-hop too. We signed the Scrotum Tighteners last week."

It didn't surprise me that Tommy had stoked the punk furies into a cash machine. Even in college, he had tapped into the mainline between profit and vice, investing in overpriced concert tickets and scalping them to kids on financial aid. Winning over a mercenary scumbag like Tommy required me to speak his language. He would never buy into what attracted me to the Mega-Stars: that a visionary band of African *salseros* could suspend tribal feuds, promote reconciliation, and provide a sanctuary from the loneliness of human existence. The only thing that impressed Tommy was money.

"It's your loss," I told him. "I bet the guy who repped Buena Vista Social Club is living large on a beach somewhere. They sold a ton of records."

By this time, the Scrotum Tighteners were winding down, and like water pouring down a drain, the punk crowd disappeared from the club, not even curious as to what the Mega-Stars might sound like.

Tommy stretched his arm fully around his girlfriend to check his watch. "All right, tell your guys to bust a move. I've got a Japanese hip-hop act to catch in Chelsea."

"It won't be long. Let me try to speed things along."

Hustling back to the green room, I found the Mega-Stars huddled together, still traumatized, warily waiting for their turn on stage.

"Big news, *compañeros*. There's a music industry rep out there who's dying to hear you play."

My announcement lifted the mood. Shaking off their unease, the guys pressed me for details on what other acts Tommy had signed, what kind of sound he preferred. Delacroix rubbed his hands. "This is very exciting, Shalom. To have this man in attendance is very good news." Even Ismael put down his sax and locked in on my every word. For their benefit, I offered an unusual bit of insight:

"There's something else you should know. Tommy has a big pair of balls, and I mean really huge." I cupped my hands for dramatic effect. "Back in school, he used to show them off at parties. That's what made him successful: a willingness to take risks."

In reality, I couldn't recall a single risk ever taken by rich boy Tommy, or anything notable about him at all, beyond the famed testicles, which truly were the size of grapefruits, far more male genitalia than I ever cared to see. Those balls, however, served as a symbol of the potential at hand.

The guys all rushed to get ready—except, that is, for Pascal. His legs crossed, he lounged in his chair and smoked calmly, the cigarette ash tripping out onto the floor.

"Come on, Pascal, we don't have much time. The guy's going to bolt."

He took a long drag and exhaled slowly. "Shalom, you do not understand anything about performing. The audience must feel fortunate to hear our music. We should not appear until the people are shouting our names."

It had always seemed counterproductive to bait the paying customer. Tonight, given the fleeting nature of our opportunity, it was positively self-destructive.

"Pascal, they don't even know your name. How can they shout it out?"

He breathed out a fresh lungful of smoke. "We cannot change to please your man. If he leaves before hearing us, he was never serious to begin with."

For months, Pascal had pestered me about a record deal. Now, as the brass ring dangled within reach, he wanted to screw around.

"Fuck it. We can't blow this," I told the rest of the guys. "If Pascal doesn't want to go out, we'll just have to start without him. Let him stay here and play with himself."

If my outburst accomplished one thing, it was to propel Pascal out of his chair. "If you want this man with the big testicles to treat you with respect, then you must stop running to him like a servant. You must grow some balls of your own."

I slugged him. Hard. Around the eye. Dad's old boxing lessons came back to me as muscle memory. As soon as my fist met Pascal's temple, knocking off his sunglasses and laying him out flat, the green room seemed to implode. A dozen arms reached for me. Everyone started yelling in languages I didn't understand.

At the heart of the scrum, Delacroix wedged his body between us and bellowed for peace. "Shalom, are you mad? Do you want to destroy everything we have created?" His hand planted into my sternum, he propelled me backward. "This is not how civilized men should act."

Before I could issue a single word of apology, I felt someone grab my shoulders and wrest me toward the door. It turned out to be Ismael, his saxophone dangling from his neck like a giant medallion. With one hand he steadied the horn, with the other he shoved me through the exit: "Get out. Now. And be glad that you did not strike Pascal in the mouth. At least he will still be able sing tonight."

Lifting my arms in surrender, I accepted the terms of my expulsion. Skulking out of the green room, I felt the entire club glaring at me, annoyed over the delay and the presumption we were wasting their time. All I could do was pray that the sound of our scrap hadn't reached Tommy.

It was after midnight, well into our appointed slot, and I had no idea whether the band would actually emerge from the green room. When the door opened, the African Refugee Mega-Stars trickled out, somber and brooding, making a forced march to the stage. There was no waving to friends or clapping hands to stir up the crowd. As Ousmane and Abdoulaye tuned guitar and bass, Pascal sulked in the shadows, hiding behind the sunglasses that somehow had survived the altercation. I started to despair that the evening was lost, when Ismael stepped into the void, kissed his horn, and belted out the beginning of "Dounya." His sax sizzling in the bright lights, he powered through the melody as if it were a narrow escape from rising floodwater. Smiling after every burst, he shook his head, his face alternately amazed and outraged, pleading and perplexed, drawing the crowd toward the pied piper of Dakar. A whole raft of our supporters surged forward. It wasn't just his countrymen, but a column of world music fans we had collected along the way. The crowd jumped and swirled, led by two hippy ladies wearing cork-soled sandals. All the rancor of backstage fell away.

I glanced over at Tommy. His attention had moved from his girlfriend's ass to her chest, the wrong direction for us, since now he could bury his whole face in her. My only recourse was to intervene before that piece of shit missed the entire set. Snaking through the crowd, I reached the bar as Ismael's sax embarked on a call-and-response with Ousmane's guitar.

"Be sure you catch the great Ismael Camara," I said, leaning against the bar. "He's a fucking genius: Cuban salsa interwoven with traditional African melodies. People used to stand in the rain to hear him play in Senegal."

Uncurling from his girl, Tommy glanced at the stage. "Too bad we're not in Senegal."

Right on cue, Pascal came in with the vocals and began wagging his finger at the audience to testify to his conviction, that the singer of odes speaks the truth in his heart.

"Who the fuck is he shaking his finger at?" Tommy asked.

"It's a cultural thing, his way of shouting out to the audience."

"What's the song about?" Tommy's blonde asked, embarrassed by her boyfriend's behavior. She seemed polite enough, so I made some shit up.

"It's about the persecution of his people, like Marley's 'Redemption Song.' Listen to that voice; you can just hear the sorrow."

"He sounds constipated to me," Tommy said.

I could have decked him, but my fist still ached from its dance with Pascal's cheekbone.

A Senegalese watch dealer jumped up on stage with a wad of dollar bills, which he flicked one by one at the band. Ismael found this ritual crass, erasing the line between artist and servant, but Pascal gobbled up the attention. He bit at the bills like a snapping turtle, before they fluttered away and left him with a mouthful of air.

"What does he think this is: a strip club?" Tommy asked. Fucking comedian.

"Tommy, stop," his girl said, pushing him. "Be nice."

I wanted to explain it as a sign of respect, but Tommy wouldn't have understood.

The watch seller pressed a bill to Ismael's forehead as if taking the measure of a fever, while the real heat was building inside me. I had sacrificed too much to let this evening go to waste. When Tommy rose to leave, I stepped close enough to chomp my teeth into his neck, a level of intimacy that nearly matched his position with his girl.

"What ever happened to those big balls of yours, Tommy? Do you really want someone else to take these guys to the top?"

"Hey, your friend on the sax can bring it, but like I said, world music's not my thing. I gotta pass."

If I could purge one euphemism from the English language, and impose a beat-down on anyone who dared utter it: it was this particular usage of "pass." Tell me to fuck off, admit to being a closed-minded jackass, or to being afraid of Africans, but don't tempt fate by "passing." In honor of my mother, who had instilled in me the power of diction, and my father, who had instructed me not to take shit from anyone, I reached down to squeeze Tommy's big balls. He bounced around, but, trapped against the bar, all he could do was to knock a stool onto his girlfriend's leg. She cried out in pain, giving him an opening to scamper away, "passing" right out of the club. His departure turned what should have been a triumph—our biggest crowd to date, a strong show built upon a shaky opening—into an abject failure. Terrible as it was to admit: Pascal had been right all along. Groveling before an industry rep revealed only our weakness and despair.

Tears overcame me. Thankfully, the crowd was too caught up in the music to notice. Defeated again, I could barely appreciate Ismael hitting the heights of his "Coumba." His thunderous finish was met by riotous calls for an encore. Alas, our time was up, and the next band was itching for its turn. I had done all I could.

28

Mugunga Refugee Camp, Zaire
October 19, 1996

DUDU LUMBERED DOWN THE FIELD, SHOUTING AT THE ORPHANS to pass the fucking ball. Who knew whether they followed his stew of Russian and Arabic curses, but the louder he yelled, the faster they ran, the higher they jumped, the quicker they kicked the soccer ball to their teammates. Somehow, he had managed, as if by magic, to transform their disjointed rabble into an organized team. The rumor that he had trained the Italians, reinforced by his red-and-black-striped shirt with the name "Weah" on back, seemed to have had a powerful motivating effect.

"It is hard to believe how much he has accomplished," Dr. Chantal said, standing on the sidelines beside me. "I never thought the boys would listen to him."

The doctor, still wearing her white coat, had joined me for the practice, happy to reminisce about her life in Butare, before the war, watching her brother play football.

"It's true. Dudu has a way of making himself heard," I said.

He divided the squad into two sides for a scrimmage, and let them loose. There was a scramble for possession until that little devil Fulgence broke free with the ball and streaked away from his pursuers.

"He's a real mosquito, that one."

"We do not like mosquitoes very much," the doctor said with a slight smile. "They are responsible for spreading malaria."

"I'm not sure how much I like Fulgence either."

As two defenders tried to tackle him, Fulgence shot the ball between the goalposts of sticks wrapped in white plastic. In celebration, he held his arms open like Atlas while his teammates jumped on his shoulders. Even the doctor let out a cheer, which she quickly covered with her hands, the thrill cut short by the arrival of two pickup trucks.

The vehicles rolled right out onto the little field, and from the flatbeds jumped a dozen men clothed in scraps of military apparel. A few had on army shirts, others wore combat boots, and they all waved machetes and spears. Forming a dense, chanting pack, they swept up the soccer boys into their angry parade.

"What do these jackasses think they're doing?" I said, starting toward them.

Dr. Chantal tugged hard on my arm. Her tenderness had turned to desperation. "Please, do not approach them," she said. "We must leave right away."

"Why should we leave? They're the ones interrupting practice."

The sound of their chorus made her shudder. "What those men are singing is . . . it is what they sang when they went . . ." she paused, searching for the right word, "when they went hunting, during the genocide."

It was the first time I had heard anyone this side of the border use the term "genocide." From her lips, the word sounded heavier than ever.

One of the men, a big goon wearing the same colored soccer shirt as Dudu over his camouflage pants, broke away from the pack. He shouted something at Dr. Chantal that seemed to stun her. Her mouth snapped shut, her shoulders looked weighed down by a heavy sack.

"Chantal, who is that man?"

"His name is Gescard Mbarushimana," she said without looking up. "He had been a friend of my brother Michel. They played football together, until Gescard brought the Interahamwe to our house. He is the one who murdered my brother, when Michel refused to join them against the Tutsis."

As the thugs rolled along the field, singing their songs, dancing like conquerors, I called out to Dudu, standing with the soccer ball against his hip.

"We better go. The doctor says these are the genocidaires, and this song puts them in a killing mood."

Dudu didn't have any rooting interest in Hutu or Tutsi, but it bothered him to abandon his team. "We can't leave the boys here, Aba."

"Come on, the doctor's worried. There's nothing we can do for them anymore."

"*Cus emek. Ben-zona,*" he grumbled, flinging the soccer ball at their line. It didn't weigh much, but the marchers jumped out of the way.

We had turned back toward the tents when Germaine appeared, charging across the field with the force of a river. She passed us without word, perhaps without even noticing our calls to stop. So focused was she on the loss of her boys that she pressed straight toward the center of the phalanx.

Heading after her, Dudu paused only to call back. "Wait here, Aba. I'll help Germaine with the boys."

"I'm coming too."

"No, you stay with the doctor. She needs you more than I do."

Turning around, I saw Dr. Chantal staring at her feet, too frightened even to formulate an objection.

"Don't worry, I'll be right back," I told her, feeling an echo of every time I had abandoned the women in my life. Susanna had never forgiven me for my choices. With Judith, I had never forgiven myself. And now my reassurances to Chantal sounded as empty as any I had ever issued.

Rushing across the field, we caught up to Germaine as she confronted the mob.

"We must have our boys back," she said. "They cannot miss their afternoon lessons."

The genocidaires seemed gleeful, as if our presence was cause for celebration. Their circle tightened around us until their chief, Gescard, pushed through the ranks.

"The boys will stay with us now. We have other things to teach them."

His men seemed to find this funny, as did the soccer players now interspersed among them.

"These boys have lost too much already," she said. "Give them a chance to learn something besides war, so that one day they can help rebuild your country."

Her words cut off the laughter, as if she had sucked the oxygen from a fire. For a moment no one said anything, and I clenched my fists to prepare for the confrontation. It would have only taken a whisper to set off an explosion, but Gescard suddenly stepped away and waved his hand in concession, a signal that Germaine took to gather her boys. Soon she had accounted for the entire team, except for one.

"Where is Fulgence?" she called out. "I must have Fulgence too."

"Him we need for our football squad," Gescard said.

Germaine would not be moved. After a shove and a few more laughs, the little mosquito emerged from hiding. Before we could turn away, the Interahamwe struck up another song, which made Germaine jolt around again.

"Gentlemen, this is no place for rallies. We will lose our funding if we allow any political demonstrations."

His patience failing, Gescard sneered. "But who will know we are here?"

"God will know, as well as the donors who generously provide our assistance." She motioned in my direction, casting me as the big shot who filled the aid pipeline. As the killers turned my way, I tried to mimic the arrogance of the rich donors corralled by Salik. My act must have been credible enough, because Gescard called off his men and they took their rally elsewhere.

The soccer boys groaned and griped, and Germaine tried to shush them, but they resisted until Dudu offered some consolation. "Come on, you nudniks. Football will be there later. Let's see how the girls are doing with the Shakespeare."

The promise of engaging a tent full of actresses helped the boys shake off the disappointment. As they joined their coach in a rush to rehearsal, Germaine called out for them not to interfere with the girls' lines.

Rejoining Dr. Chantal by the sideline, I offered her my arm for the walk back to her clinic. With her clinging tight to me, we must have looked like a couple of lovers, stumbling across the volcanic rocks that left no footprints behind. She watched her every step, as if worried the earth itself might swallow her up.

When we reached her examining room, I needed to find out why the incident had seemed to crush her. "Dr. Chantal, what did that man call out to you on the field?"

Shushing me, she hurriedly checked the ward for eavesdroppers. It all seemed quiet, as if the camp was still brooding after the genocidaire flare-up. Then she spoke at such a low level that I had to read her lips to confirm her words.

"He reminded me of my part in the genocide."

"Your part? What did you do?"

"I treated the Interahamwe who came to the hospital. They had only minor injuries—twisted ankles, lacerations from a stray machete, dehydration—but I did not refuse them."

"Didn't your oath as a physician compel you to treat their wounds?"

"Of course, but if I had turned them away, more of their victims might have escaped."

Considering the vast number of souls filling this city of tents, I wondered how many would have expressed the slightest pinprick of contrition, confessed the tiniest droplet of sin. At least in Chantal's case, there were mitigating factors.

"No one could blame you for what happened. It must have been absolute chaos," I said. "If you'd like, I could try to arrange safe passage back to your old hospital in Butare. I'm sure they'd be happy to have you."

It was a rash offer, one that exceeded my rights. Dr. Chantal shook her head. "No, no. I cannot leave. I am responsible here."

"Responsible? For what?"

"Someone must tend to the sick and the injured. I could not stop Gescard and his men during the genocide, but they also could not interfere with my vow as a healer. Not then, and not now."

The slight billowing of the tent made her look sharply around. It was nothing. No one was listening. No one but me.

"Why are you telling me all this?" I asked.

"It was important for me to inform someone, before it's too late, and you seem to have come to pass judgment on us."

"You make me sound like King Solomon. Do I seem that old?"

"No, not that old." She smiled, that lovely coy smile of hers. Then something changed, the warmth vanished, her focus hardened, steeling herself to loss. "I'm sorry, Mr. Jacob, I must return to my patients. It was irresponsible of me to abandon them to watch the football practice."

It had taken me until now to realize that nothing would happen between us. Nothing could happen, given the vast difference in age. Old fool that I was, I had read her all wrong. She was a professional, devoted to her art; how could she be enticed by an *alter kocker muzungu* suffering from stress? With my treatment now complete, there wasn't any further reason to stay.

In the classroom, I found Dudu standing guard while Germaine assigned the boys to parts in *The Tempest*. Making fun of the girls as they rehearsed, the soccer players didn't seem terribly serious about the project.

"Come on, let's go," I said, pulling Dudu outside. "We've spent enough time in this hellhole."

"What now, Aba? You want to go back to the hotel to stare at the lake?"

"Better that than to dig ourselves in any deeper here. "

The ladies of Blessed Relief would have to solve their own problems. We had never had any business getting involved. It sure wasn't part of the proposition Salik had laid out before me, and truth be told, it couldn't be seen kindly by our Tutsi friends, who even now were fighting to liberate North Kivu.

Dudu didn't give a shit about the politics of this place. His only response was to shrug and to start back toward Mugunga's main gate, where Patrice had parked his car. We walked in silence; but before reaching the entrance, we passed the Interahamwe's café, now filled with the same thugs who had invaded the football field.

"Let's have a beer," Dudu said, stopping before them.

"Here? Are you crazy?"

"You're always asking how these guys could have killed so many people. Now's your chance to ask them."

Dudu strode right into the café, invited himself to a central table, and called out to the waiter wearing a zebra-striped shirt: "Hey, Baggio, bring beer for everyone."

Within moments of his invitation, we found ourselves surrounded by new friends, with more arriving every minute. Showing up with the new wave was Gescard, the killer of Chantal's brother. He was thicker around the upper chest than most of his compatriots, not fat so much as fit, and he squeezed my hand hard enough to leave an impression. In my day, I would have leveled him with a left uppercut. Now was not the time to start a brawl. Not here, on their field.

Dudu stood for a toast: "To football."

The whole crowd agreed, and Gescard, captain of their team, presented his best players: the balding banana farmer Ignace who was a midfielder, and their striker Pio, a former university student.

"What about the goalie? Where is your goalie?" Dudu asked.

"We don't have a regular goalie anymore," the ex-student said. "What about you? They say you played in Italy. Why don't you be our goalie?"

Dudu smacked Pio's bottle with his own, sending beer frothing over the top. "You guys don't know anything about football. All you know is killing."

The chatter stopped. The phony camaraderie dissipated. The men all stood to defend themselves, crowding around us and protesting angrily, until Dudu let out a huge laugh and slapped Pio's back so hard that the kid nearly smashed his face into the table.

"It's a joke. Can't you take a joke?" He called for more beer, and the Hutus demanded Dudu tell them exactly what he had heard.

"They say you guys fucked up the others, what you call them, Tutsis?"

The Interahamwe started shouting again until Dudu jumped up and jerked his arms wildly, like Samson shaking off his chains.

"Don't yell at me. I don't care about this. All I know is what Jacob tells me."

Everyone turned to me. In this moment, I recognized one mandate: not to bullshit them. Like angry dogs, they would sense any whiff of fear or deceit. All I could do was speak the truth, and trust that my age and my fortitude would hold off their machetes.

"Look, I've seen plenty of war. You kill your enemy before he kills you. But not the women and children, not the civilians."

I left out the magic word, genocide, but even so they were all over me, yelling on top of each other, making it hard to distinguish who was saying what, until Gescard made them pipe down. He put his hand on my wrist, both as vise and guide.

"Let me instruct you what happened. The Tutsi cockroaches shot down the president's plane. We had to fight back. We could not let them take over the country." He went on to justify the genocide, arguing some horseshit about how the Tutsis had always acted superior to the Hutus. "They had their cattle and their property, and they wanted to control everything. I tell you this: what we did to them, they would have done to us."

His men kept quiet, bored by a lecture heard a thousand times. Gescard pressed on until Dudu slapped his hands on the table.

"Enough of this shit. Who cares what you did or the others did? All I want is more beer."

The rest of the crowd sided with Dudu. Better a fresh drink than an old argument. Armed with a new bottle, Dudu offered up a toast. "To war."

The whole place paused a moment, then exploded in laughter as they finally caught on to the crazy *muzungu*. Then Dudu pounded his chest and demanded they clear space to wrestle. Promising not to use his arms, he called for Gescard to step forward, but the big bully wasn't going to risk being humiliated in a fair fight, so the banana farmer Ignace agreed to Dudu's rumble. The boys moved the tables, and Dudu slapped his hands together and came at the farmer in a furious burst, his arms trailing behind like the tail of a leopard. With a great heave, he jolted Ignace back, pressed him to the ground, and flopped on top of him, pinning him with his shoulders alone. It didn't take long for the guy to surrender.

Dudu lifted his fists and roared in victory. This was the moment when he usually pulled up his sleeve and narrated the stories of his tattoos, finding some new lesson to draw from the death of his friends. Not this time. Instead, he called for a cigarette. I had never known him to be a smoker, but he puffed a few times to get the flame going.

"Watch this."

He held the cigarette aloft, the magician showing he had nothing up his sleeve, and as his audience accepted the offer, he plunked the lit end straight down into his fist, directly onto the big knuckle. The sound of crinkling skin reached us before the smell, a wisp as the cigarette burned itself out, the rare moment when flesh extinguished fire. The Interahamwe, for all the blood they had spilled, started shrieking, jostling each other to examine Dudu's wound, questioning whether it was real.

"You see, no pain. Pain is all in the mind," Dudu said, tapping on his coconut, which sounded more hollow than usual.

A few of the genocidaires tried to repeat the trick, but each screeched at the first application of fire. These bastards only knew how to inflict pain, not to absorb it.

"You are crazy," Pio said.

"Well, maybe a little. Now, teach me that fucking song of yours," Dudu said, "the one from the football pitch."

They kicked off their hunting anthem, loud and raucous, like *Horst Wessel* must have sounded in Vienna after the Nazi Anschluss. Dudu tried to repeat their words, but his pronunciation sent them into hysterics. Then Pio, the one-time student, asked for one of our songs.

"What you think, Jacob?" Dudu asked, "Should we try *Kol Haolam Kulo?*"

I had witnessed terrible things in my life: camps filled with the dying, villages hounded by their enemies, and soldiers sacrificed for the greater good, or for no good at all. Through all this, I had never considered teaching a Hebraic ballad to a group of genocidal killers. Before I could object, Dudu started belting out the first two verses, slow and deep:

> *Kol ha-olam kulo, gesher tsar m'od, gesher tsar m'od, gesher tsar m'od,*
> *Kol ha-olam kulo, gesher tsar m'od, gesher tsar m'od, gesher tsar m'od,*

Waving his hands like an orchestra conductor, he urged them onto their feet, and soon we had formed a stumbling circle of drunks, our arms wrapped around each other's shoulders, dancing Hassidische style, going faster and louder and more militant.

V'ha'ikar, v'ha'ikar. Lo lefached, lo lefached klal
V'ha'ikar, v'ha'ikar. Lo lefached klal

After a couple more circles, my heart could take no more. Not indigestion this time, but a deeper kind of ache, from the sense we were dancing on the Tutsi graves. Of all the songs to choose, we should never have lit on this particular message: "The whole world is a very narrow bridge, and the most important thing is not to be afraid."

Reclaiming the privilege of age, I settled into a chair and regretted ever agreeing to have passed through the gates of Mugunga. It was too late now. A decision made in expedience could not be undone.

By the time we staggered out of the café, Dudu was barely coherent. He stopped in an intersection of lanes, steadied himself, and plucked out his prick to piss. As the flow started, he stuck his burned hand into the stream.

"What the fuck are you doing?"

"Disinfecting the wound." He wagged his pecker and flipped it back in his pants.

"You stupid idiot, we're lucky you didn't get us killed."

"You have to take chances if you want to learn something."

"So why didn't you show them your tattoo and give them one of your lectures about the futility of war?"

Dudu waved his hand to dry it. "They would have taken the wrong lesson."

The wrong lesson was a grave danger on this field of compromise. It wouldn't affect me, however. Decades of guiding the lost across the desert had taught me how to distinguish between an oasis and a mirage. Our friends in Blessed Relief, for all their good intentions, couldn't make out the difference. The only resolution now was for the Tutsis to clear the place out, punish the guilty and send the innocent home.

PART 4

29

Brooklyn
January 26, 1997

I WOKE UP SHIVERING TO THE FAINT SOUND OF MY NAME. THE bedroom was freezing, a result of leaving the window open after I dragged myself home from Mia's at 3:00 A.M. Hearing someone call for me again, I draped the blanket around my shoulders like a cape and stuck my head outside. Downstairs, waiting on the stoop, the African Refugee Mega-Stars had gathered for a rare morning rehearsal. Shit. I had completely forgotten.

"Shalom, come open the door," Delacroix called up. "It's cold out here."

The image of the Mega-Stars huddled together in the snow provided the perfect metaphor for a band on ice. Our CBGB debut had been the apex of our downtown career, confirming the theory that all bands were in constant motion, either expanding or contracting. There was no doubt of our current direction: condemned to anemic weeknight shows in one measly club after another, our audiences diminishing with time.

"Hang on. I'll be right down."

Creeping past Mom's bedroom, I noticed her light still burning. She was sleeping less than ever these days, spending all night reading while I wandered the city trying to make inroads for the Mega-Stars. On the stoop outside, I found the guys clustered together for warmth. We had scheduled practice for before our bassist Abdoulaye, fresh from a graveyard shift at the nursing home, crashed for the day. Unlike my mother, he could seize any moment for a restorative nap. Two weeks earlier he had nodded off during a set, throwing off the beat until Delacroix reached over his congas to nudge him awake.

Ismael dabbed his finger against his watch. "Shalom, what's wrong with you? We are already one half-hour past the arranged time." He didn't look happy. Then again, Ismael rarely looked happy these days.

"Yeah, sorry about that. I had to work late." None of them needed to know my business, a succession of deliveries capped off with a visit to Mia.

"No more wasting time," Ismael said. "We must practice to improve on our recent performances. This sloppy play cannot continue."

Most of the mistakes had crept in when Pascal forgot the lyrics or missed his cues. Ismael would have booted him, but Delacroix counseled patience, giving him a second chance that Pascal was working hard to blow, arriving late and acting bored, conducting business on his cellphone right before showtime. True to form, as everyone else assembled on the stoop, Pascal had failed to show up.

"Okay, *compañeros*, you go ahead and get started downstairs. I need to check in on my mom. She's been having trouble sleeping lately."

Delacroix milled his hands together, warding off the cold. "Shalom, you should have informed us that your mother would be present. We would not have agreed to begin so early."

Even on this frigid morning, Delacroix looked sharp, his suit freshly pressed, his necktie tightly knotted. Ever since the big fight at CBGB, he had been all business. He no longer shared with me the horrors of his work investigating war crimes. Nor did he show up early to confide how the job disrupted his sleep. It was as if my aggression toward Pascal had placed me in the ranks of those who degraded human life, and nothing I did could restore me to the realm of the righteous.

"Don't worry, Dela. My mom said it would be fine. She loves listening to you guys rehearse."

It was true that Mom had given her blessing for an early morning practice, but that was before the latest dose of chemotherapy plunged her into an epic battle against nausea and insomnia. She had been too exhausted lately to focus on her writing, much less to plan her grand conference on the evolution of language. Absent any guiding hand, the project was turning into a big mess. Letters piled up downstairs. E-mails went unanswered. She didn't discuss it with me, however, not after I made clear my determination to have no part in the event.

On this frigid morning, a good son would have apologized to the Mega-Stars and scrubbed the rehearsal. Instead, I handed over the keys to the basement and trudged back upstairs to rouse a woman for whom sleep was often tantalizingly out of reach. Cracking open her bedroom door, I found my mother passed out among her papers, lying sideways across the bed. The scarf had slipped off, leaving her head uncovered. The shock of her bald scalp made me question once again what the hell I was doing.

"Mom?"

She didn't respond, so I called out again. Stirring, she let out a slow slurp.

"Oh, Shally, I must have dozed off. Is it late?"

"Don't worry, Mom. It's only 9:30."

"Already? That's no good. I have so much to get through today."

She patted the bed for her scarf and saddled it unevenly over her head. The sight would have been clownish if it were not so tragic.

"Can I bring you something to eat, Mom?"

She gripped the edge of the bed as if steadying herself. "Oh no, not now. I still feel terribly nauseated."

I had offered her ganja a dozen times, but she always declined, apologizing that she was too old to recast herself as a bohemian. The longer I watched her, rubbing her eyes, adjusting her scarf, the more I hated myself.

"Mom, I need to ask you something."

Her chin dipped, signaling not assent but a nod back into sleep, before she jerked herself awake again. "Yes, of course, what is it?"

"Would it be all right if we started practice early today?"

"Practice?"

"Yeah, we talked about it a couple of days ago, a special rehearsal for the band, right after our bassist gets off his overnight shift."

Her perplexed look made me wonder whether the cancer had affected her cognition.

"If you're not up for it, that's all right," I said, trying to sound helpful.

"No, no, it will be fine. You go ahead with your friends." She reached across the bed for a stack of papers, recovered her glasses from the far pillow, and returned to reading. Her blessing confirmed me as both coward and louse.

"We won't be long," I said, lying to her yet again. "We'll try to keep it down."

Already I could hear the snap of Robbie's timbales and the thump of Abdoulaye's bass warming up a cold morning. In five more minutes, the noise would be loud enough to rattle paint off the walls. This rehearsal might have been the most misguided, reprobate act of my useless life. And yet I couldn't help myself. Things just happened that way.

30

**Brooklyn
January 26, 1997**

THE JOURNEY BACK FROM AFRICA ENDED WITH A SMOOTH landing at Kennedy Airport. The other passengers broke into applause, but this final crossing had been the least of my trials. I had survived bad roads and creaky airplanes, lumpy beds and rotten food, the smell of shit and the sight of death. Now it was over.

Taxiing to the gate, I spotted traces of snow on the tarmac and steam rising from the ground crew. Two seasons had passed since my departure, and I didn't have clothes for a New York winter. It didn't matter. A few minutes shivering wouldn't kill me. Having nothing to declare at customs, I passed through the terminal and met the driver sent by Effie to carry me the rest of the way home. He was a Russian who we had helped to emigrate decades ago, and he recognized me to be in no mood for conversation.

As the car reached our stoop, I felt a shudder in the air that seemed to be coming from my basement, of all places. So much for finding peace at last. Strange black curtains blocked me from peeking inside my apartment, so I fished out my keys and opened the door. A wave of sound and a plume of smoke overwhelmed me on entry. What I found inside was a full band assembled where my sitting chairs had been. My furniture was piled high against the corner, and the floor was covered in muck. It looked like the wreckage left after battle, something all too fresh in my mind.

The musicians—who I took to be the Africa Rumba Express—stopped playing as soon as I entered, but none of them spoke until my son approached with one arm twisted behind his back.

"Hey, Dad, welcome home. I almost didn't recognize you with that beard."

"What the hell is going on here?"

Shalom dabbed out his joint and waved his hands to disperse the smoke. "Well, you were gone, so Mom said it was all right to use your place to practice. We can clear out if you want."

It was such a ridiculous situation that I wondered whether Dudu might appear from the back, laughing at the joke. That was impossible, of course. There was no use in talking to my son, so I directed my attention to the musicians who waited in a state of suspended shock.

"Good morning, gentlemen. We're finished here, okay. Maybe Shalom didn't tell you, but I've been gone a long time, and now I'd like to get some rest."

A well-dressed fellow with a shaved head stood up from the drums and approached me in apology. "Please, Monsieur, do not be angry with your son. Instruct us in the proper placement of your furniture, and we will restore your apartment as quickly as possible."

At my direction, the drummer organized his compatriots to unplug instruments, roll up cords, and pack up equipment. They moved efficiently, like an army breaking camp. I couldn't blame them for taking advantage of my absence. It was my son who had invited them inside. And now, instead of pitching in, Shalom lounged in one of my broken chairs and waited for me to address him. Fed up with his nonsense, I picked up my bag and headed toward the bedroom.

"Dad, you might not want to go back there." Shalom tried to block the doorway, beyond which glowed a strange light. I brushed past him to find my bedroom transformed into a greenhouse, marijuana plants spreading across the floor. A string of lamps beamed down on the nursery.

"What the fuck have you done?"

"It's just a little side-project of mine. In another few weeks, I would have had it all harvested. These plants are nearing the end of their growing cycle."

What an imbecile he had turned out to be. I could have put up with his failed enterprises: filling the pipe dreams of these musicians or transporting hippies into the jungle to drink some shaman's brew. But this kind of risk was unforgivable. If the Feds had found him maintaining a pot plantation, they could have seized the entire brownstone.

"You really are a worthless piece of shit," I told him.

He sank to the floor, his legs buckling beneath him. "I know."

I couldn't decide which bothered me more, that he had wrecked my apartment or that he conceded to his own ineptitude. His behavior did have one benefit. It gave me an excuse to revisit the boundaries of my old agreement with Susanna.

"All right, start getting all this shit out of here. I'm going upstairs to ask your mother if I can borrow her shower."

He looked up at me. The mention of Susanna turned him serious for the first time. "When did you last speak to Mom?"

"Just after I left."

"Then you don't know she's sick."

"Sick, what's wrong?"

"It's cancer." He spat out the news. "Melanoma. It's spread all over. She's been in chemo for months."

Coming home, I had hoped to start anew, to forget what had happened. Instead, what faced me was the worst blow yet.

"If that's the case, what are you doing down here blasting music?"

He covered his face in his hands. "This is how she wanted it, for everything to continue as normal."

Through the years, the brownstone had always been my sanctuary, where I could take refuge among my family, even if it meant being exiled to the basement. Now it had all changed, just as I had changed too.

"Why didn't you contact me? Effie could have tracked me down."

My words must have reopened an old wound, because Shalom jumped up and rushed at me. Standing chest to chest, I could see he had filled out, but his balance was off. He never had learned a damn thing about fighting.

"Track you down?" he shouted in my face. "When did you ever give a shit about us? You couldn't clear out fast enough whenever the phone rang."

I was angry enough to belt him, lay him out cold. No, we had wasted too much time already.

"Where is she?"

"She was in bed an hour ago. Her insomnia's been bad lately."

"And this little performance down here is what you might call a lullaby?"

He sank back to the floor and banged his head against the wall. Pathetic.

Leaving him to begin cleaning, I hurried up the stoop to the front door. Our separation had never been so bitter that Susanna felt compelled to change the locks, and I had always respected the territorial limits dividing us. Until now.

"Susanna," I called out. No response. She must have been upstairs. Peeking into the parlor, I could see that little had changed. The aunts' old couch, more beaten down than ever, remained by the bay window. The Persian carpet, a gift from the former rabbi of Hamadan, lay on the floor, its reds and browns

blended into a indistinguishable mud. The piano stood in its cus-
tomary spot by the bookshelves. What a shame to have allowed a
fine Steinway to go quiet.

The stairs sagged in the middle, far deeper than on the Sunday
morning in 1964 when she had first invited me into her home.
With each step creaking, I rose to the second floor. The door to
our old bedroom was ajar. It felt rude to barge into her boudoir,
but she'd have to forgive me. I had already crossed too many
borders to care. There wasn't enough time to worry about the
damage I had left behind.

Spotting her lying atop the bed, I could tell she had lost a lot
of weight. Her face had a strange tinge, green almost. Beneath the
scarf, her hair—that luscious, wondrous hair—was gone. Not just
shaved, but vanished, exposing mottled patches along her scalp. It
was a terrible sight. She had fallen asleep with her mouth open, as
if the victim of a violent crime. If not for her slight drawback of
breath, I might have thought that I'd lost her already. My lurking
in the doorway roused her. She raised her head and smiled.

"You're back."

31

Brooklyn
January 26, 1997

A FACE SHROUDED IN WHITE EIDERDOWN BECKONED TO ME through the hazy architecture of memory. The shock of a stranger in my bedroom should have triggered a flight response in me, but something seemed familiar in the wry expression and the hulking shoulders, as well as in the bass voice wishing me a good morning.

"When did you get in?" I asked.

"A few minutes ago. I wanted to see how you were feeling."

Jacob's presence felt incongruous. He had no right to be here, and yet I wasn't angry. Perplexed, perhaps, certainly wary, but not angry. I didn't have strength for that.

"You've let your beard grow. I almost didn't recognize you."

"Well, you might say I lost faith in shaving."

It was nice to focus on someone else's physical transformation. The relief lasted only until Jacob gazed over my shrunken body with an intrusiveness that made me cover my legs beneath the blanket.

"I must be a fright to look at." My face quivered, an involuntary spasm. Stoicism is best practiced with strangers, not with those who expect more than they are owed.

"You would never scare me. Even though with that schmatte on your head, I might have mistaken you for Hassidische."

"Oh great, now you'll never leave me alone about lighting those silly candles."

The little quip made me choke on my own breath. An itch in my lungs exploded into a batch of coughing: dry, hollow spasms. Jacob weaved carefully through the scattered books and papers to pass me a glass of water. I steadied the glass with both hands. One little sip, then another.

"Thank you," I said, tugging the blanket up over my chest. "You remember how drafty this room can get."

Jacob retreated to the mantelplace, where he stood stiffly, as if on a job interview. His presence in this room violated every precept of our separation, and yet I felt no cause to order him out. "If you'd like to sit a few minutes, we could catch up."

He eased himself into the armchair and looked over my field of battle—essays on childhood syntax and primate anatomy interspersed with dirty plates and empty mugs.

"Don't you have your tenure already? What do you need with all this *mishegos*?"

"There is an essay I must finish, and dozens of submissions to review for a conference in April."

"Do you have to do it all yourself? Can't that old crank Rosenfeld help?"

"Chuck is somewhat weak on the interpersonal skills. I had to negotiate a peace treaty even to persuade him to attend."

My former husband picked up a heavily annotated article involving tracheal position in infant humans. "So, are you making progress?"

"More than you might think. Cancer has a way of concentrating the mind."

"There has to be a more effective way to get work done."

"You play the cards dealt to you. Isn't that what you would do?"

"No, I would cheat and get myself some new cards."

I had to laugh, recalling not only his permeable sense of ethics but also the lightness that illuminated our early years together. Drawing his armchair to my side, he reached out for my hand, in what first seemed like a caress, stroking my palm, then appeared to be more of an examination. My arm must have looked awfully thin, like the stick that Hansel used to trick the witch, except in my case the witch was internal, devouring my flesh from inside.

"Hasn't that son of ours been feeding you?"

It never boded well for Shalom when his father refused to utter his name.

"I don't have much appetite."

"No one's talking about appetite. You need food to keep up your strength. Why don't you let me prepare you something?"

"Please, don't trouble yourself. You must be exhausted from your travels."

Leaning over the bed, he waved me closer. "Come on, put your arms around me."

Lacking strength to fight him, I wrapped my arms around his neck, our closest proximity in a quarter century. He heaved me aloft, like the classic portrait of newlyweds crossing over a new threshold.

"Jacob, this is crazy, you'll strain yourself."

"Not with what little you weigh. We've got to fatten you up."

He backed us out the bedroom door and moved quickly down the stairs, swinging my legs wide, like a ride at an amusement park.

"Stop showing off," I said, resting my face against his shoulder. He smelled muskier than I remembered, but he retained his old solidity of body and spirit. He huffed and jerked me higher.

"Reminds me of when you were pregnant," he said.

A selective memory indeed.

"How would you remember that? You disappeared before the heavy lifting."

He paused on the stairwell. "Things were different back then."

These words, along with the solemnity of his gaze, might have been the closest he had ever come to an apology. I touched his beard lightly, just to check he was the same man and not some imposter returning from a distant war.

"So, which community of persecuted Jews needed rescuing this time?"

He flinched, like a juggler losing track of balls in the air. "No Jews this time. There were some people we tried to help, but the whole business ended badly. The less said, the better."

His hesitation reminded me of the deeper questions that had haunted our marriage.

"That's all right, Jacob. It doesn't matter anyway."

Reaching the kitchen, he lowered me gently into a chair and opened the refrigerator to rummage up some breakfast. The bare shelves made him curse our son again. "Not even a few eggs. What the hell does he do all day that he can't keep the fridge stocked for his mother? No wonder you look so thin."

Delving into lower shelves, Jacob pulled out a chop wrapped in butcher's paper. "Look what I found."

"Steak for breakfast?"

"Sure, I can't imagine those early humans of yours waited for noon to wolf down a fresh kill. Didn't you always tell me that time was a cultural construction?"

"Did I say that? Maybe it was a rationalization for missing a deadline."

He reached for the old cast-iron pan, which I barely had the strength to lift anymore. With enough clanging to compete with Shalom's band, he placed the pan on the burner and lit the flame.

"Not too much oil. The meat will render its own fat."

"Trust me," he said, laying the steak into the hot pan, "I have experience in this."

He reached into the cabinet for my apron, a birthday present from Shalom that illustrated the popular version of human evolution, a series of cartoonish silhouettes showing the progression from australopithecus to homo.

"That's a funny look on you," I told him.

"Yeah, well, I'll leave it up to you to determine which one of these characters bears the greatest resemblance."

"Come on now, your flat forehead and upright gait are dead giveaways."

He tended to the steak until it was well-done and slid it onto a plate. Reaching for my knife and fork, he carved the meat into small pieces and placed them before me.

"Here, eat."

The smell made me gag. "I haven't been very hungry lately."

"Do your best. You need the protein."

Caving in to his insistence, I bit into one of the pieces, chewing deliberately until it was reduced to rope, the juice sucked out. Then I flushed it down with some water, feeling more nauseated than ever.

"Have more. It'll do you good." He picked up my fork, speared a chunk of meat and wiggled it before my face. My second childhood had come sooner than expected. Shaking my head, I closed my eyes, turning woozy at the smell.

"Just a moment, please. I have to take it slowly."

He turned the fork to his own mouth, bit down on the meat and reacted with pointed ecstasy, as if persuading a recalcitrant child to eat her spinach. He swallowed and turned serious again. "What does your doctor say?"

"Oh, well, he's been very guarded."

"Guarded, what the hell does that mean? Who is this guy?"

"An oncologist here at Brooklyn Medical."

"Oy, no wonder. To him, you must be like some exotic reptile. He probably sees a case like yours every three years."

I remembered that the only local enterprise Jacob trusted was Effie's car service.

"Jacob, please don't push this. I am too busy to run into Manhattan."

The tenor of my refusal sharpened the distance between us, as if reminding him of his tenuous position at this level of the brownstone.

"Susanna, I have always respected your wishes, but this is crazy. There's no use being treated by some shnorrer in Brooklyn when the world's leading expert can be found right across the river. Let me get some names."

"Jacob, please, I'm managing fine."

The obvious absurdity of my defense stripped my voice of conviction. Rationales that worked magic with Shalom had no power over my former husband.

"Susanna, this is suicide. You have to fight." His voice resounded with a forcefulness usually reserved for reprimanding our son.

"I'm not sure that I have the strength."

"I can help you. If you'll allow it."

It took monumental chutzpah to burst into my home and demand license over my care, while failing to acknowledge how he had earned his expulsion in the first place. And yet, as Jacob took over my kitchen, I felt myself lured in by his old voice, carried back to a time when I fell for his promises.

"Jacob, how can I trust you? How can I ever trust you?"

He started to answer, and then reconsidered. His intentions, always opaque, were further obscured by his new beard. "Nobody said you have to trust me. You only have to let me make some calls. For Shalom's sake. For mine too."

He had no right to ask, and I had every right to refuse. Somehow, though, perhaps due to my frailty and despair, I felt myself surrender to the force of his will.

"Go ahead, make your calls."

He reached for the phone and dialed the first of a dozen numbers; the conciliatory tone falling away as soon as he began instructing Effie on his new assignment. Within minutes, Jacob had secured the home telephone of a leading oncologist at the city's top cancer center, and before I could protest, he had organized the dispatch of my medical records. We would fight like hell, Jacob pronounced, sounding promising, but I hadn't asked for promises, only the chance to make use of the remaining time.

32

Goma
November 2, 1996

LATE INTO A LONG NIGHT OF SHELLING, THE SIGHT OF DUDU'S toes informed me that the Tutsis were close to ending President Mobutu's long reign over Goma. We had been hunkered down at the Hotel Bruegel for days, waiting for the Tutsi rebels to smash through the Zairean army's lines. Shells had been landing steadily, fired by artillery pieces inside Rwanda, gunboats out on Lake Kivu, and mortars carried by Banyamulenge infantrymen marching south from the Virunga Mountains. During a break in the nighttime symphony, I heard Dudu's tap–tap–tap and opened the door to find him brandishing the leg of a broken chair, nails studded through the top.

"What the hell are you doing with that?"

Stepping inside quickly, he locked the door and put down his improvised mace. "If we have any trouble, this will be more effective than prayer."

Even in semi-darkness, Dudu looked different; shorter, his center of gravity lower. For some reason, he was wearing shower sandals.

"Is this is how you prepare for war, in those ridiculous things?"

He tilted the chest of drawers onto its side and rammed it against the door. "It was a bad night, Aba. Mobutu's soldiers robbed everyone at the bar."

"What happened? They didn't appreciate your sense of humor?"

"Not this time. They took everything, even my boots." Sliding to the floor, he braced his shoulder against the bureau. "The mood has changed out there, Jacob. We need to be careful."

"Everything will be different when the Tutsis get here."

"Maybe, but you can't be sure whether it will be better or worse."

This was the most dangerous time, during the transition. We settled in to wait out the trouble. Near dawn, we heard a loud knock, shouts to open up, and a key rattling in the lock. Dudu threw himself against the door and waved for me to hide in the bathroom, out of the line of fire. Refusing to be coddled, I joined him at the barricade and the two of us, unified for once, pressed our bodies into the breach. After a few minutes, the intruders decided to pass over our door in favor of easier marks down the hall. We soon heard the cries of aid workers being relieved of their worldly posessions.

"I bet a lot of *muzungus* will be missing shoes tomorrow," I said.

"They'll be lucky if that's all they lose."

We lingered by the door until the sky softened from black to gray and an uncertain calm settled over the town. Peeking out the window, I watched a half dozen Zairean soldiers on the lawn struggling to carry off a refrigerator laid flat like a coffin. The fridge was too heavy for them, so they turned it sideways to pour out half its contents. A cascade of beer bottles spilled onto the grass. Leaving his gun behind, one of the soldiers collected as many bottles as would fit into his cradled arms.

"At least they appreciate what is important in life," Dudu said.

"From what we've witnessed, I'm only surprised they held out this long."

When the shelling petered out, all that could be heard across the battered city was the intermittent spray of small-arms fire, the wail of women, and the sputtering of a car engine refusing to start. Dudu jerked the bureau out of the way, picked up his mace, and peeked into the hall. Edging forward, he beckoned me to follow, and we skulked down to the hotel lobby, which looked as if it had been hit by an artillery blast. The bar had been stripped bare, and there was a gaping hole in the plaster where the television had been ripped from the wall. The only light seeped in from outside.

"No power?" I asked the concierge standing behind the counter in his undershirt, his uniform having been seized by the retreating Zairean army.

"The soldiers stole the generator."

"So no breakfast either?" Dudu asked.

"They took the food, and the stoves too. We are glad to be free of them. Let them run all the way back to Kinshasa."

Outside, the streets were as quiet as Crown Heights on Yom Kippur. At the commercial district, a couple of dogs wandered through the wreckage of twisted metal, broken glass, and spent shell casings. A gang of looters darted out of a clothing store as an angry shopkeeper swung a stick at them. Nearby, a man with a military haircut was backing a pickup truck into the steel shutters of a gem shop. Stupid ass didn't realize that diamond dealers carried their inventory in their pockets.

"There they are," Dudu said, pointing down the boulevard at a formation of soldiers advancing professionally, providing cover for each other, their weapons aimed at any threat. Judging by their discipline, this must have been a unit of Banyamulenge, the Zairean Tutsis who were fronting the rebellion.

Dudu pulled me back into a warren of stone-walled streets. Off the avenue, we were safely removed from potential gunfire, but Dudu worried that bullets would bounce off the walls and turn the whole corridor into a shooting gallery.

"It's too exposed here, Aba. We need to get back inside. Now."

"Don't worry, Dudu, these are our friends."

"Maybe, but friendship won't give you any immunity from their bullets."

We hurried back to the Bruegel as bursts of gunshots sounded in the streets behind us. The rebels were wasting no time imposing their will. For them, Goma marked a significant milestone in their dual mission: to clear out the Hutu genocidaires who threatened to exterminate the Tutsis of Zaire; and to oust the Mobutu regime that treated their community as *auslanders*.

When the Banyamulenge Tutsis reached the hotel, they ordered the guests to assemble on the back lawn. Even after a triumphant day, the rebels looked stern and unsmiling, no candy for the children or kisses to the girls. They sure didn't bother casting about for admirers among the *muzungus* who had fed their enemies.

"Not much fun anymore, are they?" Dudu asked, eyeing the soldiers who guarded our every movement with their Kalashnikovs.

No, the Tutsis had never been much fun. They had always been fair, however, at least to us. Standing among the aid workers and assorted other hotel guests, I wondered whether our time in Mugunga refugee camp might cause some complications and make the Tutsis wonder which side we were on. Holding my breath, I slipped the *laissez-passer* written by the Tutsi commanders into my passport and presented it to the Banyamulenge in charge. The officer examined my papers and, without word, beckoned a soldier to escort us to the parking lot, where his troops were mustering. There, along the road, we watched an endless stream of military vehicles grinding their way out of Rwanda and heading west, toward the distant sound of fighting.

A jeep carrying Captain Ezekiel Hakizimana swung into the hotel lot. The sight of our old friend bounding from the vehicle reassured me that we would be remembered fondly. Dudu didn't share my optimism.

"Your man looks changed, Aba."

Dudu had a point. The captain had shed the slow, loping strides that carried him up Bisesero's Hill of Resistance. His shoulders had more substance to them, as if he had gained a full jacket size since we parted on an airfield outside Kigali. Now I could really picture him hauling the mag, maybe not as easily as Dudu, but well enough. Instead of the machine gun, however, he carried on his hip the Glock that had been our gift to him. Approaching us, he issued me a salute that reaffirmed my purpose in coming here.

"We have been successful, Mr. Jacob. Goma is free."

I had to stop myself from giving his cheek a fatherly little tap, a Galicianer show of affection that might not have translated across cultures. Staying my hand did little to diminish my admiration. Ezekiel had done well. His entry into Goma reminded me of the famous photograph of Dayan and Rabin striding through the old city of Jerusalem in June 1967, a moment of rebirth so powerful that it made me miss a real birth in Brooklyn.

"Congratulations, Captain. You've accomplished more than I thought possible in so little time."

The captain seemed distracted by the line of military trucks heading west. "There is more good news. Our forces have now liberated Masisi. If you would like to see what the genocidaires have done to our people, you may ride with us into the mountains."

During our travels together, Ezekiel had described his native Masisi as a Tutsi Canaan, a land of milk and honey, where his great-grandparents had migrated with their herds during the days of the Belgian Congo. It would be a blessing to visit this place and witness the restoration of Ezekiel to his people.

"We can't go anywhere right now," Dudu piped up. "I don't have the boots to be running around the mountains."

Lifting one foot, Dudu showed off his shower sandals. Then he grabbed his toes and hopped about, pretending that he had stepped on a sharp stone. Captain Ezekiel didn't smile, resisting even a minor moment of lightness on a serious day. Striding to the road, the captain flagged down a passing military truck and called up to the soldiers leaning over the railing. One of them passed down a pair of rubber boots, muddy and maybe even still warm from the previous user.

"Now you can feel how is to walk in our shoes," he said, handing them to Dudu.

Dudu plopped down on the curb and tugged them on. "Too small," he said, stamping on the ground to adjust the fit. "You guys have tiny feet."

"You are fortunate Mobutu's soldiers did not steal your clothes," the captain said. "We would have trouble finding a uniform to fit your size."

"Not me," Dudu said, shaking his head. "I would sooner go naked. I am through with war."

Dudu would have used any excuse to avoid traveling to Masisi. He couldn't contend with the serious questions: life and death, survival and genocide. The only fight that mattered to him took place over a soccer ball. I had brought him here to watch out for trouble, but all he had done was make my life more difficult. Not any more. I refused to let his petty concerns dissuade me. The world would never change if men of conscience turned away from hard truths. The least we could do, given the invitation by our friend Ezekiel, was to bear witness to a disaster averted.

33

Manhattan
March 4, 1997

BRACING MY ARM, JACOB LED ME ACROSS THE HOSPITAL LOBBY
that resembled a medieval rendering of the Last Judgment. This
was a foreign country filled with the spiny smell of disinfectant
and the listless shuffle of families too anguished to speak. An
elderly man with a fist bulging from his midsection trailed his
adult grandson; a hairless child slept fitfully in her father's powerless arms; a line of adult women awaited a radiation bath for their
empty breasts. One day medical science would curse this place
as a barbarity, as bad as leeches or lobotomies, imposing horrors
on patients who crawled through the doors as modern penitents,
pilgrims in search of an alternate ending. It was precisely this
hideous scene that I had hoped to avoid, until Jacob returned to
me like a gruff Virgil and wore down my resistance.

"Come on, Dr. Gerson's waiting," he said. "If we're late, they
may sell your chemo to the highest bidder."

"I'm sure that if that happened, you would uncover some
secret stash."

We must have looked like a couple of old lovers strolling along the strand, or maybe even a modern version of the australopithecine couple at Laetoli whose three-million-year-old footprints had been discovered in the hardened ash. In the weeks since his return, Jacob had attended to my care with an impassioned sense of purpose: prodding me to finish the protein drinks he prepared twice daily; scheduling an ever-more-taxing series of medical appointments; and interrupting my reading to pronounce it time for sleep. His interventions were highly intrusive, but I couldn't fault his dedication. He had replenished the refrigerator and inscribed checks for past-due bills. He even vacuumed the carpets, scrubbed the toilet, and replaced the bathtub washer to stop its incessant dripping. He had also crossed a more significant boundary. Without asking permission, he had taken to sleeping in the armchair across from our bed, or rather what had once been our bed.

Reaching the hospital elevators, we joined a throng of doctors, patients, and family members waiting to be locked inside a vertical boxcar.

"I could carry you upstairs if you feel nervous," Jacob said.

It was a tempting offer, to be hoisted in his arms all the way up to the sixth floor.

"That's all right. The hospital would complain about the liability."

Resigned to wait, I adjusted my scarf, tied behind the neck, befitting his antiquated sense of romance, a hardened kibbutznik tilling the promised land.

"That's a nice one," Jacob said. "I remember it from Ethiopia."

I felt for the fabric, forgetting what color I had selected this morning. "Did I take this to Hadar? I can't recall."

"That or another like it. It suits you."

"Not too Hassidic?"

"Not at all, but if you feel inspired in that direction, Effie has a guy in Borough Park who makes wigs for the *frum* ladies. Very authentic looking."

"I bet you'd like that. You always did aspire to turn me into a good Jewish girl."

"Not me. I knew better than to try to change you."

The elevator finally arrived, and I gripped Jacob's arm tight and shut my eyes. As the doors closed around us, he whispered: "Don't worry, I have a special trick to pry this thing open. It's something they don't share with the general public."

Who knew whether he was telling me another fable, but just as when he coaxed me aboard a plane to Ethiopia, his words were soothing enough to carry me through the ride. When the doors opened on the sixth floor, I exhaled deeply, relieved at having survived the first of the day's ordeals. A half hour later, Dr. Gerson breezed in to greet me with courtesy and compassion. If he had spotted the shadow of death in my scans, at least he wasn't allergic to eye contact.

"How are you feeling, Professor Sussman?"

"It hasn't been an easy week, Doctor."

"I'm sorry. These are very powerful medicines."

A dark yarmulke blended into his thick hair. The flag of his faith might have comforted some patients, but I had to squelch the urge to press him into justifying his belief in a benevolent Deity when dying children stalked the halls. My inclination was petulant. Why challenge the virtue of a man courageous enough to confront lost causes?

Dr. Gerson had me stand so he could check for new moles. Leaning on Jacob for balance, I shifted my gown and allowed the doctor's hands to work over my skin. Trying to ignore the poking and prying, my thoughts meandered back to my research on the baboons. I wondered whether Shalom remembered our times together, accompanying me through hours of observation. For a little boy, he had been so patient, listening to the baboon chatter. Only later did it dawn on me that I shouldn't have pushed so hard. Anthropology had not been for him.

"Remind me, Professor Sussman, do you have any history of cancer in your family?" the doctor asked, peering intently at a dark spot on my ribs.

"It's difficult to know; my family was lost in the *shoah*."

"I see, so we can't be certain of the genetic contribution." Opening my folder, Dr. Gerson flipped through the pages and surveyed the reports. For weeks, I had consented to his plan to hurl a full arsenal of chemotherapy at the disease. Despite his efforts, it felt like a losing campaign.

"Dr. Gerson, the treatment is having a terrible toll on me. I am hosting a major academic conference in six weeks and I barely have strength to hold up a piece of paper."

My resistance jolted Jacob into action. "Susanna, you have to give it time."

Jacob had preached overcoming this enemy through careful planning and unrelenting resolve. This philosophy might have propelled him through many past battles, but I doubted whether the melanoma cells cascading through my system would be cowed by the force of his will.

"I will not allow cancer to define my existence. It cannot soak up what's left of my life."

Interceding between us, Dr. Gerson extended a potential compromise. "We'll try to adjust the dosages to make the treatment easier to tolerate, and to schedule a break leading up to your conference. Will that work for you, Professor Sussman?"

He meant well, this man of faith, and it would have been choresome to deny my son, and my former husband, the possibility of hope.

"Yes, that will be fine."

Dr. Gerson released me to the next round of chemo, administered in an open room boasting an expansive vista of the East River. Jacob helped me into the big, cushiony armchair, and a nurse carried over bags of fluid. Her first task was to find a vein, rarely easy these days.

"Ow," I winced as she dug into my flesh.

"I'm sorry about that. You have bad veins," she said, as if the fault lay in me.

Jacob didn't like how she struggled. "All right, stop poking her. I want the Russian to handle this."

He strode down the hall to reel in the mother-superior of vein stickers, an older nurse from Moscow who chided Jacob in her language for disturbing her. He dismissed her abuse with what sounded like a sarcastic rebuke. Reaching my side, the Russian lady acknowledged me only to stroke my arm roughly and to slide the needle right in, unleashing the flow of chemicals into my bloodstream.

"You can always count on the Russians," he told me as the nurse strode off. "They know how to get under your skin."

I could have pressed him to explain his strange fluidity in a foreign tongue, but hard experience had left me wary of trying to untangle his history. It was enough that he had come back to show himself so devoted.

"Jacob, thank you for staying with me."

"Stop thanking me already. It's what I do." Sliding his chair to my side, he reached for my free hand and smoothed out my palm, as if reading my fortune in the lines. He shouldn't have needed superstition to see my future.

"I have an anthropological theory to try out on you," he said.

"Since when did you become interested in anthropology?"

"You must have inspired me through the years."

"So, what is the theory?"

He leaned in so close that his beard tickled my ear. "Your old friend Marcel had his geography wrong. He insisted on looking for hominids in the desert, but a small tribe couldn't have survived in that wasteland for long. He would have been much better off searching the mountains."

His reference to Marcel so surprised me that I jerked my arm involuntarily, pinching the spot where the needle penetrated the vein. It was hard to fathom why Jacob would blithely bring up a betrayal that had grown ever more painful over the years, given how the Hadar site had yielded one of the greatest finds in anthropological history, a whole new species, *Australopithecus afarensis*.

"What makes you want to search the mountains?" I asked about his batty theory, not so much to humor him, but to divert my attention from the poisonous juice collecting inside me.

"I've learned a few things about the struggle of the persecuted to survive. If it had been my responsibility, three million years ago, to save my people from being eaten by leopards or crocodiles, or even a competing tribe, I would have migrated into the highlands, like the famous mountain gorillas."

He had obviously given the matter some thought. Intellectual honesty, and some long-buried bitterness, compelled me to point out some obvious flaws in his thesis.

"It's an intriguing theory, but it would be difficult to prove. Those mountains are too rainy to allow fossilization. Water destroys the evidence, and the soil is acidic enough to chew through organic matter. Dry sand is the best preservative for bones."

Jacob Furman was a hard man to discourage. "Maybe when you recover your strength, we can fly back to Africa for a look. There are a few spots in the mountains around Lake Kivu that you might really enjoy."

"All right, but only if you promise not to disappear this time. You'll have to subdue your ingrained impulse to rescue anyone."

He stroked my free hand. "I'm done with the rescuing business. From now on, I'm all yours."

Something had changed in him, far more profound than the growth of beard. If he had shown himself this engaged, this reflective years ago, I might never have despaired of a life together.

The toxins flowing into my system were beginning to make me light-headed. Closing my eyes made me even more dizzy, so I focused on the vista out the window, a panorama of the East River appearing like a valley of still water, less a tributary of Upper New York Bay than a tidal pool, floating in and out of the Atlantic Ocean like breath.

"The wine-dark sea."

"What was that?" Jacob asked.

"It's a phrase from Homer, about the sea. It's so evocative, I can almost picture the Greek ships sailing for Troy, and Odysseus on his long voyage home."

He followed my gaze out the window and perceived an entirely different poetry. "I sailed with Greeks once, Jews from Salonica. After Auschwitz, we put them on boats to Palestine, but I don't remember the sea looking so wine-dark, even after the British detained us. Blood dissipates pretty quickly in all that water."

I would have reminded him to appreciate the image as metaphor, but the drip left me woozy, spinning me back to my own childhood passage across the Atlantic, when the ocean churned and the boat surged and fell, storm waves shocked the sides, and in my despair I longed for the sea to engulf the cask and relieve me of my misery. The wine-dark sea.

34

Masisi Territory
November 5, 1996

GLOCK IN HAND, CAPTAIN EZEKIEL HAKIZIMANA LED US UP A
grassy slope to his ancestral land. After hours of driving into the
mountains, we had finally reached Masisi, with its lush hills and
rich pastures, greener than the uniforms of the Banyamulenge
Tutsi troops who escorted us up from Goma.

"It's beautiful," I asked. "Did it look this way when you were
a boy?"

Ezekiel stopped to survey the landscape. "There used to be
three trees over by that stream, and all the families that lived here
are gone now, but otherwise very little has changed since my
father instructed me how to take care of the cows."

The personal tenor of Ezekiel's remembrances made me glad
that Dudu lagged far behind us down the slope. The last thing
I needed was for that loudmouth to poke fun at a soldier's sense
of nostalgia. As Dudu flopped about in his new rubber boots,
struggling to make it up the hill, I listened to the captain describe
how as a young boy he had learned the pathways through Masisi

territory, from stream to pasture, from hostile villages to welcoming neighbors. This mental map helped him to flee Zaire when his father was murdered in a pogrom, long before the Rwandan genocide, long before the world began counting the Tutsi dead.

"Your father would be proud of you," I told him. "You left here as a boy who had lost everything, but you return as a soldier defending his people."

Holstering the pistol we had given him, the captain picked up a stick lying on the ground. It was long, rising above his head, and so smooth that it seemed almost polished. The staff in hand, he tested its strength, then waved it lightly through the overgrown grass, as if ready to lead his herds again through the pastureland around us.

"It is very sad: my father's teachings were wasted on me."

"Those lessons are never wasted. My father taught me to tailor clothes as a boy, and even today I could mend your uniform."

Ezekiel gazed dreamily around us. "Let me ask you, Mr. Jacob, have you noticed any cattle on our journey?"

On the hard drive up from Goma, along the muddy scar that served as a road, we had passed neither herd nor herder.

"No, I suppose not. It hadn't occurred to me until now."

"The genocidaires have been stealing the cows and selling the meat in Goma. You may have eaten some in your restaurants."

The memory of the steaks that Sunny had served on a bed of Thai noodles made me wonder whether we had become the genocidaires' unwitting accomplices, little better than cannibals, helping to finance their pogrom against the Tutsis. A fresh wave of indigestion swelled in me, as bad as the one that had sent me running to Dr. Chantal.

"It is good we always ordered the fish," Dudu said, catching up to us at last. "Jacob doesn't like to touch the meat unless he can be sure it's kosher, and you don't have any rabbis in Goma to say the blessing."

Who knew whether the captain believed this horseshit. Ezekiel's face was placid, giving nothing away. Despite all our conversations, I still had trouble reading him. He pressed on up the hill to a series of earthen walls that rose knee-high from the ground. They looked like floor plans of an ancient settlement, blackened and charred by time. Kneeling, he plucked a piece of straw from the ground.

"These were houses until the genocidaires arrived a few months ago. Tutsi families used to live here with their children. Now they are all gone."

The ruins looked as if they dated back eons. As I had learned at Buchenwald, it didn't take long for the earth to cover up the crimes of men.

"Never again will we allow our people to be murdered," Ezekiel said. "Now we will take care of our own security."

Returning to the captain's jeep, we drove up the road to another village, this one still living. It didn't look like much. Decrepit mud huts stretched along a hilltop. Our arrival brought out the local machers, dressed in frayed suits and torn T-shirts, who reached out their weathered hands and mumbled blessings of welcome to the returning hero. Leaning against long staffs, they looked like bent trees, swaying with the wind. They had survived the onslaught; now Ezekiel's army would make it right.

As the captain addressed his landsmen, a school of little boys gathered around Dudu. Awestruck by his size, they whispered from a respectful distance, until he invited a couple of boys to hang off his flexed right arm. Then he pulled up his left sleeve to show off his tattoos. From the image stitched onto his arm, he narrated the story of the rocket attack as if it were an action movie, complete with booming sound effects.

"Enough, Dudu. You're scaring the poor kids."

He rolled down his sleeve. "Look at them, Aba. Don't you think they've seen worse than this?"

Dudu had a point. These kids must have suffered plenty. Now life would be better. This was the promise of the Banyamulenge, to save them from their enemies.

We climbed back in the jeep and rode until the muddy track descended to a clearing. There, a unit of Tutsi soldiers guarded a few dozen haggard men who sat hugging their knees, their fingers entwined behind their heads.

"These are prisoners we captured in the forest," Captain Ezekiel said.

"Good, maybe we'll find the bastard who stole my boots," Dudu said, scanning the ranks of captive men.

The captain shook his head. "Not here. Those thieves were Zairean soldiers. The men here are genocidaires."

The Hutu killers sure looked like a seedy bunch, shaking where they sat. Not so bold now, not like during the Rwandan genocide, or during their plush exile in the cafes of Mugunga. The season had turned. Like Eichmann in Jerusalem.

The Tutsi soldiers prodded forward a prisoner wearing military fatigues. His shirt was hanging out of his pants, and the collar looked threadbare. Something appeared to be wrong with his stomach. He held his guts as if to keep from shitting. A plastic card identified him as Augustin Ngarambe, a major in the old Rwandan army.

Captain Ezekiel looked over the card and nodded. "This man's name rings through our history. During the genocide, he was responsible for the murder of 237 Tutsis. He ordered them into a church and then had the building set on fire."

The major turned to me in protest, as if I had the power to amend the historical record. "Please, sir, it was not my fault what happened during the war. We tried to help the Tutsi people, but there were forces beyond our control. No one could stop the events once they began. The Tutsis would have done the same—"

An explosion cut him short. The back of the major's skull burst open, spraying out its contents like a punctured tomato. His body tumbled into the dirt and twitched a few times. From the hole in his head poured a mess of white coils stained with red.

I tried to shield my ears, but my reflexes weren't quick enough to stop the gunshot from igniting a terrible screeching. Through the shock and pain, I caught a glimpse of Captain Ezekiel, his face fixed with certainty. Not joy, not anger, simply determination. This must have been what was required to shoot a man in the head. It was something I had always lacked.

The Glock drawn, he stalked the rows of prisoners. They shook in place, still squatting, their fingers gripped behind their necks, their elbows flapping so hard that the poor bastards looked ready to fly away.

A military truck pulled into the clearing. The Tutsi soldiers ordered the prisoners to climb aboard, and the Hutus clambered up as if their lives depended on it, which in a sense was true. The prisoners crammed into the truck, and a pair of Banyamulenge picked up the dead major by his wrists and ankles, swung him like a pendulum, and heaved the corpse on board. The truck started up again and took a slow turn left, deeper into the mountains, the opposite way from the Rwandan border.

"They're going the wrong direction," I mumbled as the truck disappeared from view.

Dudu pinched my arm and raised a finger to his lips again. At the critical moment, he knew when to shut up. The next sound we heard was a bulldozer grinding its way up the road.

35

Brooklyn
March 15, 1997

IT WAS NEARLY DUSK ON SATURDAY, ALMOST TIME TO LIGHT THE Havdalah candles that welcomed in a new week, when Shalom came down to the parlor wearing a blue African shirt that looked like pajamas. This was his answer, after days of grumbling, to my demands that he take Susanna's place at the wedding.

"Have you lost your mind?" I said. "You can't wear that."

"Why not? It's a traditional Guinean wedding dashiki."

"Don't you realize this is a formal occasion?"

"So? I don't see you with a tie. And that suit looks like it's been in mothballs since my bar mitzvah."

He had a nasty mouth on him, ready as ever to tell his father to fuck off. Susanna might have accepted my renewed presence upstairs, but Shalom resisted even the slightest suggestion of how to fix the mess that constituted his life.

His head was covered by what looked like a maroon bowl, turned upside-down and embroidered with geometric shapes.

It was the style of kipah that I remembered from the shuls of Uzbekistan.

"Have you turned Bukharan all of a sudden? I thought you wanted to be African."

"You know me. I like to dip into the ocean of world culture and fish out whatever bites. Anyway, where's your kipah? I bet you left it upstairs."

He had me. Returning to the bedroom for my skullcap, I found Susanna immersed in her reading, as usual. What a shame she didn't feel up for the trek to Crown Heights; it might have been a nice reminder of sweeter days.

"What are you two fighting about this time?" she asked as I kissed her forehead.

"Nothing. Only a minor dispute over the dress code."

She squeezed my hand. More strength in her grip lately, a little better color. Maybe the chemo was doing some good after all. She picked some lint off my suit.

"Jacob, would you do something for me?"

"Of course."

Removing her reading glasses, she stroked my hand as if she were smoothing out the folds on a tablecloth. "Try to reconcile with Shally."

It wasn't an unreasonable request, no worse than Nesia's plea for me to stop fighting the world. "I can try, but the hostility runs in both directions."

"That may be true, but he has his own burdens. It can't have been easy to live in our shadows."

I could have argued, but there was no point in convincing a mother of her son's inadequacies. Daylight was fading fast, and I didn't want to miss the ceremony, so I gave her another kiss and reminded her to put away the books by midnight.

Meeting Shalom downstairs, we strode down Eastern Parkway until the black hats started appearing, drawn to the squat brick building where the Grand Rebbe used to hold court. Outside, on the lawn, we took our place among the gathering crowd.

"Dad, what the fuck are we doing here?"

I could have informed my son how this lawn had shaped his existence, how Susanna and I had once stood here for our own wedding ceremony. No, I thought, he would only have dismissed it as another of my lectures.

"We're paying respect to Effie. And you are representing your mother, who didn't feel up to coming. Plus, you've known Menachem all your life."

"I don't think I'd recognize him these days." He gazed over the assembled Hassidisches. "Actually, I'd have trouble recognizing anyone in this crowd."

He had a point. The black suits and brimmed hats made it difficult to distinguish one individual from the next. They all had full beards and pale faces, cheeks tinged with red. Too much time sheltered indoors.

"It's only the youth," I said, pointing out a couple of venerable figures. "They take on more personality as their beards turn white."

"Must be tough to grow old before you can form your own identity. Although now that you've grown your beard, you could fit right in."

"Not me. I can't pretend to follow 613 commandments."

"Only the convenient ones."

I would have struck back, cut him down over his own failings: his weakness for marijuana, his inane business schemes, his neglect of his mother, but Susanna's plea for peace gave me pause. To win back her confidence, I would have to refrain from baiting the one closest to her. It didn't seem like much to ask. I had put up with plenty of crap from Dudu over the years. I could withstand a few jabs from my own son.

By this time a host of stars could be seen above us, more than all the Havdalah candles on earth. Four Hassidisches raised a *huppah*, and a clarinet started up a klezmer tune. A black hatter who must have been Menachem, with reddish beard and glasses, approached the lawn, helping along his father, so heavy now that he barely made it beneath the wedding tent before unloading his troubles onto a chair.

"Jeez, is that Uncle Effie?" Shalom said. "He looks terrible."

Effie had never exactly been fit, but since his wife died a few years back, he had lost the one person who reminded him not to eat like a pig.

The bride's party emerged from a car. A gaggle of women surrounded a ghostly figure hidden beneath a white veil. She moved strangely, jerking along on what turned out to be crutches.

"What happened to her?" Shalom asked. "Twisted her ankle chasing after Tevye's milk truck?"

"Apparently she broke it climbing out of the *mikvah*."

"You're kidding?"

I had to laugh with him on this one. It was a little crazy, this *mikvah* business. If you needed a bath, take one at home. "Supposedly it can be very slippery."

Despite the bum ankle, she stuck to the tradition of circling her groom seven times. She hobbled around him with the wedding party in tow, as Menachem mumbled prayers as if in a trance.

"You'd think they could give her a break until the leg heals," Shalom said. "Doesn't she have a lifetime of marriage to run around in circles?"

I hated to let him see me laugh again, but my son had a decent sense of comic timing. When the girl completed her procession, the rabbi recited the conjugal blessings and read from the *ketubah*, a contract we could only hope would last longer than the one sitting in my closet downstairs. After slipping a ring on the girl's finger, Menachem stomped on a glass and the wedding party departed to the strains of *Siman Tov and Mazal Tov*. By the time we caught up to them at the reception hall, parted down the middle, Effie was sitting alone on the receiving line. Paying little notice to the strangers offering their blessings, he looked like one of those dogs that hung low, barely able to drag his body down the street. His bottom lip fell open to allow him to breathe easier.

"What, no greeting for Dr. Hausmann?" I asked.

The reminder of our shared past seemed to revive him. "Jacob, Jacob," he said, straining up from his seat to hug me. "I can't tell you how happy I am to see you."

"We wouldn't have missed it, even if I had to swim back from Africa, although Shalom might have lost his way between the continents."

Freeing one arm, I waved Shalom into our embrace. Effie slapped one of his legendary oozing kisses onto him. "Shalom is welcome however he wants to dress." For once my son didn't pull away.

"It's been a long time, Uncle Effie." Shalom seemed genuinely happy to see him. He had always been fond of the men who passed for uncles, Effie and Salik. Chuck Rosenfeld too.

"Let's find you some friends your own age," Effie said. "You don't want to spend the whole night with a couple of *alter kockers*."

Shalom looked as if we were dropping him in a foreign land with no map and no currency. "Don't worry about me, these aren't exactly my type of people."

"You should keep an open mind. If you want, I can make some inquiries, and see if there are any prospects for you across the wall," Effie said, nodding at the barrier that marked the boundary between sexes. "There must be a few girls around here looking to rescue a beardless guy."

"I don't know, Uncle Effie; when it comes to women, I'm pretty much spoken for these days. Ask Dad, he'll tell you."

It was hard to believe, but essentially true. This girl Mia had come around every day to help him clean up the basement. She was pretty, a dancer type with long hair that she stroked as if it were a tamed animal. Apparently she had been one of Susanna's graduate students, but the lovebirds both begged me not to mention their relationship to his mother. They thought it might upset her, so I assured them I could keep a secret.

"It's true," I said. "Shalom's found himself a hard worker."

"Good for him. A nice Jewish girl?"

Shalom lost the cocksure look. This Mia might have been a lot of things, but Jewish was definitely not one of them. At this point, I didn't give a shit. It was enough that he found himself a girl willing to put up with his nonsense. Whether that would suffice for his mother was another question entirely.

"Come on, Effie," I said, "don't ask questions that you don't want to hear answered."

Effie arranged for one of the bride's cousins to look after Shalom and led me to the head table, where a bottle of Slivovitz awaited us, just as in times past. I had to help Effie up the riser to his seat overlooking hundreds of guests.

"Did you have any idea Menachem was so popular?" I asked.

"They do seem to like him. It's a shame he won't eat at my house anymore."

To me, Effie always seemed plenty religious. He went to shul now and then, and could even carry on a Talmudic discussion with the bearded guys. His big concession to treif was the occasional ham sandwich and shrimp lo mein, but only outside of the house. This wasn't good enough for Menachem, who had rediscovered his faith in college and now refused to use the plates that Effie had brought back from Bavaria.

"Well, at least Menachem's found himself," I said. "That's more than I can say for my boy."

"You want Shalom to turn religious? Jacob, you would go crazy with all the rules."

"No, not religious. But something."

"Looks to me like he's found plenty."

Across the hall, my son had struck up a heated debate, probably over the morality of circumcision or the rights of the Arabs. Leave it to him to provoke an argument on a happy occasion.

The Hassidisches were pushing past each other to shout at him, and Shalom was slapping some on the back, waving his finger at others, ignoring a few entirely.

"He'll be okay," Effie said. "You should have more faith in him."

"You sound like Susanna. She thinks I'm too critical."

"She should know. She raised the boy after you left."

"I didn't leave. She threw me out."

We were interrupted by waiters serving plates of boiled chicken and potato salad. As we ate, the rabbi who had officiated at the ceremony stood for a long, incomprehensible speech, filled with references to the Torah. When he finished, he handed the microphone to another rabbi, leading me to shift close to Effie: "When does the groom's father get to make a toast?"

He looked as if I had suggested screwing the bride's mother. "What I need to say, Jacob, I'll say to you."

I patted him on the arm, and we took another swig of brandy. It was sad how poor Effie, all these years after Buchenwald, still felt so alone. His drivers, enjoying dinner at the tables below, had come to pay their respects, but they were employees, not comrades.

When the rabbis ran out of speeches, the band started playing, so loud I could barely hear myself shouting into Effie's ear. Rolling up the tables, the Hassidisches formed a succession of dancing circles, arms around each other's shoulders. They threw off their black jackets, and let white shirttails hang out, as the circle spun faster and faster. Through their midst whirled a flash of blue, visible for only a moment, like a bright colored sock in a washing machine. It was the blue of a Guinean wedding dashiki. Before we knew it, Shalom was sitting atop some Hassid's shoulders, pumping his fist and belting out the words to *David Melech Yisrael*.

"It doesn't take Shalom long to make friends," Effie said.

"He has the advantage of having no shame. Look at how he dresses."

"He's a grown man. Why do you care what he wears?"

The dancing carried on past midnight, long after I had promised to return home. Susanna had encouraged me to have a good time, but I worried for her spending so much time alone. Anything could happen, the least of which was her wearing herself down with endless reading. Effie insisted on escorting me out, even if he wasn't in any shape to be standing. As he staggered to the doorway under the influence of too much Slivovitz and boiled chicken, I propped him up by his sloppy waist and considered how far we had traveled since we stood at Buchenwald reciting kaddish for our lost families. After all our years together, I had a lingering question only he could answer.

"Do you remember that girl who showed up at my house in Bavaria?"

"Sure, the one who survived Auschwitz. We never saw her again."

"Her name was Judith. And you know something strange. Susanna looks like her now: the weight loss, the sadness in her face, the scarf."

"Jacob, don't act crazy. The girl came to your place for one night. You can't still be thinking about her fifty years later."

"She left an impression."

"For all you know, she never made it out of Bavaria. Survivors were dropping from every little sickness back then, and no one was keeping count of the dead."

Effie was right. There was only one thing for certain: allowing her to slip away had been the greatest mistake of my life. After the war, Salik had searched the passenger manifests of all the ships trying to break the British blockade of Palestine, and checked periodically with the Ministry of Absorption for any new immigrant bearing her name. Nothing ever came of it. By this point it wasn't fair to any of us, least of all to Susanna, for me to dwell on ancient regrets, or even on more recent ones.

"You're right, Effie. I shouldn't get so sentimental. It must be the beard."

"You did what you could, Jacob. The same as always. There's no use starting to regret now. You're not a man who changes with time."

Effie dispatched a Hassidische to summon Shalom out of the dancing circle, and my son emerged with his shirt dark with sweat. All of Effie's drivers were enjoying the party, so we started the long walk down Eastern Parkway, with me reflective and Shalom full of energy, another mark of our differences.

"So after all the complaining, you had a good time."

"You know what, Dad, these crazy Hassidisches throw a hell of a party. They even gave me a new idea for the Mega-Stars: African klezmer."

"Oy. That sounds like a winning move."

He stopped and adjusted the big Bukharan *kipah* on his head. "Think of it as a way to share your Galicianer traditions with the world: Judeo-African rhythms as grand 'fuck-you' to Hitler."

"I hate to tell you, but these Hassidisches weren't exactly our kind of Galicianers."

Gripping my elbow, he pulled close to me. "We can dress the Mega-Stars in black hats. That would be a bad-ass look."

"You're crazy."

He released my elbow and turned away, as if I had crushed him again, just like during his childhood when Salik called me away and Susanna had to make excuses for my absences. He couldn't keep up the veneer of outrage for long.

"I'm just messing with you, Dad. The Mega-Stars are way too sophisticated for this crowd. Plus, can you imagine finding an audience for African klezmer? It's hard enough booking venues as it is."

As he spoke, something struck me about his expression. Shalom had always had a stubborn streak, boldly telling me to fuck off. Now he showed me something I hadn't noticed before, maybe because I hadn't been looking. It was a sense of purpose, a focus and a resolve that must have been how I appeared years ago, when the whole world needed rebuilding and it felt like my job to do it. Maybe this was what had divided us—father and son warring over the same territory, with the old king reluctant to pass along the keys to the realm. Mindful of Susanna's call for reconciliation, I considered a path that would serve both our interests.

"Listen, if you want, I can ask Effie for help finding you a new rehearsal space. I would even spring for the rent."

"Well, if he can find a place, that would be useful."

The offer extended, I informed him of the cost. "There's one condition: you have to help your mother with the conference."

"Come on, Dad. Mom made it pretty clear she wanted to handle it all herself."

"She can't. She needs someone to do the dirty work so she can concentrate on finishing that damn paper."

"Find someone else then. After the way those bastards treated me, I wouldn't be caught dead at another academic conference."

"No one said you have to show up, just make it happen for her. These professors are pestering us every day, complaining about the arrangements. At least you can make sense of this Australo-pithecus-smithicus business."

My offer may have been a honey trap, but once extended, he couldn't resist. Much as Susanna needed assistance to corral those pompous windbags into a conference hall, Shalom needed help as well, and not just with the music.

"All right, Dad." He held out his hand to seal the bargain. "I'll do it. Not for you, but for her."

We walked the rest of the way home and found Susanna still at work, eager to hear Shally's stories about the hobbled bride, the boring speeches, and the wild dancing. If I hadn't tossed him out, she would have listened all night.

36

Goma
November 10, 1996

LAKE KIVU WAS A SEA OF TRANQUILITY COMPARED TO THE tumult all around me. For the first time, I could no longer trust my senses. Ever since Captain Ezekiel had imposed summary justice in Masisi, I had suffered through an incessant ringing of the ears, exacerbated now by the shelling in the distance. What made my tinnitus particularly bad was the hysterical carping of aid workers hanging around the Hotel Bruegel's back lawn. Convinced they knew how to separate good and evil, the do-gooders were yelling into satellite phones for an army of Blue Helmets to come save the Hutu refugees from the Tutsi rebels who by this time had encircled Mugunga camp.

Facing the dark lake, I tried to rub away the whine in my eardrums. It was no use. Much as I wanted to cry out for some peace and quiet, the damage was done. I couldn't pretend nothing had happened.

"I can't believe Ezekiel did it, that he just blew that man's head off."

Dudu was shoveling a sandwich, the third this morning, into his mouth. Nothing we had witnessed affected his appetites. "Jacob, I warned you this trip would be too much for you."

I wanted to slap the smug smile off his face, but Dudu had a point. He could recognize my weakness, even if no one had ever informed him about the Nazi rocketman in Bavaria, when I faltered at the critical moment and let justice slip away.

"I thought we could do some good here, help people."

"It takes a hard man to suffer through a war like this," Dudu said. "You were never ruthless enough for the impossible decisions."

The decisions sure had become impossible. The Zairean army may have melted away, abandoning Goma to the Tutsis, but the Hutu genocidaires had dug in to defend Mugunga. The worst part of it, as the sirens kept cycling through my ears, was that the only doctor I could trust, Dr. Chantal Kayiranga, was stuck on the wrong side of the front lines. What a shame we couldn't have persuaded her to leave before Goma fell. Our only option now was to wait for a break in the impasse.

"We're all trapped here," I said. "Every one of us. We're each forced into a role: Dr. Chantal, Captain Ezekiel, even me."

"Not you, Jacob. Nothing is making you stay."

"Salik wants us to see what happens."

"Tell Salik to go fuck himself."

"It's not so easy. I owe him better than that."

"Ach, you don't owe him anything. Any debt must have been repaid years ago."

There was no use explaining what Salik had done for me, how he had given me back my will to fight, my purpose in life, my chance to leave something more to this world than a bag of bones. No, Dudu wouldn't have understood. The slightest hint of doubt would just have given him another excuse to torment me.

Rescuing me from his cynicism was Germaine Buzera, who strode onto the lawn looking resplendent, as Susanna would have said, in a bright yellow outfit that wrapped around her big body and made her skin gleam. Passing up a dozen invitations to join the tables of do-gooders, Germaine wound her way down to us. "Ahh, my friends, we are happy to find you here. So much has changed since we last met." It must have been a shock for her, after decades of Mobutu's corruption, to watch the Tutsi rebels seize control of her hometown of Goma. The governance of city affairs seemed improved, albeit with plenty of scores to settle, but Germaine didn't take much comfort.

"We are so worried what will happen to our orphans," she said. "They have already been exposed to too much war."

There wasn't much I could say to console her, so I tried to change the subject.

"Did your girls ever get to perform their *Tempest*?"

"Yes, it was very lovely. The girl who played Prospero did a wonderful job."

"What about Fulgence, and the other boys on the football team?" Dudu asked.

Her radiance clouded over. "We lost them."

"Lost them? I thought the Banyamulenge had the camp surrounded."

Sighing, she informed us how the Interahamwe leader Gescard had spirited away the footballers. "I tried to stop them. I begged the boys to stay with Dr. Chantal, but it was impossible. All they wanted to do was to fight."

"That's what boys do," Dudu said. "They like to play with guns, and if there are no guns, then knives and sticks are okay too."

"They have been traumatized by war. They see it as their only future." She shook her head, refusing to cave in to easy comforts. "This tribalism will kill us all."

Germaine's lament was interrupted by arrival of her boss, Karina Bronkhorst, lugging along a heavy satchel. Plopping herself down into a chair, the Dutch lady related how she had tried but failed to persuade the Tutsi rebels to halt their advance. "We had hoped to appeal to their humanity, to convince them that their goals can never be achieved by military means."

I didn't like to argue politics, but Karina was acting more unrealistic than usual. "It seemed to me the battle for Goma was pretty convincing. These rebels know what they want, and they've waited a long time to get it."

"That was only a skirmish," Karina said. "A true resolution will be possible only through peace between the warring parties. Unfortunately, the rebel command refused to meet with us. That is why we have come to you, to help us reach them."

I considered reverting to our old act: as naïve adventurers in search of mountain gorillas. That guise didn't fit anymore, not after our actual visit to the highlands. These women saw us for who we were and didn't seem to hold it against us.

"You have some unrealistic ideas about our influence," I told them. "We're just observers here."

On the road, a Tutsi military truck revved into higher gear, picking up speed as it headed west to the front.

"We have some intelligence you must see." Reaching into her satchel, Karina pulled out a stack of folders and began to describe a terrible series of massacres. The relief groups had uncovered evidence that Banyamulenge soldiers were executing great numbers of Hutu refugees and dumping the bodies into mass graves. The Tutsi rebels were trying to cover it up, blocking every attempt to investigate. It was the local Zairean villagers—forced to bury the dead—who were speaking out about what was happening in the forest, how Hutu men, women, and children were being struck down as they fled.

"Mr. Jacob, you consider yourself to be a man of principle," Karina said. "If that is true, then you must act now to protect the innocent. Our orphans were not responsible for the genocide in Rwanda. Nor was Dr. Chantal."

As she finished, I heard the clunk of paddle against canoe. The sound of the fishermen rowing out for their evening catch didn't bode well. The last thing I needed was for another body to be caught up in the nets, and for Karina to raise a fuss over its origin. Thank God, the fishermen paddled on without impediment.

"Look, I want to help the doctor, and your orphans too, but it's too early to talk about peace, especially with the genocidaires controlling Mugunga."

Germaine clasped my hand as if she could squeeze out my consent. "Oh, no, Mr. Jacob, it is never too early to talk about the peace. Otherwise the hate will be passed on to the next generation, and that will lead to more war, worse even than what we have already seen."

"I'm afraid that hate and war have always been with us. They're in our bones, dating all the way back to the earliest humans."

Releasing my hand, she shook her head. "I can never accept that. The possibility of reconciliation is what defines our humanity. We have a mutual friend who can prove that to you better than anyone."

Before I could object, Germaine opened up one of the satellite phones that had become part of the aid-worker arsenal. She dialed a number.

"Dr. Chantal, we are sitting with him at the hotel. Is it safe for you to talk?"

I couldn't make out the response, but Germaine leaned close to me, her full bosom brushing against my arm, and prodded me to speak, as if urging a child to overcome his fear of deep water. Raising the receiver to my left ear, a little less damaged than the right, I greeted the doctor, who immediately inquired after my health.

"How are you feeling, Mr. Jacob? I hope there has been no recurrence of tachycardia."

I assured her not to worry about my heart. Given the circumstances, it didn't seem worth mentioning my tinnitus. "It's good to hear your voice, Dr. Chantal. How are you holding out?"

"Conditions have become more challenging. Our medical supplies are no longer sufficient, and the armed men insist that we preserve what remains for their wounded. I am trying everything possible for my patients, but they are watching me all the time."

She paused, as if to check whether anyone might be snooping on her conversation. In a hushed voice she described a rising state of panic. "Every day the fighting comes closer. The refugees all wish to flee, but many have been shot as they try to escape."

I was considering how to advise her when the line went dead. Hearing no response, I called out her name. We tried to redial, but she was gone, as surely as if she had disappeared into the ruins of Bavaria. At least back then, I had been able to give Judith a pistol to protect herself along the way. Dr. Chantal had nothing but her white coat and her good fortune. They had carried her this far, but her luck couldn't last forever. She had become like so many I had met in mountains of Gondar or the displaced-persons camps of Europe. She needed to be rescued.

37

AN HOUR OR SO AFTER MOM LEFT FOR CHEMOTHERAPY, ISMAEL announced his intention to kick our singer out of the African Refugee Mega-Stars. Trouble had been brewing for months, as Pascal wore us down with his vanity, his endless griping, and his inability to show up on time. His voice had never been good enough to justify the diva shtick. Even now, with his future in the balance, Pascal kept us waiting in my mother's parlor for much of the morning.

"We are finished with you," Ismael said when Pascal arrived at last. "You will not play with us any more. Go start your own band."

Ripping off his sunglasses, Pascal started puffing hard, his standard cool evaporating. It took him only a few moments to recognize his principal adversary. "You are blaming me for the mistakes Shalom has made," Pascal said, pointing my way. "From the beginning I have said that we need a real manager. This is why we have not had success."

I wanted to defend myself, but Delacroix, the peacemaker, shook his head, reminding me not to interfere. Ismael would

275

handle this. Our musical director, for all the sweetness of his saxophone compositions, could be utterly cold, bloodless even, when it came to band business.

Cleaning his horn, Ismael allowed Pascal to rant, saying some awful things about me. It was only when the singer reverted to Wolof that he must have crossed a forbidden line, because Ismael suddenly put down his sax, sprang to his feet and unleashed a tirade so furious that the kufi seemed to levitate on his head. His barrage sucked the protest right out of Pascal, who stepped toward the door with one parting shot: "Shalom is a fool. You will never go anywhere with him."

After he slammed the front door, no one said a thing. Ismael reviewed his fingering on the horn, Delacroix tapped softly on his congas and Sang Froid sat at the piano, sliding his fingertips along the ivory as if measuring the keys.

"Well, that wasn't much fun," I said at last.

"You should be happy," Ismael said. "You have wanted to be rid of him for many months."

I had certainly campaigned for Pascal's dismissal; but now that he was gone, a twinge of guilt came over me. "I know, but I feel bad that it worked out that way."

"It had to be like this," Ismael said. "We must return to playing at a higher level." Ismael's thinking, never explicitly shared with me, finally became clear. The emergence of the guitarist Ousmane, who contributed vocals on a growing number of songs, had allowed our musical director to cut loose the insufferable Pascal. Ousmane didn't speak much English or French, but he was heir to a rich griot tradition, like the Talmud but with better stories and without all the legalisms. His voice bore the gravity of generations, his fingers carried the calluses of thousands of songs. I would need to shift my pitch for this iteration of Mega-Stars, and aim for a headier bunch of World Music types. Maybe the Renaissance Faire hadn't been such a bad idea after all.

The sound of footsteps on the stoop made me wonder whether Pascal was returning to go postal on us. Thank God, the pace was slower, heavier too. When the door opened, it was my father who stepped inside.

"What the hell's going on in here? You guys look like you're sitting *shiva*."

The Mega-Stars rose to greet my dad, whose stature as an authoritative elder had flourished in recent months. Since returning from his travels, Jacob Furman had squashed all doubts over who was the man of the house.

"It's nothing, Dad. Just some trouble with our singer. Ismael had to give him the boot, and he put up a big fuss."

"Good, because the only one who's allowed to make a fuss in this house is Professor Sussman. Even I have to be on my best behavior." Dad said, winking at me. Then he turned to Ismael. "So, what did that idiot do to get himself fired?"

Ismael was standing at attention with his horn, like a soldier on review. "He did not respect the music."

"Then you did right," Dad said. "Without respect nothing is possible. Or at least it's much harder than it should be. And life is hard enough."

My father looked forlorn, a mood I had never considered to be part of his emotional makeup. These past few months must have worn him down. He was used to gallivanting around the globe, engaged in his various surreptitious enterprises. Now his world had shrunk to tending to a sick wife, confronting the grueling realities of chemo and cooking, nausea and diarrhea. These responsibilities seemed to age him, a burden he couldn't hide, not even behind that new beard of his.

Delacroix, sensing the mood, offered to clear out. "Forgive our presence here, sir. We do not wish to be an intrusion. None of us should interfere with the professeur's recovery."

Waving him to relax, Dad informed us there was no rush. "Don't worry, my wife will be stuck at the hospital for another couple of hours. She only sent me home to collect some papers. In a few minutes the car is going to take me back."

I had only faint recollections of the time when my father made his home in the upper reaches of our brownstone. The sight of him lately, parading around, directing Mom's care, moving back into her bedroom, conflicted with a lifetime of my dealings with a mercurial, neglectful patriarch. Through the years, he had always been disengaged, uncommitted to being around the next hour, much less the next week. Now, before tromping upstairs to retrieve Mom's missing papers, he patted my cheek, not hard, but not lightly either.

"Where's your girl?" Dad asked. "I thought she came over whenever Susanna was out of the house."

"Mia will be here soon. We're going on a supply run."

"Good. Thank her for those blintzes she brought last week. Your mother really enjoyed them."

Mia had shown herself to be a real mensch, or whatever the equivalent was for women. She had helped me scour the basement and harvest the weed, which we turned over to Uncle Effie for disposal. Twice a week, she drove me around town to fulfill the various items demanded by my father: protein powders and eggs, high-calorie foods, prescriptions and medical supplies. Through her labors, she had developed a sweet rapport with Dad, who met us in the basement to drop off his directives. The cynic in me wondered whether her dedication was merely a sneaky means to creep closer to Mom, and thereby to restore herself to the good graces of her onetime thesis adviser. My suspicions, however, were allayed by watching how hard Mia took the news of my mother's illness. She wept repeatedly and unrelentingly, having lost her own mother a few years earlier. Afterwards, Mia insisted that neither me nor my father ever mention her role to Dr. Susanna Sussman, recuperating upstairs.

"Are you sure that's what you want?" I asked her. "You deserve some credit for all this work. My mom is bound to find out eventually."

"Not yet, Shally, not in her condition. She was never that crazy about me to begin with. Give her time to recover before she has to hear about me dating her son."

I opted not to involve Mia in my main mission these days: attending to Mom's impending conference on language evolution. That was my job alone. Per my agreement with Dad, I coordinated flights and hotel reservations, booked conference halls, printed programs, and negotiated with scholars from dozens of universities, all in the service of language itself. It was a miserable, thankless task that cast me back into the world of my enemies, but it accomplished its principal goals: to lift the organizational burden from my mother and to secure my father's support for the Mega-Stars.

True to his word, Dad arranged for Uncle Effie to rent us a rehearsal space near a Russian smokehouse in Red Hook, the old port neighborhood where worse crimes took place than a few noise violations. I had never known my father to harbor any musical affinities, but he seemed to have developed a real fondness for the guys, for Delacroix in particular. I even returned home one afternoon to find the two of them hanging out together in the parlor. We didn't have a meeting that day, but our conga player was sitting on the couch with his necktie unbound, his head in his hands. The conversation stopped as soon as I entered, and Delacroix immediately straightened himself out and pronounced a need to rush back to the war-crimes tribunal.

"Your father understands what I face in my work, and he advises me in how to confront it," Delacroix told me later, when I asked what had brought him out to us. "He is a wise man."

"Really?" I said, unsure whether to dissuade him. "I mean, I love my dad and all, but that's not how I would have described him."

Delacroix nodded. It had been months since he had confided in me. Now he had found a better match, someone who could appreciate his stories of brutality and killing.

"He has a great capacity to listen," Delacroix said. "Your father has helped me understand the roots of genocide. I do not say he was a witness, but he has real insight into the massacres. He has even shown me on a map where the crimes have transpired."

How it was possible, that Dad had any intimate knowledge of genocide in Central Africa, was beyond me. Whatever my father had been doing all those months away, he sure hadn't shared any of the details with his son. Some part of me wanted to warn Delacroix that Jacob Furman might not be the genial sage of recent appearance, that whatever crime I might have committed by slugging our former singer at CBGBs was nothing compared to my father's lifetime of nefarious activities. I stopped myself. It would have served no use, beyond exposing me as a bitter son, overcome by the past. If Delacroix and my dad found common cause in stories of children being murdered by their neighbors, it didn't feel like my place to interfere.

"I'm glad that you found someone to talk to," I said. "It's probably good for both of you."

After procuring my mother's papers, Dad came back downstairs and stood among us one more time. He must have been overdue to drive back to the hospital, but he seemed distracted by the heaviest gravitational body in the room.

"So, maestro," my father said to Sang Froid, "what do you think of our Steinway?"

Sang Froid, who spoke most fluidly in the language of music and mathematics, stroked the keys with affection. He tended to turn coy around the piano, as if smitten by a childish crush, but now revealed a discontent that must have been brewing in him for months.

"Forgive me for speaking frankly, Mr. Jacob, but this instrument has not been maintained as it should have been. The soundboard is in a very fragile condition. It needs to be played much more regularly."

Dad lay his hands upon the piano lid and looked deep into the black lacquer. For one who acted so hard-boiled, he sure had a mystical attachment to this Steinway.

"For many years we had an old man named Stolbach who attended to its care," Dad said. "He's gone now, poor man, and we've waited a long time to find someone to take his place. If you are willing, Sang Froid, you could fill in for Stolbach, whenever you have time. I can promise you it would give Shalom's mother a lot of joy."

Sang Froid limbered up his fingers with a little ditty that pulled us closer as if by sheer magnetic force.

"It has a beautiful sound," Delacroix said, leaning with the rest of us against the trunk. "May we ask why you acquired it, if you did not yourself play?"

"It came back with me from Germany after the war. I had hoped one day to meet a girl who deserved it."

"Is that really what happened, Dad? Mom always said you won it in a card game."

I expected him to lash out at me, but my father seemed lost in a kind of reverie.

"No, it wasn't a card game," he said. "It was the restitution of stolen property. Believe me, it's better off with us. This way it stayed with the Jews."

The Mega–Stars, given their deference toward their elders, weren't about to ask my father what the hell he was talking about.

"I would like to teach you gentlemen a song," Dad said, "something from our tradition, so you may understand us a little better." He started to sing, his voice slow and rich, deep as the foghorns that rumbled over our Red Hook studio.

"Hine ma tov u ma na'im, shevet achim gam ya'chad."

Not wanting to let him sing alone, I joined in and surprised myself over how alike we sounded, down to the vocal stylings. Two repetitions in, Dad put his arm around my shoulder and began rocking side to side, his free hand conducting everyone to follow along. By the next round, he had the guys humming with him, trying to mimic the words, their bodies swaying with ours. Sang Froid picked out the melody on the keyboard, and Ismael raised his sax to take up the tune, tweaking the scale and the timing like a Senegalese Coltrane, putting in a little Mandé variation to bring out something distinct, floating in the ether between Galicia and Dakar.

"What does the song mean?" Delacroix asked when they finished playing.

"It's about gathering with your people," Dad said, "how good and sweet it is for us to sit together as brothers."

We heard a rumble of approval. The spirit of *Hine Ma Tov* as an ode to fraternité matched the aesthetic sensibilities of the Mega-Stars, so much so that I could imagine Ismael melding the tune into our set. African Klezmers after all. Leaving us to pick up my mother from chemo, Dad parted with the guys one by one, each of them now an heir to his Galicianer heritage. Before leaving, he whispered to me, "One day, Shalom, the piano will be yours. All of this will." And then he was gone.

38

Gisenyi, Rwanda
November 11, 1996

FROM A HILLTOP INSIDE RWANDA, I SQUINTED TO MAKE OUT
Mugunga in the distance below. Through the haze, the fires
rising from the field, I imagined the final hours of a long
siege: the tension, the fear, and the testy recognition that many
wouldn't survive the ordeal. There was a prayer for this moment,
recited during Yom Kippur, that listed all the various ways of
dying—who by fire and who by drowning, who by sword and
who by stoning. It all seemed possible down on the plain. My
only comfort lay in the next few lines of the *piyyut*: that repentance, prayer, and good deeds could lighten the severity of the
decree. This was the best I could hope for Dr. Chantal, protected
only by her white coat: that we might forestall the day of judgment, at least for a little while.

"Jacob, are you sure you want to do this?" Dudu asked.

"I have to, I have to do it."

Dudu rolled his shoulder and winced, as if the very consideration of our role here caused him deep pain in an old wound. "It

makes no difference to me. I just don't want you to get upset again. We can't go back so easily to your pretty doctor for treatment."

I didn't appreciate being reminded of that shameful episode. My heart had remained steady since then, but now suddenly, as I considered our impending meeting, I felt the return of a terrible thumping in my eardrums, worse than before. God damn it. The last thing I needed was to turn back into a nervous nudnik.

"What the hell am I going to say to the general?" I asked.

We had traversed thousands of miles, witnessed terrible sorrows, weighed enough ethical dilemmas to perplex Maimonides, and yet this was the first time I had asked Dudu for moral support. My need seemed to amuse him. I expected him to offer another lecture about my lack of ruthlessness, but instead he pulled up his sleeve to reveal the full extent of the tattoos twirling around his left arm.

"Show him this. Maybe he can learn from our mistakes."

On the back side of the battle scene was an inscription in Hebrew: the names David, Shachar, and Edo.

"Who the fuck are they?"

"My brothers from the army. The ones who died from the Hezbollah." He rotated his arm to match the names against the bodies illustrated in the rocket attack.

"What about the other writing, the business in Arabic?"

Inspecting his arm again, he admired the words as if encountering them for the first time, a different hand drawing this part. "That's the family that didn't deserve what I did to them."

He pointed to a rudimentary illustration of a table, which looked like it had been scratched by a prisoner in the Soviet gulag, and explained how one morning in Lebanon his unit had come upon a farmhouse. Assigned to clear the area, he kicked open the door and interrupted a family at breakfast.

"They were just sitting there, when the grandmother dropped a pot on the stove, and then click." His arms shook to illustrate how the machine gun erupted in his hands and unleashed a torrent of fire that blew away seven members of the Shomali clan.

"That's why I hated the mag, Jacob. It was too heavy with memories."

When it was over, he had laid down his weapon and sat at their table to finish their breakfast, just as he had finished their lives.

"How the hell could you eat after what had just happened?"

He breathed deep, eyes closed, as if he could still smell the cocktail of ammunition, dust, and blood. Then he smiled, almost fondly. "I wanted to taste how their life had been. And you know what: it was the best fucking hummus I ever had in my life. The grandmother had probably spent all day making it, rubbing the skins off the beans, mixing in the tahina, and the parsley and lemon from their garden."

It must have been a ghoulish sight, and his commander wanted to send him for psychological evaluation, but there was no time for shrinks, not in the middle of a war. His unit fought all the way to Beirut, where, during the siege, he scratched out the image of a table onto his own arm with a needle and some ink from a pen.

"So you think that by putting all those names together, you'll make peace between nations?"

"I don't have your ambitions of saving the world, Aba. All I can do is pay tribute to the dead. My arm will be the only place in the universe where their names will be read together, because they all died the same way: for nothing. And when I am finished, they will be buried together, in the same grave."

Dudu dropped his sleeve and looked out at the distant camp. "Just like your friends down there. They'll all be buried together."

A Tutsi soldier approached to beckon us inside the former elementary school that now served the military command. As we entered, General Roger Gitarama and his staff were bent over a table mapping out their campaign. The meeting broke up, and the aides retreated to the fringes of the room. The general reached out his long bony hand and invited me to sit and to tell him all that had happened since our last meeting at Bisesero.

"I had been wondering how you were finding things," the general said. "My understanding is that you have had some interesting encounters. I hope they proved illuminating."

Whether he was referring to our travels through Masisi or our repeated visits to Mugunga, I could not be sure. My only certainty was that the ominous thump in my ears seemed to grow stronger with every breath.

"Yes, we've learned a great deal in our time here."

The general leaned forward to pat me on the knee. "And you requested this meeting because you have an urgent issue to discuss."

There was a joking familiarity to him now, without any sign of his old aloofness. This guy must have known our reason for coming. Salik had told me that he had kept tabs on every little detail under his command. It was what had made him so forceful a leader, able to dictate the terms of the conversation.

"There is a concern." I weighed my words deliberately, one after another, finding that speech helped ease the pounding in my ears. "That many innocents will suffer in the fight for Mugunga."

My comment seemed to leave a stench in the air. The general adjusted his glasses to observe me more closely. The wary smile melted into an implacable stare.

"I am surprised to hear a man of your experience defend the genocidaires. You, better than anyone, should appreciate what it means to face extermination."

There was something damning, even terminal, in his tone, an indication of how few drops of poison it took to contaminate an entire lake. Maybe I had crossed the front lines too many times to be trusted. Or maybe I had simply overestimated my influence.

"No, General, I don't mean to defend them. When it comes to the genocidaires, you should do what is needed. They deserve no less."

He stared blankly at me, his expression nearly catatonic. It was as if he were lost in thought, but there was no dreaminess to this man. "It is a relief to hear that we have your blessing." His tone had shifted again, his sarcasm rising, as if I were no different from any other whingeing do-gooder pleading for him to have mercy on the killers. In the space of a few breaths, I had squandered something irreplaceable, the trust between comrades.

"Believe me, I have no words for the genocidaires." The thumping had nearly vanished by now; my speech had regained its normal pace and pitch. "My concern is for the civilians who took no part in the genocide, but are now held captive in the camp."

"What are you asking, Mr. Jacob?"

Germaine and Karina had sent me with a mandate for peace and reconciliation, but I couldn't go that far. The ladies were dreamers and could never comprehend the dynamics of a military campaign, or the difficulty of defending a persecuted community. Unwilling to be cast as a peacenik, I had come armed instead with a more tangible proposal.

"Hold off the attack until the innocent can be evacuated. Let us procure for you a list of all the inhabitants of Mugunga, so you can check those names against those who committed crimes during the genocide. In this way, history will record that you did everything possible to separate the innocent from the killers. Then you can get right back to the campaign."

The idea had hit me the previous evening, as I sat staring at the lake after Germaine and Karina had left. It would take an organizational masterstroke, but it offered a chance. Better than nothing.

The general looked befuddled. Then he shook his head and started laughing to himself, enjoying a private joke. "That is quite an ambitious undertaking, Mr. Jacob. Let me ask you, however, what makes you so confident the aid agencies that have sheltered our enemies will be inclined to share their records? Not only that, would the genocidaires truly relinquish their most significant strategic asset: the civilian refugees they have used to garner world sympathy?"

The general gazed across the former classroom, as if he could still see the Tutsi children who had studied here before the genocide, seated beside their Hutu classmates. "It is as I informed you at Bisesero. The longer we delay, the more we give an opportunity for the genocidaires to regroup. Every day costs us more lives, and stops us from moving toward a future where tribe is no longer part of our consciousness."

I couldn't contend with the general's strategic assessment, nor his vision of a future without tribalism. All I could do was testify to the merits of Dr. Chantal, a righteous woman in the city of Sodom, who had confessed culpability for her part, however tiny, in the genocide. It wouldn't do any good. The more I argued for her, the more the general would have dismissed me as naïve, a simplistic do-gooder, a romantic old fool. And so, once again, I abandoned the woman who I had promised to protect. This time, it wasn't out of cowardice or a misplaced sense of duty: it was just irrelevance. There was nothing I could say, nothing I could do, to change the course of history. As I retreated into silence, another voice spoke up in my defense.

"General, you should not doubt this old man," Dudu said, stepping out from behind my chair. "Jacob is the greatest friend the Tutsi people could have. He spends his days worrying about your future, and if he is upset that the innocent will die in Mugunga, there is a reason for his concern. He knows that whatever happens down there—the good and the bad—will stay with you forever."

Dudu's emergence caused grumbling among the gallery of military officers who filled the room. For this crowd, it must have represented a clear violation of protocol. Dudu didn't much believe in protocol. Ignoring the hostility, he thumped his chest and raised his voice even louder.

"I don't give a shit what happens, but Jacob loves you, better than he ever did me, and he has been like a father to me. He speaks as if you Tutsis are the chosen people, and you, General, are another Moses, leading the Israelites to the promised land."

The general glared at him, that vacant hostile stare of his. It didn't stop Dudu. Nothing could stop Dudu. He rolled right along:

"Jacob wants to win an argument with history itself, to make sure that in ten, fifty, even a thousand years from now, you Tutsis will still be considered as a light among the nations. I keep telling him it's all bullshit, that a man like him—who has no education, who has always avoided the hard decisions a soldier has to make—will never know how it all turns out. He doesn't listen to me, though. Jacob can be very stubborn."

The shuffling in the room stopped. The general and his staff no longer grumbled or glared. They endured Dudu's lecture out of pity for me, but the last thing I needed was their pity. It made me feel older than ever.

"Come on, Dudu, that's enough," I said. "We've done our best."

The general and his staff returned to their battle plans. We were led out, pausing one more time to look at the broad panorama over the field below. Dudu had exposed too much, but I couldn't be angry with him, not this time. He had recognized, long before I did, when a cause was lost.

39

Brooklyn
April 19, 1997

As time wound down on the morning of my conference, I couldn't stop tweaking my essay on the evolution of the human vocal tract, fearful that the slightest oversight—an imprecise assessment of existing data, a false analogy, a mistaken citation— might undermine the broader thesis and sabotage my vainglorious hope of patching together the feuding factions of my field. Jacob, standing by me with a devotion unseen during our troubled decade of marriage, had finally run out of patience.

"Susanna, enough already. You can't show up late to your own event."

"All right, let me print this and I'll be right with you."

I pushed the buttons for the computer to inscribe the essay to paper, but with a perfect comic irony that made me reconsider my disbelief in evil spirits, the printer refused to function. After inspecting the apparatus for obvious defects—a lack of ink, a paper jam, a faulty connection—I couldn't figure out what was wrong.

Jacob checked his watch again. "Leave it alone. Shalom can fix it while you're in the bath."

For the past month, without any prompting from me, Shalom had taken charge of the conference planning, evincing a mastery for logistics that matched Marcel's guidance of the Hadar expedition. My great regret was in failing to have recognized his talents sooner, when it might have made a difference.

Responding to his father's call for help, Shally came down to my office, tinkered with the printer, and brought it back to life with an electric whirr.

"Thank you, Shally. I couldn't have done this without you."

"Stop thanking me, Mom, and get dressed already."

Giving in, I allowed Jacob to assist me into the bathroom. He averted his eyes as I dropped my robe and stepped into the shower. This had long been one of my minor pleasures: the hot water soaking up my persistent chill. It never lasted, the sense of warmth, but for the moment it felt glorious. Then, as I spread soap across my hip, something disconcerting drew my attention: a fresh constellation of moles, surfacing like a breaching whale in an area protected from direct sunlight.

As panic flushed over me, the warm shower turned into an oven. "Oh, Jacob, this is no good."

He slid open the shower curtain and bent deep to examine my hip. Covering my chest in shame, I watched his face for guidance. There was no surprise, no fear, only clarity.

"Don't think about this now. We'll show them to Dr. Gerson next week." He wrapped the towel around me to pat me gently dry. "We'll get through this. But first you need to get ready. You have a big day."

Jacob propped me up until I was fully clothed in the severe gray suit reserved for academic events. The outfit that had once fit snugly now hung like drapery. He brought in a chair so I could rest while dabbing rouge onto a face that had rarely indulged in cosmetics. Better to resort to subterfuge than to face the cloying sympathies of strangers shocked at my physical deterioration. In the corner of the mirror, I spotted Jacob staring at me.

"Is it too much?" I asked.

"No, it's fine. I was just admiring how beautiful you are." He brushed the back of his fingers against my cheek. I shied away. The last thing I needed was to have to reapply this ridiculous mask.

"Even without the hair you loved so much?" My fingers reflexively touched my bald head.

"It's still there for me, in my memory." He held out a scarf, a lovely piece of lavender silk, which he draped over my head and knotted into place behind my neck.

A honk outside alerted us to the arrival of Effie's driver. Shalom assembled my papers and accompanied us down to the stoop, but no further. His refusal to attend the conference saddened me. As the car pulled away, I wondered whether Jacob might have prevailed on him to end his boycott. No, it wouldn't have been fair to place father and son into conflict again, especially since they had been getting along so much better lately. Besides, Shalom had the right to make his own decisions.

When we reached the university, Jacob guided me into a packed auditorium framed by a banner: "The Biological Roots of Babel: A Multi-Disciplinary Investigation into the Evolution of Language." The boisterous crowd quieted upon our entrance. My pale figure, unsteady bearing, and head scarf, a Jolly Roger in lavender, must have answered all questions about my state of being. We had made it only a few feet when the silence was broken by an applause that surged into a sustained ovation.

"Susanna, look up," Jacob said. "See how much they appreciate you."

"I'm embarrassed. They shouldn't be clapping."

He squeezed my ribs tighter. "Of course they should. You've earned this honor."

The crowd converged around us as we made our way down the aisle. Long-time colleagues clasped my hand and told me that

I looked great. Younger scholars greeted me with gratitude for my guidance. Assembling this dissonant collection of voices constituted an achievement in its own right, one for which my son deserved primary credit. Shalom had cast the net in all directions, ensnaring evolutionary biologists and cognitive psychologists, physiologists and surgeons, and, most of all, physical anthropologists and linguists, an act of diplomacy so profound that I wondered whether his true calling shouldn't have been to forge peace between nations.

"What a wonderful job Shally did bringing them together," I told Jacob. "I don't know how he managed it; these people hate each other."

"You must have inspired the best in him."

I wished Shally could have shared in this moment. If only he had allowed me to defend him when he stood before the department with his terribly flawed essay, which was crushed without consideration. My intervention might have failed to make any difference, but his decision to have me recused, however honorable in academic terms, haunted me still. A mother should be allowed to support her son at his moment of crisis.

Caught up in regrets, I wasn't prepared to be approached by Mia Greystone, of all people, weaving her way through the crowd. I had dismissed her brusquely in our last encounter, but she still sidled up to me with an implied familiarity and clasped my hand.

"I'm so glad you made it to the conference, Susanna. I hope you are feeling better."

She wasn't dressed as flirty as on previous occasions but appeared to be as self-indulgent as ever, flipping her hair around with her typical nervous glee. One day, were Mia ever to be in my position, she might understand how painful it was to watch her flaunt her health and vanity. I hated to seem vindictive, but the sight of her left me more distrusting than ever.

"Nice to see you, Mia. I'm sorry for withdrawing as your thesis adviser. As you can tell, I wasn't really in the position to commit to a long-term project."

Unlike the rest of the crowd, Mia didn't seem surprised. She sniffled and told me she understood, and then, in a strange moment, she greeted Jacob, just a polite "good morning." Embedded in their tone was a flicker of mutual recognition.

"Jacob, what was that all about?" I asked as my former student returned to her seat. "Do you know Mia?"

He turned passive, the old blank expression familiar to me from each time I broached his zone of secrecy. Then, with a bemused smile, he transformed back into the reformed husband of recent vintage. "She's a friend of Shalom's. She helped him clean up the basement. Without her, it would still be a mess down there."

I was stunned. Never would I have guessed that this vain little waif had any connection to my son. "It's very nice of her, but you could have mentioned something." Watching Mia, seated apart from her fellow graduate students, I wondered what else he hadn't told me. "Is there more to this story, Jacob? You have your old devious look."

He raised his hands, as if I were a brigand holding him up for ransom: "I've been sworn to secrecy." He stood captive to my glare for only a moment before caving: "We wanted to tell you, but the girl begged us not to. She didn't want it to affect your professional opinion of her. For some reason, Mia thinks you don't like her."

It was enough to sour my morning, the idea of this terribly manipulative girl enveloping Shally in her web. I would have to warn him somehow, give him some final guidance, but a mother could only so much do to shield her grown son.

Of more immediate concern was the combustible presence of Chuck Rosenfeld rushing down the aisle to snatch me from Jacob's care. Blowing my husband a kiss, Chuck wrapped his arm around me and escorted me to the dais. "My dear Susanna, I know it may be fashionable, but you have taken this American obsession with weight loss a bit far."

Despite the auditorium's chill, Chuck left the top buttons of his shirt open, showing off the tanned skin and bleached chest hair of an academic Houdini who had escaped the classroom to retrace the ancient odyssey of cetaceans from land to sea.

"My dear Chuck, I could never have coaxed you back without a dramatic change in my personal well-being."

Helping me into a seat, he handed me the formal program of panelists and drew his finger down the long list of speakers. "You've assembled so much hot air here today that we'll be lucky if the building doesn't float away."

"Oh, you old grouch, behave yourself until you've heard what they have to say."

Pulling the microphone toward me, I welcomed the congregation with a secular invocation, a plea to look past our divisions. "Let us hope that these discussions help us to reevaluate our place in the natural world and to refine our definition of what it means to be human. We may not resolve all the answers today, but one day. . . ."

I paused, overcome by emotion and embarrassed that my words were showing me to be a sentimental fool. After a moment's breath, I felt myself lifted once more by the sound of clapping, the audience rising for another ovation. The response was so generous, so indulgent that my only graceful escape was to cede the floor to Chuck. Invited to begin, my old adviser didn't waste a moment recounting his work on bottlenose dolphins, among which he had learned to distinguish grammar, even culture, in their signature whistles. If he could have designed a better means of breathing underwater, he would have swum with them forever, searching for interspecies dialogue. When he finished, the audience applauded his contribution. Surprised, Chuck clasped both hands above his head, like a political prisoner freed from detention after a long, unjust conviction.

"I told you times had changed," I said as he returned to my side.

"Before you get too excited, let's hear what these walking apes have come up with."

The morning was devoted to the animal studies: chimpanzee sign language and vervet monkey alarm calls, followed by the big draw—a parrot named Socrates, who had learned to use a hundred words.

"They have filthy mouths, those damn birds," Chuck said, watching Socrates yawn and expose a pink tongue. He had a primal disdain for any non-mammal species.

"Be nice. This research has some fascinating implications."

"I meant it literally. Their mouths are full of bacteria."

Ignoring him, I wrapped my shawl tighter to ward off the chill and watched Thaddeus Walker, Socrates's researcher, call on the bird to perform. Waving his wings to maintain his balance, Socrates showed us his capacity to differentiate between blue circles and green circles, and to count up to six items. Not language, but perhaps a strain of the cognition that flowered in us.

After lunch, the lineup shifted to modern humans: from the marvel of childhood language acquisition to the tragedy of aphasia in stroke victims. As the afternoon wound down, I summoned my remaining strength to deliver my own contribution, speculative in essence, charting the odyssey of the larynx from high in the primate palate down into the throat of modern humans. Citing research that gorillas, chimps, and even goats could drop their voiceboxes to threaten an adversary or to seduce a mate, I wondered whether the laryngeal shift in early hominids might have been a game, a way of entertaining the tribe, which offered such an evolutionary advantage that the larynx became stuck at its lower depths, igniting the explosion of syntax and generative grammar and brain mechanics that allowed us to create language.

When I reached the final paragraph, it was over: my essay, the conference, the months of preparation. The audience offered a valedictory round of applause to celebrate the airing of our debates, now bound in time for future generations.

Jacob met me on stage and reasserted his authority as the guardian of my physical state. Insisting on my need to rest before the evening's festivities, he granted me only a few farewells before bustling me out to the waiting car. Riding home, I leaned back in the seat and exhaled deeply.

"You know, Jacob, this may have been the last time I see those people."

My husband didn't contest my conclusion. He understood the significance of the fresh moles around my hip. "If so, then they've had a glimpse of the woman I've always known."

"And who is that?"

"A survivor."

"That's all?"

"That's a lot. Survivors get to leave their legacy in words and deeds. And you, Susanna, have tried to tell the story of all of us."

Jacob had sat through the conference without complaint, never budging from his perch in the first row, never disappearing to answer some mysterious telephone call. Watching him now, with his full beard, he reminded me more than ever of the Holbein poster hanging in our kitchen. His broad chest and confident brow was a mirror image of the burly lead ambassador armed with the imprimatur of power. More significant, I recognized for the first time the identity of the painting's second ambassador, thinner and more scholarly, but every bit as commanding. It was Shally, whose firm hand had reigned over every detail of the conference. And finally I understood the meaning of the skull, twisted and distended, a trick of refraction cast onto the space between them. The skull was me. Or at least it soon would be. This was the nature of things. I took comfort in accomplishing what I had set out to do.

Laying my head against Jacob's chest, I listened to his heart beat with steady, powerful strokes, a stately grandfather clock undimmed by new technology. A sturdy heart was a gift in a man his age, and his was marvelously constant, devoid of the doubts and uncertainties that affected the rest of us humans. Shutting my eyes, I felt myself drift off, able to sleep at last, relieved to have made it through the turbulence of the passage.

40

Brooklyn
April 19, 1997

I WORRIED HOW MOM'S FRATRICIDAL COLLEAGUES WOULD squeeze their monumental egos into the narrow frame of our brownstone. The last thing my mother needed, after the collegiality of the conference, was for the concluding party to splinter along traditional academic fault lines. My means of forestalling that discord rested with the most Jewish of solutions: a good spread. Mia drove me over to Bay Ridge to pick up a Lebanese meze, and then on to Red Hook, near our new studio, where Uncle Effie's Russian pals prepared schools of smoked fish.

As the guests trickled in, I put together a plate for my mother sitting beside Dad on the parlor couch. She had never been crazy about Middle Eastern food, part of her general aversion to anything borne of either house of Abraham, but she did love lox. Bagel in hand, I folded a double layer of salmon atop a healthy shmear of cream cheese.

"Shally, that's too much."

"It's good, Mom. We need to fatten you up."

I waited for her to correct my grammar, but she focused instead on scraping half the cream cheese off her bagel.

Dad leaned over to inspect my work. These days my parents acted like a couple of old nudists, so comfortable in each other's presence that they no longer bothered to stare. They related to each other like two halves of a broken plate, or, better yet, two mismatched parts of different plates glued together.

"She should have some blintzes," he said. "Didn't you get any blintzes?

"Dad, who serves blintzes at a party?"

He shrugged. "Maybe it was different back in my day. So, you don't bring your father anything?

"What do you want, Jewish or Middle Eastern?"

"What's the difference?"

At my father's table, even food tasted of tribalism. It wasn't worth negotiating my way through his garden of forking paths that traversed the holy land, not on an evening devoted to Mom, so I fixed him a plate of whitefish salad and stuffed vine leaves, with a wedge of sweets in the corner, basbusah and baklawa, rugelach and honeycake, as if the Arabs and the Jews were making peace at last over dinner.

"Sit with us," he said, when I delivered the food. "You don't need to run around so much. The conference is over."

"Not yet, Dad. I have to keep an eye on things."

He looked disappointed, hoping for a sympathetic ear among the gathering crowd. By now, the conference guests were lining up to offer cheery greetings to my mother, before moving swiftly out to the kitchen where Mia was tending bar. None of them appeared too keen to linger over Mom, partly because of her fragile health, but also because Dad glared at them like a watchdog. The only one who stood up to him was Uncle Chuck, greeting Dad with a boisterous smack on the shoulder. Then he dropped back into a boxing stance, and the two of them started bobbing and weaving like a couple of aging palookas, too old and punch-drunk to do any real damage. It wouldn't have been a fair fight. Dad must have had fifty pounds on him. Besides, Chuck was all talk, while Dad was all action, still able to land a blow and absorb one too.

"Look at you, you old spook," Chuck said, "What's the word from Mossad headquarters?"

Dad parried Chuck's jab and measured a cross to his chin. "I wouldn't know. I've been too busy taking care of my wife while her oldest friend was off screwing dolphins."

Opening his fists, Chuck tapped Dad's cheek. "I wasn't screwing them, God damn it. I was listening to them screw each other, and recording their sounds of ecstasy."

"Both of you, stop," Mom said, yanking at Dad's leg for him to sit back down.

I pulled Chuck away to remind him of his promise to deliver a copy of his conference paper. "I'm going to need that essay before you leave town, Uncle Chuck. We're moving fast to publish a book from the proceedings."

"Don't worry, Shally, you don't have to pester me for it. I'll get it to you."

Mom had tried for years to coax him to contribute to various anthologies, but not even their long friendship could thaw his resistance. Time didn't allow me to be so indulgent.

"You better follow through this time. We wouldn't want an unfortunate accident to happen to your scuba gear."

He looked surprised, less fearful than delighted. "You little devil. When did you start taking after your father?"

"It was always in me: it just took time to bubble to the surface."

I gave him a little pop to the gut, still tightly coiled. Tough old bird didn't flinch. Before I could exact a more definitive commitment, two of my former classmates called out to me, and Chuck sneaked away. Molly Epstein and Sam Melendez, now married, had led the campaign for me to be tossed out of the department, on grounds that I had breached clear ethical boundaries by sleeping with my informants: the European girls in Cuba. Much as they had done me a favor, I never appreciated the personal animus they had brought to my trial.

"Hey Shalom, we missed you at the conference," Sam said.

"Your mom said you coordinated the whole event," Molly said. "You really did a fantastic job."

They were awfully chirpy, encircling me like vultures around a famished child.

"Yeah, well, it was Mom's show. My involvement with all things anthropological ended a few years back."

"You cut your hair," Molly said. "I barely recognized you. What have you been up to these days?"

"You'll see soon enough. Best not to spoil the surprise."

Excusing myself, I sneaked behind Mia serving up stiff cocktails to faculty members who would one day judge her thesis, if she ever got around to writing it. Sidling in close enough to smell her shampoo, I slid my hand beneath the flirty little top that barely covered her belly.

"You haven't poured anything for Chuck Rosenfeld, have you?"

Covering her mouth, she gasped, having forgotten my dad's warning that the old crank couldn't hold his liquor. "Oh my God, I'm so sorry. Do you think it's a problem?"

"Not yet. We better keep an eye on him, though."

Across the kitchen, Chuck was holding a double of scotch and provoking the birdman, Thaddeus Walker, who had brought along his parrot, Socrates, as party prop and chick magnet. The bird himself didn't seem to appreciate Chuck's demands to submit to another test of his numeric skills.

"How many, you silly bird?" Chuck asked, holding up his fingers.

Socrates issued a sound that could have been "four," but might well have been "bugger." Chuck wasn't impressed.

"All right, Walker, stop bullshitting us. This damn bird is nothing but a cheap vaudeville act."

I wanted to keep tabs on Chuck, but my attention was diverted by the arrival of the African Refugee Mega-Stars. On this night, Delacroix, Ismael, and Sang Froid were joined by our new singer, Ousmane, who had swapped his electric guitar for a traditional 21-string kora. Dad embraced each of them, Delacroix in particular, as if they were the nephews he would never have. Then Delacroix knelt, so he could address my mother at eye level, and announced that they had prepared a special set in her honor.

"Madame Professeur, we have been hoping to perform for you for some time. To celebrate tonight, we have learned to interpret the ballads traditional to your people. And Sang Froid will present a special composition he has completed for this occasion."

Mom wouldn't have recognized a klezmer tune as part of her cultural heritage, but she seemed delighted at the chance to hear the Mega-Stars perform, rather than just rehearse in the basement. "It's a wonderful treat for me," Mom said. "I'm so happy that Shally invited you."

I couldn't allow myself any undeserved accolades. "Actually, it was Dad's idea."

She looked at my father as if he had developed a sudden passion for orchids or Persian cats. "Since when did you discover an ear for music?"

"I needed something to spice up my retirement," Dad said, nodding at me. "I couldn't just sit around gardening all day."

She cuddled into his side and they both grew quiet, more affection than I had ever witnessed between them, but before it became too intimate, Mom lifted her head and turned to Sang Froid. "I must thank you for your lovely music during the afternoons. Your piano playing has brought back memories of my father in our parlor in Łódź. The house has become awfully quiet in his absence."

No one was quite sure what she meant. To spare her any embarrassment, Dad invited the Mega-Stars to set up wherever they could find room. Sang Froid took his seat at the piano, while

Delacroix positioned himself against the bookcase with his congas before him. All Ismael had to do was clip his sax around his neck, but it was Ousmane, the smallest among them, who needed the most space, setting himself down on the carpet with the kora that he plucked like a harp. As Ousmane tuned his twenty-one strings, a houseful of academics crammed into the parlor.

Before I could introduce the band, Mia tugged my arm to remind me of the big cardboard carton we had stowed beneath the piano. "Shally, don't forget." She helped me haul out the box and distribute the final memento of the conference: a white T-shirt with a brown silhouette illustrating the ascent of man from knuckle-dragging ape to bipedal hominid, the design pinched from Mom's kitchen apron. On the front was printed the conference title, on back a full list of presenters.

"What a delightful shirt," Mom said, as my father held it out before her. "You really thought of everything."

As the shirts sprayed out in all directions, someone called out that there was a problem, and I bent over my mother to see that, indeed, the text had been printed as "Evoltion of Language."

"Shit."

I should have checked the sample, but, caught up in the conference preparations, it had completely slipped my mind. Once again the anthropology gods had cursed me and turned me into the butt of jokes; that is, until my father spoke up in my defense.

"It doesn't make any damn difference." Dad's voice boomed through the brownstone. "Everyone knows what the shirt means."

The titters of laughter stopped; no one dared to challenge my father, not in his house, not with his hard edge. The junior scholars tugged on the T-shirt over their clothes, a final show of unity before they returned to their monkey talk and baby babble and computer models.

As Ismael kissed his horn and started to play, Mia nudged my shoulder with her chin. "Don't you want a shirt?"

"Not me. I washed my hands of anthropology a long time ago."

She held my hands close to her face, inspecting my palms. "They don't look so clean to me. This place is filled with your handiwork."

I edged in to kiss her as Ismael launched into "Coumba." She backed away, but found herself trapped against the wall.

"Shally, what are you doing? Your mother is right there."

"Don't worry about it. We can't hide forever. Besides, my dad gave away the farm."

"I thought he knew how to keep a secret."

"Yeah, well, he seems to have adopted a new policy against deception. My mom spotted his reaction when you greeted him at the conference."

Mia and I glanced over at my parents holding hands on the couch. For a moment, they stared back at us, and the two sets of couples gazed at each other in astonishment, wondering how to make sense of the other's relationship. Then we all grew embarrassed and went back to pretending nothing had happened.

By this time, the Mega-Stars were in full swing, and in a fitting coda to the conference, the assorted anthropologists and linguists came together in dance, a ritual Mia claimed to be more ancient than language itself. Not wanting to miss out, I tugged her toward the center of the parlor.

"Come, let's show these jokers how it's done." I reached low to roll her hips.

"Oh, so you think I don't know any salsa?"

Stepping into the open space, we put on a clinic, me drawing on memories of Havana clubs, Mia adapting a lifetime at the barre. Unable to compete, the gang of academics formed a circle around us and started clapping like chimps, driving us to ever more daring moves until Ismael wrapped up his saxophonic journey.

"Ay," he said, taking a big breath.

The crowd whooped and hollered, and when the clapping ebbed, Delacroix stood up from his congas to address the room.

"Our homage tonight is for Professeur Susanna, a great lady who we wish to recover very soon."

My mother waved in appreciation, and the guests applauded before the Mega-Stars kicked into the next song, this one an Africanized version of a klezmer classic. When the set ended, the guys put aside their instruments and went into the kitchen to socialize. I could have joined them, to protect them from the clutches of my former classmates, but another task loomed. It felt long overdue to come clean to my mother, so Mia and I could stop skulking about, especially as Mom now knew the truth about us anyway.

"Come on, we might as well get this over with," I told Mia, starting toward the couch.

"Really, right now?"

"Would you rather do it when no one else is around?"

As we approached, Dad rose from the couch to allow Mia space to sit beside her former adviser. At this stage, there was no use in pretending any longer. All pretenses could be dropped.

"Mia, I understand from my husband that you've been a great help to us these past few months."

"Thank you, Susanna, I've been happy to do whatever I can."

For some strange reason, Mia was enunciating every syllable, smiling too hard, raising her voice, as if my mother had lost her cognitive faculties. It made Mia come off a little unhinged.

"What about your thesis?" my mother asked. "Have you made any progress narrowing it down?"

Here was an open wound. All the days that Mia had spent driving me around should have been devoted to refining her incoherent premise on the origins of dance.

"Not as much as I would have liked. You would still consider my topic to be a little speculative."

"That's no good. Mia, you need to dedicate yourself, or time just slips away. You can't rely on anyone else to do this for you. Sometimes people look out for your best interest, but often they wage their own battles at your expense. You have to make your own possibilities, and tell the truth, no matter what happens."

My mother went on like that, dispensing wisdom that had Mia dabbing at her eyes, quickly, as if afraid to bawl in front of her former adviser. It was harsh medicine, far harsher than any my mother had ever issued to me, and I had been a terrible student. Mom had spent decades sparing me even the slightest criticism, but as she called out poor Mia for her strategic cycles of manipulation and obsequiousness, of venality and servility, I had to think that my mother's message was meant for my edification as well. As much as it might have been unfair, I could feel my perspective begin to shift.

Watching Mia face my mother, I wondered what the fuck I was doing. For all Mia's enthusiasm and generosity, we didn't have anything between us. I couldn't live forever on a sense of gratitude alone. Sure, we had fun together, but it wasn't based on any substance, anything solid, just the adolescent rebelliousness of hiding out from my mom. Once the secret was revealed, there wasn't much left. It would be awkward to cut her loose, but I didn't see any other way. Mom had shown me that much.

My mother sighed and rested back against the couch, a sign that it was time to move along, so Mia excused herself to make sure the Mega-Stars had enough food and drink. She was nothing if not helpful.

As she moved off, I felt a sharp pang in my thigh, where my father had just jabbed me with a fork.

"You little shit, you're going to dump that girl because you think you're too good for her."

"What? You mean Mia? No. It's not like that, Dad."

"Sure it is, I can read it on your face. You want to move on to another one."

My mother had always warned me about Dad's uncanny prescience, but I had passed it off as her way of getting me to behave when she had no alpha-male presence in the house. "Better not do that or your father will know" was as effective a warning in our home as in any intact family, and, strangely enough, it gave me pause in many a precarious situation, like when some of my pals began to dabble in smack. The fear of Dad tracking me down often kept me from going too far over the edge.

Before my father could poke me again, Mom grabbed the fork out of his hand and placed it back on the coffee table. "Oh, leave Shally alone. Let him come to his own conclusions. I will say this for him: at least he likes to take a girl dancing. Not like you. And anyone who could have juggled all the competing agendas around here must have some clear talents."

"Talents, eh." Dad looked bemused. He would have been loath to admit it, but he always seemed somewhat charmed by the excesses of my social life. If nothing else, it allowed him to assume the mantle of paternal opprobrium, spiced with few sly winks.

"You know, Dad, it's not as if I ever actually do anything to deceive women. They just all want to save me."

"Save you from what?"

"From a dissolute life, I suppose."

Mom had heard enough. Reaching across Dad's lap to squeeze my wrist, she connected the three of us in her stubborn grip. "Shally, your life is not dissolute. Although I don't quite follow what you see in Mia. She may mean well, but I had hoped you might find someone a little more inspiring, more your equal."

"Susanna, give him a break," Dad jumped in. "Would any girl ever be good enough for a Yiddische Mama like you?"

Before she could answer, a commotion in the kitchen broke through the low hum of party chatter. We heard a male voice shout: "Scram!"

"Hey, don't do that," a second voice called out.

"Then keep that filthy beast out of the food," the first one said, recognizable now as Chuck, feeling the full impact of one stiff drink.

"Fuck you," the bird squawked.

The next squawk was cut short. A blur of gray flashed through the air.

"Oh, no," Mom said.

There was a loud scramble, the scraping of chairs, shouts for them to stop. The light flickered and beer bottles crashed to the floor.

"What's happening?" Mom asked, too weak to stand on her own, straining to see through the havoc. "What's happening back there?"

By the time I twisted my way to the kitchen, I found Delacroix, a half bagel sticking out of his mouth like a giant hook, forming a wall between Walker, who cradled his poor parrot, and the still fuming Chuck. Recognizing the aggressor, Delacroix wrapped an arm around Chuck and escorted him outside for what was sure to be a lecture on the pressing need to resolve human conflict through dialogue. I reported back to my parents that the Mega-Stars had calmed the situation.

"What's wrong with that old fool?" Dad asked. "I thought Chuck liked animals. He's always talking about swimming with them."

"Chuck is something of mammalianist," my mother said. "He's so focused on dolphins and whales that he can't consider that birds might have something to teach us."

"A mammalianist, eh? Well, if he doesn't behave himself, I'll feed his mammalian self to the crocodiles."

I assured my father that wouldn't be necessary. As I knew from experience, Delacroix would be working to instill in Chuck a sense of decorum. Delacroix's strong hands, along with his recounting of the brutalities catalogued in the war-crimes tribunal, could coax even as hardened a fighter as Chuck onto the peace train.

The party winding down, it was hard to avoid a sense of mourning as the anthropologists started leaving. Soon the only guests who remained were those closest to us: Chuck, Mia, and the Mega-Stars. Returning to the keyboard, Sang Froid presented a special composition, one I had heard only in fragments. It traversed continents and cultures, a gumbo of Chopin, Monk, and Les Ambassadeurs d'Amour, his first band in Dakar. Sang Froid announced the piece was called "The Susanna Variations."

"What a lovely gesture," my mother said, folding her hands against her chest, as if she could absorb the notes into her heart. "I'm touched."

She closed her eyes and leaned against Dad, old lovers reunited at last on a ratty couch, as if nothing had ever separated them. If this had been their life together, it was a shame it couldn't have lasted.

PART 5

41

Goma
November 15, 1996

THE RUMBLE OF HEAVY GUNS AT DAWN WOKE ME TO THE TUTSI advance on Mugunga. Within minutes of the opening barrage, a tap-tap-tap sounded at my door. Entering quickly, Dudu tilted his ear toward the distant thunder like a piano tuner, measuring pitch and pace, trying to deduce a pattern to the shelling.

"It sounds busy out there," I said.

"Your friends told us it would not be long."

When the guns settled down to a testy quiet, I waited for confirmation that the siege had been broken. The Tutsis would surely send word to update us on their progress. Unless of course, our recent visit had soured the scope of relations between us.

Soon we heard pounding on the door, and I looked out to find not a Tutsi soldier but a pair of women: Karina and Germaine, in a desperate state.

"We cannot reach Dr. Chantal on the telephone," Karina said. "Have you heard what has happened?"

"Only what everyone else in Goma has heard."

Germaine clasped her hands together, as if appealing for divine intervention. "We must reach the camp right away. Please, will you help us?"

"It's not safe yet. You don't want to be caught in the crossfire."

"Mr. Jacob, you can't imagine how Chantal and the children are suffering. Please, if there is anything you can do for them, you must act now."

I sure had tried. As the general stood over his battle plans, I offered a vision that didn't appear on his maps. Unfortunately, my pleas had failed.

"Dudu, what do you think?" I asked. "Can we make it through the lines?"

He shrugged. If it had been up to him, we would have left Goma long ago. "We can drive out to check whether the roads are clear," he told the women, "but if it looks bad, we will have to turn back. I cannot risk Jacob's life."

We met Patrice downstairs and talked him into one more trip out to the camp. Crowding into his car, we drove west until the way was blocked by a great wave of humanity. Rushing toward us were thousands, even tens of thousands of Hutu refugees, the young and the old, all walking with great purpose to reclaim their place in Rwanda. With them, they carried the meager fruits of exile: plastic jugs and metal pots, blankets and bedding. They marched in amazing quiet, no anger or shouting, no fights along the way, no pushing or cries for sympathy, not a parade as much as a scramble, the whole population of Mugunga determined to escape before the gates closed on them.

"Well, that ends that," I said. "Let's hope these people can figure out how to live together."

Dudu surveyed the faces moving past. "You've always been an optimist, Aba."

Suddenly, he recognized someone, one of Gescard's men, the university student named Pio. This fellow, who had been such a chatterbox back in the bar, turned glum as we pressed him for details about the final hours of Mugunga.

"The Tutsis attacked from the west, where no one expected them. Mortars first and then shooting. A lot of shooting. It happened so fast, we could do nothing to stop them. So I ran like everyone else."

Pio's account matched what we knew of Tutsi military strategy: pound the enemy from three sides, and force them to flee in the one remaining direction. At Mugunga the only exit faced east, back to Rwanda. The genocidaires, for all their determination to retain the refugees as human shields, were overwhelmed by the crush of humanity desperate to escape. The dam burst open, and the refugees poured forth.

"What about the boys on the football team?" Dudu asked.

"They ran into the forest with Gescard."

"But you escaped the other direction."

"I didn't want to fight any more. Gescard tried to cut me, but I was too fast for him. This is why I played striker and he was defense."

"You're not worried what will happen next?" Dudu asked.

Pio looked downriver at the masses walking quickly into the thousand hills of Rwanda. "The Tutsis can't kill us all."

His voice wobbled; false courage was the curse of the big talker. I could have assured him the Tutsis would be fair, but what did I know. No matter what his future held, Pio wasn't going to waste any more of it with us. He hoisted his blankets onto his head and rejoined the stream of walkers.

Pio's story made Dudu want to scale back our mission. "Aba, the whole camp is marching this way. Why don't we stay here? Maybe the doctor will come to us."

With refugees stretching to the horizon, it could have taken days for her to pass.

Germaine begged us to keep going. "Please, we must continue. I have a terrible feeling."

I agreed to press on, and Patrice steered us through back routes until we reached the no-man's-land surrounding the camp. As we approached, Dudu waved for the car to stop. When he got out to inspect the scene, I joined him to look over what must have been the front line. What had been a free-fire zone was now dead quiet. Across the field were scattered bodies, some of them swollen, their skins bursting after days in the open.

"They must have shot anyone who tried to escape," he said.

"Who did?"

"Who knows? They'll probably be arguing about that for years."

Across the field, a couple of dogs were digging into a rack of white ribs. Dudu hurled a rock to make the dogs scamper away, but soon they were back, shaking the intestines free, like birds plucking worms from the earth.

"See, Aba, that's all we are in the end: dog food."

The old gate of Mugunga was no longer guarded. In reality, there was nothing left to guard. The gate itself had imploded from the sheer force of human panic. Inside, a city of tents looked like the remains of a fairground after the carnival had left town. Piles of splintered wood, torn clothing, and plastic tarps were strewn across the field as if churned together by a mighty hand.

"What a mess."

"It never was going to end in honey and flowers, Aba."

"No, I suppose not."

The car could go no further, so we left Patrice with the engine running and made our way across the wreckage. Scrambling ahead of the women, Dudu reached a big mound of debris and waved for me to hurry. What he had discovered was a collapsed tent wrapped like a mummy around some heavy objects. Unwinding the tent, we uncovered three corpses, Germaine's girls, one of whom looked to be her Prospero, her charms truly overthrown, her yellow dress soaked with splotches of maroon. Dudu turned her onto one shoulder and poked at her back.

"Shot from behind."

I wanted to shield the ladies, but Germaine, stumbling along with Karina, began to shriek as soon as she spotted the girls laid out side by side. Flinging herself upon her dead Prospero, Germaine tried pleading her back to life. Karina hugged her shoulders, but Germaine shook her off and moved on to the other girls, caressing their faces, calling out for them to come back to her. Her cries carried through the ruined camp.

"Jacob, we can't stay here," Dudu warned, scanning the horizon for activity. "Anything could happen."

He was right to be mindful. Scavengers were already arriving, not just the dogs, but the locals from Goma salvaging anything they could sell.

"We'll go as soon as we find the clinic."

Leaving the women, we headed toward the medical tent, now nothing but open sky. The tent was gone, but the cots remained in rows, filled with men of fighting age, several of them in uniform, shot where they lay. Some were still hooked up to bags of clear fluid, the solution dripping in as the blood poured out.

"What the fuck happened?"

"Did you expect a birthday party?" Dudu asked.

Germaine screamed again, louder than ever this time. Down the line of cots, another body lay twisted in the debris, this one draped in a white shroud. It was Dr. Chantal's medical coat, transformed into a *kittel*. Rushing to her, Germaine wrestled the doctor onto her lap. As Germaine cradled her head, we saw that Chantal's mouth was open, as if she had something left to say, but the rest, as the saying goes, was silence. Germaine tried to press the jaws back together. They resisted, like an overstuffed sandwich. Karina searched for a pulse and listened for a heartbeat. Failing to find either, she fell to her knees and buried her face in her hands.

"She knew they would kill her."

Who "they" were, I didn't ask. It didn't matter. Both sides used the same bullets, and there was no way of tracing their provenance, not even with a list of clandestine shipments to the warring parties.

I bent down to touch Chantal's cheek. She was lost to me, like the others; the only difference here was that I had to face her amid the wreckage.

"Aba." Dudu prodded my shoulder. "Aba."

"She's gone," I said.

"Yes. She's gone. But look who's back."

Dudu pointed to the distance, where a line of soldiers was emerging from the forest. Fanning out, they appeared to be Banyamulenge carrying out a mop-up operation. It didn't seem wise to wait around.

"We have to go," I told the women. "It's not safe."

The sight of the soldiers turned Karina into liquid, her resistance oozing away. Not so Germaine. She rocked back and forth, eyes closed, mumbling psalms as she held the doctor. Karina and I tried to pry her away, but it took Dudu to lift her from the dead. Regaining her senses, she stood straight, wiped her bloody hands on her dress, and came to a clear conclusion.

"Dudu, you must carry Dr. Chantal for us."

"But Mama, where will we take her?"

"We will bury her in our cemetery, next to my mother. We will not leave her here for the dogs."

She looked back at the school tent, where her three students lay in state. "As soon as it is safe, I will send my people back to gather our young daughters."

Germaine wiped Chantal's face clean and closed her eyes, a hurried cleansing of the dead. She tried once again to straighten the broken jaw, but it was no use. Refusing to wait any longer, Dudu folded the doctor's body over his shoulder and hoisted her aloft. I raised my hands to help his balance, but Dudu brushed me off.

"I have her. All of you come now. Let's go."

As he led us back through the rubble, Chantal's arms swayed side to side, a final wave to the ruined camp. A million souls were now rushing down the road to Rwanda, but she, the best among them, would never make it home. Survival depended much more on luck than grace.

42

Brooklyn
May 17, 1997

JACOB WAS TRANSFIXED BY A TELEVISION REPORT SHOWING African soldiers parading down the boulevards of a capital city. Young men raised their guns and cheered as the announcer described the culmination of a thousand-mile campaign across the forest. The rebels, referred to as Banyamulenge, had reached Kinshasa. The war was over; the old dictator Mobutu had been ousted. A new era had begun. A new Congo.

Pressing the button to elevate my new bed for a better view, I thought these victorious soldiers looked familiar, like any other band of warriors in the throes of triumph. Such men were capable of terrible brutality, from the Wehrmacht to the Ethiopian Derg to the executioners at Jebel Sahaba in the upper Nile before humanity learned to record history. It made me feel hopeless, the unending nature of it, the failure to learn from our past.

"Friends of yours?" I asked my husband.

Jacob peered ever closer at the rebel troops sloshing black paint over posters of the deposed president.

"None that I recognize."

The report cut to pictures of dead bodies in the street, and then to crowds watching the parade, whispering warily to each other, until one of the liberators broke away from his comrades to put his hand over the camera lens.

"I'm surprised to see you so engaged," I said. "Your interests were always confined to the tribe of Abraham, Isaac, and Jacob."

"Maybe I've come to appreciate your view of humanity as one single tribe, stretching all the way back to our last common ancestor with the chimpanzees." He pinched my arm lightly, careful not to bruise it. "Did I get that correct, Professor Sussman?"

"Close enough. For curiosity's sake, what brought about this change in perspective? I've always known you to be a man of implacable conviction."

Muting the television, he leaned his forearms against the metal bars of my bed.

"Let's just say I've come to appreciate my mistakes."

My thinking hadn't been entirely clear lately, but it was hard to believe what I was hearing. "Jacob, is that guilt I detect in your voice? Or possibly even regret? I never thought you shared these basic human frailties."

Smiling, he scratched the strange beard that still seemed so alien to me. "Oh, I have plenty of regrets, but my greatest strength has always been to squirrel them away into a little box near my heart, like a pacemaker, but with the opposite effect."

My curiosity over his endeavors had ebbed during the long desert of our separation, but now, far too late to make any difference, he began to confess, as if he sensed that I might not last until Yom Kippur. As he recounted his adventures, I tried to follow the brutal history of Hutus and Tutsis, the long despotic rule of Mobutu, the uprising of the Banyamulenge, aided by the Rwandan Tutsi army, that flushed the Hutu refugees out of Congo and mounted an epic march to Kinshasa. It was hard to make sense of the politics. Even Jacob found it confusing.

"I'm a fool, an old romantic fool, for thinking it would all end neatly," he said. "Those young men who took Kinshasa will be back fighting soon enough, and when that battle's finished, they'll send the next generation to take their place. Just like we do, just as we all do."

I didn't believe in anything as mystical as a soul, except as a manifestation of our collected experiences; but even as metaphor, his soul seemed to be in a parlous state. It didn't matter whether I shared his politics, or his elevation of one clan over another. As my husband laid out his regrets, I felt no need to condemn him.

"Jacob, you know that the concept of absolution is alien to me, but I'm sure you've done some good in your time, saved the lives of those who otherwise would have perished. That sounds, to borrow a phrase, like a mitzvah."

He seemed amused by my correct usage of "mitzvah," just as I had been when he dropped words like "esoteric," "languid," or "resplendent." Then he shook his head, not to reject my comfort as much as to purge a latent image from his mind. He cupped my hand in his. "All I can promise you is that I'm done. From now on, my only travels will be by your side, so that you can keep me out of trouble."

"This might surprise you, but I'm not planning any trips anytime soon."

"Not even a visit to the mountains around Lake Kivu to search for the bones of our ancestors?"

"Our last visit to Africa was hardly memorable for its success."

"This time it'll be different. We'll have a whole army to support us; and if we don't find any bones, we can still visit the gorillas hiding in the Virungas. You can even bring your tape recorder to figure out what they're saying to each other."

We both laughed at the idea of me hiking through his magic mountains. These days I could no longer make it up the stairs without help.

"All right, but only if we allow Shally to organize the expedition, since he did such a beautiful job with the conference, completely of his own accord."

Jacob thought about it for a moment, as if doubting whether to play in my dollhouse. Then he nodded. "No harm in that, I suppose."

It was a sweet notion, that we could turn this trek into a family enterprise, like the Leakeys in Olduvai Gorge. Even if the journey took place only in my imagination, I still enjoyed the fiction of traveling high into the mountains to map out a hidden chapter of hominid evolution.

Jacob excused himself to go downstairs to prepare another of those awful protein shakes, but instead of the sound of the blender I heard the front door open. A few minutes later he returned to my bedside bearing a picture frame, what turned out to be our ketubah, the old marriage contract that had once bound us together.

"Remember this?" he asked.

"Of course. I'm surprised you didn't use it to plug a hole in the wall."

"Not a chance. It's taken me this long to figure out what it actually meant."

The document looked familiar, a central chart of Hebraic characters surrounded by a bucolic image of forests and rivers, a fiction of paradise in marriage, certainly not anything discernible from my experience.

"Should I hang it, for old time's sake? We could use a change of scenery." He had never cared for the image of Yorick's skull presiding over the room.

"All right, you old romantic, but only if you can assure me I'm not giving up anything in the bargain."

He rested the frame against the bars of my bed and studied the Aramaic text, his finger ranging right to left through the letters. "According to the ancient contract, you are committed to three goats and a camel. It's a good price, given your current condition."

"All right, it's a deal, but I'll have to pay on the installment plan."

"You can take all the time you need."

He plucked the pins from Yorick's four corners and hung the ketubah back in its old spot. It fit snugly into the outline of faded paint.

"There, not bad."

"No, not bad."

He did love me, he always had. The pity of it was that it hadn't been enough. Returning to my side, he reached through the bars to warm my hands. For a moment I thought he was going to say something more, but he swallowed hard and clamped my hand tight to let me know he would stay with me as I drifted off to sleep.

43

Lake Kivu
November 17, 1996

A SHIFT OF MY HIPS NEARLY CAPSIZED THE PIROGUE. THE OLD fisherman called out for me to stay still, and I raised a hand to say: okay, okay, no more sudden jerks. Struggling to compensate for my weight, the old man took easy strokes. He wasn't going to kill himself for a *muzungu*'s joyride, even if I had paid him for a week's worth of fishing. We were barely out of shouting range from shore when he laid down his paddle.

"Okay?"

"No, no. Out there."

The old man grumbled and went back to paddling, toward the center of Lake Kivu barely visible through the fog. As we pressed farther out onto the lake, Goma seemed to melt away, obscured by an approaching storm. The wind picked up, carving ripples into the inland sea. In the deep water, I wouldn't have to worry about being caught up in anyone's nets.

Calling out to the fisherman, I patted my hands downward, as if testing the firmness of a mattress. He stowed his paddle and gripped both sides of the canoe to steady it as I yanked off shirt and pants. It seemed ridiculous to fuss with underwear, so I shed them as well and slid my legs over the side, letting them dangle for a moment. The water felt brisk, but a little discomfort wouldn't matter. Not for long anyway.

The cold water took me back to Coney Island on New Year's Day, when I plunged into the surf to try to impress Susanna. She fell for my bravado, but then I failed her, just as I had failed Judith, and now the poor doctor as well. These acts stuck to me, as binding as the tattoos marking Dudu until ten days after death.

Easing my weight over the edge, I slid in and dropped beneath the surface. Arms floating higher, toes pointing to the bottom, my body became a corkscrew, winding slowly down. I let my last breath escape. At these depths, I wouldn't have to worry about the Tutsis pursuing the Hutus across the forest, exacting a terrible revenge for all they had suffered. Dudu had been right. I wasn't ruthless enough to live with these decisions: who would live and who would die; who by bullet and who by fever; who by starvation and who by drowning. All these possibilities washed away from me now. The doubts too. This way, I wouldn't have to watch it unfold. I wouldn't have to be part of it.

I could have drifted down forever, or so it seemed until a deep thud resounded in my chest, not the tachycardia that had sent me scrambling to Dr. Chantal as much as the concussion of an artillery shell, or maybe even the recoil of Dudu's mag. It felt like a reflex, embedded within my body, a resistance to being swallowed up and churned into another set of bones washed clean by the lake.

My body made its own choice, arms groping higher, legs kicking up a froth, eyes straining for the luminous green above. Bursting through the surface, I gasped hard, breathing in so much water that it left me coughing and panting. The first thing I heard was the old fisherman shouting like a maniac. My underwater escapade, and the prospect of explaining to the Tutsi authorities how he had lost the old *muzungu*, must have scared the crap out of him. Rowing up beside me, he tried to haul me back into his little boat. It was no easy trick to revert to fish from human. I flopped around until the fisherman wrenched my hip and rolled me on board.

The storm caught up to us. As the rain smacked down upon the lake, the fisherman turned the pirogue about and paddled hard back to Goma. Naked in the belly of the boat, I covered myself with my wet clothes and watched the shore as the old man returned me to face the burdens ahead.

44

Brooklyn
July 28, 1997

ALL I COULD THINK ABOUT ON THAT FINAL DRIVE HOME FROM the hospital, as Mom rested against Dad's shoulder, was the lock of hair that I had pinched after shaving her head. It was ridiculous to fixate on something so trivial after Dr. Gerson had informed us that the cancer had spread to her liver. Dad pushed for an experimental treatment, but Mom shook her head. She'd had enough. All she wanted now was a lifetime supply of morphine and a ride back to the brownstone that had been her sanctuary these past fifty-eight years.

When the car dropped us off, Dad carried her straight up to the bedroom, and I sneaked past to conduct a frantic search of my dresser drawer. There, hidden behind the underwear, was an envelope containing the lock of hair, bound up by the anthropological tweezers that had doubled as my roach clip. The hair looked strangely unconnected to her, as if it belonged to another eon, already long past. Mom had taught me that hair didn't decay as long as the conditions were right.

I peeked into her bedroom to find her already asleep, the morphine shrouding her from us. Heavy stuff, that morphine, much more potent than the weed I'd been offering her for months. A good son would have pulled up a chair and waited for the moment to hand her a sip of water, now that her time had winnowed down to the unquantifiable "not long." Yet standing at the threshold, all I could think about were reasons to flee.

In the kitchen, Dad was working the phone, instructing Uncle Effie to send help. The nurse who showed up was a Hassidische lady, trained in hospice care, who seemed to have a long history with Mom.

"I remember you before you were born," Drora told me. "I helped your mother during her pregnancy, and after she came back from the hospital."

I had no idea what to say to someone who claimed intimate attachment to me *in utero*, but who now declined to shake my hand. *Shomer n'gia*: don't touch the women, a wise precaution considering my history.

I had been dodging Mia for weeks. She beeped me repeatedly, but I couldn't deal with her, with her gratitude, with her neediness, or even with her generosity. This was the time for family, except I couldn't even manage that.

Drora's presence allowed Dad to stay by Mom's bedside and gave me license to avoid the whole scene altogether. Two days passed before Dad caught me slipping past the bedroom door.

"You haven't spent five minutes with her since we came back from the hospital. Go in to see her. She's been asking for you."

I didn't respond, except to flinch as he drew closer, expecting him to punch me. Instead he wrapped me in his arms and leaned heavily upon me, as if for the first time he needed my support.

"Don't think about the future," he said. "Go be with her now."

I had no answer. Shamed into action, I entered her bedroom to find her reading not evolutionary biology or linguistics, but poetry, searching for a song beyond the genius of the sea.

"Shally, come." She moved a few light volumes aside. Poetry never weighed much, not with all its straining over words. I could have used a touch of the poet to figure out what to say. All I did was fall back on banalities.

"How do you feel?"

"The morphine makes me very woozy, like being tossed in the ocean."

It sounded nice, the sense of floating. "Maybe you should let me try some, for anthropological purposes, of course."

"Oh, Shally," she laughed, a positive sign. "I thought you had broken with anthropology."

"Not entirely. I still have some fairly close relations with anthropologists."

We both laughed this time.

"Speaking of anthropology, there is something that I've always wanted to discuss with you."

I dreaded what was coming. It didn't seem worthwhile to bemoan "Sex on the Beach," and my successive exit from the department, when every moment represented an increasing percentage of her remaining time. She had the right, however, to talk about whatever she wanted. It was her life, and her death as well.

"Shally, I've always regretted my failure to speak up for you. You deserved another chance; no one should be condemned for one mistake."

"Mom, you don't have anything to feel sorry for. Academics weren't for me. I probably followed you into the department for all the wrong reasons."

She squeezed my hand. It was hard to look at how bony and discolored her arm had become.

"You had such an unusual childhood. I worry that I did you a disservice with all my talk of baboons and bipedalism. I should have allowed you to watch Curious George and Magilla Gorilla in peace."

"I have to admit, I always did want the gorilla in the window."

She didn't get the reference to the cartoon's opening jingle. It was all right, I said, not wanting to expend any more precious time explaining.

"I should have been more attuned to your needs," she said, "or at least have recognized that you're closer in spirit to your father than to me: his resourcefulness, his authority with people, his determination too. That's what reassures me that you will find something that gives you meaning, that puts all your talents to use."

The terminal tenor of her assessment made it difficult to absorb.

"I can't imagine what talents you're thinking of."

"Oh, Shally, don't say that. You have real gifts that simply didn't manifest themselves in an academic setting. That's what I've come to realize, watching you pull together the conference and manage your musical group, that you have found your own way, separate and distinct from anything I could have imagined for you."

Heavy stuff, which I wished we could have put off until tomorrow, but her stack of tomorrows was quickly running out, so I breathed deep, stared at my sneakers, and tried to avoid breaking down in front of her.

"There's something I have to give you," she said.

"I don't need any presents, Mom. It's enough to sit here talking."

"Don't worry, it's not exactly a new bathrobe. Only something you should have."

She directed me to her bottom drawer, where I pulled out what looked like an old shoebox, covered in dust, the cardboard crushed along the sides and bound tightly by a greasy piece of string. She yanked off the string, releasing more dust, and opened what appeared to be a box of letters and knickknacks. The first thing she produced was a piece of cardboard hanging by a string of yarn. It was inscribed with the number 44, marking the seat assigned to her on the plane that had carried her out of Poland. This number, in a very real way, defined her existence.

"I never showed you this because I wanted you to have a normal life, free from fear, not to have to worry whether the Nazis might knock on the door. Your father and I disagreed about this. He would have marched you to Buchenwald for your bar mitzvah, but I insisted on protecting you. I never believed the *shoah* should be the essential lesson for humanity. It is only one lesson among many."

Looking over the medallion, I realized it defined my life as much as hers. Without it, I would never have come into existence. Mom tried to put it on one more time, but the yarn no longer fit over her head.

"I suppose there aren't any more flights that can deliver me to safety," she said. Placing the medallion back in the box, she removed a stack of letters, written in a language incomprehensible to me, the words fading into the delicate paper.

"What do they say?" I asked.

"They document the last few years of my parents' lives. If you're interested in a translation, I'm sure your father could help."

"Dad doesn't speak Polish, does he? I always thought his Galicianer shtick was a bunch of wishful thinking."

"If he doesn't, I'm sure he can find someone who does. You know him."

The conversation must have taxed her. Closing her eyes, she nodded off, the drugs elevating her to an opiate dream-state. Taking the box with me, I carried off the legacy of the Sussman family. There was one item I needed to add: the envelope containing her lock of hair.

The following weeks felt wrapped in a gauze of partings: a few colleagues and students called to pay their respects. Sang Froid showed up almost every day to play the piano, not just Chopin and Bach, but also the Susanna Variations and some of his other African jazz compositions, providing music to fill the gaps between doses of morphine. Mia stopped by to check on us. Apologizing for my distance, I explained that I just needed some time.

Chuck reached out by satellite phone from somewhere off the Aleutian Islands, his voice breaking as he related how his life already felt diminished. His conference essay had arrived by mail, the last missing paper for the compendium, the rest of the book already laid out. The printer delivered some early proofs, rushed into typeset. Mom lacked the strength to go through them line by line, so I sat by her side correcting the grammar and diction, consulting her but mostly doing what I considered best.

Her periods of lucidity dwindled, as did her capacity to eat. When her liver began to fill with fluid, Dad informed me it wouldn't be long. It was a shock to me, that the end could come so quickly, but Dad had seen enough death to recognize its footsteps. Sending Drora home, he declared it time for us to be alone as a family. He and I took shifts by her bedside, careful never to leave her by herself. He had been sleeping in the armchair beside her for months, and now I made my bed on the carpet, resting my pillow a few feet from her face.

We stayed with her as she slipped into longer spells of sleep. The morphine was both blessing and comfort. A few nights later, I woke in the darkness convinced I had heard something. Rising to my knees as light filtered in from the street, I looked at the bed to see her smiling at me.

"Shalom, Shalom, Shalom."

She said my name as if she had found religion: Kadosh, Kadosh, Kadosh. Holy, Holy, Holy. Each word was a full breath, a lifetime unto itself, beginning with excitement, ending in resignation, the cycle of birth-to-death embodied in a name.

"What is it, Mom, are you okay?"

The word "okay," malleable and meaningless, could not have counted for less at this moment. She smiled, as if absorbed in some sweet internal joke, a blessed contentment, a bliss that may well have been the drugs. I held out a glass of water, the simplest of tasks elevated to a sanctified role, replete with the blind hope of replenishing her. She didn't respond, and her eyes slowly closed, her head settled deep into the pillow. I stayed in place, watching her face and awaiting any further communication, beginning to doubt whether she had actually spoken at all. It seemed a dream, impossible that she could have produced a moment of clarity after two days of delirium. Also improbable was that my father, with his falcon reflexes, could have slept through it. Hearing nothing further, I lay down again on the carpet and went back to sleep.

I woke with the morning light to find Dad sitting beside her. His head was down, like he was praying, and he seemed to be crying.

"Dad, what is it?"

He wiped his hands across his face and breathed in deeply. "She's gone."

And she was. I could tell right away, her body shrunken beyond her already withered state. No need to feel for a pulse, or stick a mirror beneath her nose. Dad knew how to separate the living from the dead. He placed her hands by her side, raised the sheet over her head, and called Uncle Effie to make the arrangements.

45

Entebbe
January 24, 1997

STANDING IN FRONT OF THE INFAMOUS ENTEBBE TERMINAL, NOW abandoned to the weeds, Dudu and I scanned the skies for any sign of the approaching plane. A stiff wind blew across Lake Victoria. By force of habit, I stroked my beard, fully grown by now. Dudu hounded me one more time to stop looking back.

"Do yourself a favor, Aba, shave off that fucking thing before you return home. Your wife shouldn't see you mourning another woman."

"Mourning is what we do. We remember our dead."

Dudu put his arm around my shoulders. "Aba, I warned you this would be hard. You have to forget the doctor, and the other girls too, and focus on those who are left. Remember what it says in the Torah: A living dog is better than a dead lion."

I didn't bother correcting him that the line came from Ecclesiastes, Kohelet, that all was vanity and a striving after the wind. It didn't take scripture to put doubts in my head. We had witnessed the fastest migration of souls in history, so many refugees crossing the border after Mugunga's collapse that it promised to change the future of two nations. If I had been watching from 35,000 feet, I would have called it a grand success, a victory for humanity. From our vantage point, so close to the action, all I could see was bodies. A million Hutu refugees had returned home to Rwanda, but hundreds of thousands more had escaped into the forests of Zaire. As they fled west, hunted by the Tutsis, there had been enough horrors to wipe out all our certainties. My only conclusion was that Germaine had been right all along: hate and war would kill us all, and genocide would haunt this place.

Ready to depart at last, we stood in the shadow of the old Entebbe terminal, vegetation creeping down the façade. Now it was just another ruin, but twenty years ago, during the infamous hijacking, I had studied every facet of this building, the runway, and the control tower. After the terrorists separated Jew from gentile, with a hundred lives in the balance, all that observation helped us mount an epic rescue, one of our greatest operations, in an era when victories were easier to define.

"You were too young to take part in Operation Thunderbolt, but it was glorious."

Dudu glanced at the terminal and turned right back to the sky. He never did care about history. "That was a long time ago, Aba. Things are different today."

They sure were different. Different enough to make me miss the days of clear villains, now that crazy Idi Amin was dying of syphilis in Saudi Arabia and Mobutu was fading fast on the French Riviera, done in by his prostate as the Tutsi rebels moved on Kinshasa.

"So what will you do now?" I asked.

The decision he had been pondering for weeks was upon him at last. "For the next few months, I'll stay with Sunny in Nairobi, while she plans her next restaurant."

"Have you come up with that recipe for Yiddische-Thai chicken?"

"Not yet. For now she needs my help with security."

I could picture his life on the African aid circuit, flying out to dusty shitholes in Sudan and Somalia, months in the field serving up lemongrass noodles, broken by a few weeks whoring in Mombasa, roasting in the sun until his skin marbleized.

"I'm sure she'll be glad to have you around. It's an insecure business she's in."

"Everything in life is insecure, Aba. The most important thing is not to be afraid, like the song goes."

The plane appeared over the lake and landed on the runway before us. They wheeled up a set of steps, and the arriving passengers began to disembark.

Dudu pulled me in for a hug that threatened to crush my ribs. "Take care of yourself, Aba. Go back to your wife and son, and live a good life. Try to forget what happened here."

"I couldn't do that even if I wanted to."

He released me from the embrace but held on to my neck, bending our foreheads together, the boy from Odessa now a free man. "Ach, Jacob, let people find their own resolutions, good or bad."

When they finished unloading the arriving flight, my fellow passengers for Paris lined up to board the airplane. Dudu spotted a full-figured stewardess heading back to the main terminal. Winking at me, he drew commas in the air to illustrate her hips squeezed into a tight blue dress-suit. As she boarded the bus, he smacked his lips, imagining the taste of her prize, and bounded after her, catching a lift right as the doors closed. No sense wasting an opportunity. My final vision of Dudu was of him leaning over her, whispering something in her ear that made her pull away in disgust.

46

Brooklyn
August 17, 1997

THERE WAS NOTHING LEFT TO SAY. WE DROVE TO MOUNT Lebanon in silence, a whole caravan trailing behind the hearse like a chain of weak links, broken several times by the traffic along Eastern Parkway. It made sense to have the ceremony graveside, even on a gray day. Susanna wouldn't have felt right in a *shul* or a funeral home. If no one else showed up, Shalom and I could have covered her ourselves, with as much help as Effie could manage. As it turned out, cars filled with mourners kept arriving, parking along the narrow paths, as we prayed the rain would hold off long enough to put her in the ground.

Word of her death had spread fast, an epilogue to her conference. Her colleagues in anthropology, as close as she came to a tribe of her own, mumbled their sympathies and hurried away, as if I might eat them if they lingered. Her chairman informed me they were planning to dedicate a Susanna Sussman prize, to be awarded at a conference in her honor.

Her students cried to Shalom how his mother had inspired them, given them a model of a strong, visionary woman who had transformed academic conflict into shared wisdom. Shalom barely looked at them, lifting his head only for Mia, who hadn't been around much in recent weeks. Wearing sunglasses on a cloudy day, she kissed his cheek and whispered in his ear before moving a few steps away, respecting this as time for father and son.

It wasn't just Susanna's people who came. There was the Hassidische lady who helped care for her, as well as Effie's son Menachem, who left behind his bride, already pregnant. I was surprised to see many of Effie's drivers who we had rescued through the years: Russians, Syrians, and a few Ethiopians who had all found their way to Brooklyn.

The Mega-Stars gathered around my son. The pianist, Sang Froid, had offered to perform at the funeral, but Shalom explained this was not our tradition. He meant well, and even though Susanna could no longer hear him, I invited him to keep coming over to practice on the Steinway. It comforted me as it had her. I might have even willed him the piano, if not for the hope that Shalom might one day leave it to his children.

Effie passed out the kipot, worn by me and Shalom and the Mega-Stars who joined us in brotherhood, as well as a few of Susanna's colleagues. The rest of her people watched us like we were chimpanzees performing strange rituals to pull termites out of a log. We slid the pine box out of the hearse. With Effie directing traffic, I lifted one side with two of her colleagues, while Shalom and his bandmates—Delacroix and the pianist—took the other. With short steps, we marched the coffin to the grave and laid it down atop the straps.

The rabbi described a woman he had never met, his voice sounding over the sniffles and wiped eyes. Susanna would have hated this, all the fuss, all the attention, all the talk of her eternal reward which, if it existed, she so richly deserved.

The public nature of the ceremony made me uncomfortable as well. My eulogy would stay private, within the family. Standing above the coffin, I thought back to our first encounter, when she fell into my arms, what seemed like a planned bit of clumsiness, if not intentional then at least *bashert*. From that initial meeting, I recalled the last, at the funeral home shortly before they loaded her into the hearse, when at dawn I relieved the old lady who had spent the night reading psalms by her coffin. After the rebbitzin put away her prayerbook and departed, I pried open the lid and slid it down far enough to expose her head. Reaching into my pocket, I unfurled her green scarf, the one from Hadar, and wrapped it over her, more kerchief than shroud. Effie's orthodox ladies, the ones who had washed and prepared her body, might not have approved, but it didn't matter. This was how I wanted to remember her.

The rabbi led us through a mourner's kaddish and then stepped toward me, blade in hand. I offered my shirt, and he sliced the fabric just above the heart. After the rabbi cut Shalom, the gravediggers loosened the bands and lowered her in spurts, one final short trip before the coffin hit the bottom of the pit. Effie passed me a shovel, but I wanted to feel the earth itself. Brushing off the hands trying to support me, I knelt in the dirt, still wet from last night's rain, and held a handful over her coffin without releasing it. What made me hesitate was the irony, that we should bury one who had sought wisdom by pulling ancient bones from their repose. Susanna had resisted the idea of being interred, arguing that cemeteries took up vast expanses of arable land that were needed to feed an expanding human population. I had told her not to worry: future generations could reclaim more land from the sea and make the desert bloom. She didn't raise the subject of cremation, knowing I would never have allowed Hitler a final victory. No, she would have the burial denied her parents, and rest among my Galicianers, the section of Mount

Lebanon reserved for the Nowy Sacz society. And right beside her, relieved of his duty to the piano, was our old friend Stolbach.

I opened my hand and released the dirt onto the coffin. It made the traditional hollow thud. Shalom followed my lead, first pushing the earth with the back of his shovel and then heaving a full load of dirt into the hole. Behind us the other mourners lined up to help: her colleagues and students, the émigré drivers and Hassidisches and the African musicians all joined in, with Effie directing them to fill in the gaps, to cover the four corners. Soon the thump of dirt on wood faded, replaced by the muffled sound of earth on other earth, so that she grew further and further away, relegated to her own place, gone from us, at least until the day I joined her side.

When it was done, the mourners drifted back to their own families. We would have *shiva* calls to receive and memorial services to attend, but soon, after we uncovered the mirrors and returned to sitting on the furniture, Shalom and I would be left to our memories and our mementoes, the photos and writing, as well as the brownstone where we had spent our lives together.

Standing over her grave, I gazed across the thousands of headstones and was struck by how much they reminded me of the tents of a refugee camp. The exile on this field, however, was permanent.

Shalom put his hand on my shoulder. "Come on, Dad, let's get out of here. People will be showing up at the house soon, and Uncle Effie ordered a whole smoked whitefish for us."

The hole in the earth restored, and Susanna packed away within, there was nothing left to keep us. Effie handed me a foot-long candle that would burn for the entire week of shiva. It was thick and heavy, not at all like a Havdalah candle. We'd light it as soon as we got back home.

Acknowledgments

THIS BOOK CAME INTO BEING WITH THE SUPPORT AND COUNSEL of many keen commentators. Rob Spillman mentored an early draft of this novel at the Tin House Summer Writer's Workshop and guided me on shaping the narrative. Joanna Scott saw the book's incipient stages at the New York State Summer Writers Institute, and believed in its voice from the outset. Karen Shepard read the opening chapters at the Tin House Festival and helped me hone the varying perspectives.

The descriptions of conflict in Central Africa were informed by my work producing a documentary for PBS Frontline World in the Democratic Republic of Congo. My thanks go to Frontline's Ken Dornstein for his support of that 2006 piece: "Congo: Hope on the Ballot." I remain grateful to those who tried to guide me through the complicated realities of Eastern Congo—Jason Stearns, Petronille Vaweka, Anneke Van Woudenberg, Thierry Kambere, Baudouin Kipaka, Dr. Mathilde Muhindo, Lena Slachmuijlder, Dupont Ntererwa, Tharcisse Kayira, Michel Kassa, Deo Buuma, Kapeta Benda-Benda, Nancy Bolan, and others who must remain anonymous. Any errors in interpretation are my mistake, not theirs.

I am also grateful to Christiane Amanpour, my former anchor at CNN, for her descriptions of the refugee camps in Zaire and the return of hundreds of thousands of those refugees to Rwanda in November 1996. Invaluable to this novel were several powerful accounts of Congolese history, most notably Gerard Prunier's *Africa's World War*, Michela Wrong's *In the Footsteps of Mr. Kurtz*, and Jason K. Stearns's *Dancing in the Glory of Monsters*. Also essential were Howard French's *A Continent for the Taking*, Stephen Kinzer's *A Thousand Hills*, and Philip Gourevitch's *We Wish to Inform You that Tomorrow We Will Be Killed with Our Families*, as well as the war reporting from Eastern Congo by John Pomfret in the *Washington Post* and James C. McKinley Jr. in the *New York Times*. Significant influences came from "The Arms Fixers," a 1999 NISAT/PRIO report on the middlemen in the arms trade by Brian Wood and Johan Peleman, and the 2010 United Nations OHCHR's "Mapping Report" that documented the vast scope of human rights violations in the DRC from 1993 to 2003.

A profound debt is owed by me to the musicians who shared their experiences and allowed me a glimpse of their challenges: Sylvain Leroux and Fula Flute, the Mandingo Ambassadors, Martino Atangana & African Blue Note, and Kékélé. Much gratitude as well to Rick Shain for his rich study of African salsa, and to Scott M. X. Turner for his stories of the New York music scene.

Susanna's views on language evolution came into being through readings of Christine Kenneally's *The First Word*, as well as Philip Lieberman's *The Biology and Evolution of Language*, Steven Pinker's *The Language Instinct*, and Noam Chomsky's *Language and Mind*. Donald Johanson & Maitland Edey's account of the Hadar dig—*Lucy*—was invaluable to the story, as was Richard Leakey & Roger Lewin's *Origins Reconsidered*.

Chiwoniso Kaitano-Price and David Mills each offered camaraderie and a forum to read before wider audiences. Marcy

Schwartz and Evelyn Spence gave me extensive notes and invaluable feedback on an early draft, and Diane George guided me through the anthropological twists of human evolution. Sasha Abramsky, Victoria Lancelotta, Christie Aschwanden, Charles Fox, Martin Rowe, Carl Deal & Tia Lessin were compatriots and sounding boards throughout the course of this book.

Jessica Case at Pegasus Books believed in the book and propelled it forward with vision and passion. Pegasus' publisher Claiborne Hancock showed immense faith and commitment to this project. My agent, Miriam Altshuler, advocated for this novel with wisdom, foresight, and great compassion. Reiko Davis gave me an incisive analysis of Holbein's magnificent painting.

More than anyone, Leila Lerner encouraged my writing and raised me with an enduring love of literature.

Most of all, to my wife, Alyson Shotz, who shared her life with these characters and who believed steadfastly in my fight to tell their stories. Her love and inspiration made it all possible.